A SPELL OF DUST & SMOKE

ELORA BURRELL

BLOTTED QUILL PUBLISHING

Also By Elora Burrell

THE NEVERLANDER SERIES

Neverlander

Nevernever

TRIGGER WARNING

A *Spell* OF *Dust & Smoke*

ELORA BURRELL

eloraburrell.com

BLOTTED
QUILL
PUBLISHING

First printing, January 2022.

ISBN: 978-1-915044-00-6 (Ltd. Hardback)

ISBN: 978-1-915044-02-0 (Hardback)

ISBN: 978-1-915044-01-3 (Paperback)

ISBN: 978-1-915044-03-7 (Ebook)

Book, Cover Design, and illustrations by ArtByKHuggs

Blotted Quill Publishing.

www.eloraburrell.com

To the survivors.
We found our strength in the darkness.
We are stronger than we realise.

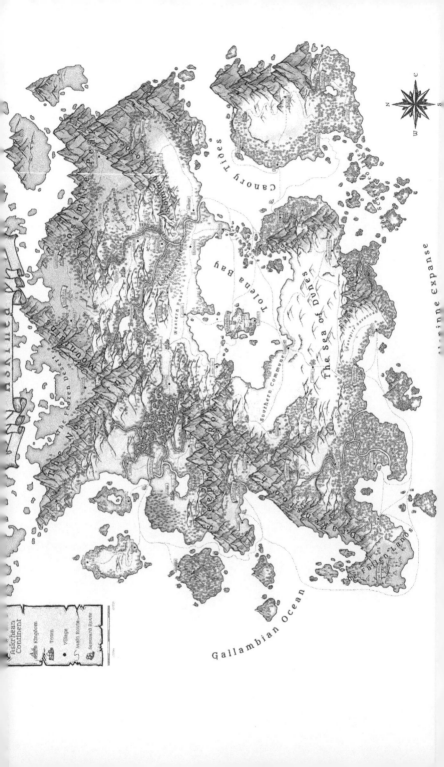

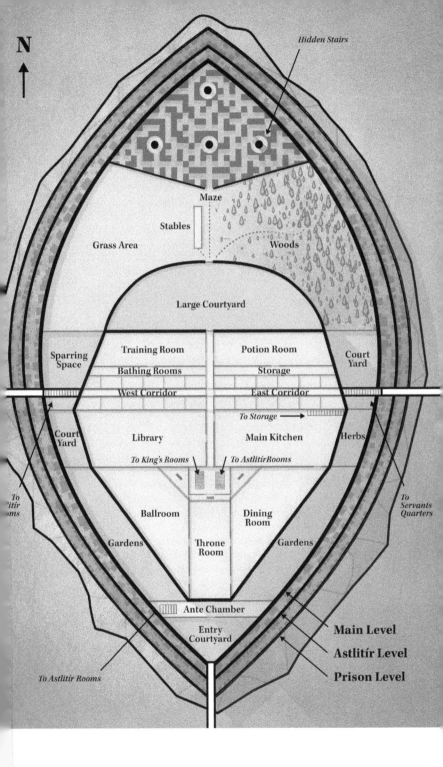

Contents

DREAMGAZER

NESRYN

CHAPTER ONE

The copper taste of blood swirls with the saltiness of the sweat sliding down my brow. My footsteps are quick and light as I spar with my adversary. The steel of our blades connects and parts over and over, the sweet clang of steel colliding echoes across the courtyard.

His feet shift blindingly quick, closing the gap with a blow that I know I will feel the force of. My teeth judder as I lift my arms up high to block the attack, my elbows threatening to buckle as the full force of his weight bears down on me.

"Hold your defence," Jarek barks at me.

I have no time to react as he suddenly pulls away and swings again. Unprepared for the change in tactics, I stumble forwards and the hilt of his sword slams into the back of my head, sending me reeling. Black dots appear in my vision, hindering me for a second too long as the sword comes flying towards me again. I try to manoeuvre out of harm's way but Jarek throws out a leg and I stumble backwards to the floor, my own weapon flying from my grip. The clean sound of steel cutting through the air sings in my ears and the sword stops, the tip hovering right over my pounding heart. I look at the hand gripping the blade before glaring up at him.

"You need to work on your stance if you're to ever get a shot at the upper hand," he lectures.

He drops the blade and the clang of metal rings out across the courtyard as he holds out a hand for me to grab. With a huff, I take it and clamber to my feet, rubbing away the dull ache at the back of my head.

"You didn't have to fight so dirty, you know."

"It's a kill or be killed world out there," Jarek says, sending me a pointed look.

I roll my eyes and reach for my weapon laying on the small patch of grass under the black cherry plum tree. The beautiful centrepiece of the courtyard.

"So you keep saying," I grumble.

"And I'll keep saying it until you best me in combat, young lady. This world was—"

"—Was not built for the meek-minded. I know, I know."

I'd heard the words a thousand times.

Jarek sends a bland look in my direction, a few loose strands of his ebony hair draping across his slightly flushed cheeks. He tucks some behind his ear and cracks his neck—a sign that our lesson may be coming to a close.

I debate whether or not I want to call it a day, but ever since I awoke, I found myself full of nervous energy and I'm willing to keep going if it means that I can get it out of my system. I feel the tension in my shoulders as I roll them back and I know I'll have to massage it out later. But, right now, I welcome the distraction.

I wipe away the sweat dripping down my temple, brushing it away with my shoulder as I stride closer. I stare at him with an impish grin. He recognises the invitation immediately and shifts his footing. Just as I'm about to raise my sword, a voice cuts through the tense silence.

"I think that's enough practice for one day, don't you, Jarek?" my uncle comments.

Jarek freezes, his shoulders stiffening as his eyes fall on his employer.

"Evidently not, by the look of Miss Havenore," he replies, inclining his head towards me.

I spin on my heels to face my uncle to see him give me a stern look. I answer with a pleading look of my own. Beneath his well-sculpted beard, his wide lips are set in a serious line and I know that he's not going to change his mind.

"Please, Uncle Erathon, just for another hour?"

"As much as this is music to my ears, you haven't time," he replies, something shifting in his gaze.

My shoulders slump and I glance back over my shoulder at Jarek who holds out his hand for my sword. I hesitate, but he nods reassuringly, and with a defeated sigh, I hand it over.

His shoulder drops with the weight of it and he shifts to balance the blade over his shoulder, holding the hilt loosely.

"We will pick it back up at dawn," he tells me.

I bite back a frustrated sigh and nod curtly. Without a word, I make my way across the courtyard towards my uncle. As soon as I reach him, he turns and strides towards the double doors that lead to the cool corridor, and I speed up to match his pace.

"Have you forgotten what today is?" he asks, glancing over his shoulder at me.

"No, I haven't," I reply quietly.

"Then you know you have to at least try to look your best."

"Why have you even accepted an audience with His Majesty? He's hardly your favourite person," I mutter.

My uncle remains silent for a few moments, though neither of us is willing to speak the words aloud. Not when the walls have ears and the servants have loose tongues.

"Regardless of my political stance, he is still our king. We mustn't bring attention to ourselves by refusing tradition. The Choosing is the law, by the will of the king," he answers, his eyes trained on me. "And don't even try to wear that grey gown. You will not convince me, no matter what your reasons," he adds.

"Why not? It's modest and comfortable," I counter.

"Nesryn, you will not sway me," he warns, though there is the smallest hint of an amused smile tugging at his lips.

I roll my eyes and groan.

"I have already told Ragna and Ceryl not to take it out. I have given them orders to take out the gown I hired the dressmaker for."

"You had one made?" I ask with a hint of humour.

"Altered," he corrects me, his tone stiff.

I notice the sudden change in his demeanour as we amble down the hall, the slight slump in his shoulders and the dullness in his eyes are the only tell-tale signs of his sadness. Deciding not to press him on it, I walk silently beside him, my body now beginning to ache from my sparring session.

When we reach the place where the corridors form a crossroads, he stops and glances down at me. His brown onyx eyes shift as they move over my face. *I know that look.* The look of concern twists my already fraught nerves.

"Uncle Erathon, what is it?" I ask quietly.

The faraway look in his eyes disappears with two quick blinks and he shakes his head dismissively. The corners of his mouth turn up in a flash of a smile before he carries on down the corridor. Only this time, I hold back.

"Clean yourself up, I'll see you in a short while," he calls over his shoulder.

When I reach my room, my stomach is still in knots, my body aching from skipping my warm-up stretches. I can hear Ragna and Ceryl busy tending to my bath in the adjoining room as I stroll through the doorway. I scan the room, brushing over the numerous rows of leather-bound books and staring longingly at the neatly made four-poster bed.

I stop short when I see the dress that my uncle has picked out for me, carefully laid out on the silken sheets. My heart speeds up as I recognise the gown. The dusky blush fabric and the detailed embroidery takes me back to the portrait hanging in the main hall. It hangs proudly in the main corridor leading to the drawing room, where my uncle likes to host guests. It's impossible to miss. The image of a young couple, the man with thick coiled dreadlocks and rich mahogany skin; and the woman, with an olive complexion and long waves, woven into a crown. Even now, with the oil painting far below me, I envision my father's face, tilted down towards my mother in his arms, his onyx eyes alight with adoration. My mother's gaze is fixed on the beholder, her hand resting on his and her womanly frame wrapped in the very same dress that has been prepared for me.

I silently pad closer to the bed, my fingertips brushing the embroidery and fabric petals that run down the length of the dress in a soft pink shade. I suck in a breath, holding it to my chest before releasing it shakily. My nerves ease slightly though the thought of wearing her dress leaves me with a bittersweet feeling.

The soft chimes of the clock hanging on my wall bring me back to the present. With a final touch of the fine material, I reach down and peel off my training soles. As my aching, bare feet meet the cool, wooden floor, I let out a heavy sigh. I savour the feeling for a moment before peeling off the sweaty tunic and loose cotton trousers. The tight band of fabric around my ankles gets caught on one of my heels as I hop about, eager to soak away the dull ache seeping into my muscles.

Losing my balance, I tip over and land on my backside as Ragna appears in the adjoining doorway. Her lips twitch with amusement but she recovers quickly.

"Your bath is ready, milady," she informs me.

"Just a moment and I'll be with you," I reply as I free my foot from the pantaloons at last.

"Will you be wanting the jasmine soaps or the honeysuckle?" she asks.

I glance up at the dress with a thoughtful look before I get to my feet, shimmying out of my undergarments.

"Both I think, please. Thank you, Ragna," I answer, wrapping the nearest robe around myself.

She nods once and turns, disappearing back into the washroom. I wait until I'm alone again before letting my eyes drift back to the dress. I should be worried, anxious, afraid even, of His Majesty's impending visit and what his attention might mean for me. Yet the small, proud smile on my lips is hard to shift.

It is easily well past mid-chime when Ceryl finishes the criss-crossing braiding across the front of my hairline, and steps back to admire her work.

"There, miss. Would you like to have a look?" Her voice is light and airy as she gestures to the beautiful mirror across from us.

The skirts of my dress swish lightly as I stand, skimming against the floor as I make my way over to gaze upon my reflection. I'm taken aback, my fingertips grazing the plait that forms a circlet around my head. My arms glimmer with the golden shimmer that Ceryl and Ragna have dusted me with. My corset is tight and restricting but the dress is still surprisingly light. My skin glows beneath my sheer puffy sleeves, contrasting well with the dusky blush fabric. The dress is modest, buttoning up my back to the nape of my neck with a low sweetheart neckline beneath the sheer fabric at the front. My curves are accentuated by the lavender bodice and softened slightly by the floaty top layers of fabric. I finger the embroidered petals once more, unable to peel my eyes away. As someone who prefers wearing loose training gear, I normally dislike dresses of this style and find them to be too much. But knowing who this once belonged to fills me with adoration for the dress and a burning sense of pride.

"This is the closest I'll ever get to be with you, Mother," I murmur to myself.

"Is it to your liking, milady?"

I turn my head from side to side, my coiled curls bouncing freely. I trace a finger along one of the plaits twisting across my forehead and smile.

"It's beautiful, Ceryl, thank you."

She dips her head and takes a step back, falling in line with Ragna and folding her hands neatly in front of her.

I step away from the full-length mirror and walk towards my vanity, glancing out of the window behind it to where the small clock tower stands proudly. I look down at the crystal bottles aligned neatly in a row on my table before reaching for the one with a golden liquid inside. I pull the wand free and press it behind each of my ears, my teardrop earrings swinging back and forth.

The smell of citrus wafts through the air and I close my eyes and inhale deeply, my mind taking me north from here, to the beautiful orange orchards settled in the Ezrolm Glades. The sharp chime of the clock reverberates in my room and my eyes snap open. I'm late.

"Thank you, ladies," I say as I place the bottle back and turn towards the servants.

Both women dip their heads in acknowledgement and leave the room in silence, one in front of the other. I watch them leave, my stomach coiling into knots as I think of what the next few hours may bring.

"Asteria, preserve me," I mutter to myself, nervously flattening the front of my dress before taking in a deep breath.

Despite the nervous energy coursing through me, I maintain my pace through the halls of the manor towards Uncle Erathon's study. I fiddle with the fabric petals around my waist, afraid of displeasing our king on his visit, the pools of my skirt swishing around me with every step.

I turn the corner and hurry to the door at the end of the short corridor, not bothering to knock as I reach for the handle, turning it and stepping inside.

The musty smell of books fills my nostrils as I enter, filling my chest with a warmth that little else can summon from me. Light fills the space, bleaching the tops of all the books a tea-stained colour. The yellowed volumes look odd, stacked in neat rows within the redwood bookcases. My uncle is standing at his desk in the centre of the room, his foot tapping against the enormous rug covering most of the hard floor.

"I was beginning to wonder if I should have one of the servants summon you," he says from behind his desk, his studying the scattered papers before him.

I ignore his remark and edge closer to peer at the papers littering his desk.

"Merchants giving you trouble again?" I ask casually.

He chuckles and shakes his head. "Disgruntled merchants are hardly a matter for you to be worrying—" he stops short as he finally looks up at me. His frown falls away, replaced by a look of complete wonder.

"You look just like her," he says softly as he stands up straight.

"You think so?" I ask as I look down at myself, my cheeks warming.

When he doesn't say anything, I speak up, eager to fill the silence. "Thank you. For the dress, I mean... it's truly the best gift."

"She would have wanted you to have it," Uncle Erathon manages.

His eyes shine with unspilled tears, his expression full of pride as he gazes at me. I notice how his wide smile wobbles a little as he takes in my mother's dress.

A dense blanket of quiet settles over us, fuelling my already erratic nerves.

"Did you wish to speak with me before our guests arrive?" I ask, stepping around the desk.

"Yes, there are a few... matters that we need to discuss," he replies.

I move towards the shelves, brushing the spines of the books as I wait for my uncle to continue, but he doesn't. His eyes follow me as I stop at the slim spine of one of my most favoured books. He steps forwards as I draw it from its place between the others, admiring the intricate gold foil on the front.

"The Princess and The Starweaver," he reads over my shoulder.

I smile up at him as he holds his hands out for the book. The nostalgic look in his eyes mirrors my own as he lays a hand on the cover.

"I remember the nights of reading this to you as a child," he murmurs, relishing the memory.

"Few loves held as true, though none could ever compare, to the love the princess and her Starweaver shared," I reply, quoting the final page.

"Nix." His voice is strained.

The knots in my stomach tighten despite the use of my pet name.

"Yes, Uncle."

"I already expect this afternoon to go smoothly and you have always acted as expected. You already know my views of our king, but please let us show none of this disapproval with His Majesty or his court upon his arrival," he says quietly with the smallest hint of shame.

"I wouldn't dream of it, Uncle Erathon," I reply.

"The Choosing can be a right of passage, but it requires sacrifice should you become one of his Chosen," he says, "I fear the sacrifices you may have to make, should this come to pass," he adds, placing a warm calloused hand on my cheek.

"I hope I will make you proud, whatever the outcome," I reply, determination rising within me.

"I know you will… no matter the outcome," he answers, though the smile doesn't reach the hollow look in his eyes.

LYSAN

CHAPTER TWO

The king is in one of his moods, but for the first time in months, I don't care.

My mind is focused as I stroll along the wide corridor of the east wing, making sure that my pace is relaxed; lazy even. I push my hands further into the deep pockets of my trousers, the heels of my boots making no sound against the stone floor.

I know the guards have their eyes on me as I saunter past—I can almost taste their distrust, hear the unspoken words that they wish they had the balls to say to my face. I smirk to myself, relishing in their fear.

Fear is power.

Barilius was certainly right about that.

When I'm far enough away, they utter the very words that I've been waiting for. They must know that the distance between us won't save them if I choose to strike them where they stand. Yet it seems that they can't help themselves.

"Shadowcasting *bastard.*"

It has a bite to it, but it's nothing I haven't heard before. Only now, it isn't a meek child that they're saying it to. The monster now standing in that boy's place is far worse than any hiding under their younglings beds in the darkest of night.

I consider, if only for a moment, teaching the man a lesson. It would only take the tiniest fraction of my power to have him huddling in his own piss. Fortunately for him, I have other things on my mind and I'm not bored enough to rise to the bait.

So I carry on, allowing the fool to have his tiny victory, knowing there will not be a second.

I'm surprised at my own calm considering what today will bring as the final days of Warmwell shift into the growing heat of Sunreach. It has already been a long two weeks of travelling, of visit after visit to arse-kissing nobles and their meek daughters.

King Barilius has been pickier than the last Choosing, which so far has resulted in him becoming even more unbearable, and the whole ordeal has barely even begun. This is my first in my new role and this time I will be much more involved in the process, though the thought doesn't sit well with me. My first Choosing had been when I was six, the following at sixteen. This time though would be different, this time I wasn't an uninformed, petulant child.

'*One more visit,*' I remind myself as I turn the corner.

The doors to the east library are slightly ajar and I frown. Slowly, I draw a hand from my pocket and flick it ever so slightly. A swirl of shadows darts across the space, forcing the door wide open.

I spot one of the kitchen servants meandering through the rows of books before she sees me, staring at me with wide coffee-stained eyes.

"M-my lord," she acknowledges, dipping into a quick curtsey.

I step into the room and raise a brow in silent question.

"Please, my lord, His Highness gave us permission to seek out some recipes in preparation of our guests. The chef sent me in his stead. I don't mean no offence," she hurriedly explains, tucking a loose strand of hair behind her ear.

I notice the way she avoids eye contact, the way she shrinks into herself at my mere presence. Such a small thing already, a timid rabbit in the presence of a wolf. I find myself equally amused and disgusted by the thought.

"Find what you need, then be on your way," I bark.

"Yes my lord, of course," she answers.

She quickly grabs three large cookbooks off the shelf behind her without so much as looking at them and scurries off like the subservient little woman she is. I watch her as she disappears out of sight. I hesitate, only for a moment, before a tilt of my head has the trails of shadow pulling the doors closed and sealing them shut with a barrier of swirling darkness.

With the knowledge that I won't be bothered for a while, I pull my eyes from the door and move through the rows of books towards the midsection. The stone pedestal rises up to greet me, shining with a flurry of colours from the stained-glass windows behind it.

With my finger I draw out the Elven sigil, murmuring the incantation with taut effort before the mark glows and melts into the stone. I hear the familiar scrape of shifting stone and I pass the numerous rows of books until I see the familiar opening in the far wall. As soon as I'm through, the wall begins to close up behind me, brick by brick, as I descend into the darkness.

My eyes adjust to the gloom, but after years of exploring these catacombs, memory serves me better than sight as I make my way through the echoing halls. Every once in a while I hear the scuttling of a beetle or the squeaking of a rat—common enough sounds in a place like this. I follow the winding path, its layout a perfect map imprinted in my mind.

I know that I've arrived when I feel the shift in the air, the unsettling quiet of this place and what it holds. In mere moments the torches are lit with elvynfire and the space is illuminated with blue flickering light.

"Aflora livitus," I command, my voice echoing along the darkened halls.

The spell takes a moment and despite the skill that it takes to conjure elvish magic—even the light magic. Purple-petalled flowers begin to float down from above and land softly on the earth before me. The shade of them is so deep that I almost mistake them as black.

My small gesture of respect makes little difference to the turmoil that I feel. No matter how many times I come here and no matter what horrors I witness at the king's side, the sight before me causes a sickness that I can't quell. There are eight graves in total, their headstones jutting out from the ground in a cumbersome row. The unmarked stones have never sat well with me, but then again, the dead can't speak. If only they could.

'*Soon there will be more of you.*' I shudder at the thought.

I stare at the graves, my hands bunching into fists. Despite my best efforts to restrain my power, the shadows snake from me and fly out in spearing tendrils, cracking against the stone walls with enough ferocity that it causes debris to crumble away and sprinkle across the graves. Dust flies everywhere and I stifle a cough as I reign in my anger, still sickened by the thought of unnecessary blood spilt.

'*This time will be different.*' I remind myself. A vow that I intend to keep.

The carriage ride is filled with tense silence as we're pulled to the outskirts of the kingdom, towards the countryside. King Barilius has not said one word since he sat down, his thick brow bent into a frown as he peers out of the window in disdain. I notice how he wears his usual glamour, the visible signs of ageing no longer present no matter where I look.

I'm smart enough not to bother him when he is in one of his moods. It had been especially torturous these past several months of chasing after the numerous whispers of a supposed heir to his throne. I had travelled across the kingdom, indulging the king's obsession with this supposed true heir only to find my hands bathed in the blood of innocent young men. Though a part of me is curious as to what's caused it this time, I still find myself wary, and I'm glad for the excuse to remain silent. Having found myself in a brooding mood of my own after my trip to the catacombs, the last thing I want to do is share stilted conversation with him. After a while, however, King Barilius has a change of heart.

"This shall be an interesting visit. Erathon, for the most part, has kept the Havenore girl out of reach. It will be nice to watch him squirm in my presence."

"You've never mentioned him," I answer, turning away from the window.

"He is an earl, mostly irrelevant. But now it would seem he has something worth my interest," King Barilius flicks a speck from his shoulder, the gesture as dismissive as his tone.

"You think her the twelfth?" I sit up straighter, my attention piqued.

"Let's not jump ahead, Lysander," he replies, his harsh gaze now on me.

I bite back the scowl that threatens to eradicate my neutral expression, matching his gaze. I learned a long time ago that holding your ground in moments like these paid off with the

king. Though he had only ever tolerated it from a select few—
me being one of them.

"Your interest in her seems unwarranted, then," I say, if only
to fill the silence and for the satisfaction of having the last word.

"My interests are more than warranted and hardly any of
your concern, *boy*. I am king, and The Choosing is mine to
orchestrate as I see fit. You will do well to remember your
place," he growls, his amber eyes burning like wildfire.

At this I dip my head into a low bow, restraining my temper as
best as I can, though the shadowed tendrils still curl around me,
cowering away from the natural light and waiting for my next
command. The king turns away from me again, his expression
now bored as the carriage rolls through the country towards
Havenore Manor.

The carriage stops before a magnificent build of white and pale
grey stone. I stretch as I step down from the carriage, grateful to
be free of the tense energy.

A number of windows break the rhythm of stone with high
curved arches and neatly painted sashes. Sweeping steps lead up
the gravelled courtyard and up towards the rich, stained-wood
doors. They stand slightly open, if only by a hand's width, and
on either side stand armed guards, their postures stiff.

I turn at the sound of cascading water and the image of the
fountain we'd ridden around flashes through my mind. A typical
centrepiece to such a courtyard. My attention shifts to the splash
of green to the left of the manor where a glade of Flarak fruit
trees stands proudly, the golden fruit hanging plump and ripe on
the low branches.

A path leads from the courtyard through the trees and I notice
flashes of black and silver and recognise them as more guards
standing dutifully at their posts.

'*A wealthy family will always hire sword and shield... but
why so many*?' I wonder.

I turn as a man pushes through the doors and hurries down the
steps towards us. A flicker of movement above him captures my
attention. I squint to see a flag flapping above the archway of the
entrance, a blur of gold, purple and black with a puma at its
centre.

'Reliability, Generosity, Honour, Nobility, and Valour. An impressive family crest.'

"Have you announced our arrival?" King Barilius questions the footman as I turn back to help the king down the steps.

I send a sideward glance to the nervous man hopping from one foot to the other under the king's discerning gaze and watch as he shakes his head and scrambles back up the steps. With a raised brow, I shake my head in disapproval, aware of the king's sour expression. Today is definitely going to be a long day.

"Useless fool," I hear Barilius mutter beside me.

Mere moments later, the footman emerges again from the manor, this time with two others; a man and a woman. King Barilius takes a step forward, and as always I hang back, allowing him a head start, my hands respectfully behind my back.

"Presenting His Highness; King Barilius Saurhen, First of His Name," the footman calls aloud.

As we reach the top of the stairs, I'm finally able to see our hosts' faces. The man is tall and broad, his brown skin rich and his braided hair darker than the blackest ink. His matching onyx eyes watch us from where he stands, his lips pursed beneath a well-kept beard that coils across his jawline. He is well dressed in a suit jacket of blue and gold, and trousers of pure white.

'The markings of a soldier of the Elven War,' I observe.

He steps forward, his voice deep and rich as he speaks with a bow. "Your Majesty, I would like to introduce you to my niece, Nesryn Adella of the House of Havenore."

My eyes flick to the young woman in a sea of sheer, dusted pink. She is a sight to behold with smooth tawny skin glittered with gold, and innocently wide eyes, the hue of new spring, bright and soft all at once. Her hair is a tumble of curls woven into a crown above her head, the deep shade of brown coming to life under the bright sun. Across the left side of her chin, I notice, is a splash of darker skin. It only seems a few shades deeper than the rest of her, and yet it stands out. Her slender neck and long fingers are the only parts that are free of the embroidered fabric and I find myself wondering about the shape of her beneath the fan of her long elegant skirt.

'Certainly prettier than some of the others,' my mind whispers to me.

The king clears his throat beside me, which tells me that I've stood silent for too long. I'm about to make a snide comment or an excuse of some sort when her gaze moves to me and pins me in my silence. I sweep into a bow, noting the king's simmering anger, but refusing to acknowledge it.

"It's an honour, milady. I am Lysan, Second to His Majesty, The King, and his most faithful servant." I straighten, turning my attention to her uncle.

"Erathon, I presume. Thank you for hosting us this Choosing."

"You'll forgive Lysander, he seems to have lost his head today," Barilius grumbles beside me.

A warning of harsh words to come.

For now, I push them aside, directing my attention towards Erathon.

"Please, allow us to invite you in," he says, gesturing behind us to the open doors.

"Lead the way," I answer.

I feel Nesryn's wary eyes on me as her uncle leads her back into the manor, a protective hand on the small of her back.

I hang back and wait patiently for the king to follow after them but he eyes me suspiciously, his brow furrowed in distaste.

"Act accordingly or I'll be in need of a new Second."

"My apologies, Your Highness," I answer with a bow.

He mutters something beneath his breath and strides after Erathon and his niece. I hold back for a few seconds to pull myself together and remind myself why I'm here. I count to ten before following after Barilius, maintaining a mask of indifference as we're led down a long corridor.

Erathon leads us through a number of halls, turning left past a painting of a man and woman. It catches my eye momentarily and I recognise the same features that I saw in the Havenore girl. I glance towards where she walks ahead, eyeing the back of her perfectly pinned hair.

We're led into a drawing room where a table of light refreshments and plattered hors d'Oeuvres lay waiting. It seems that the earl has spared no expense as I eye the foreign morsels that have been so delicately placed on the silverware.

"Can I offer you a drink?" our host asks, gesturing for a servant to attend to us.

"Wine, I think," Barilius drawls.

"Red, preferably, thank you," I add quickly.

"That will be all, then," Erathon nods to the young man.

The servant nods once before scurrying away through the far doors and out of sight, returning promptly with four glasses of red wine. Once his tray is empty he bows and leaves.

My attention shifts as Barilius and Erathon begin to talk idly, and I wander away from them a little as I survey the place between small sips. The wine is rich and fruity on my lips, a dry kick as I swallow. I swill it around in my glass as I study it, considering its origin.

'Perhaps Cregvale, in the Northern Isles,' I consider.

Peeling my eyes from the crimson liquid, I take in the array of artwork that hangs on the walls. Each piece depicts a different landscape, a collection of beautiful scenery from across the Askrhean continent. Barilius had me tutored by the finest scholars in his kingdom, teaching me all about the vast lands mapped out on thick rolls of parchment. But I had yet to see past Akhozian borders, and as I take in the paintings, I wonder just how many of them are sights from outside these lands.

I draw further from the conversation, stopping in front of the huge tapestry facing the east wall. Sunlight streams across the centre of the fabric, illuminating the specks of dust floating in the warm air. I recognise it as the story of the gods and goddesses.

"Are you familiar with the story of the Goddess Asteria?" Nesryn asks.

I hide my surprise at her sudden presence and her stealth. I steal a sideways glance at her face. Her eyes are focused on the tapestry, flitting over the images woven into a beautiful tale before us.

"There are many versions," I answer, taking another long sip.

Nesryn gives me a sideward look but says nothing about my remark.

"She fell in love with Ciel, God of the Skies, and to confess her love she lit up the sky with golden starlight. Some of the gold flecks of light fell from the sky like shooting stars, blessing a handful of humans with the goddess's gift.

But when Ciel rejected her, devastated and brokenhearted, the light within her faded. From that day forth, where she once wielded light, now there was only shadow. Those who had been blessed by the goddess also suffered in her curse. For when they too suffered great loss and pain, they would become rulers of shadow just like Asteria before them."

I watch her as she recounts the story. Something that I can't quite read shines in her eyes.

"Asteria's love for Ciel had been so powerful and so true that although the starlight couldn't shine through the brightness of the day, as night fell, it would appear through the darkness as the last testament of her affections."

Despite myself, I scoff, a wry smile sneaking across my lips as I shake my head.

"You don't like the tale?" Nesryn asks, a defensive note to her question.

"It's definitely one of the soppier versions I've heard," I reply with a chuckle.

"I think it's beautiful," she retorts.

"You would."

I feel her hardened stare as she turns to face me. I raise a brow in silent question.

"What exactly is that supposed to mean?"

I sigh and lower my glass from my lips, turning as I slip my free hand comfortably into my trouser pocket.

"It means, *princess*, that fanciful tales of woe and romance were made for women like you, to keep you doe-eyed and soft.
"

The outrage on her face is evident and I snort through my nose as I look down at her.

"I'm not a princess," she scowls, "And what do you know anyway? You're just the king's dog," she practically growls, anger reverberating through the words.

The words are vicious and yet again I find myself surprised. I never imagined words like that coming from such a small, pretty thing. I open my mouth to speak but she swiftly turns on her heel and strides away, her head held high.

I watch as she leaves, amusement tugging my lips into a smile which I quickly cover with the rim of my glass, suddenly aware that the king is now watching us. Though perhaps he'd been watching the whole time.

Without another word, I saunter back towards them to where Nesryn Havenore stands, refusing to meet my eye.

NESRYN

CHAPTER THREE

I can feel Lysan watching me, his blue eyes roaming over me in lazy strokes. Anger simmers beneath my crawling skin. I try to cool my frustration by ignoring the bait. I refuse to give him the satisfaction. Instead, I focus on the small talk between the king and Uncle Erathon, and on occasion, me.

'Ignore him. He's a waste of energy,' my mind tells me.

I try my best to focus on the chatter between the other men, aware of my uncle's tense posture and the strain in his smile. My attention shifts back to the king. He is hardly the most intimidating man I'd ever come across, and younger than I'd imagined him to be. His olive skin is tan, but I see no signs of ageing. No laughter wrinkles crease his mouth, there's not a single stray grey hair in sight, only deep creases line his forehead from his constant frowning. His dark hair stretches to just over his shoulders and surprisingly there's no hint of a receding hairline beneath his solid bejewelled crown. Even his well-groomed, triangular beard is full and rich in colour.

The only indication of his true age lies in his mannerisms, though even then I have a hard time understanding how someone could reign over a kingdom for almost two decades and look no older than thirty. As I ponder this, his amber eyes fall on me, and I fight the urge to shudder at the molten pools regarding me so intently. Something within them causes my stomach to clench uncomfortably.

"Pardon me for overlooking you, my dear, I mean no disrespect," he says with a flash of teeth.

His tone seems friendly enough, but his smile doesn't reach his eyes. His eyes, I realise with a start, are hollow. All eyes turn to me and I try my hardest not to look away. I hold my ground, fighting the urge to shuffle uncomfortably on the spot.

"It's no trouble, Your Majesty," I answer with a small curtsey.

"So well-mannered. It seems you have raised quite the young lady," he observes, turning back to my uncle, though his eyes remain fixed on me.

"I have certainly done my best by her," Uncle Erathon answers.

I dare to glance over at Lysan who seems more interested in his empty wine glass than anything going on around him. My dislike of him only grows as I take in his bored expression and I bite my tongue before I show the king how ill-mannered I truly can be.

Lysan looks up from his glass towards us as he pulls his hand from his pocket and combs it through his black curtain of hair. Something wild flashes across his features, but it's gone before I can blink.

"The Choosing is more than an array of well-mannered girls," he comments, dropping his glass into the hands of a passing server.

"Lysander is right. I take it, girl, that your uncle has made you aware of what is expected of you, should you become one of my Chosen twelve?" King Barilius watches me closely.

I glance at Uncle Erathon who gives me a tight-lipped smile. My eyes flit back to the king as I rub anxious circles over a petal on my skirt.

"I am aware of my duties as a Chosen maiden, should you bestow the honour upon me, Your Highness," I answer.

Out of the corner of my eye, I notice Lysan watching me with a solemn gaze.

"Good. Then I shall leave you with this parting verse. You have until sundown tomorrow to give me an answer," he informs me.

"His Majesty won't be joining us for supper?" Uncle Erathon asks in surprise, though I can see the relief in his loosening shoulders.

"I have far too much that requires my attention, Erathon. Perhaps another time," King Barilius says dismissively.

He turns to me, his expression growing serious as he steps forward.

"I will only say it once, girl, so listen closely," he says.
I nod once, my eyes never leaving his face.

"The beast alone cannot be fed,
Upon the mark, the faces tell.
Once the beast has but yester's dead,
It cast but one, imperfect spell."

As the words leave his lips, I stow them away to contemplate in a moment of quiet.

"You have until sundown tomorrow," he warns me again.

"Thank you for this opportunity, Your Majesty," I reply, dipping my head.

"I await your response then. A pleasure," King Barilius replies, his eyes scouring my face greedily.

The gesture unnerves me and I shift on my feet. After a moment his attention returns to my uncle and they converse amongst themselves. My mind is already busy dissecting the riddle as the chatter dies down and Uncle Erathon begins to escort the king and his Second out of the drawing room and into the main hall.

I follow after them, keeping a good distance as I turn over the riddle in my mind. I'm so preoccupied that I hardly notice when Lysan glances back at me and slows down.

'The beast alone cannot be fed / upon the mark, the faces tell / Once the beast has but yester's dead / it cast but one, imperfect spell.' I mouth the words to myself over and over as I try to make sense of them.

"Try not to ponder too hard, or those eyes of yours will turn in on each other," Lysan mocks with a wink.

I glare at him as he saunters past and releases a breathy chuckle as he slows beside his master. Deciding to ignore his childish taunts, I focus on the riddle, repeating the four lines in my head in an attempt to familiarise myself with it, to slowly understand it.

'It can't be an animal, that would be too obvious,' I deduce.

We round the next corner, my parents' portraits coming into view, before we continue on, moving further along the lengthy hall towards the front door.

"But if it isn't a real beast, then it's a metaphor," I mutter to myself.

'And if it's a metaphor then...'

I stop mid-stride.

"The answer is the shift in seasons," I blurt.

All three men stop and turn to look back at me. The king with a raised brow, his lips curling into a smile, an expression more daunting than warm and kind. Beside him, Uncle Erathon looks crestfallen, while Lysan's expression is one of mild intrigue. I see a flash of surprise in his eyes and a smug smile blankets my face.

"From Snowhold to Warmwell," I finish.

Silence blankets the space, my heart racing as I wait for a response.

"Interesting," King Barilius mutters, cutting through the silence. "Seems she certainly has her wits about her, hey Lysander?" he says, glancing at the young man by his side.

My eyes flit to Lysan and the glowering look in his eyes. I stand my ground, head high and shoulders back.

"You shall receive my correspondence in a short while, Nesryn Adella of the House of Havenore," he says with a dismissive wave.

Lysan's eyes remain trained on me for several more seconds before he turns and follows after the king, his shoulders tight and his hands clenched. As I glance down at his shadow I blink in surprise as I watch it writhe around before returning to its original shape. I'm stunned into silence, what I had seen was no trick of the light. The king's Second is truly a Shadowcaster.

'Perhaps the rumours are true? Perhaps he truly is as powerful as people say.'

"It has been an honour. Until your next visit, Your Majesty," Uncle Erathon says with a low bow.

The king doesn't turn back to acknowledge him but instead waves a lazy hand over his shoulder before he strolls through the open door and down the sloping steps, out of sight.

The breath that I didn't realise I'd been holding escapes my lips in a heavy breath. My heart continues to pound even as I hear our guests return to their carriage and their horses pull them across the courtyard and through the gates.

"I did it," I mutter to myself in disbelief. "I actually did it."

LYSAN

CHAPTER FOUR

The palace is buzzing with life and the nervous energy is contagious. There have been extra hands about the place for days, scrubbing and shining everything in sight in preparation for this year's Choosing. Servants rush about the east wing, popping in and out of the long corridor of guest rooms. They flit about, opening the balcony doors and arched windows to allow the rooms to breathe in the fresh air. Fresh linen is laid out, beds are stripped and remade, floors are scrubbed and bathrooms are polished until the whole wing smells like the fresh beginnings of Warmwell.

My room is dark despite the open curtains. I lay sprawled on my disturbed sheets, not yet dressed for the day, wearing only a pair of trousers that hang comfortably low. My tousled hair slips repeatedly into my eyes and I comb it back with my fingers as I flick my other wrist, the tendrils of shadow whipping forward and piercing the glass on my desk. Glass flies and chimes as it sprays across the floor in tiny shards and I smirk at my bored attempts at target practice. The shadows smother my room, drinking in the light and coating everything in a swirl of inked darkness.

Over the past few days I've tried my best to keep to my quarters, or busy myself with my duties, far away from all the commotion. Barilius, however, seems to have other plans for me and I find myself being summoned by him again and again. Summons that I choose to ignore.

I lift my hand in silent command, watching as a wave of shadow creeps along the ground, drawing them up into the air and swallowing up the shards. The shadow shifts, curving effortlessly into a large sphere that floats just at the end of my bed between the two posts. The pieces of glass collide against one another, tumbling around and around with a tune of tinkling sounds. I tilt my head to the side, watching as it spins, feeling a soft breeze to brush against my face. With another flick of my wrist, the ball spins in the opposite direction. The movement barely takes any effort after so many years of honing my talents. I sigh and clench my fist tight, the sphere evaporating into thin air, while the shards of glass float to the floor in a pile of ground-up dust.

A rapping at my door pulls me from my agitated boredom and I roll off the bed and pad towards the door. The dust swirls across the stone floor, a loose shard nicking the heel of my foot as I stride past. I brush it away, cursing under my breath as a speck of blood beads on my foot.

"Yes," I answer as I pull the door open.

My eyes fall on Melek, the king's most favoured messenger.

I raise a brow at the old man darkening my door. His expression is bored, though there is a youthful spark in his eyes that has always surprised me. His lips curl up into a smile beneath his wiry beard. The light catches his spectacles as he pushes them further up the bridge of his hooked nose.

"What do you want, Melek?" I ask as I lean against the doorframe.

"His Majesty requests your presence in his private study in a half-chime," he informs me.

"A request rather than a summon. Barilius must be in a favourable mood today," I say dryly, folding my arms across my chest.

His eyes move from my crossed arms to my face, unimpressed. "Just get dressed and don't be late. You're already on thin ice," he warns me.

He spins on his heel and walks away.

"Aren't I always?" I call after him.

I hear him sigh and catch the shake of his head as he continues on, turning the corner and disappearing from sight.

Looping my belt through the buckle, I fasten it securely and glance over at my blades laid out neatly on my desk. Sharpened, shined, and ready for action. With a deep inhale, I decide against them and pull my eyes away, grabbing the loose black shirt on top of my hastily made sheets instead.

I shrug it on and button up the front in a daze, my mind on the king and what arduous task he's picked out for me next. My only guess is that it has something to do with The Choosing and the twelve girls he's been picking out over the past several weeks.

I think of what's to come and frown. Diplomacy isn't my strong suit, though neither is attending events, and I have no doubt that King Barilius expects me to be a part of the whole spectacle—just like the last time.

Her face isn't something that torments me often but it appears clear in my mind's eye before I can push it away. My chest tightens at the sight of her. Shadows unfurl around me, covering every inch of the room. They twist and writhe slowly as if they have a mind of their own, but the truth is, when it comes to thoughts of her, I can never keep my emotions in check.

"I made a promise, Loísia, and I intend to keep it."

With a deep breath, I retract the shadows encircling me, watching as they pull the darkness from the room and soak into my skin. Sunlight streams through the windows once more and I let out the breath in a shaky sigh.

'Get it together, Shadowcaster,' I tell myself.

Once again, my eyes move to the array of weapons lining my desk and I consider arming myself. I dispel the thought quickly. I know exactly what the king would say if I arrived emblazoned with steel.

'You are the weapon, Lysander, not these measly trinkets,' I hear his voice clear in my mind.

The halls are busier than I'm used to as I weave through the maids and servants milling about the halls. Even the guards are too preoccupied to hurl insults at my back as I saunter past. I'm surprised when I pass a group of six soldiers on patrol, accompanied by a familiar face—their captain, Keelhan.

He's tanner than I remember him, with darkened freckles splashed across his face, cut off only by his thick facial hair. The dark beard is a stark contrast to his bright blue eyes and blond braided hair that tapers off past his shoulders. It's long enough now for him to be mistaken for one of the Nruk warriors of the north.

"Aren't you supposed to be in Trlló doing real work?" I call to him, unable to fight the smirk tugging at my lips.

He stops barking orders as he catches my eye. A wide smile spreads across his face as he breaks rank and strides over. He pulls me into a strong embrace, slapping between my shoulderblades in a way that only he can get away with, before stepping back.

"Shadowmongrel, it's been an age!" his voice booms along the halls.

A few servants glance our way, but a quick warning look from Keelhan has them moving along, busy with their tasks once again. I glance over at his men who remain banded together, though their suspicious eyes continue to shift towards me in particular when their captain isn't looking.

"Quite the disciplined group you have there, what's the occasion?"

"King Barilius ordered my return as soon as he picked the twelfth broad for The Choosing. He's upped all the security around the castle, what with those so-called rebels popping up left, right, and centre," he explains. The fire in his eyes reveals the words left unspoken.

I raise my eyebrows in surprise. The king had mentioned his concerns several times over the past weeks, but I had never expected him to pull his best soldiers from the ports of Trlló to deal with some mediocre troublemakers in the capital. Despite myself, I wonder what this may mean, and what the king's true plans may be if this is just a tactical play.

"Not the best move tactically speaking," I comment, glancing at the soldiers once more.

"Try convincing our king of that," he scoffs. "He'd probably listen to you over me anyhow," Keelhan grumbles, unusually bitter.

"And yet it's you who wields the title of captain," I retort.

He sends a deadpan look my way and I can't help the laughter that bubbles up from my throat.

He glances around, suddenly wary of those around us. I follow his lead, scanning around us for an unknown threat as he leans in to speak.

"The men I have stationed here are more than capable of dealing with a few petty rebels. It's the ports we need to be watching, these so-called organisations rely on what sails into those docks," he informs me, his voice softer than before.

"Does the king know? Surely he wouldn't have pulled you from your duties in the city if he knew that your work here is important to the effort."

Keelhan shakes his head, a sombre expression on his face. "Supposedly, what we know is nothing more than rumours and word of mouth." I frown, sceptical. "But I have a contact and thus far, he has yet to lead me and my men astray," he answers.

"I see," I say, rubbing a hand across my chin. "Well, I'm on my way to see him now, perhaps I'll run it by him... see if he's still set on keeping you in the capital."

"Then it sounds like I owe you a drink or two," Keelhan grins, slapping my shoulder.

"Or more," I reply, my smile returning.

He throws his head back in laughter and when he looks at me again, I see that the usual brightness has returned.

"Then I won't keep you," he says with a grand sweep of his hand towards the palace.

"I'll find you later and you can tell me of all your exciting adventures on the road," I smirk.

"I look forward to it."

Keelhan's demeanour shifts as he turns back to his men who stiffen under his gaze. They stare straight ahead as he leads them in a disciplined march down the hall, moving as one towards the south doors and the gardens beyond.

My trip through the palace becomes quieter, the bustle of servants dwindles as I leave the east wing. I make my way through the familiar halls towards King Barilius's rooms with a vague sense of dread. I think of how full the palace will feel with twelve noblewomen and how each of them will fare in the weeks to come.

It's been so long since the last Choosing, yet somehow I remember it as clearly as the days in which it happened. I had been a young, naive teenager at the time, but even then I appreciated the seriousness of the occasion. I shudder inwardly at the thought of it. I never could've predicted what was about to happen during those long weeks ten years ago.

I shake away the lurking thoughts as I pass the throne room and then the ballroom, the sound of sweeping and polishing muffled behind the closed double doors. I continue on towards the twirling stone steps that lead to the room in the tower. The king's private study. I notice with a chill that the torches are lit— a sign that Barilius has spent all night up here doing whatever he does behind closed doors.

Despite the many years that I have lived inside these palace walls, I still find myself curious about what goes on in this secluded corner of the palace. The noises that would wake me as a young boy and carry me to the foot of this stairwell in the dark of night still plague me and make my imagination run wild. Even now, I feel tense as I climb the steps. In all the years I have been under the king's service, I have only ever been summoned to his private study a mere handful of times. He tended to prefer the throne room or the dining halls for his usual places of discussion. His private study had always been off-limits.

When I reach the top of the stairwell, I stop outside the large door and glance warily at the gold knocker, shaped like a three-horned demon. I rap my knuckles against the thick wood whilst eyeing the creature. I wait but no voice trickles through the door. I frown and try again. Silence. My hand hovers over the door knob for a couple of breaths before I brace myself and twist the knob to the right. I expect the hinges to creak as I push the door open, but they remain silent as the door swings wide open. I fight the shudder threatening to run through me; I've never liked this part of the palace.

I'm once again surprised at how dark and big the room is. The tower has always looked small from the outside. As I step forwards, the door closes with a sharp bang behind me, causing me to whip my head around. Satisfied, I turn my attention back to the room, wander about the space, drinking in its details.

Bottles of strange liquids and vials of pale powders are lined up before countless volumes of thick, dusty books. In the far corner stands an iron cauldron, lifted up off the floor by four claw feet. To the left stands a table of solid polished stone. The small window beside it is open, releasing fresh air into the space.

As I walk deeper into the room, I can smell the heavy metallic taste of dark magic clogging the air and I try not to gag from the staleness of it.

I stop and listen as I scan the space, expecting the king to step out from whichever dark corner he has been hiding in, but he doesn't and I realise that, for once, I'm entirely alone. I feel the rush as the rebellious voice inside my head whispers to look around more closely. I don't need to be convinced. I peer closely at the bottles on the shelves, trying to decipher the scrawly handwriting on the label, and taking in the embellished gold jackets of the hardbacks behind them.

Slowly, I run a fingertip along the spine of a faded volume. *No dust.* It looks like one of the more frequently used books on the shelf—especially compared to the ones on either side of it that are covered in a thick blanket of the stuff.

"Magic: A Guide By The Ages. Volume Four," I read aloud.

I tilt my head to the side to read another title when I hear heavy footsteps climbing the winding staircase. My chest constricts at the thought of getting caught snooping about the king's items and I step back into the safety of a dark corner, my shadows drawing out of thin air and wrapping around me until I am nothing but a living, breathing extension of the darkness.

I wait in silence as the door opens and slams shut as the king strides into the room. His boots strike the stone as he makes his way to the pedestal hidden behind the cauldron. I watch as he opens the closed book, his expression serious and his brow furrowed as he flips through the pages.

He pulls out an envelope wedged between the pages about a third of the way through and turns it over in his hands before edging closer to the cauldron. I recognise his personal seal on the back as he drops the envelope into the depths of the cauldron. It takes on a life of its own as it sparks and rumbles at the incantation that he utters. One that I'm not close enough to hear. Sparks fly out of the cauldron as Barilius finishes the spell. Mist or steam floats over the lip and spills over as the scent of magic grows thicker. I watch as he steps away from it and returns to the pedestal.

'*What did he do with that letter*?' I wonder.

He busies himself with flicking through the pages of the volume once more, murmuring something else under his breath.

Just as I begin to wonder how I'm going to present myself after hiding here for so long, King Barilius decides for me.

"Stop hiding away in the shadows, boy. I taught you to wield them, not become them," he snaps.

'*If he knew I was here and was willing to cast in front of me, why the usual secrecy with this room?*' I wonder, the sting of embarrassment making me feel like that timid boy again.

At his request, I step out from the corner, the shadows unfurling around me and shrinking back into the darkness. I dip my head, hoping that my face isn't burning as brightly as I feel it is.

"For a supposed exceptional Shadowcaster, I'm disappointed by your occasional sloppiness," he says, glancing at me over his shoulder.

"My apologies, Your Majesty."

"You will stop this foolery at once and act accordingly, or you won't like what I'll do to you," he warns.

I swallow, choosing to say nothing. Without prompting, he continues on.

"I summoned you here as I have an important job for you. These need to be delivered to each of the recipients as soon as possible. I trust that I can leave you with this simple task, Lysander?" the king asks.

I wait patiently, obediently, as he walks over to the cluttered writing desk and rifles through it for several long moments. I try to peer around him to see what he's looking for, but soon enough he gives a triumphant grunt and I straighten just in time. He whirls around, holding out a small stack of sealed envelopes for me to take.

"Of course, Your Majesty. I will take my leave immediately."

"See that you do."

I bend into a low bow that he doesn't acknowledge before I leave. The door slams shut behind me as I glance down at the wad of letters. I rifle through them, reading each name under my breath in the quiet of the stairwell.

Reverie Zouvsa

Vena Astalón

Zariya Gladdreiys

Lesya Raviffete

Ovie Montallet

Rohana Duhrannes
Maskia Lockport
Erryn Drulfeard
Twyla Drullanon
Chandra Roquenet
Mallon Vythierre
Nesryn Havenore

My eyes hover over the final name as I recall the young baroness who had unravelled the king's riddle in mere minutes. I think back to the triumph lighting up her eyes and the smug smile she had directed at me in the moments after.

She had wanted to show me up, to make a point. But she was wrong. The Choosing would be making a point of showing them up, and she would find that out soon enough. They all would.

'*King Barilius is not one to be trifled with,*' the words float around my mind.

"Goddess help them," I mutter.

I begin my descent down the curving stone steps, my mood sombre as I glance down at the stack of letters in my hands for the third time. I step out into the hall, my mask of calm slipping back onto my face despite the grim feeling settling in my stomach.

The maidens have been chosen, the letters have been written. There will be no turning back for any of them now.

The Choosing has well and truly begun.

NESRYN

CHAPTER FIVE

I wait with bated breath from the moment that King Barilius's carriage rolls through our gates back to the capital, until the arrival of my letter. My veins had been thrumming with nervous energy ever since answering his riddle.

My rigorous training with Jarek is constant and yet it seems that it isn't nearly enough to keep my head firmly on my shoulders, instead of up in the clouds, anxious and anticipating. I make stupid, amateur mistakes that cost me bruises and the scorn of my teacher, whose lectures start to become longer than the lessons themselves.

The wait is unbearable.

Uncle Erathon has barely said a word since King's Barilius's visit. He has taken on a sombre mood that travels with him wherever he goes, like a grey cloud that looms overhead. Even the farmers working the orchards and the servants running the manor weren't graced with his usual friendly demeanour. Instead, he is stiff, distant, and much more tight-lipped than I'm used to. I watch in growing concern as he begins to miss meals and stay up late into the evening, holed up in his study, the elvynlight glowing through the keyhole and the slim gap beneath the door.

It takes five days for the letter to arrive.

I'm in the gardens, practising yet another round of drills—courtesy of Uncle Erathon. Despite me not seeing him for more than a few moments a day over the past week, my uncle has not let up with my training. If anything, he's encouraging Jarek to be harder on me, to work me until my body is a trembling mess of bruises and shallow cuts. I feel the exhaustion rooted into my bones and finally demand Jarek to let me take a rest. For once, Jarek doesn't argue with me.

The news that a letter has arrived for me finally reaches my ears and I'm surprised to find myself visibly relax after hearing the news from the excited maid who hurries to find me. I rush through gardens and into the coolness of the manor, speeding along the halls in search of the person who has it. I'm trying to slow my breathing and stay calm when I round the corner and almost bump into the maid I'm looking for. She smiles and drops into a short curtsey as she hands me the envelope adorned with the king's seal. I waste no time as I rip it open in front of her, my eyes flitting left and right on the page as I drink in the words.

"Dear Nesryn Adella of the House of Havenore, I invite you to the palace as my honoured guest and twelfth member of this year's Choosing. I congratulate your efforts and wish you well for your upcoming trials," I read aloud, my voice breathy from my run and the tension.

"Congratulations, milady," the maid utters, embarrassed.

I look up from the paper and give her a wide and warm smile before she mumbles an excuse and scarpers off, leaving me reeling from the news.

Uncle Erathon is nowhere to be seen at dinner. I try not to show my frustration and disappointment at being unable to share my news with him over our meal.

My body aches beneath my dress from the gruelling training, my shoulders stiff as I try to get through my meal with as little movement as possible. I glance across the table for the fifth time to the empty chair and the steaming bowl of rich beef stew waiting beside two rolls of fresh, fluffy bread. I look down at my own half-eaten bowl as I break off another chunk of the bread and soak it in the stew.

I savour the rich flavours as they roll across my tongue, my eyes flitting to the door as I hear the familiar twist of the handle. My hopes are dashed as Mina, one of the kitchen staff walks in and picks up the food sitting across from me.

"I take it that means he won't be joining me. Again," I say, filling the silence.

Mina gives me a half-smile that doesn't reach her eyes. "Sorry, milady."

I sigh as I put down my silverware and shake my head in disappointment. As if she can tell that I'm not done, Mina stays, hovering with the bowl and plate balanced on her arms. An idea sparks in my head in the midst of the silence.

"Please could you bring me a bottle of white and two glasses, Mina?"

"Of course, milady, which white will you be wanting?"

"My uncle's preferred white, if you don't mind," I answer.

"Of course, milady. I'll be back shortly," she replies before turning and leaving the way she came.

When Mina returns, my bowl and plate are empty and I'm leant against the corner of the table, drumming my fingers against the thick wooden surface.

I notice how flustered she looks as her gaze flits to me, and away again bashfully.

"I'm sorry for the wait, milady. The stores seem to be low on the wine you wanted... it took me a while to find some," she explains.

She places two dusty bottles down on the table with a clunk.

"That's alright, Mina, thank you. Perhaps we can order some more for the next trip to port," I suggest as I collect the bottles and crystal glasses.

"Of course, milady. Will that be all?" she asks after collecting my dinnerware.

"Yes, thank you," I answer, giving her a small smile.

Without another word, I turn and leave, pushing my way through the doors and into the darkened hall.

The air is cool as I walk, servants lighting the sconces with orbs of elvynlight as I meander past, the bottles clinking together in my grasp, matching my steps.

In the impending dusk, the shadows begin to scale the walls, turning the framed portraits and landscapes into gloomy, ominous versions of themselves. Apart from the scuffle of shoes, the manor is quiet; the majority of the servants are probably prepping for bed in their quarters on the southern side of the manor.

As I wander the halls, mapping out the route to my uncle's study in my mind, a ghost of a smile appears on my lips. I remember rushing along these halls as a child, afraid of the monsters lurking in the darkened spaces, raring to strike when I least expected them. How I would run when my mind twisted and distorted things into the shapes that my imagination brought to life.

My uncle had swept me up in his arms when I ran to him, tearful and afraid, hiding my face in his chest.

"Oh, Nix, the darkness is nothing to be afraid of," he would tell me while stroking my head.

"It isn't the darkness that frightens me, it's what's hiding in it," I had said.

He paused, a thoughtful expression on his face as I pulled back and looked up at him with wide eyes. Finally, his eyes met mine and a warm smile spread across his lips.

"That is quite the clever perspective, little one, but know that whatever may be lurking in the shadows would never dare to cross you," he explained.

"Why?" I asked.

"Because you're going to smite them like the fearless little warrior queen I know you to be," he answered as he rubbed his nose against my own, making me giggle. "In time you will see that it is they who should be afraid. Hear the unheard, see the unseen, and endure."

I smile to myself at the fondness of the memory, gradually stopping at the doors to his study. I glance down to see the light spilling out from under the door and release a short, weary sigh. I lift my hand, tapping the top of the bottle against the door in a quick knock.

I hear shuffling as he gets up from his chair and walks towards the door. He pulls it open enough for me to see his face and he gives me a surprised look. I raise a questioning brow.

"Nix," he cries, pulling the door wider.

"If I didn't know any better, I'd think you were avoiding me," I say dryly.

A shadow moves across his eyes as he smiles guiltily at me. But before he can mutter one of his usual excuses, I hold up the bottles and the two glasses.

"I come bearing gifts," I say with a smirk.

Uncle Erathon releases a tired sigh and smiles at me while shaking his head, a little light coming back to his onyx eyes.

"You'd best come on in then," he says, stepping aside.

As soon as I'm inside, I stop short. My eyes are wide as I take in the chaotic state of the room.

The desk is overflowing with papers, some screwed up into balls and scattered about the floor, others littering the walkway. A pile of messily stacked books lean against one side of the desk, while two books lay open on top of the sea of papers.

"What in the seven continents is this?" I demand, looking back over my shoulder at my uncle.

Shame is written all over his face.

"Uncle, please... what is going on?" I ask, my tone much gentler than before.

"I've been scouring the books. Searching for a clause, a rule, anything to find you a way out," he answers after a long pause.

"A way out of what?" I ask.

I move over to the desk, push some papers out of the way, and place the wine and glasses down. As I straighten, he walks over to me, taking my hands in his, a fearful look in his eyes.

"The Choosing," he says.

I pull my hands out of his grasp, frowning with confusion as he reaches for me, pleading.

"Uncle Erathon, I am one of the twelve. It's my duty to the king to be a part of this year's Choosing. Why would you wish to rob me of this opportunity?" I ask, the hurt in my voice clear as day.

"You know my views of the king and his politics," Uncle Erathon replies.

"It doesn't matter what you think, he is still our king," I argue, shaking my head.

"He is a dangerous man, Nesryn," he warns.

"So are most wealthy, titled men," I counter.

"*Nesryn*—" he starts. A warning.

"—This is something you can't change, Uncle. I accept my role as a Chosen, you have no right to stop me from doing so," I point out.

"I'm just trying to protect you," he argues, his frustration evident.

"Protect me from what? Have you forgotten the years of vigorous training?" I argue, eyes narrowing. "What is it that you're not telling me?"

"There are things that your training won't have prepared you for," he tells me, rubbing a hand across his face. If I didn't know any better I'd say that he was afraid.

"And there are things that you have no control over, things that I must do," I say, marching through the door with my head held high, ignoring his pleas to come back.

The night is quiet and peaceful as I sit beside the rippling pond, the fish nibbling at my ankles, hopeful for a treat. With a sigh, I sprinkle another dusting of food across the surface and watch as they scramble amongst themselves, their little mouths popping up to the surface. Bubbles bloat and pop as the frenzy dies down.

A warm breeze rifles through the trees, a shushing sound moving across the orchard to my right, the leaves whispering as I watch from the sidelines. My mind echoes the words Uncle Erathon had said, my head ringing with it all as I try to fathom his views.

'*I could never decline, even if I wanted to,*' I think to myself.

For the first time since I received the letter, I think of what accepting my place in The Choosing will mean, what I will have to leave behind. I consider what our tests may be. Intelligence? Endurance, perhaps? I have no clue what is in store for me, and I feel both excited and anxious at the thought of stepping foot into the unknown.

'*Eleven others will make the same sacrifice*, it's only a few months,' I remind myself.

I hear his footsteps before I see him and I brace myself for another round of debates, something that I realise I'm not ready for.

"I had a feeling I would find you here," he says as he stops at my side.

I glance up at my uncle who offers an apologetic smile.

"If you've come to continue our debate, then don't," I say with resignation.

He says nothing as he removes his shoes and seats himself beside me, hissing as he dips his feet in the cool water. Without a word, he pulls out one of the bottles of wine and pops the cork, taking a long swig straight from the bottle before offering it to me. I take it gladly.

"Do you remember those stories I would tell you when you were much younger?" he says finally.

"About the Starweaver and his perilous adventures. How could I forget?" I take a swig, feeling the liquid warm my throat.

"Those stories..." he trails off, his expression distant.

He blinks and sighs sadly as he comes back to himself. He turns to me, taking in every inch of my face until he eventually turns back to the pool.

"Those stories were told to me by your father."

There is a sadness in his voice that stirs something within me and I lower the bottle from my lips, looking at him with silent, wary curiosity.

"He once said that his father had told them to him as a boy and that when it was time, he would tell them to his children."

My throat constricts, the wine suddenly difficult to swallow.

"When he died, he entrusted the task to me. I've done my best to do it with honour and dignity, as he would have," he continues, choking a little on the words as they leave him. I place my hand over his and smile when his eyes meet mine.

"I promised them that I would take care of you—that—that I would protect you until I saw them again," he explains, raw pain in his voice.

"And you have, you have kept your vow from the moment I was thrust upon you," I tease, feeling an overwhelming sense of gratitude.

"You remind me of them both, you know? They would be so proud of the young woman that you've become," he says gently, his hand reaching for my face.

He wipes away the stray tear that falls and smiles lopsidedly at me.

"Promise me you will be careful, Nix," he asks.

It's a simple request but I can feel the depth behind his words. It's a declaration of trust, one that I'm glad to hear.

"Hear, see, endure," I reply, quoting the words that he'd taught me as a child.

NESRYN

CHAPTER SIX

The next day Ragna and Ceryl spend the morning flurrying around my room, helping me pack. I weave around them as they rush back and forth between my wardrobe and the open chests at the base of my bed. I watch as they slowly fill up with gowns folded neatly into squares. Since the moment I had awoken, the two women had been rifling through my clothes, helping me pack the necessary belongings for my time at the palace.

"You'll need plenty of evening wear," Ceryl tells me over her shoulder, pulling out a gown of shimmering emerald green.

"She'll also need a few more modest ones for during the day, should she be called upon," Ragna cuts in.

I watch as she draws out my favourite grey piece, the silk of the skirts shimmering in the light.

"What about my training gear?" I ask, gripping the black leathery clothing in my hands.

"What about it?" Ragna queries.

"I'll need it as well," I point out.

"I should think not," Ceryl exclaims.

"I'd like to be prepared for all outcomes," I explain as I move towards the closest chest.

I hear her huff of disagreement but she dips her head as I look over my shoulder, brows raised.

"I'm sorry, milady, but if you don't mind me saying, you're one of the Chosen twelve. You won't have time for any of that vulgar training the master insists you do," she argues.

"First of all, Ceryl, I happen to enjoy the training, vulgarity and all," I start, regaining my posture. "Furthermore, there may be trials that require a little less finesse and silk skirts. I've heard that there are more to the trials than just standing around and looking pretty." A bitter laugh bubbles free. "So I'll be taking my gear."

"Very well, milady," Ceryl replies, her head dipped, a blonde curl slipping free from under her bonnet.

"I will see to it that they are packed," Ragna informs me.

"Thank you, ladies."

I hear the clock sound, marking three chimes. Just as I'm about to help them with my packing, a swift knock on my door halts me. I glance at them in turn, both clueless, before striding over to the door.

"Jarek," I say, the surprise evident in my tone and expression.

His serious eyes find mine immediately and he hesitates.

"Nesryn... I hope I'm not disturbing," he says, glancing past me curiously at the bustling women behind me.

"We're just in the middle of packing for my trip," I explain. "Is there something that you wanted?" I press when he doesn't speak.

At my words he snaps back to attention, his temporary distraction forgotten. "Yes, your uncle asked me to bring you to him."

"He needs me now?" I ask, confused.

He nods once, drawing his hands behind his back as he waits for me.

I turn back to Ragna and Ceryl.

"My uncle has asked for me. My escort will be here at five chimes, do you think you can manage to gather my things without me?"

"Of course, milady. We'll have this done in no time, we're more than capable of getting this done on our own," Ragna replies for the both of them.

Ceryl nods in encouragement.

"Alright then. Thank you both," I smile.

I turn back to Jarek and gesture for him to lead the way, pulling the door shut behind me.

The halls are quiet as we walk side by side.

Sunlight filters through the large arched windows, illuminating the space and warming the air. Dust particles swirl through the air, catching the light as we disturb their path. The familiar musty smell of oil paintings catches in my nose and I realise that soon I'll be surrounded by unfamiliar halls and paintings of people that I have never met, of landscapes that I have never seen. My stomach snags as I realise how everything is going to change, how I'll be alone amongst a group of strangers, deep in the capital, away from the beautiful countryside that I've always called home.

As we pass by yet another window, I slow my pace and glance out at the Flarak orchards beyond the gardens, watching the workers as they climb the ladders and pick the ripened fruit. I'll miss sitting beneath the shaded branches of those trees, reading my books while feasting on the sweet fruit.

I contemplate what to expect when I arrive at the palace—if there will be gardens as vast and beautiful as the ones on my doorstep. I think of how my uncle will now walk these paths alone with no one to hear about his favourite literature or his strong political views. I wonder if he will find himself lonely, if he will miss my presence at our evening meals.

"Is everything alright, Nesryn?" Jarek calls, a few feet ahead.

I pull my eyes away from the vast stretch of land and focus on him with a tired smile.

"Yes, of course," I answer, closing the gap.

Jarek stays silent.

"Will he be alright?" I ask with a nervous look towards my tutor. "My uncle, I mean."

"Erathon only worries for your sake. He'll be fine."

A sigh escapes my lips and I feel Jarek's eyes on me once more.

"You worry for him," he surmises.

"He's hardly been himself since the king's visit," I reply.

"That may be true, but he's a lot more resilient than you believe him to be," Jarek tells me.

We round the corner and slow as we reach Uncle Erathon's study. The door is slightly ajar and Jarek stops as I step forward to push the door further open. I send him a questioning look when I realise he doesn't plan to follow.

"There's no need for me to be in there with you. I was just the messenger," he shrugs.

I stop mid-stride, my hand hovering over the doorknob as I begin to protest, but Jarek cuts me off.

"I wish you all the best in The Choosing, Nesryn, but know this... if you don't make the cut, we will be right here waiting for you," he says with a reassuring smile and earnest eyes.

I give him a small smile and dip my head to him gratefully to which he returns the gesture own and with hands held behind his back, he turns on his heels and wanders down the hall and out of sight.

I'm happily surprised to find Uncle's study back in order. Books are displayed neatly along the shelves, papers are stacked in neat piles and I can finally see the rich oak desk underneath. The windows on either side of the far wall are wide open and carry in a delicious breeze that caresses my neck.

My uncle stands facing the closest window, holding his hands behind him as he stares out at the view. As I round the desk I see the pensive expression on his face. His dreadlocks are tied in a half ponytail, the shorter coils sticking out horizontally, while the loose ones taper off at his shoulders.

"Uncle, you called for me?" I call gently.

He starts at the closeness of my voice, the shock soon turning into a smile that lights up his face.

"Nesryn, yes—yes I did," he answers, taking my hands in his.

He leads me to the chair by his desk and sits me down before moving across the room to the far bookshelf. To the safe. I try to peer past him, my curiosity piqued as I hear the sound of a magic sigil being carved. I hear the soft sound of the lock clicking open before he turns and strides back over to me. In his hands he carries a black box, the sides adorned with intricate gold swirls.

"I have waited for this day for a very long time," he tells me as he kneels down in front of me.

"What is it?" I ask, leaning forward.

"A gift. From your father." The pride in his voice is impossible to miss.

My heart skips a beat in my chest and I glance between the box and my uncle in disbelief. Words surface for a brief moment before flurrying away, leaving me with nothing.

"Why have I… You never mentioned…" I trail off as my eyes fall back on the box. My hands tremble as I reach for it.

"I was instructed that this was to be given to you when you were ready," he explains. "I think now is as good a time as any," he adds, watching me closely.

I run my fingers over the smooth wood, feeling the grain beneath my fingertips before clicking the latch open, my breath catching in my throat as it opens to reveal a sheathed dagger laid out on a velveteen cushion. I remove it with careful fingers and turn it this way and that as I admire the fine details in the sheath and hilt.

The sheath is decorated with a breathtaking pattern of golden swirls and teardrops, interspersed with tiny dots. The handle of the dagger is carved from some kind of bone and curves up into the head of a roaring puma, fragments of gold sliced into the cream of the bone. I run my fingertips over its face in awe.

As I unsheathe the blade, I hear the satisfying hiss of steel cut through the air. My eyes travel the length of the blade, noticing my distorted reflection in the shining silver metal.

"It's beautiful," I breathe.

"Quite a weapon to behold. I remember the day your father ordered it to be made. Back when we were both foolish young men," he chuckles as if recalling a fond memory.

"He wielded it?" I ask, snapping my head up to see my uncle's expression.

"And your mother, on the odd occasion," he says ruefully. "Faolán named it Stormtip," he adds.

'*Stormtip*,' I repeat in my head.

Pride swells in my chest as my eyes flit back to the dagger balanced in my hand.

I think of it in my father's hand and I feel closer to him than I ever have before. I sheathe it once again and just hold it, unable to put it down just yet.

"And now it's yours," Uncle Erathon announces, patting my knee as he gets to his feet.

A thought crosses my mind and I place the dagger in my lap as I look up at him with wary eyes.

"You mean for me to take it with me." It isn't a question.

"You have no idea what could be waiting for you the moment you leave through those gates," he states.

"I will take it for the trials along with my training gear... but I'll be protected by the king and his laws as one of his Chosen."

"And as I've told you time and time again, Nesryn, the king cannot be trusted," he argues.

"Uncle, we've been over this. You forget that I'm fully capable of taking care of myself. What have you against me giving the king an heir, or even being married off to an earl or baron beyond our lands?"

"Those are just rumours, Nix," he reminds me with a warning tone.

"All rumours are bled from truth, and need I remind you again, I can take care of myself just fine, Uncle," I repeat.

I think of all the training I've done with Jarek and I know that he's thinking about it too.

"And you'll do even better with Stormtip."

"If I'm found with this on my person, Uncle, it could get me into all sorts of trouble." My stomach drops at the thought.

'*I could be disqualified from participating,*' I consider.

"Please, just take it with you. Pack it with the rest of your things if you must," he pleads.

I watch him for a long, hard moment before I let out a frustrated sigh.

"I'll pack it at the bottom of my trunk, it will be less conspicuous there."

The relief on his face eases the tightness in my chest a little, though the risk of getting caught with such a weapon keeps me on edge.

The clock sounds four chimes as we watch each other across the space and it hits me suddenly how little time we have left together. As if he's read my mind, he steps forward and places a hand on my shoulder, squeezing reassuringly like always.

"It'll be rather strange without you here," he says softly.

"It'll be strange for me too but I'll write to you," I say, lifting my chin to look up at him.

He smiles. "One last thing," he says, drawing away and striding across the room.

I groan. "If it's another weapon, I might just hurl it at you," I warn.

His chuckle is deep and rumbling as he stops in front of the shelves again and reaches up, though I can't see what for.

"Don't worry, I think you'll find this much more suitable," he replies.

He holds it out to me and I gingerly take it from him, holding his gaze for several moments before looking at the book in my lap.

"The Princess and the Starweaver," I murmur.

"A little piece of here, for when you miss home," Uncle Erathon explains in a soft voice.

I sense the lump in my throat before it grows and I try to choke back the sudden wave of fear that threatens to overwhelm me. Before either of us can utter another word, I spring out of my chair and wrap my arms around him tightly, burying my face in his collarbone. His strong arms hold me just as tightly.

The silence is thick, and time ticks by, not caring to wait. We remain embraced, neither one of us willing to be the first to let go.

CHAPTER SEVEN

The goodbyes are long and tearful when the carriage arrives but my tears stop when I see who has arrived. I rub my bleary eyes to see Lysan climbing up the sloping steps to meet me.

"A pleasure to see you again, Nesryn," he greets me, swooping into a low bow.

"Lysan, I'm surprised to find you here," I answer, standing straight.

"The king requested I personally escort you all to the palace," he answers.

I turn to my uncle and we share a look, his expression is muted but I can still see the pain lurking there. Suddenly I just want more time.

I glance past Lysan towards the entourage of three carriages, one wagon and two carts holding luggage lining their way along the brick road just outside of the gates to Havenore Manor. My gaze is pulled back to the carriage again before returning to the seafoam eyes watching me with slight interest.

"Thank you ladies, my men can take it from here," he says to Ragna and Ceryl, his eyes never leaving my face.

They step back from my trunks as Lysan holds his hand up and four soldiers who had been waiting by the gates, make their way up the steps towards us. They're dressed in the familiar maroon and gold of the king's army, the golden thread catching the light as they lift the heavy trunks and carry them towards the carts.

"Be careful with those."

One of them pauses, his eyes turning to me before he ducks his head down and carries on down the steps.

"They're in good hands," Lysan reassures me. "The others will be getting impatient, are you ready to go?" he asks, holding his hand out to me.

I glance over at my uncle who has remained a silent bystander throughout this. He dips his head, a ghost of a smile on his face. Before he can react, I throw my arms around his neck and squeeze him tightly to me. His arms wrap around me almost immediately and he murmurs in my ear.

"Hear. See. Endure. Remember that, my sweet Nix."

"This isn't goodbye, Uncle. Just farewell for now," I promise him, and I feel him hug me tighter.

I let out a sharp exhale as we separate and I turn back to Lysan, taking my skirts in my hands.

"I'm ready."

I ignore Lysan's outstretched hand and brush past him, earning me a devilish smirk from the king's Second. The amusement dancing in his eyes distracts me for a moment, like being seduced by a snake. But, fighting my growing nerves, I quickly regain my composure and continue down the stairs towards the carriage. I grip the material tighter, my hands clenching into fists as I move further away from my uncle. The tears that threaten to spill keep my eyes fixed in front of me. If I look back now, I fear that I'll fall apart where I stand.

Lysan sidles up beside me, matching my pace until we're right in front of the carriage. He opens the door in one smooth motion and I glance up to see three pairs of eyes peering down at me.

"In you get, princess," Lysan's voice travels over my shoulder.

I scowl at him before climbing inside, seating myself in the empty seat by the far window. I want one last look at my home before I go. The door closes after me with a final click that makes all of this so suddenly real.

'Calm yourself, Nesryn, you'll succeed in the trials and make Uncle Erathon proud,' a little voice reassures me, filling me with renewed excitement.

The carriage shakes as the footman cracks his whip, the horses drawing the carriage slowly around the fountain. Out of the window, I see Lysan astride a beautiful stallion, its coat a shade of black so dark that it would blend in with the night.

'How apt,' I think.

He leads us forward and I dare to steal one last glimpse at the three figures still standing on the steps of Havenore Manor, watching as the carriage is pulled out of the gates. My chest squeezes as they disappear from view and I turn to the three girls sitting around me.

The two girls across from me are polar opposites; the one on the left has an air of elegance about her, and her dark skin reminds me of chocolate, rich and smooth. Her face is a mixture of soft lines and curves with her rounded lips and almond eyes. When she glances at me I notice how her eye colour mirrors her skin, but where her skin is warm, her gaze is ice cold as she sends a defensive look my way. Her hair is a staggeringly beautiful silver shade that gleams in the dim light. It's twisted into multiple tight braids that run across her skull and wrap into two knots on either side of her head.

The girl beside her is as pale as a porcelain doll with long, warm blonde hair that cascades over her shoulders in waves. Even sitting down I notice how shapely she is, and I find myself slightly envious of some of her more exaggerated curves. The shape of her face is not as smooth as that of her darker friend, with her sharper cheekbones and rounded chin. Her grey-blue eyes reflect the light from the window as she catches my eye. Her lips are small but full as they spread into a tentative smile.

I blink in surprise before returning her smile with a small one of my own. Before long, her gaze drifts away from me and back to the young woman beside her as she shifts in her seat. The darkest night and brightest day. Their entwined hands don't go amiss and I wonder how they know each other if they seek comfort from one another like this.

My attention moves away from them as I glance to my right at the third girl, sitting beside me.

Her head hangs low as she stares down at her lap. Her lips are set in a thin line as she fiddles with her fingers. She is different from the other two in both looks and demeanour: her mottled brown hair is divided into two sections; the top part is woven into several braids that run from left to right across her head; and the bottom—the rest of her hair—flows loosely past her shoulders, ending abruptly at her breasts. She looks younger than the others, I know this can't be true; the twelve Chosen must be no younger than twenty-one. Those were the rules.

I don't recognise any of them and I wonder which areas of Akhozia they are from. I think of the other two carriages.

'Maybe I'll recognise one of the others…'

Though I'm not sure if that would be a good thing or a bad thing since they're all about to become my competition over the next few months.

Questions float through my mind as I try to decide which noble houses each of them represent and what it will be like for us now that we are away from all that is familiar to us.

The carriage tilts, the wheels crunching as the horses pull us along the uneven country roads. The warm breeze filters through the window, drawing in the sweet scent of wild lavender and honeysuckle. The silence hangs over the carriage in a thick cloud, and though I'm partially grateful for it, I see the opportunity to learn the names of my competitors. I sit up straight and clear my throat, drawing the attention of all three of them.

"My name's Nesryn."

I look at the others expectantly, but after several moments of waiting, silence still ensues. Sitting back, I try not to feel disappointed at their lack of enthusiasm to share even their names. I resume my earlier position, watching the landscape soar past when I feel the girl beside me shift.

"I'm Lesya," she says, her voice sweet and soft.

I look over to her and she glances at me shyly, a small smile playing on her lips. I return the smile before she lowers her head again and continues fiddling with her hands.

"Nice to meet you both. I'm Reverie," the blonde girl says with a wider smile and a twang in her voice that takes me by surprise.

"Vena," the ebony girl says begrudgingly, her expression deadpan.

Before I can even reply, her eyes flit back to the window, her disinterest in the conversation evident. I blink in surprise, making a mental note not to rile her.

'Quite the character,' my mind murmurs.

Reverie gives me an apologetic smile. She turns and tries to subtly dig her friend in the ribs, unsuccessfully.

"Vena, there's no need to be rude," she hisses under her breath.

"Reverie, grow the hell up. This is The Choosing, we're not here to make friends," she cuts back.

"Vena—"

"—Don't *Vena* me, Ria. You listen to me and you listen well," she starts, her hand flying out to point at me accusingly.

"She wants to play pretend and draw you into a false sense of security and then she'll stab you in the back to gain a footing in the trials. I know her *type*," she spits.

She turns to me, glaring with a viciousness that sounds warning bells in my mind. Something tells me that letting her see me intimidated would not be a smart idea. I hold her stare, keeping my face impassive.

"The sooner you accept that every girl here is your rival, the better," she bites at me, twisting sharply back to the window.

I absorb her words with a sense of unease, turning to glance out of the window as a tiny part of me wonders if I've gotten in over my head.

The hours drag by slowly as we travel through the countryside, the fields merging into one another in a seemingly never-ending sea of green.

Since Vena's outburst, the journey had been spent in an uncomfortable silence and avoided gazes. Through the hours of travelling I had expected longer breaks, perhaps even a stop for water and food, but we had been handed refreshments through our carriage window by one of the footmen and expected to eat with our fingers. That hadn't gone down too well with some of the other passengers.

Two more hours drag by and I find myself itching for something to do. I mentally kick myself for not bringing one of my books into the carriage to read along the way. It's only when I start to notice the breaks in the scenery that I sit up from my slouch, suddenly alert and eager. The nervous excitement that had worn off earlier comes back in full swing as I spot tall, wide buildings sprouting up between the wide fields of wild grass and half-grown crops.

As we're nearing the next hour, there is a shift as the wheels suddenly hit smooth stone streets and the ride becomes a lot smoother than the dirt paths or uneven cobbled roads from earlier. The sound of the horses' hooves clipping against the stone is quickly overshadowed by the noises of the bustling kingdom. I'm eager to see the capital for the first time, drinking in everything that I lay eyes on as our train of carriages, carts, and wagons makes its way through the chaos.

I'm surprised at how many people are here at this hour, the sky already darkening past dusk. The shop windows are dark behind the clusters of people, tavern doors are open and drunken men knock their steins together as they call drunkenly to those of us peering through the windows at them. Others stand on balconies or hang out of windows to wave at the Aslitír and their cargo of noblewomen as we pass them on the street. Some wave as we pass while others cheer and it suddenly dawns on me.

'They've come to see us.'

I'm amazed by how many buildings are crammed together in the streets as we climb uphill. I press my nose to the glass to see how high the buildings are. This place is a stark contrast to my home in the Talló countryside.

"Make way!" I hear one of the Aslitír on horseback yell to the people.

I feel a tap on my knee and start, pulling back to see Reverie's concerned face across from me.

"Your first time in the city?" she asks.

I nod, my brows dipping in confusion.

"You may want to prepare yourself for this part," she warns me.

Before I can even ask what she means, a strange sensation ripples across my body as a flash of blue light blinds me momentarily. The carriage groans as we drown in the light, but it's gone as quickly as it arrived and I'm back in the carriage with the others, blinking the stars from my vision. My head feels strange and pins and needles prick at my hands and legs as goosebumps break out all over me. I blink repeatedly as I try to readjust my eyes to the growing darkness of the evening.

"I don't think I'll ever get used to that," Lesya mutters beside me as she shudders.

"What was it?" I ask, my mouth dry, a strange metallic taste coating my tongue.

"It's the portal to the castle," Reverie explains, gesturing to the window. "There are several spread out across the city. It's the only way in or out of the palace."

Suddenly, the door closest to Lesya and Vena of the carriage opens and one of the soldiers pops his head in. "Lysander has instructed that you have five minutes of fresh air before you're to return to the carriage. It would seem not all of you agreed with portal travel."

He disappears from sight and Lesya breathes a shaky sigh of relief.

"Thank the goddess," she mutters as she moves towards the door.

"Weak," Vena mutters under her breath.

I glare at her but she ignores me. Before I say something that I might come to regret later, I move towards the door, eager to stretch my legs. Though the thought of being far from Vena is equally as appealing.

The wind howls softly as I step out into the night air. I stop in amazement. We're high in the sky, on a bridge that looks to go on forever. I step towards the wall and reach up on my tiptoes to peer over to the bustling kingdom below. My stomach drops at the sight but I cannot seem to pull myself away. From here I can see the layers of the city, hexagonal shapes jumbled atop one another in a way that fits with the steep incline. Pinpricks of light are dotted along the streets, illuminating the crowds of tiny people celebrating the arrival of The Chosen twelve.

When I finally pull back from the view below, my jaw slackens at the sheer size of the palace.

It is staggeringly huge, bigger than anything I've ever seen, with sharp, pointed towers cutting up through the clouds into the sky like a newly sharpened arrowhead. There is nothing soft or friendly about the design of it. Orbs of elvynlight hover in place within the outside walls, illuminating the pale grey stone in a rich teal blue, giving it an ethereal yet ominous feel.

"My lady it's time to return to the carriage," the soldier from before says as he stops beside me.

I blink, turning to him in a daze. I shake my head and snap out of it, giving him a quick nod of acknowledgement. "Yes, of course."

I grab my skirts and follow him back to the carriage. He holds the door open for me and I climb in to find all three girls waiting inside.

"Quite the sight, isn't it?" Reverie comments when we start to move.

"It's…" I trail off, unable to find the words for what I'd just seen.

Reverie smiles slowly at me and nods in understanding. Beside her, Vena rolls her eyes and returns to quietly brooding. I ignore her, finding myself still in a state of awe as we pull into the palace gates and into the courtyard beyond.

We're escorted in rows of two into the palace by Lysan and a handful of Aslitír soldiers. He walks up ahead, in front, while his men crowd around us in a protective circle. We're led through the threshold, out of the wind and into a long echoing corridor. The ceilings are high and the space is open—though instead of being inviting, there's a feeling of foreboding, as if the space was *too* open. The furnishings are fewer than I imagined and made with bold, dark colours that only serve to leech more of the natural light. Unease settles in the pit of my stomach as I see the detailed tapestries hanging on the left wall. They depict the Elven War, each one more gruesome than the last. Eventually, I can't stomach it anymore and turn away.

Our steps are muted by the long rolls of carpet, though the same can't be said of the surrounding soldiers. Their heeled boots clatter loudly against the stone floor, and the steel at their belts smack against their legs as they walk beside us. I glance at Lesya beside me and she catches my eye as her lips curve upward at me in a tentative smile. I offer her a weak smile of my own before I look forward again, focusing on the back of the girl in front of me.

Some of the girls ahead of us speak in a jumble of hushed, excited tones. I think back on what Vena said in the carriage and I wonder how many of these unfurling friendships will eventually wither and perish under the pressure of the trials ahead.

'*Hear. See. Endure,*' I remind myself, standing a little straighter.

As we march down the halls, I realise how barren they are. There are no servants bustling about the halls, just the echoing sound of our footsteps and the bleak dusty tapestries hung along the walls. It's eerie and cold, almost clinical, with no sense of homeliness or life about it. I am, however, surprised at how warm it is as we continue to follow Lysan along the corridor, though I shouldn't be. I assume that magic is keeping the heat within the large halls and rooms around the palace.

Lysan leads us into the throne room. The space is vast and elegant, the marble floor gleaming as we each step into the room. At the end of the wide, wooden floors are the curving steps of gleaming marble streaked with gold that lead to the throne; a masterpiece of twisting gold with black velvet cushions. Twelve chairs are arranged in a semicircle with colourful banners hanging over the backs. Each banner displays one of the twelve family crests.

I take them in one by one, recalling my lessons on the noble houses with ease. On the far left, an orange bull for the Zouvsa House; next, a blue peacock and white arrow for the Astalón House; then, a golden snake for the Gladdreiys House; and the maroon stag for the Raviffete House. I glance towards Lesya again after noting her family crest, but she's busy staring ahead. I follow the line of colour, noting the green eagle and blue and white arrow that forms the crest of the Montallet House; the grey swan for the Duhrannes House; and the purple hare for the Lockport House. It takes me several moments to place the orange horse, though I eventually remember that it belongs to the Drulfeard House.

I watch as the other young women squint and bite their lips as they try to place each of the twelve banners with their respective houses. Some figure it out quicker than others, while some even dare to look bored and uninterested.

I turn to examine the final four banners along the right: a crimson bear representing the Drullanon House; the golden fox for the Roquenet House; the black wolf for the Vythierre House; and finally, my eyes stop on the familiar black puma of my own. The Havenore House. The powerful creature sits on a purple stripe with brilliant gold edges. A small proud smile stretches my lips as I think of all that my family crest represents.

Suddenly a scrawny scrap of a man steps forwards, unfurling a roll of parchment that falls to his chest. He begins to read aloud in a surprisingly deep voice, drawing the attention of all twelve of us, as well as some of the Aslitír.

"Please stand behind your assigned seat when I call your name. The king's presence is imminent."

He starts to say each name aloud and I watch as one by one the others stride purposefully to their seats. They sit up straight, their gaze fixed on the large throne standing at the far end of the room. Just as I'd been taught. Just as all of us had been. Finally, he calls my name and I step forward with my head held high, moving without hesitation towards my seat.

I walk past the seated girls, whose eyes follow me across the hall to my seat along with Lysan's, his arms crossed over his chest as he leans against the king's throne, cocky as always. I avert my gaze, taking the opportunity to assess the other girls as they begin to do the same. My eyes fall on Vena, her sharp gaze holding me until a throat is cleared ahead of us pulling my attention from her icy gaze.

"I thank you all for your swift cooperation. So without further ado, I declare the arrival of His Majesty King Barilius Saurhen, First of His Name," the speaker announces.

He steps aside as the king stands in the doorway, his frame casting a long shadow across the room. His face is serious as he steps into the room, the heels of his boots clipping against the marble floor as he marches through the room.

Something in the air shifts at his presence, something dark and ominous with a hint of magic. I scan the room and see how each of the girls looks straight ahead, their eyes tracking the king's every move.

I notice how some hold their breath, while others fiddle nervously with their hands. When he finally takes his seat, I notice how his eyes move to Lysan who quickly rights himself, his posture now rigid. Where his arms were hanging limply by his sides before, they're now folded across his chest, his eyes steely and focused as he stares at us from his place by the king's side.

"Welcome all to the palace, my home," he calls, his voice booms across the space. "This will also be your home for the coming weeks. My staff have been tirelessly preparing your suites for your arrival. Your safety and comfort are of the utmost importance, so I have organised for my men to patrol the halls." King Barilius smiles, and I feel every one of us hanging on to his every word, myself included.

"Please rest and get to know your new home tonight. Tomorrow you shall begin with the first test of The Choosing.

Good luck to you all, I pray the great goddess holds you in her favour," he says, looking at each of us in turn.

When his eyes stop on me, a chill runs down my spine and I fight the urge to shrink beneath his gaze. As his eyes continue on across the rest of the girls, I wonder why he has dismissed us so quickly. We remain seated as we watch the king discuss something with Lysan, who listens closely, nodding once when the king has finished speaking. His gaze wanders back to us, and he unfolds his arms as King Barilius stands and strides along the long roll of carpet, and out of the large doors behind us.

I swivel in my seat with the rest of the girls, following him until he disappears from view. Almost in unison, every face turns to Lysan, expectant.

The Shadowcaster stands beside the throne watching us.

LYSAN

CHAPTER EIGHT

Twelve pairs of eyes stare back at me. I heave a sigh, unfolding my arms and dropping them to my sides.

'Always leaving the dull jobs for me,' I think.

"Follow me, pair up and get into a line. One pair behind the other."

When I see that they're still sitting there, I slap my hands together. "Let's go girls, I haven't got all day." I skip down the steps and stride towards them as they get to their feet.

I walk past them, knowing that they will follow my orders. I stop in the doorway, eyeing the soldiers loitering in the corner. With a smirk, I gesture for them to follow. They send a dark look in my direction, the hate clear, but they do as they're told, begrudgingly.

Glancing behind me, I notice that the girls have formed a line along the length of carpet, waiting quietly for me.

'Let the fun begin,' I think dryly.

The journey through the castle is uneventful and I can't help the boredom that seeps

into my veins as we move through the halls on the same tour that I do every Choosing.

"Everything you need can be found in the east wing of the palace, though there are some things you'll need to venture out for," I call over my shoulder.

I'm met with several hushed giggles, so I continue, encouraged by the attention. I may have some fun yet.

I point toward the kitchens, the ballroom, dining hall and even the training room, which the king had reluctantly added to the girls' amenities after the fourth time of it being suggested. From the way a few of the girls react gleefully to this news, I can tell that is a welcomed feature.

We reach the east wing shortly after, where the girls' rooms have been carefully prepared for each of them. The number of girls begins to dwindle as I drop them to their designated rooms. Some squeal with excitement, others are much more withdrawn as they enter their room without so much as a backward glance, the soft click and lock of their door a signal to leave them alone.

Finally, there is only one left and I turn towards her with a flirtatious smile as we stop outside the final bedroom along the hall.

"Welcome to your room, *Lady* Havenore," I purr, leaning against the wall.

She rolls her eyes at me, one hand on the door handle.

"Will that be all?" she asks, bored.

"Well, if you'd ever like to see what other services I provide, I'd be happy to oblige. My room is on the western corridor, not far from here," I wink and she scowls at me.

"You're a pig," she snaps, stepping into the room and slamming the door in my face.

'*So easy to ruffle,*' I think.

I can't help chuckling to myself as I make my back down the hall.

'*She has quite the spunk,*' I muse, revelling in all the ways that I might push her.

My breaths are laboured as I thrust into the woman, pinning her against the wall as her legs tighten around my hips. She buries her face into my neck, her spiralling curls tickling my arm as I move inside her. She digs her nails into my back with a groan, creating a trail of half-moon shaped scratches along my shoulder blades.

I block out the finer details, like the shade of her blonde hair, the sharp angles of her face, the high pitch of her voice and replace it all with the image of *her*.

I close my eyes and imagine her hair is lighter, her face softer, her voice deeper and accented. I imagine it's her I'm buried deep inside. If I close my eyes for long enough, the shape of her comes back and the illusion comes to life beneath my fingertips. I growl with pleasure as I throw myself headfirst into the fantasy, my rhythm quickening as my right hand grabs her wrist and pins it above her head.

A moan slips from the woman, threatening to shatter the illusion, but I shake it off, sewing it back together, until it's her once more, only her.

Loísia.

I hold fast to the name, like a beacon of light beckoning me closer, as my mind begins to focus on the divine pleasure of filling the tight warm space between her thighs. With the next thrust, I unravel with the climax, the tightness easing in soft throbs as she finishes too.

When I dare to pull away and open my eyes, the fantasy shatters as I'm met with a pair of eyes the shade of swirled caramel, curtained by thick dark lashes. Gracie pats my chest twice and I push away from the wall and lower her to her feet. I watch her curls bounce as she saunters across the room, reaching for the metal pitcher and pouring its crimson contents into two of the goblets that I'd brought with me. She turns and hands me one, drinking from her own as I gulp down mine, relishing the warm kick at the back of my throat.

"You're certainly full of energy today, my lord," she comments as her eyes linger below my hips.

"I was having a dull day, it needed a little spice," I answer, closing the gap.

She watches me as I move towards her, her eyes fixed on mine as I place my empty cup on the table. I watch her as she bites her swollen lip and I feel myself swell with need once more.

"How big is your purse today, my lord?" she asks coyly, batting her lashes.

"Big enough for at least another round," I answer with a smirk.

Gracie squeals as I lift her and throw her onto the bed. I follow quickly after, climbing over her and brushing the peaks of her breasts with my chest. I press my mouth against hers and a small gasp escapes her just as I fill the space between her thighs once more, seeking to devour her.

Shuddering at the pleasure, I delve back into the fantasy once more.

I'm sitting at the bar, ale in hand, when Keelhan finds me.

I feel Gracie's curious stare from across the room where she sits with a few of the other girls. But I don't return the gaze, my attention instead on Keelhan as he props himself on the seat beside me and orders himself the same as me.

I know Gracie isn't the only one watching, and with a spot beside the king, I remind myself once again that those with less have more to gain by stealing my secrets.

"You do like to spend an excessive amount of time in some real shitty places," he comments with a distasteful look.

"I'll have you know that The Velvet Feather is one of the *finer* establishments," I reply, jokingly repeating the words of the establishment's owner.

He scoffs at me as the server hands him a stein of ale, the golden liquid spilling as he brings it to his lips.

"I've just come from the palace," he tells me with a knowing smirk and he places his drink down.

"The Chosen are certainly a *delight*, aren't they?"

"How do you expect to get anywhere with women if all you do is berate them?" Keelhan asks, bumping shoulders with me.

I mutter a curse under my breath and make a vulgar gesture at him as I take another sip and he laughs heartily. All of a sudden, his smile falters and his eyes darken as he stares at the drink in his hand.

"There've been whispers of The Righteous Hand moving shipments on the docks. King Barilius has agreed to let me travel back to Talló the morn after tomorrow."

"Why does it sound like you're building up to something?" I ask, taking another gulp of ale.

He meets my eyes over the rim of his glass, a coy smile playing on his lips. "You're to come with me."

NESRYN

CHAPTER NINE

I awake the next morning to see the weak sunlight filtering through opened curtains and a handful of maids scuttling about my room. I bolt upright, pulling the quilt to my chin as I watch them warily. Not one of them pays me any mind and I watch as two of them disappear into the adjoining washroom. The sound of pouring water filters through the space while plumes of scented steam begin to float out from the doorway and into my room.

I clear my throat as a third maid walks across the room, her hands full of neatly-folded fabric. Her head snaps up at the sound.

"Oh, Miss Havenore, you're awake!" she cries, her eyes wide.

"I am. What is it that you're all doing?" I ask, peering past her to the washroom.

She blinks in surprise.

I take her in, noting her warm brown hair and matching eyes. Her cream skin is a stark contrast to her chestnut hair. She can't be any older than I am, though if she is, her small button nose shaves several years off her face.

"Perin, Sarleigh and I... We've been assigned to you, my lady," she answers after a moment.

"Assigned to me?" I repeat, slipping out from beneath the sheets and craning my neck around the bedpost to see the two girls peeking around the bathroom door and giving me a small smile and shy wave.

"We'll be providing you with our service during your stay at the palace, Miss Havenore," she explains.

"And if they are Perin and Sarleigh," I gesture to the women bustling around the bathroom, "Who are you?"

"I'm Hesta, Miss Havenore," she answers with a small curtsey, before striding across the room and placing the fabric on the table beside the vanity.

"Please stop calling me that," I grimace.

Hesta twists at the hip to look at me, her head tilted partially to one side.

"And what would you like us to call you then Mi—"

My disapproving frown stops her mid-sentence. When she falls quiet, I realise she's waiting for me to speak.

"Nesryn will do, thank you, Hesta," I say quietly.

"Very well," she replies with a curt nod before striding towards me.

"This will need to come off," she says, tugging at my nightgown.

"Hey—" I start, my cries of protest silenced by the cotton fabric over my mouth.

She tugs it over my head, my senses momentarily disoriented as she pulls me free. She tries to reach for me again, this time with Perin beside her, and I step back as their hands move towards my more personal garments.

"I think I'm able to take it from here, Hesta," I say, raising my voice.

Hesta and Perin glance at one another, a silent conversation taking place between them before they turn back to me and nod.

"The bath is drawn," Sarleigh announces as she steps back into the room.

My eyes flit to the elegant clock face hanging from the wall reading the time, aghast.

"It's barely six chimes!" I gasp, turning back to my servers with wide eyes.

"So it is," Perin answers, her expression unchanged.

"The king's Second said the first trial wouldn't start before noon," I point out.

The images of laying between the sheets until hunger dragged me from them fade as quickly as they had come. My hopes for a relaxed morning are dashed with her next words.

"A simple trick. The king gave orders to have you and the other eleven bathed and dressed by breakfast. He wishes to dine with you before his hunt."

Irritation sweeps through me at Lysan and his games. My clear lack of preparation meant I had already lost my footing with the competition and The Choosing had barely begun. I rush to undress, all sense of propriety gone as I strip my undergarments off in front of them.

"Let's get you in that tub," Hesta says, drawing me from my thoughts.

I barely open my mouth to agree before they lead me into the washroom and shove me towards the bath. Before I know it, I'm chest-deep in the sunken tub. Steam rises, drawing up the smell of amber and cinnamon as I hiss at the heat of the water.

They waste no time in lathering me in soaps and lotions and scrub me raw until there is not a single inch of me that hasn't been thoroughly cleaned. They comb through the knots in my curls, the coils bouncing back as they comb through the ends. There's no time to soak in the hot water as the maids pull me from the tub, muttering about being on time for the king. Gratefully, I take the towel offered to me and wrap it around myself as I'm ushered back into my room. The sudden wall of cold hits me and my skin prickles from the abrupt and unwelcome change.

I look over at the clothes laid out across my bed and stop short.

"Those aren't mine," I say, turning to Sarleigh.

"It's called a vaita. They're new, courtesy of the king. All Chosen are expected to wear them throughout The Choosing," Perin explains airily.

"Alright," I answer with a small nod.

I pad the rest of the way over to the bed and collect the vaita and modest garments in my hands. Rushing to get dressed, I slip into them easily, fastening up the three pearlescent buttons lining the nape of my neck as I step out to take a look in the mirror. My hands run over the clothing as I twist this way and that to get a better view. The tunic wraps around my neck and across my chest, cutting off abruptly across the top of my ribs. Its sheer black sleeves puff out and close with a thick band of fabric around my wrists. The trousers start just above my navel, hugging my figure around my hips and thighs before fanning out and ending in the same way my sleeves do with a length of fabric wrapped around each of my ankles. The fabric of my pants is a rich purple with a sheer black layer over the top, the hems rounded off with a scratchy golden thread that shimmers when the light catches it.

I realise as I take in my reflection that I'm dressed in the colours of my family crest: black, purple and gold, and pride swells in my chest, though I admit as my heart twinges it makes me miss home.

With an impatient huff, Sarleigh takes me by the arm and pulls me over to the vanity. She sits me in front of the small mirror and begins to dry my hair with an impressive speed. I sit quietly while she works, her caramel fingers pulling the curls apart as she towel dries them, before reaching for the pointed comb and parting it into sections.

"You have beautiful hair, my lady," she says almost wistfully.

"Thank you."

A ghost of a smile flashes across her lips as her eyes find mine in the reflection. I see the sincerity in her warm brown eyes and the slightest hint of blush creeps along her cheeks, standing out against the rich caramel tone of her skin. She holds my gaze for several long moments before she focuses on her hands once more. Her fingers move swiftly and consistently, like a dance she has not only learnt but mastered. She weaves my hair into a number of braids, working painlessly and tirelessly with my thick locks until she has twisted them to her will. When she finally steps away, it takes me a few moments to realise her work is done. I lean forward and take in the four ropey braids twisting across my head and snaking down my spine, the ends brushing against the small of my back.

I'm reminded of the female warriors of the Sand Dune tribes. Those of the eastern path of the Southern Commune. I think of the pictures of them in the textbooks from my history lessons years ago.

"That should keep until tomorrow, milady," she tells me over my shoulder.

I draw back and get to my feet, the trousers of my vaita swishing about my legs from the movement.

"Thank you, Sarleigh. They look wonderful," I smile gratefully.

She dips into a curtsey in reply as Hesta strides past her to hand me a pair of black shoes. I take them from her, turning them over in my hands curiously.

I sit down and pull the rubber-soled pumps onto my feet, stretching my toes and rolling my ankles in surprise at the comfort of them. I'm impressed at how well they fit my feet, the high ankles fitting snugly over the band of my trousers, giving off the impression of it all being one complete piece. I glance at the clock again when a soft, clear knock sounds from the door. All three ladies look at one another before Hesta marches across the room to let the person in.

I watch as a middle-aged man in long murky brown robes steps into the room, offering me a low bow. His tawny face is pale and greyish as he straightens. His beady black eyes, non-existent lips, and greasy hooked nose remind me of a raven.

"I apologise for the intrusion, Lady Havenore. I take it that your servers have you ready?"

The question sounds more like a statement but I answer anyway.

"We were just finishing as you arrived, my lord."

I glance over at the three of them, Hesta having rejoined their ranks.

"I'm no Lord, milady. Just a simple messenger of the king. You may call me Vilkha," he says, though from the way he puffs out his chest I see that I may have stroked his ego.

"As you wish," I reply.

He nods briskly. " I shall escort you to the dining hall, if you are ready then," he offers.

I frown, glancing behind him to find none of the other girls waiting, part of me dubious. Something about his bleak complexion and beady eyes makes me uneasy.

Hesta, Sarleigh and Perin each give me a reassuring smile and I take a deep breath, drawing it in through my nose and then out through my mouth before I close the space between us.

"Please lead the way, Vilkha," I lift my hand, gesturing to the door.

The hall is grand and breathtakingly beautiful with a black marbled floor and scarily high midnight blue ceilings. Tall twisting glass sculptures are lined proudly along the walls. Each one holds up a giant orb of elvynlight, illuminating the space with a cool glow.

A single table stretches along the centre of the dining hall, splitting the room in two. The huge surface is laden with numerous platters of all sorts of foods; from rich meat pies hailing from the east, to plates stacked full of sweet plums and juicy crimson berries. Each plate originates from a different part of the kingdom. As we're guided into the room, I pick out delicacies I recognise from Tralló, others I recognise from the vast orchards of Treburg and some I presume to be traded in from outside of our borders.

When we arrive, I'm glad to see others join Vilkha and me by the entryway. I pick out the familiar faces of Vena and Reverie, the latter responding to my smile with a small wave and the former ignoring me entirely. Curiosity gets the better of me and I peer at their attire. Vena's vaita fits across her curves graciously, leaving little to the imagination. I find myself envious of her womanly shape and how the rich blue fabrics and the sheer pearlescent material covering them suit her beautifully. Her hair is braided similarly to mine, though hers wraps around her head like a sleek crown of brightest silver.

Reverie's vaita is brighter and bolder against her rosy skin—a combination of red and orange film that flickers with her movements like an open flame. Her long blonde tresses are pulled back into a high ponytail, the end flicking out as she turns her head.

It isn't hard to see that our new clothes are designed to represent our families.

We filter into the room, our escorts disappearing from beside us as we move towards the same half-moon layout of seats as before. I check each place setting and for one ludicrous moment, I panic.

'What if this is the first test? What if this is some cruel trick to pick out the smartest Chosen?'

I scan the seats and decide that if it was a test, I would know; Uncle Erathon made sure that I was observant. I surmise that there are no designated seats and take my seat on the next chair that I pass. My stomach rumbles with hunger and yet again, I curse myself for not rising sooner as I take in the delicious smells of ripened fruit, rich meats, and fresh bread.

Time passes and we wait in nervous silence. The anticipation is a living breathing entity hovering over the entire table. After several agonising moments of waiting, a man in the king's colours strides into the room. His boots clip against the marble and his sheathed sword clatters against his thigh with every step. He stops at the centre of the table, gaining the attention of each of us.

"His Majesty sends his apologies but he will not be joining you this morn. He wishes you luck with your first trial," the messenger announces, his voice echoing along the hall in waves, each softer than the last.

A soft murmur erupts in the hall as speculations are shared amongst the girls. I watch them quietly until something catches my attention from the corner of my eye. Vena rises from her seat to pick out a sweet pastry from the banquet before us. She takes one, then two and places them on a plate before seating herself once more. Utter silence ripples across the room before it erupts into a clatter of plates and cutlery as the other girls follow suit.

I pick out my own plate, piling it with starfruit, sliced bread and a selection of meats before devouring it. Waiters pepper the room, filling our glasses with nectary drinks as we eat, while soldiers stand rigidly on either side of the hall, staring ahead at nothing. As I take another bite, I look about at the competition, wondering what the king has planned for us.

I glance across the table at the girl sitting opposite me, recognising her as Maskia. As if she feels me staring, her bright blue eyes dart to me and a tentative smile spreads across her face. Her vaita is a blend of deep purple and gold, the sheer fabric glinting in the morning light. The colours accentuate her pale complexion, giving the impression of her being a porcelain doll. Though I would bet that underneath that friendliness, she's anything but fragile.

After several moments of intense studying, she says: "Colours of the Havenore House, if I'm not mistaken."

"You would be correct," I reply.

"Lockport," she says, gesturing to herself while tucking a pale golden strand of her hair behind her ear.

"Quite the prestigious family," I acknowledge, dipping my head in respect.

"Please, we're all equals here, despite what some may say," Maskia remarks, glancing along the table.

I follow her gaze to the far end of the table where four girls are clustered together, talking quietly amongst themselves. I recognise them from yesterday's introductions: Rohana, Mallon, Chandra and Erryn.

"I wonder how long they'll last," the words are out before I can stop them.

I look back at Maskia, surprised at my own words. I'm about to apologise or come up with some other meaning for my words when she smiles knowingly. Her eyes sparkle with something that I can't name as if the two of us share a secret.

"I suppose we'll have to wait and see… but isn't that half the fun?" She grins. "The sooner we find out what the next trial is going to be, the sooner we can feel out the competition," she adds casually.

I want to believe that we're on the same side but I know that her remark is aimed at me as much as the others.

'*We're all competitors here,*' I remind myself.

We don't have to wait long.

The answer comes as we finish our breakfast. The plates are taken away and a server places another silver plate down before me. Just as I'm about to ask him to take it away, he lifts the tray to reveal a sealed envelope, the king's seal embellished in gold and maroon wax.

I glance across the table, eyeing the other girls as their servers reveal identical letters beneath their silver covers. With my heart pounding in my chest and urging me to hurry, I waste no time opening it. I break through the seal and pull open the parchment to read the contents.

> *Hark the only letters yell,*
> *You will find what once you sought.*
> *Before you step where letters fell,*
> *That which letters forge hath wrought.*

Beneath the riddle, I notice, are a handful of scattered squiggles on the page and what look to be letters, though they look odd. I realise they may be in a tongue I'm unfamiliar with. The style almost seems foreign, possibly even hailing from another continent entirely. Murmurs and gasps ripple across the table as the other Chosen open their letters. I turn my gaze to Maskia, still reading her own letter, and breathe a sigh of relief.

'*If she hasn't figured it out yet, it must be difficult. It's not just me.*'

The others are the same. I see a mixture of serious and confused expressions. No one has deciphered it yet—or at least they haven't made it known. I silently wonder if the others have received the same mysterious riddle as I have when Vilkha steps into the room, making his presence known.

"I see that all of you have received your second task. You had two days to unravel the riddle that got you here, now you have one. Your answer will be expected no later than the twenty-four chimes from now. Make sure to pass your answer to one of the messengers when the time comes."

Silence falls as we absorb this information.

"May Asteria serve luck to you all," he says with a flourish.

Without another word, he turns on his heel and leaves. The room erupts into chatter as the others begin putting together a plan of action. Once again, Vena is the first to move as she leaves the hall with a purposeful stride, her envelope tucked in between her fingers.

My mind whirs as I stare at the scattered letters on the parchment before looking across the space at Maskia and grinning.

"It looks to me like you already have a plan."

"I think I do," I answer, locking eyes with Reverie.

LYSAN

CHAPTER TEN

I rush around my room, collecting items and throwing them in the trunk in no particular order. My mind whirs with the conversation I had with Keelhan and the king's orders that I accompany him. In all my years of servitude, I'd never been permitted to stray far from the king's side. Having kept me within arms reach for so long, it was unusual for him to request that I seek out the truth behind these rumours circling around The Righteous Hand.

I made my confusion known when I'd sought out Barilius earlier that morning in his study.

"I hate to question your authority, Your Grace, but to send me away just as The Choosing begins..."

"You don't trust my methods?" he replied, arching an eyebrow at me from his seat.

"Won't I be more useful to you here?"

"I think I'm capable of handling a few spoiled girls, Lysander," his tone warned me against pushing any further.

"I want you with Captain Keelhan. If he's so sure of the movements of these so-called rebels, then I want my best and brightest there to handle them," he continued.

"Handle them?" I repeated, not liking the sound of it on my lips.

King Barilius stopped writing and set down his quill. His face was serious, his eyes the colour of molten lava and steely with an iron will.

"You are to execute any member of this Righteous Hand group on sight."

"But Your Highness, they'll need to be questioned," I reasoned.

"Allowing them to believe they ever had a voice was a mistake I won't make again so easily," he said with a sneer.

I remained quiet. There was no point in fuelling his silent rage.

"You will report back in a week with your findings, or earlier, if you intercept them before your deadline."

"As you command, My King," I answered, sweeping into a low bow.

As I had moved to leave, he'd stopped me and called me back.

"Oh and Lysander, when you find them I expect proof," he'd stated calmly, his eyes steady as they fixed on me.

I dipped my head and slipped from the room with grim anticipation.

A soft knock against my door pulls me from my thoughts and I turn towards the door.

"It's open," I call, chucking a few more things in the trunk.

There's a slight pause before the person knocks again and I raise a brow at the closed door, cocking my head as I wonder who the hell it could be. I drop the tunic in my hand and march over to the door, flinging it open with an annoyed grunt. I look down at an extremely serious-looking Nesryn. I suppress the surprise that I feel, adopting my usual mask of boredom—though it soon falters, betraying my amusement.

A movement behind her catches my eye and I flick my gaze to where the Zouvsa girl and the Lockport girl hover in the corridor. The pair of them shift nervously on the spot as they do their best to avoid my gaze.

'You're smart to be afraid,' I think as I recognise the tell-tale signs.

"Hello *Princess*, I wasn't expecting a visit from you so soon," I drawl as I slowly drag my eyes back to meet hers and give her a wink.

They flash with irritation.

"Where can I find the library?" she snaps.

"Now, you're a smart little thing, what would you need the library for?" I query, raising my brows at the other two before returning my attention to Nesryn.

She taps her fingers against the paper in her hand—a sign of impatience—and I find my interest piqued as I recognise the maroon and gold wax seal.

"You came to ask me for help with your first trial? I'm touched," I remark, folding my arms as I lean casually against the door frame.

"I only came because you're the only one I could find in this labyrinth," she explains, gritting her teeth.

"Struggling so soon? Or maybe you just missed me," I retort with a smirk.

"Does it ever tire you out being this difficult?" she demands, her brows knitted together.

"About as much as it must tire you being so highly-strung," I reply, my smile widening.

She rolls her eyes and mutters 'prick' under her breath.

"Temper, temper," I chuckle as I tut at her.

"You're insufferable," she grumbles as she turns to leave.

"Oh, you'll find that I'm many things, Nesryn Havenore," I remark.

She rolls her eyes and scowls, spinning on her heels and storming away. The other two watch me warily for several moments before they follow after her. I watch them go, my amusement dying as I begin to wonder how long it'll be until they turn on one another.

Hours later, I find Keelhan in the stables arguing with the stablehand.

"Where are the horses I brought you ten moons ago?" he demands, the anger in his voice tangible.

"They're wild brumbies, Captain. Ain't been trained properly yet," the boy explains as he cowers beneath my friend's shadow.

"Dammit boy! I have men in need of horses. We are to leave tomorrow morn."

"I'm sorry m'Lord, I—" the boy stammers.

I decide to step in at that moment, before Keelhan loses his temper completely.

"You throwing your toys out of the pram again, Keel?" I call as I saunter in.

He turns, throwing me a tight, amused smile, but even as I close the gap I can see the anger simmering beneath.

"How about I settle this?" I offer, placing a hand on his shoulder.

He gives me a curt nod and stomps away, while I turn my attention to the boy. If he'd been fearful of Keelhan, he was terrified of me—hardly surprising given my reputation.

Reaching into my pocket, I pull out a handful of buckles and hand them to the kid.

"Go to the breeder at the edge of the city, tell him I sent you, and buy as many of his beasts as you can," I instruct him.

He glances down at the money in his hands with wide eyes and a slack jaw, before returning his dazed expression to me.

"There is enough here for more than thirty stallions," he breathes in disbelief.

"Then buy as many as Captain Keelhan wants and keep the rest for your family," I answer with a dismissive wave.

The boy nodes eagerly. "Yes, right away m'Lord, thank you," he bows twice and scarpers from sight, clutching the buckles in his scrawny hands.

"I'm not a—oh to hell with it," I dismiss the words, realising that he's already gone.

I turn back the way that I came, a niggling thought resurfacing in my mind as I search for Keel.

'I'm hardly keeping my promise to Loísia if I'm off playing executioner with Keelhan,' my mind taunts.

I push back the bitter thought, scanning the palace grounds in search of my friend. As Warmwell takes hold, the patches of nebiulas fill the flower beds and creep in amongst the shrubbery with their fluffy petals that billow out like clouds plucked from the sky. The sight is quite something to behold, though I don't have the time to stop and enjoy them or the beautiful scene that is the gardens at this time of year.

As I make my way around the back of the stables, I find him deep in conversation with two lower-ranking soldiers. Their voices filter through the wall and I realise that their discussion revolves around the preparations for our impending trip.

They stand to attention as I waltz over, attracting the wary, hate-filled gazes of the two soldiers, as I stop beside Keelhan.

"—move in groups and don't stray from the path no matter what may…" He slows mid-sentence, distracted by my arrival.

But I glance at him and gesture toward his men in a bid to have him finish giving them his orders.

"As I was saying don't stray from the path, there are many a bandit and rebel scum about those parts. Remain vigilant and follow the rest of the party, and we shall arrive as planned."

Only when his men stride away at a faster pace than usual, does Keelhan finally turn to me.

"Your men will have their horses by the end of the day."

"Your usual vendor?" Keel surmises.

I shrug as I flash him a devilish grin and he shakes his head, fighting the smirk tugging at his mouth.

"Do you like putting the fear of the goddess into people, Lys?"

"Fear will always last longer than respect," I tell him with a small shrug.

His steel-blue eyes lift to meet mine, his smile slipping.

I see the familiar look of pity and misunderstanding in his eyes that returns every time the topic of my upbringing under Barilius's keen eye is brought up.

I sigh, too tired to have this fight with him again. We could be brothers-in-arms for a lifetime and he would never truly understand my place in the king's court.

Since the moment that we met I'd seen the leader in him, his potential to reach further than even I'd dared to think about. He could be the hero, whereas my abilities forbid even the opportunity to do good. There had been too much horror, too much fear and death.

"Have you spoken with our king about the nature of this trip?" I ask him, glancing sideways.

"You're changing the subject," he observes.

"This subject is more important," I answer.

"Lysander," he warns.

"Keelhan," I retort.

He huffs in exasperation before shaking his head. I can tell he won't put off this conversation forever, but today, like most days, I seem to have won.

"He hasn't made the time for it. I guess you'll have to play messenger for me, like always," he answers, glancing my way, a smile returning to his lips.

"He's given the order to execute on sight," I tell him, all the playfulness gone from my voice.

Keelhan turns and stares at me, the alarm in his eyes mirrors my feelings on the matter. He glances around us for unwanted listeners even though we are the only ones here. I understand his caution; there are eyes and ears everywhere they're not wanted.

"That isn't the best course of action, Lysan. It's not even the right one!" he exclaims.

"I agree with you, but you know how Barilius can be."

"This is foolish, not to mention dangerous," he continues, beginning to pace up and down the path as he chews the tip of his thumb.

"If the information proves to be false or we're trapping the wrong people—"

He stops short, his hand hovering in front of his parted lips as the horror of my potential scenario comes crashing down on him.

"We'd have innocent blood on our hands and The Righteous Hand would only have more fuel to add to the fire," he cuts in with wide eyes.

"It could lead to an outright rebellion of the people," I continue. "Or worse. A civil war."

He shakes his head violently as he strides over to me, grabbing me by the shoulders.

"We can't let that happen. If we find these rumours to be true, if we're fortunate enough to get our hands on one of these so-called freedom fighters then we gather intel *first*. Death must be a last resort. At least until we can confirm or deny anything," he says, his eyes trained on mine.

"He won't like it, he'll treat it as an act of treason," I point out.

Even when I disagree with Barilius's methods, the thought of disobeying doesn't sit well with me. Not when I know what he's truly capable of when his orders aren't obeyed.

"To hell with him, the man's a bloodthirsty fool," Keelhan scowls.

"You're the captain," I shrug.

"Then you agree," he counters, watching me closely.

"On your own head be it," I reply.

"And on yours too," he retorts with a grim smile.

NESRYN

CHAPTER ELEVEN

After wasting a few hours wandering the halls in search of the library, we run into Melek, another of King Barilius's messengers. He's a smaller man with a wiry beard and spectacles I notice he is constantly pushing up the bridge of his nose. The old man leads us through the east wing, straight past the two guards stationed on either side of the grand double doors, to the modest library within. I'm surprised at the size of it in comparison to the luxurious rooms in the rest of the palace. It looks cosy enough with its simple décor, musty smell of old books, and the rich green leathery chairs. It almost makes me feel at home. The walls are lined with hundreds of books with topics ranging from literacy to history and fiction. I study the spines, my fingers running across them with fondness as I pass by.

As I look around the room, I see that Vena and a few of the others are already sitting with several books spread out around them. Sunlight pours through the windows along the far wall, radiating warmth into the space and bringing out the array of colours filling the shelves. I glance over at Reverie, expecting her to join Vena across the room. But to my surprise, she doesn't. Her lips are set in a thin line as she strides across the room to the opposite corner where a cluster of armchairs is tucked away beside a beautiful lamp of colourful glass on an equally beautiful little table. Maskia soon follows and the pair make themselves comfortable in two of the armchairs as if they're settling in for a long day.

I glance over as they begin to talk amongst themselves. Over the course of those few hours scouring the halls for the library, they had shared endless details about their homes, their families and their lives. They seem like nice enough girls and in an ideal world, we could have been real friends. Whatever we have now, in the midst of The Choosing, is fragile and fleeting like an ice-covered lake at the end of the Snowhold months. I try to cast the thought from my mind; it's dangerous and foolish of me to want to make ties with my competitors, and yet I can't help imagining it.

I think of the strange letters and jumbled scribbles on my folded parchment and I scan the shelves, skimming across the languages section where there are several spaces. I glance over at the table where Vena has a handful of texts splayed open around her.

"Just because something isn't where you expect, doesn't mean it doesn't exist at all," I murmur, recounting an old lesson my uncle had given to me.

An idea sparks in my head as I think of my growing theory forming in my head, as I begin to rifle through the volumes on languages.

I grab several books on dead languages and olden texts, including Elven ones. Without a word I take them over to the others and drop to my knees, placing the books out in front of me.

Maskia draws out her envelope and pulls out the piece of parchment. "So I suppose we're working together?"

"I don't see the harm in it, it's only one trial," I answer with a shrug, opening up my own envelope.

Maskia shrugs once and leans back into the curve of the armchair, propping her leg up on the arm as she begins to scrutinise the paper.

"Why are we teaming up again?" Reverie asks distractedly.

I look over to find her sitting up straight in her chair. I follow her gaze and my eyes fall on Vena and the cluster of girls who have just joined her at the table. She looks vaguely interested before her eyes slide back to the texts laid out in front of her.

"There aren't any rules against it. We can work faster if we put our minds together. Besides, it seems that we aren't the only ones," I point out.

Reverie pulls her gaze back to us and blinks as if she's returned from her inner thoughts. She throws me a weak smile as she shuffles in her seat, leaning down to reach for one of the volumes on the floor.

"You have a point," Maskia shrugs beside me.

"Let's try not to waste any more time," I tell them as I smooth out the letter.

The trip to Lysan's room had been a complete waste of time. The slim hope that he would actually help rather than tease and stall had been eradicated as soon as that infuriating smirk had crawled across his lips. Reverie shifts in her seat, her brows knitting together as she flits between the book of dead languages in her hands and my face.

"What is it? Have you found something?" I ask.

"Why did you go to the Shadowcaster?"

I pause, wondering why it mattered, and briefly, what tactic she might be using.

"It's the only place I could think of. It's not exactly like this place is heaving with servants to ask," I explain, not liking the looks I get from them.

"Shadowcasters are made from fear and pain, and they inflict those very same things onto others," Maskia says, her voice grave.

"Your point?" I ask, my attention shifting to her.

"They aren't to be trusted, Nesryn."

"Did no one ever teach you about them?" Reverie asks curiously.

"My uncle believed them to be misunderstood," I say, my tone defensive.

"Dangerous and unpredictable are the words I'd choose," Maskia remarks.

"Your uncle seems to have rather controversial views," Reverie adds.

'*So it would seem,*' I think to myself.

"So... where should we start?" I ask, giving her a pointed look.

Reverie puts the book in her lap to one side and leans in, peering at my splayed out letter and comparing what's on it with hers. Her brows knit together and I watch her bright eyes as they flick between the papers.

"They don't seem to hold anything out of the ordinary other than squiggly lines and dashes," she says finally.

"What about mine?" Maskia pipes up.

She leans across, her pale gold waves tumbling over her shoulders as she passes her envelope to Reverie. I sit back patiently as she compares the papers, eventually shaking her head and lifting her gaze to meet ours in turn.

I hold out my hand and she passes them to me swiftly. I study the riddle and the jumble of incoherent lines and swirls below. There are similarities in the way that some of the lines curve, but with a defeated sigh, I realise that Reverie is right.

"We have nothing to go on. Where do we even start?" Maskia grumbles.

"From the beginning," I quip, dropping the letters into my lap.

She sends me a sorrowful look and I respond with a sympathetic smile before handing her one of the thick books from the pile beside me. In the other chair, Reverie resumes her earlier reading while I reach for the Elvish textbook at the top of the pile.

The hours slowly traipse by as we scour book after book with no sign of getting any closer to unravelling the king's riddle.

Tension creeps into the air as others around us leave and return, becoming more frustrated and agitated as time slips by. Maskia is restless in her chair and Reverie becomes more and more interested in the angsty chatter buzzing across the table from where Vena sits, her nose still deep in books.

I shift and stretch, my bones complaining as I try to stave off the stiffness taking over my limbs. I switch positions for probably the tenth time, my feet pricking with pins and needles as I cross them in front of me and force myself to return to the open texts in my lap.

"Perhaps we should take a break," Reverie suggests as Zariya, Chandra, Rohana and Erryn file out of the library.

"My eyes could definitely use one. Plus, I'm starved," Maskia grumbles as she smacks the book shut and tucks her envelope into her sleeve.

I look up from my page, glancing between them. "You go ahead."

"You're not coming?" Reverie remarks, surprised.

"I'll catch up," I reply before dropping my gaze back to the book.

Out of the corner of my eye, I see the girls glance at one another and Maskia simply shrugs.

"We'll see you in a little while," she says as she steps around me, Reverie close behind her.

I manage to make it another hour—with no success—when I finally decided to take a break. I look up, surprised to find that I'm alone. Even Vena has gone. With a groan, I stand and stretch, grabbing my envelope and stepping out into the hall to ask for directions from one of the soldiers standing watch.

I emit a happy sigh when I manage to find the palace gardens, the fresh air a pleasant change from the stuffiness of the library. My legs are stiff as I walk under the trees and along the paths that weave through the beds of flowers that perfume the air. As I move under the arching branches, I listen out for signs of wildlife, only to hear the hushed sounds of the city below. I notice the high walls encircling the outer edge of the gardens and casting long shadows across the neatly trimmed lawns. As I delve deeper into the grounds I hear people along the gravelled path, searching keenly when I hear the familiar sound of hooves.

I follow the sound to some stables where a beautiful stallion stands in its paddock. His intelligent eyes watch me as I take the last cautious steps to him and rub along his side. A stable boy saunters past, stopping short as he catches me with the horse.

"He's a palomino that one. He's called Fencer. Very friendly. Beautiful too, ain't he?" he asks, striding over.

I smile at him before turning back to admire the majestic beast, stroking his soft caramel muzzle.

"Oh he is, you must be very proud of caring for such a fine beast."

"Oh I am, I take good care of all my horses, m'Lady," he boasts with a wide, toothy grin.

I answer with a grin of my own and return my gaze to Fencer, his dark eyes already watching me.

"Do you ride, m'Lady?" the boy asks, peering at me.

"Occasionally."

My mind drifts back to pleasant rides on my beautiful chestnut steed, River, through the orchards in the middle of Sunwake, the warm rays tanning my skin and bringing a smile to my face. We would go for miles before resting beneath the shade of the Flarak trees and reading my favourite books.

'*Books!*'

The thought startles me out of my daydreaming and I rush through an excuse and leave, making my way back through the gardens and back into the looming shade of the palace as quickly as I can.

The evening sun filters through the windows and scatters sunlight across spine after spine, catching the glint of the gold and silver foiled letters running along them. After their break, some of the other Chosen, like us, chose to stay amongst the books in search of an answer, while others like Chandra and Rohana only returned to take what books they could and left.

As time passes by, more and more filter out with mentions of returning or searching for another angle to tackle the riddle from. The pile of books in the middle of our small triangle grows as we pull more books from the shelves, comparing the strange characters penned beneath the riddle with the faded images in the books. Out of nowhere, my grumbling stomach cuts through the heavy silence, drawing the unwanted attention of the others.

Maskia raises her brow in silent question. Reverie only smirks.

"I must've forgotten to eat," I explain with a bashful shrug.

"It *is* getting late…" Reverie comments, putting down her book with a thump.

"I'm not even sure that it's scripture. Are we sure it's even a language? Perhaps it's just symbols or a code. I'd even consider numerology at this point." Maskia groans.

"I would take anything over opening another of those wretched books," Reverie adds, glaring resentfully at the piles in front of me.

"Well, it's only eight chimes. We have ten hours left to work this out." I offer.

The groans and muttered words that I get in reply tell me that's not what they want to hear.

Maybe we should rest, eat, and regroup later tonight?" I suggest.

The two of them exchange glances, a shrug passing between them before they nod at me. Maskia then jumps out of her chair with a surprising flourish and claps her hands together.

"I'll see you girls at dinner," she says, before striding from the room.

Reverie gets to her feet, none of Maskia's energy evident. She throws me a tired smile and places the book that she'd been scouring through on the pile.

"Remember that dinner's in an hour," she comments with a smirk, glancing down at my stomach.

A rush of colour stains my cheeks and I give her a lopsided grin. Without another word, she leaves and I'm sitting alone once more. A sigh escapes my lips as I get up, collecting a handful of the books and taking them back over to the shelves. On my third trip, I stop when the title of the book in my hand catches my eye.

"The Moonshard History: A Reflectional Study of Symbolism, Lost Tongues, and the Complete Language of Glyphs," I read aloud.

I briefly consider shelving it before pulling it back into my arms. The weight of it surprises me and I have to shift it onto my hip to bear the weight as I leave.

My room is lit and warm when I return, the bed neatly made, and a fresh nightgown folded at the bottom of the bed.

Despite the proof that they had been here, Perin, Sarleigh and Hesta are nowhere to be found, and I find myself grateful for the chance to have my room to myself.

Incense floats about the room as I walk through, layering it with sandalwood and vanilla. I draw it deep into my lungs with my next inhale and I realise as the clock chimes eight just how exhausted I am. My eyes feel dry and my body aches from being curled up on the floor for hours on end. A dull ache throbs at my temples from having spent the day staring at dusty old books and scrutinising the most minute differences.

I place the book and the riddle on the vanity and run myself a bath, dropping in some soothing salts and sweet soaps as it rises, forming a layer of bubbles on the surface. The water is welcoming as I slip into the bath and I hiss with pleasure as I lower myself all the way down until the water kisses my chin. My eyes feel heavy as I soak, the bubbles swirling around me, and the water rippling out with each breath.

My aching legs feel much less stiff when I finally exit the bathroom, and I feel clean and refreshed as I face the grand double wardrobe. The clock behind me rings out signalling nine chimes and I realise I'm late for dinner. I throw open the doors to reveal several more vaitas like the one I'd been wearing hanging neatly within. I blink in surprise and grab the first one that I see, flinging it onto the bed.

I walk past the vanity with a cursory glance towards the riddle. I have to look again to make sure that my eyes aren't deceiving me. I stand in front of the vanity and bend down until my eye line is level with the surface. My breath hitches in my throat as my thoughts are confirmed.

The sky outside is a rich deep blue and the light of the moon filters through the window, shining squarely on the parchment. Slowly, the riddle begins to glow and the ink of the squiggles below begins to sparkle as the paper comes to life.

"Moon glyphs…" I breathe.

Something in me snaps to attention and I reach for a scrap of paper and the quill and begin to copy out the glyphs, scribbling them quickly onto the crumpled piece of paper in my hand.

"They're verses… it isn't a message at all. It's a poem," I murmur in realisation.

I glance over at the book on moon symbols that I'd brought back with me from the library, and a short surge of laughter bubbles up out of me. When I've finished copying it out, I step back, my eyes greedily scanning the page.

"Moon dust in your lungs,
stars in your eyes,
you are a child of the cosmos,
a ruler of the skies,"

As I read the words out loud, they flash and fade, some of the lines remaining as ink that hadn't been there a moment ago. They suddenly begin to shine through the paper, connecting one by one until the familiar curving letters of the elvish language appear.

"What's this?" I breathe, my brows knitting together as I scrutinise the paper.

I rush through the open doors leading to the dining room, zeroing in on Reverie and Maskia at the far end of the table. I feel the eyes of several Chosen follow me as I rush over to them. They look up from their plates in mild concern as I double over, catching my breath.

"I worked it out," I announce breathlessly.

They sit up straighter, their eyes widening in surprise. I scramble for the letter and the crumpled paper with my untidy notes sprawled across it.

By now I've attracted the attention of the others, their chairs scraping against the hard floors as they stand up and move closer, their curiosities piqued. I ignore them, too excited to care if they overhear me.

"They're moon glyphs," I explain, showing them the papers together.

"They can't be. I've never seen a moon glyph presented like this," Maskia utters, taking the papers from me to analyse them herself.

"That's because they've been altered in translation. They're moon glyphs in Elvish script," I explain, the excitement leaking into my voice.

An uneasy murmur and several gasps erupt throughout the room at my words. Maskia's jaw slackens as she stares from me to the papers in her hands.

"The traitor's tongue," she says finally, her brows furrowed with concern and something else.

The hall begins to rumble with an uneasy buzz.

"You know Elvish?" Reverie gapes at me.

"My uncle demanded that my tutors teach me a little bit of everything," I admit. "Including the controversial subjects," I add.

The smile that creeps onto her face surprises me, but her next words surprise me more.

"Smart man," she chuckles.

"Show us," Maskia requests, passing the papers back to me as she stands.

I nod and stand in front of the closest window, feeling the presence of Reverie and Maskia, as well as several of the others, behind me. I hold the letter up to the pale moonlight and let the magic take hold. Gasps erupt once again from behind me as the glyphs begin to glow, the verses revealing themselves just as they had done for me before.

I read the verses aloud, clear and precise, and watch as the verses fade, relinking the swirls and curved lines to reveal the hidden message.

"What does it mean?" Reverie asks as she pushes past the girls who have tried to get a closer look. She stops beside Maskia, reading the papers over my shoulder.

I look back at her, noting the shock on her face as I speak.

"*Lanta Ho'Aman*," I read aloud. "It means fallen from grace."

"Well done, Lady Havenore, it seems that you have completed the trial," Vilkha announces, stepping into the room.

Chaos ensues after my revelation of the moon glyphs and Elvish text.

Dinner is forgotten as The Chosen split off. Some remain in the dining hall, talking rapidly amongst themselves with furious expressions, while others dart out of the room and I can only presume they mean to discover their own messages and complete the task. Vena is among the ones who leave, throwing a dark look over her shoulder directed straight at me.

"What is her problem?" I ask no one.

Heated voices from the other end of the dining hall distract me from Vena, and I look over to where Rohana and Mallon are arguing with Vilkha.

"I didn't realise they were all so... political," I murmur as I glance towards the other end of the table.

"Elvish is called the traitor's tongue for a reason, Nesryn. Some of the families view the politics of Elves and the removal of their culture from the curriculum as law," Maskia points out.

"Several families have very strong views on it all. I'm surprised that the king allows for this level of controversy, especially during such an occasion," Reverie adds, picking at her plate.

Rohana and Mallon's voices get louder and I'm drawn back to their conversation.

"...and I'm telling you that I will *not* be participating in a trial meant for heathens and traitors!" Rohana yells, pointing a finger into Vilkha's chest.

"It's a trick. It's a way to test our values and I wish to have no part in it," Mallon adds beside her.

Vilkha's face is calm, but I can read the anger swirling in his eyes as he surveys the room, his eyes falling on each of us in turn.

"Failure or refusal to complete the task will result in the immediate disqualification of the Chosen party," he calls to us, his voice loud and clear.

He turns back to Rohana and Mallon, drawing his arms behind his back as he looks down at them in a way that reminds me of a vulture again—this time, it's a vulture assessing its next meal.

"Is this what you wish, Lady Durhannes, Lady Vythierre?" he asks them. There is a warning edge to his voice.

A thick silence suddenly envelopes the room as everyone waits for their response. In moments, the girls hold their heads high as they nod stiffly at the king's messenger. Their defiance is a tangible spark, dangerous yet daunting to all in the room. A mixture of shock and disdain ripples through the rest of us, breaking the thick silence with frantic whispers and quiet murmurs.

This may have been a controversial challenge, but they were now going against the king, against The Choosing. It was an act of defiance against our ruler, an act that could very well be declared treason.

"Very well, I shall inform the king," Vilkha says finally.

"You will gather your things. Transport to return you home will be arranged for the morning," he continues.

Neither Rohana nor Mallon say a word as they stalk from the dining hall, refusing to look at any of us as they leave. Vilkha hesitates as he scrutinises the rest of us, his lips now set in a thin, wispy line beneath his greying moustache.

"As for the rest of you, preparations for your next trial will be underway tomorrow. I expect it to begin in two days' time. Take until then to do as you wish within the perimeters of the palace," he says, before leaving through the same doors as the girls.

CHAPTER TWELVE

After a long few days on the road, we arrive in Talló.

The salty air fills my lungs as Keelhan directs us through the streets towards the harbour. Even from a distance, I can hear the sound of the marketplace in full swing: buyers and sellers haggling over the prices of fruits, fish and exotic wares from across the Gallambian Ocean.

Curiosity urges me to look at everything as we ride past and I take in the rows of little bakeries, butchers, and independent shops. With the next bend in the road, I spot a horizon of deep glimmering blue, and after spending so much time confined within the palace walls, I find myself unable to look away from the rippling waves. I'm in awe of its sheer size and beauty. I watch the gulls fly above, cawing and swooping in the hopes of picking out their next meal and large ships rock from side to side as the waves pull them to and fro, their masts soaring high up into the skies above.

"Can you see why I love it here?" Keelhan asks with a grin as he sidles up to me.

"It *is* beautiful," I admit, staring out at the vast blue. "But I'm pretty sure you don't love coming here just to admire the scenery like a tourist," I add, flashing him a knowing grin.

"You're right, that's not even the best part. You wait until we try the local taverns tonight," he says with a chuckle and a flash of amusement in his eyes.

"I look forward to it. But first, there are matters that require our attention," I reply as I glance at him sideways.

His amusement remains as he waves a dismissive hand at me, shaking his head.

"Oh, Lys! Learn to live a little. You're all work and no play these days," he chuckles.

"I'll even take you to one of the seedier places, find you a nice broad to warm your bed if it'll make you lighten up," he jokes.

"This is certainly ironic coming from the upstanding captain of the Aslitír," I tease.

"Yes, well we can't all be so serious and sombre all the time. You're like a walking, talking dark cloud of misery,"

"And you're a pompous pretty boy," I laugh, bumping his shoulder with mine.

"Try and take it all in. I'm sure you'll learn something eventually," he quips.

I laugh as he rears his horse and surges forward before I can retort. I watch as he gallops to the front, weaving around the carts and soldiers until he's out of sight. It isn't long before I've lost interest and I gaze at the view, realising once more how different this seaside town is to Akhozia's capital. It's brighter and louder, and I realise that I prefer this to the silent halls of the palace.

People watch as I ride past, their eyes following me warily. It's a common occurrence these days and I barely pay them any mind. It doesn't matter where in this world I go, there will always be someone afraid of what I am.

A few hours later, Keelhan busies himself with speaking with our hosts as I help several soldiers unload the carts. The inn we're staying at is humble at best, with a sagging roof, creaky floors, and wonky steps.

I glance at it distastefully as I carry another crate of supplies towards the open door. As I reach it, one of the soldiers meets me in the doorway and takes it off my hands, though from the expression on his face I can tell he'd rather be doing any other task, as long as it was far from me.

"Take that inside, store it with the weaponry," I order him.

The look in his eye is a mixture of distrust and disgust, but he nods curtly and follows my orders without question. I wait until he steps inside the inn before I turn on my heel and stride back to the cart. Out of the corner of my eye, I see Keelhan making a beeline for me so I slow my pace and wait for him to reach me, shoving my hands into my pockets.

"Our board is all arranged, courtesy of our hosts and a few extra buckles," he says.

"It's adequate enough," I reply, trying not to grimace.

"You've been spoiled and pampered too long in the palace, my friend. It's a bed with a roof. What more could you ask for?" he asks.

"A large glass of something strong," I answer. He lets out a booming laugh, dropping a hand onto my shoulder.

"That will come later," he answers. "For now, get settled and rest. I'll come find you tonight."

"Tonight?" I repeat, my interest piqued.

"I'll explain later. Dress casually," he says, glancing down at my filthy clothes.

I raise a brow as I glance down at his own mud-stained coat and boots and an understanding smile crosses his lips.

"Point taken."

The floorboards creak and groan under my weight as I survey my room. It's small and cramped, with a cot in one corner with a flimsy-looking quilt. A rickety-looking chair sits in the other corner in front of a small window looking out at the bustling centre. Beside it, a side table with a cluster of half-melted candles stuck to it. I find a tiny wardrobe behind the door as I close it behind me and I notice begrudgingly that one of the doors hangs off. The space is surprisingly light considering the only source is the tiny window. I'm grateful that I won't have to waste time finding a light orb.

The bathroom isn't much better; a tiny room adjacent to the bedroom, with a bathtub that fills almost the entirety of the space and a flush toilet and sink squeezed in beside it.

Without a word, I walk over to the bed and drop my bag on the quilt, before sitting beside it, rubbing a hand over my face. My eyes trail over to the open doorway leading to the bathroom and I sit staring at it for several moments as I think of Keelhan's words. I consider bathing but quickly toss the thought aside. With one swift movement, I flick my wrist and tendrils of darkness begin to crowd the room, trailing through the air like ink in water. I watch them move lazily above me before bringing my hands down sharply in a silent command.

In seconds, the room is in complete darkness, my shadows blocking out even the sounds of the other men trundling about the inn around me. I let myself wonder what Keelhan plans are for tonight before I let the subject go and close my eyes.

I'm woken up by someone shaking me roughly, and my eyes fly open as I recognise Keelhan's voice.

"By the goddess, Lysan, it's like a bloody tomb in here. Can we let in a little light?" he asks.

I retract my shadows in seconds and I'm surprised to find the room still dark, the window showing a rich blue night sky.

"And you haven't even bathed," he observes, with a deadpan expression.

I rub my face as I stand from the cot, blinking the bleariness from my eyes as I turn to face him.

"You haven't even told me what it is we're doing," I reply groggily.

"We're meeting a contact of mine, they have news on our target," he explains plainly.

"When and where?" I ask, my focus sharpening.

"In an hour," he answers.

"We have time," I observe.

He shakes his head. "It's on the other side of the docks and we aren't taking the horses."

"Too conspicuous?" I look at him and he nods. "Alright, I'll meet you outside in a few minutes.

Keelhan opens his mouth to say something, but at the last moment, he decides against it, nodding instead before slipping out the door.

We walk through the streets, side by side. The nights in Talló are vastly different to what I'd seen earlier this afternoon. The lit streets are mostly barren. Several people litter the streets, gathering around the rows of houses.

The comfortable silence is interrupted only by the sound of our steps. Keelhan slows and with a tilt of his head, gestures to the alleyway to our right. We turn into it and keep moving, but I come to a stop several feet in, my eyes travelling up the wall.

It's been sprayed with some kind of paint, a deep emerald green background with a purple handprint at its centre. It spreads across the wall over a few feet, large enough to stand out, to be noticed. The colours that have been chosen are as important as the symbol itself, as I realise it's a message of hope and justice.

"More and more of these are popping up across the kingdom. If we're not careful, all of Akhozia will be overrun with The Righteous Hand movement," Keelhan tells me, staring at the wall in disgust.

'How much different would it be to Barilius's reign?' I consider silently.

The mere thought alone is treason, and yet the smallest part of me revels in the tiny act of rebellion. Despite my oath to the king, my views differed greatly from his.

"With time, it will come to an end. We'll fight this together," I say.

"It'll be great fun fighting beside you again, my brother," he answers.

The smirk on his face makes him seem so much younger, the fierceness in his eyes bright and daring. It takes me back to a time when we were both young and hungry to make a name for ourselves. Keelhan's aspirations had laid out a path for him that, while it moved in the same direction as my own, had never crossed with mine. There had once been a time when I had hoped to share the same path, but I realised soon enough that that could never be the case. The king had his own plans for my future, plans that had given me the name Diaboli.

The demon's shadow.

When we reach the centre, it's like reaching the beating heart of Tralló. Taverns doors are splayed wide open with men and women spilling out of their doors, drinking ales or hurling them along the cobbles. Music echoes through the street and I recognise a few of the sailors' songs and shanties, despite spending most of my time in the capital.

Keelhan points to one of the taverns further along, its sign jutting out from the bend, high and swinging in the wind for all to see: The Buckles and Brass.

As we march towards it, a huge man emerges from within, carrying a much smaller, drunken man by the scruff of his collar and the belt of his pants. He grumbles something to him before tossing him aside into the street with little effort, before wiping his hands and going back inside.

"That's where we're going?" I ask, glancing warily at Keelhan.

"It was my contact's choice of venue," he replies.

"That's certainly brave of you, Keel," I reply.

"Sometimes you need to take a risk to get answers." His eyes dart to me.

I can tell by the stiffness in his stance and his quickened pace that he's uneasy. I look at The Buckles and Brass, scoping it from afar. From here I can see two exits on the ground floor as well as several windows.

'*A last resort*,' I consider.

"Keelhan you don't need to lecture me of all people." I pause. "If there's trouble…" I trail off, waiting for an answer to my unspoken question.

He holds his hand up and shakes his head, giving me a warning look.

"You let me handle it," he answers.

"Keelhan, we need to be prepared for the worst-case scenario," I argue.

"And I am. If we run into trouble, I need you to answer the threat with steel instead of shadow. We don't need any more enemies here, Lysan," he adds with a grave tone.

His words sting but I understand why he says them. I take a breath and nod.

Keelhan leads us in silence through the doors into the tavern. The noise is louder than expected and the place is heaving with all sorts of characters. I keep close to Keelhan, watching his back, but my eyes scour the room for an easy way out, should we find ourselves caught up in trouble that we can't fight.

The place is busy as people scramble to grab the attention of the barmaid rushing up and down the bar, filling steins with ale and taking coin in return. Booths run along the far wall, bending around the corner. Tables are scattered through the open space, everyone taken. The atmosphere is loud and stuffy and the stench of spilt ale and unwashed skin fills the air.

'*He wanted me to bathe for this place?*'

My nose wrinkles at the smell, but I say nothing as we weave through the crowds towards the only empty booth, sheltered away in the far corner. As we move closer, I realise that there is already someone waiting, a hood over their head and their hands clasped in front of them. I notice the large man from earlier as he pushes through the crowd and places several steins on the table, the froth from the ale sloshing over the side as he puts them down roughly.

"Now that's someone you wouldn't want to meet in a dark alley," I comment dryly.

Keelhan sends me a warning look but says nothing as we make our way to the booth.

As we move closer, the brutish man steps out in front of us, his brows knitting together as he surveys us. The hooded person behind him must have said something, as his attention shifts momentarily to them, before we're back to being scrutinised. The man doesn't say a word, but steps out of our way,

Keelhan slides in first, with me close behind him. The stranger draws in their hands, lifting them to pull back the hood shrouding their face. I'm unsure what I expected, but I find myself shocked to see the face of a striking woman beneath the shadows of her hood. Her heart-shaped face is framed with a tangle of raven-black curls. Her hooded eyes are the cool brown shade of the forest trees deep in Snowhold and set beneath wide brows. A long jagged scar runs across her bottom lip, across her olive skin and trailing to the start of her collarbone.

She can't be much older than us, yet there is an aura about her that seems older, wiser.

"Esmeray," Keelhan says in greeting.

"Keelhan, it's good to see you," she replies, tilting her head.

The jagged scar twists and pulls with her movements, her eyes then flitting to me with a flash of curiosity.

"I see you brought a friend," she continues, leaning forward to rest her chin on the top of her hands.

"Yes, this is Lysan. A member of the court," Keelhan answers, introducing me.

Her eyes flash with interest at this new information.

"The king's Shadowcaster, interesting," she murmurs.

"What news have you got for me?" he presses, changing the subject as he leans forward.

"Coin first, answers after," she states, holding out her open hand.

I glance from her to Keelhan as he reigns in a sigh and reaches into his back pocket, drawing out a small leather pouch. It jingles as he places it on the table and pushes it toward Esmeray.

We wait in silence as she opens the pouch and rifles through, checking each piece before she's satisfied. She smiles at us, slipping the pouch beneath the table and into her pocket.

"They call themselves The Righteous Hand. They have many faces and many people in their pockets," she starts as she hands us each a stein.

"We already have this information. What good are you to me if you only tell us what we already know?" Keelhan snaps.

The large man glares at him over his shoulder, a growl emanating from him as he sneers at my friend. I place a hand on Keelhan's shoulder and give him a small shake of my head. Esmeray holds her hand up to the man, and he glares at us once more before turning back around.

"I'm simply catching your friend here, up to speed," she answers with a wry smile.

"Just get to the point," Keelhan mutters.

"Word is that there is a shipment waiting in the docks for them. Supplies, no doubt. It came in yesterday morn and has yet to be retrieved by their people," she says.

"Surely this shipment is valuable to them? Why would they delay collecting it?" Keelhan ponders aloud.

"Perhaps because word spread of a troupe of Aslitír heading to town," she answers casually.

"That was hardly common knowledge. How did you come by the information?" I ask sceptically, putting down my ale.

"A spy never shares her secrets," she says with an ominous smile as she turns to me.

"It's hardly relevant now, Lysan," Keelhan sighs, turning back to Esmeray. "How do we use this to find The Righteous Hand, Esmeray?"

"You'll have to find the messenger. Find him and you'll have the information you need to find the others of this little movement," she replies.

"You're not giving us very much to go on," I comment dryly.

Keelhan glares at me but my attention is already on Esmeray, who watches me from across the table with a thoughtful expression.

"Dunira' Peshuwar," she says finally.

"You'll have to elaborate," I tell her.

"The docked ship," she smiles, as though it's all the explanation that I need.

Slowly, she gets to her feet, her hands resting on the table as she appraises us. Her dark curls fall across her shoulders, curtaining her face as she speaks.

"Well, it's certainly been fun, boys. But I must take my leave. I'm sure you understand."

Keelhan stands to argue but gets a threatening grunt from Esmeray's companion, which swiftly convinces him to take a seat again. I watch in silence as she leaves the booth, waves a hand over her head and cuts through the drunken crowd, her hefty bodyguard trundling behind her.

"For fifty buckles, that was rather unhelpful," Keelhan mutters.

"You gave her fifty buckles?" I ask, incredulous.

He sends me a warning glance as I slap my hand against the table releasing a burst of laughter.

"Well, we best start using her information wisely. I don't want to be around when you tell the king you wasted coin on a name," I chuckle after downing the rest of my ale.

NESRYN

CHAPTER THIRTEEN

My arms burn as my fists collide with the dummy, sweat beading at my brow and traipsing down my temple. My breaths come in short, heavy bursts as I try to time them with my jabs. I try to remember what Jarek would say in our lessons, doing my best to keep my form.

'Elbows up, shoulders squared, lunge with your body, not your arms,' his voice tells me as I swing again.

I shift then jab, duck, then jab again, focusing on pressure points and weak points as Jarek had taught me. I finish with a spinning kick, sending the dummy skittering backwards as it slides across the marble floor. But my moment of pride is short-lived as I mess the landing, sprawling backwards onto my behind and winding myself.

"Shit…" I wince, rubbing my hip.

"Elegantly done," Reverie chortles, as she walks over to me.

"I told you my hand-to-hand combat wasn't the best," I grumble as I take her hand.

"Just keep practising your balance," she replies.

"You sound like my teacher, Jarek," I grumble.

"We all have flaws to remedy, Nesryn," she reasons.

"I just need to keep trying," I tell her as we cross the training room.

I drop down to the floor when we reach the other side, pressing my back against the wall as I gulp down the water that Reverie hands me. I watch her as she keeps glancing up at the clock.

"What is it? How much time do we have?" I ask as I finish another mouthful.

Reverie lifts her head to read the clock before she looks back at me.

"We have plenty of time," she says.

"Shall we go again?" I ask, getting to my feet.

I watch her glance at the clock once again and I bite back the curiosity that tugs at me.

"Do you need to be somewhere?" I ask, leaning forward.

"No, no of course not," she replies, too quickly.

'You're going to meet someone,' I realise.

I eye her suspiciously, noting the blush running across her cheeks and tinging the tips of her ears as she stares at the floor.

'But who, I wonder?'

Without a word, I lean back to glance at the clock myself, noting nine chimes. I blink in surprise, realising how long our training session had become.

"Actually maybe we should call it a day? I think three hours is long enough," I suggest.

The relief in her eyes is enough to confirm my suspicions but I keep my mouth shut as we leave the room together. The past few days have been a refreshing distraction from The Choosing, and I find myself grateful for Maskia and Reverie's company. Though I know deep down that they are my rivals, I can't ignore the small buds of friendship that have tentatively bloomed between us.

As we make our way out of the east wing, we spot a familiar face coming our way. Maskia's eyes light up as she recognises us and her golden tresses fan out behind her as she runs over. She's already dressed in her vaita of purple and gold.

"I was on my way to find you both," she says with a flourish.

"You're dressed early," I note.

"I just wanted to get it out of the way," she explains with a shrug.

"Well, we were just heading back to bathe and change ourselves," I tell her.

"And what am I meant to do while you two take your sweet time preparing yourselves?" Maskia pouts.

"Actually, I think I left something back in the training room. You go, I'll catch up with you both later," Reverie speaks up, shuffling a few steps back.

Maskia's loops her arm through mine. "Well, I guess I can lounge around with you while you're getting ready."

Reverie gives us a tight smile and walks away with a purposeful step. I watch on with a knowing smile as she glances back at us and disappears down another corridor.

Maskia pores through my trunks as I bathe my aching muscles in a welcomed hot bath of essential oils and bubbles with the scent of honeysuckle.

"It's such a bore wearing these vaitas instead of our own clothes," she calls from the other room.

Though we haven't known each other for long, I can tell by the way that she speaks that she's pouting again.

"I don't mind them so much," I call back in answer.

"That's because if you aren't in your vaita, you're in those beloved training leathers of yours," she retorts.

"And what would you wear then, if our choice of clothing was our own?" I call.

There's a pause as she considers her options and I hear her slap her palms against my dresser as she slumps down at the vanity in defeat.

"I wouldn't even know where to begin, there are simply far too many choices for me to make such a decision without help," she replies dramatically.

I chortle, my chin brushing against the surface and causing the water to ripple around me. One part of me wishes to stay here for the rest of the day, while the other wonders what trial is coming next. I wonder whether we'll compete against one another and risk breaking the fragile bonds we have just begun to build.

"You're rather quiet in there, do I need to come in and fish you out?" Maskia's voice drifts through the open doors.

"That won't be necessary, thank you," I giggle. "I'll be out in a few minutes."

"You'll soak yourself away at this point," she grumbles.

"What do you think the king will have us do next?" I ask, changing the subject.

"Well, if it's anything like the last one... something unorthodox," she replies after a moment's hesitation.

"I tend to agree with you there. I had no idea that the king had such an open mind," I say, as I think of Rohana and Mallon probably grumbling back in their respective homes.

"I think it's less to do with the king having an open mind, and more to do with what we will stand by in the face of controversy," she answers thoughtfully.

"Such wise words," I tease.

"You'll get wiser ones in a moment if you don't hurry up. I'm sure your wrinkles have wrinkles by now," she calls. "You have one more minute and then I'm coming in to drag you out myself!"

I laugh and quickly lift myself from the bathtub before she makes good on her threat.

The nervous energy is palpable as we stand in a neat line across the room.

We're on the north side of the palace in a room that I've never seen before. Large orbs of elvynlight hang low across the ceiling, illuminating the navy walls decorated with a gold swirl pattern. The room seems to wait with bated breath, the musky scent of old potions clinging to every surface.

Ten tables are spread evenly around the room with a multitude of items placed on each one. Along the wall behind us are rows upon rows of glass jars full of a multitude of different powders, liquids and more. They seem to be organised by tiny labels, each one inked neatly. My attention is pulled from my surroundings as Melek stands before us, splaying his arms wide.

"I welcome you all to your next trial. It will take more than just your wits to keep you from failing," he explains.

"This time, however, the challenge will require a rare book of great power. Once you have read through the terms of the trial, you will each, in turn, step up to the pedestal at the end of this room and call upon the Book of Requirement. Its magical properties will give you what you need to go forward," he continues.

Murmurs and hushed gasps ripple through The Chosen as some of the girls begin to gossip amongst themselves. Vena, I notice, stares ahead, unwilling to involve herself in the conversations around her.

"Isn't that the most powerful spellbook in Estóreah?" I whisper to Reverie.

"There's only four in existence. There used to be more but that was before the Elven War," she murmurs back.

"Alright, settle down," Melek calls, but no one seems to listen.

Out of the corner of my eye, I notice one of the girls step forward, her brown hair is wrapped up in a neat bun, her vaita black with a sheer maroon overlay; the colours of the Raviffete House. When I look at her face, I immediately recognise her from the carriage ride. Her meek expression from five days ago is no longer present.

"Is it wise to allow us to use such a powerful book? Not all of us were trained in the magical arts," Lesya says evenly, glancing toward Erryn and Ovie whose eyes are cast down to the floor with embarrassment.

"The point of The Choosing, Lady Raviffete, is to weed out those unfit to bear the title. The shortcomings of your competitors should be no concern of yours," he replies with a single raised brow.

"How much time do I have?" Vena cuts in.

We all turn in her direction, but she ignores every one of us, her onyx eyes holding Melek's gaze. The king's messenger regards her thoughtfully for several moments, intrigued by her eagerness to separate herself from the rest of us.

"Three hours," he answers.

"But that isn't nearly enough time!" Ovie exclaims.

"It's time enough," Melek answers with a dull expression.

He pulls out a sand timer from within his robes and places it on the top of the pedestal, sealing it there with a spell. He strides back down the walkway, looking at all of us in turn with an ominous smile before he steps to the side and gestures to the tables. In the next moment, there is a scurry as all of the girls try to push in first. All the while, Vena moves calmly past the kerfuffle and seats herself at one of the tables closest to the front.

Reverie, Maskia and I share a look as the others around us begin to claim tables and we move toward the closest ones, silently choosing to stay as close to one another as we can. Maskia chooses the table in front, and I take the seat behind her while Reverie seats herself at the one to my right.

I glance at the items spread out across the surface of the table. Dried herbs and flowers are organised in neat rows on the left, a cluster of crystals and precious stones in the far right corner. But what truly catches my eye is the carved box of mahogany wood with a white folded letter balanced against one of its corners.

"May Asteria bring luck unto you all," Melek calls before leaving the room.

The old man is swiftly replaced by two armed guards.

I pick up my envelope at the same time that Reverie and Maskia pick up theirs. I break the wax seal and open it in a wild frenzy, my eyes scanning the looped letters of the verse scrawled across the thick paper.

> *One to save and one to spread,*
> *Before you step where irons fell.*
> *To the feet where irons wed,*
> *Cast but one, and perfect spell.*
> *Watch the kingdoms do the same,*
> *Upon the mark, the kingdoms tell,*
> *Of fire attire trimmed with flame.*

I glance past the letter at the box, noting the four iron strips fixed into the wood, one on each side. They meet at the top, wrapping the box like a gift and unfurling into a pattern of intricate swirls that spread across the surface of the lid. In the centre of the lid is a tiny fire ruby held in place by a claw of welded iron.

"Watch the kingdoms do the same," I mutter to myself, my eyes looking around the room at the other Chosen.

I look on in silence as some analyse the box, twisting it this way and that in their hands, while others pour over the letter. Ovie seems to be the only one standing around, not doing much of anything. I watch as she picks up a crystal warily, turning it around in her hand before putting it back down. She flinches and her eyes meet mine across the space, but it doesn't last. Her cheeks redden and she promptly looks away.

"The kingdoms must mean us," I realise as I look back to the riddle.

'*Cast but one, and perfect spell,*' I repeat in my head.

"We have to unlock this box with a spell from the Book of Requirement," I breathe in realisation.

It seems as though I'm not the only one who has worked it out as Zariya steps out from her table and marches across the room to the pedestal. Silence falls across the room as we all peer towards her in anticipation.

She utters something quietly and opens the book. There is a flash of golden light and a soft sigh as the magic flips the page and fades. She reads the words in front of her, before writing something down on a scrap piece of paper. Without another word, she thanks the book for its knowledge and shuts it with a soft thud and steps away, back to her table.

"What did she say to it?" Maskia asks as she turns back to me, leaning in as she speaks.

"The opening incantation, most likely," I reply.

"I don't remember learning about that," she replies, her brows knitting together.

"I remember it from my lessons on books of power," I reply as I try to recall the teachings from Professor Reahn.

Lesya is the next to step up to the book, then Vena as I try to recall the incantation my tutor had taught me.

"Wish me luck," Reverie whispers before she too walks over to the book.

We hear as she murmurs the incantation, followed by the flash of light and the pause of silence as she reads the spell that the book has given her.

She comes back with a troubled expression on her face.

"What is it?" Maskia presses as she stops at her table.

"The book gave me an Incedis spell," she tells us.

Maskia and I share a concerned look.

"Those can be so unpredictable," Maskia acknowledges.

"Just be careful," I warn.

Maskia gestures to the book with a wary smile, worry lines creasing her forehead.

"After you," she tells me.

I take a breath and collect the quill and letter from the table, before skirting around it and walking up toward the pedestal. An orb of elvynlight shines above as I step up and face the book. It's surprisingly plain, with worn leather stretched across the front and back. It has raised embellishments across the front and the title is made up of large gold letters pressed into the leather.

I release the breath that I didn't realise I'd been holding and chant the opening incantation.

"Knowledge required, knowledge to keep. Show me that, for which I do seek," my voice is quiet but clear.

I feel the magic wash over me and I open the book, the pages fluttering as it reveals the spell that I require.

The letters slowly begin to appear across the page as the golden light seeps into the parchment. As soon as it's legible, I feel a wave of shock and my pulse hammers in my throat.

Lencaluith Potion

'An unbinding spell?' My brows knit together in confusion as I read through the conditions of the potion.

I glance back at the locked box on my table as I wonder whether the book made a mistake. I look back at the book but the pages don't change.

"If you're wondering if the book is wrong, it's not. The Book of Requirement never lies," Vena says clearly from behind me.

I turn to her, aware of her hard eyes on me, her expression set. I don't bother replying before I copy down the spell and give thanks to the book. As I close the leather cover, the magic ceases with a hushed sigh.

Maskia brushes past me as I return to my seat. I steal a glance at Reverie who has already moved towards the rows of ingredients, her face scrunched up with concentration. I look between the spell in my hand and the iron seals wrapped around the box. Then I remember the sand timer. A jolt of shock hits me as I notice how much has slipped into the bottom of the glass already.

I shake my head, trying to clear my mind of the image of falling sand. I focus all of my attention on the ingredients needed for my potion.

Organic matter of the creator

Liquid truthbane

Syre Acid

Strix Dust

Witchbasil

Mugwort Root

"Seems easy enough," I mutter.

I quickly get to work, joining Reverie as she scours the rows of sealed ingredients, searching beside her for my own. Neither of us says a word as we collect what we need. As time passes more of the girls join us by the shelves.

Bottles clink against each other and jars are knocked this way and that as each of us studies the labels. Unsurprisingly, the shelves are well-stocked and all of us return to our tables, hands full.

No one speaks for the final stretch. The only sounds are the shuffling of feet and the clinking of glass as The Chosen measure out each item and pour them evenly. I filter through my ingredients with careful precision and the last ingredient is several strands of hair. I pluck a few from my head and watch them sizzle in the flask. I lift the flask by its stem and swirl the ingredients around, watching the colours twist and merge until the shade is a warm glowing orange.

I squint at the paper on the table and pick it up for a closer look. With a deep breath, I invoke the words scribbled there.

"*Lenca'si angwedh nista opto'ni al Rúna lanwa i'tor osto,*" I read aloud, my eyes flitting between the flask and the incantation in my hand.

I hold my breath and wait, watching intently for something, *anything* to happen. After several more moments, my shoulders slump in defeat. When my failure becomes mortifyingly obvious, I set the glass back down on the table, sloshing some of its contents in my frustration. A few droplets land on me in the process. I look up, searching for a distraction, but Reverie and Maskia are still busy with their own potions, their heads down and their expressions focused.

Straight ahead, I notice Vena's gaze directed at me, her lips cast in a prickly half-smile and I note the amusement dancing in her eyes.

'*She's enjoying my failure,*' I realise. Fury bubbles within me.

Slowly, she turns away from me and back to her own potion, though I continue to glare at the back of her head before I huff and glare at the emptying sand timer instead. I note the shrinking sand in the top and begrudgingly turn my focus back to the flask and paper beside it, my swooping letters curling across the page.

"Why didn't it *take*?" I scowl, picking up the flask and peering at the swirling liquid inside.

I pick up the paper again, reading over the words as I contemplate.

'*It might be an Elven incantation but nothing was said about it having to be read in Elvish,*' I realise.

"I wonder…" I mutter, trailing off as my mind whirs.

"Unbind these chains… repress me not… free within the secret locked."

The liquid begins to glow with my words and I stare at it in wonder with widened eyes until a searing pain in my hand draws my focus and I watch, only half-aware, as the amber liquid splashed across my wrist glows brightly like the flask and soaks into my skin. The glass in my hand suddenly shatters.

The energy hits me with a sudden and overwhelming strength and I feel my body become weightless as the force of it hurls me backwards against the wall, knocking out the shelves with one almighty blow. The air rushes from my lungs as I hear the crunch of bones breaking from the impact and I fall to the ground like a limp doll. My hearing is muffled as though I'm beneath water, though I can still make out the screams and crashes as chaos ensues around me. I try to lift myself up, my whole body trembling from shock, as glass and loose ingredients fall off my clothes in an array of clatters as my body shifts and I stop short.

I feel weak and empowered all at once as something within me stirs, flickering into existence like a tiny flame. Without warning, I feel it rear up into an incredible unseen force, like a caged beast fighting for its freedom. I heave in shuddering breaths as I fight the power rising within me. In a blind panic, I shove it back down with my remaining strength, instinctively recalling my magic defence lessons with Jarek, creating a mental wall and locking whatever the thing is back inside before I do any more damage.

"I screwed up the spell… Goddess, forgive me," I manage in a rasping, broken whisper.

Dark spots creep across my vision as I sway on all fours and I slump to the floor.

When I slowly come to, I realise by the sloping curtains over the bed and the sweet incense burning that I'm in my room. I try to sit up and immediately regret it, pain cutting through every sense as I try not to writhe, a gurgled groan slipping past my lips.

"You're awake!" someone yells and I hear a scuffle of feet as someone rushes toward me.

I try to turn my head to look, but I'm met with another wave of pain.

"Easy, you've just been through something awful," a kind voice says.

The person with the kind voice helps me slowly into a sitting position and brings a ceramic cup to my lips. I swallow the minty liquid obediently and sigh as the ebbing pain begins to ease.

I tentatively open my eyes to see a relieved Reverie watching me closely.

"Reverie, you're here!" I croak.

"You weren't technically allowed visitors, but I insisted," she replies, shuffling to sit beside me.

She winks with a reassuring smile as she bumps soldiers with me and I groan as the pain washes over me with an immensity that turns my stomach.

"Oh! Sorry," she says, wincing.

Silence falls over us and I take a deep breath, preparing myself for the answer to the question circling around my head.

"What happened?"

Reverie hesitates, her expression one of confusion and uncertainty.

"No one actually knows what happened, it all happened so fast," she shrugs. "Your flask exploded and threw us all back. Every glass in the room shattered and well…"

"Well what?"

"Not all of us got out so lucky," she mutters, scanning my face before looking away with a shuddering breath.

"Who?" I demand, my voice trembling.

"Erryn. She was still holding her flask when the surge hit her and—" she makes a gesture with her hands. "I—It took a while for them to douse the flames," she says after a long pause, shuddering at the memory.

"She went up in *flames*?" I say incredulously, my jaw dropping.

"She's gravely injured. I doubt she'll be able to continue," Reverie admits.

"By Ciel," I breathe, my heart pounding in my chest as tears prick in my eyes.

"It isn't your fault. That potion shouldn't have surged like it did," she reasons, placing a hand on my knee.

I peer at her, unconvinced.

"To be honest, I'm shocked you're still standing," she continues.

"Don't hold your breath," I answer grimly as I lift the loose tunic to peer at my blackened ribs.

"No. Nes, your body suffered the brunt of that force. It should have *killed* you."

I wrinkle my nose at her in vague amusement. "Nes?"

"That's what you take from that?" she cries in disbelief.

I shrug and she shakes her head at me.

"I think we're way past formalities now, don't you think?" she comments dryly.

I laugh and nod in agreement. "I suppose so."

"So, just call me Ria from now on," she says, smiling at me.

Her smile warms my chest, and I find myself unable to stop the smile curling my own lips as I look warmly at my friend. I watch as she reaches down to pick something up. The mahogany box, clad with iron. It looks awful. The iron is bent and twisted outwards, curling at the ends like a vine and the outside of the wood is black, burnt as charcoal.

"I managed to salvage this for you. The room was cleared out a few days after the blast," she explains.

"I've been out for that long?" I answer, shock rendering me speechless.

"Four days," she frowns.

I take it from her with a tentative grasp, and with a shaky breath, I push open the lid. The contents take me utterly by surprise and Ria answers my questioning look with a grim nod. I note the fury in her eyes. Not at me, but at what lies inside.

Inside is a simple eye mask designed for a masquerade ball. It's black and emerald green and seemingly untouched by the magical blast that caused such damage. I stare at it in disbelief.

"This?" I try to shout but my voice cracks. "This is it?" I cry, throwing it to the floor.

"There was one in each of our boxes. Apparently, it's our ticket into the next round of The Choosing," she tells me, an edge to her voice.

"We could've died over an accessory," I breathe, the reality hitting me even harder as the shock begins to subside.

"I'll let you rest. The healers should be by this afternoon. They mentioned bringing along some stronger tonics to help with the rest of your treatment," Ria says as she moves to the doors.

"But Ria—" I start.

"—The king has announced that the next trial will begin when you're healed and up to strength, seeing as Melek informed him that you passed the last test," she announces, her eyes flitting to the box in my lap and hardening.

"Can't you stay a bit longer?" I press.

The flash of anger disappears as quickly as it had come as her eyes meet mine. She heaves a heavy sigh, a tired smile creeping across her face.

"I'm happy you're alive, and I'm happier still that you're alright. But you haven't fully recovered yet and you need your rest," she reasons.

"I'll come see you soon, I promise," she vows before slipping from the room.

As a heavy silence fills the space, I think about what she said had happened, of the words we've just shared.

'*It should have killed you.*'

Her words ring in my head.

Something within me flickers at the thought. Something foreign, unknown, trapped behind a wall of ice and glass, waiting to be set free.

"I fear it may have awoken something instead."

CHAPTER FOURTEEN

The morning is cool and damp with sea mist as me, Keelhan, and a few of his men make our way to the dock in search of the Dunira' Peshuwar. Gulls fly overhead, cawing and screeching as they fly in circles above us. The soft sound of the waves lapping against the ships as we pass is, for all the sound in the kingdom, like a beating drum. We match our steps to the soft beat of the waves as we stride along the harbour.

We've changed out of our usual attire—our uniforms of visibly rich fabric, as well as the tell-tale signs of royal servants —and swapped it for the attire of average, inconspicuous merchants. Courtesy of our hosts.

"We won't get very far wandering about in Aslitír uniforms and riding palace horses," Keelhan had stated, faced with the grumbling men he'd handpicked for this assignment.

"We'll still look strange, surely? I mean, a group of merchants all travelling together through the docks, searching for a messenger boy, may gain a few unwanted ears listening," I had argued.

Despite this, I glance down at myself and then to the others around me, unconvinced of our supposed blending-in job. From a true merchant's perspective, we most likely stick out like a sore thumb. The people who travelled here to sell their wares wouldn't look so well fed or look as brutishly trained as we do, even in our fraudulent clothing. I scowl, already missing my uniform of maroon, gold and black, as Keelhan leads us along the water's edge in plain view of everyone.

"People can see us," I grumble.

"There's no one here to see us, Shadowmongrel," Keelhan points out.

"Remind me again how the fuck you dragged me into this? Why are we doing this when we could just as easily split up and have their messenger surrounded? It would save chasing after him if he tries to give us the slip," I argue.

"Just because you don't like my plan, doesn't mean it won't work," he reasons.

"You haven't told me your *full* plan," I snip.

"I gave you the basic summary."

"You're a pain in the arse."

"Quit getting your panties in a bunch, would you?" he grunts.

For probably the fifth time, I consider his plan, and I wonder if the rebel messenger will spot us from a mile off, or if, somehow, he'll fall victim to the captain's wild plot. Before I can think about it further, we reach the docked boat, seemingly void of any crew members.

Keelhan turns towards several of his men, nodding at them with a meaningful glance. Without another word, they move towards the ship in perfect synchronicity, climbing aboard with ease.

Seconds later, I hear their not-so-subtle clumping footsteps and things crashing as they search the upper decks.

Keelhan and I stand to the side, keeping watch and waiting impatiently for them to return with a report. One of the men barks out a surprised cry and the sound of scuffled footsteps soon follows. We look toward the commotion, Keelhan's hand hovering over the hilt of his blade as I instinctively reach for my shadows. Just as I recall the captain's words on using steel before shadows, all of a sudden, a blur of movement jumps over our heads and slams to the ground behind us.

We whirl around, the person already out of our reach. The rest of the men try to grab at the perpetrator but miss as they weave easily around the grabbing hands and sprint back the way we came. Whoever it is they're fast, and I find myself impressed at their lead while the Aslitír make after them as quickly as their feet allow, as I stare at Keelhan.

"What?" he demands.

"Quite the plan there, Keel, worked *wonderfully*," I say dryly.

"Would you just go after him?" he demands with a scowl.

"I thought you said no shadows, Captain," I smirk.

"Just do it, smartarse."

I tease him with a salute as I call upon my shadows. He rolls his eyes and breaks into a run as the darkness rears up, swirling around me until suddenly, I'm gone.

Following the sounds of barked orders, I land ahead of Keelhan's men and the escapist. But the runner catches sight of me and swerves out of my reach. Clutching at thin air, I mutter a curse under my breath and shadowfold again.

When I appear this time, the individual crashes into me and I punch them square in the face, disorienting them. I grab them by their collar. Only then do I notice their size.

A boy, no older than fourteen moons. Shame forms a tight lump in my throat.

"Let me go!" he shouts, blood streaming down his face.

Keelhan and his men reach me a minute later, and one of the soldiers takes the boy off my hands. I note his surprise as he takes in the boy.

"You sure this is the one?" I ask the Aslitír.

He glances at me, before gesturing to two of his fellow men to step forwards. They lift his sleeve with a yank, right to the elbow and they knock him in the head again as he tries to fight them. He reels from the second blow as they twist his arm. There, on the inside, is an inked mark of a tiny handprint.

"This is the one alright," the soldier announces to the group.

I stare at the boy, masking my surprise and disappointment. He's a child, and yet, somehow, he's still the enemy. His scrawny limbs and his eyes, too wide for his sunken face, tell me that this messenger job is the only thing keeping him from starving.

Even from here, behind the swirling fear and hatred in his eyes, and the dagger held loosely in his long fingers, I can tell that he's no threat at all. Even with the information he apparently possesses.

"Look at him, he's harmless," I laugh, gesturing to him.

He looks up at us both from where he's perched, two of Keelhan's men still flanking him. I can tell he's considering attempting an escape, but he knows as well as I do that there's no escaping now, especially not with me here.

"Harmless or not, what do we do with him?" Keelhan mutters, rubbing his fingers across his chin.

As the words leave his lips, the king's words from our meeting high in the tower ring in my head with a clarity that unnerves me. As if he can read my mind, Keelhan turns to me, his eyes sharp.

"Well I'm not killing him, that's for damn certain. He's an asset. He has information we could use to gain the upper hand," he reasons.

"The king isn't going to like it when we show up on his doorstep with the complete opposite of what he demanded we do," I reason, raising a brow.

"He's not going to tell us anything here. Perhaps we should take him back to the castle? Explain to the king that we had no choice," Keelhan answers.

The boy leans forward with purpose and a bright spark in his eyes. "You'll never stop us, we're everywhere and more join every day. In every tavern, inn, every nook and cranny."

"I do love a good game of chase the mouse," I answer, staring the boy down with a dark smile before turning back to Keelhan.

"I'd rather not face the king's temper any day soon," I counter, meeting the boy's furious gaze.

"We don't really have a choice. We're ill-equipped for this. I'll have my men remain here, take a few of them on the road with us back to the king."

"Fine," I sigh, furrowing my brow as I point a rough finger at Keelhan. "But you can tell him this was *your* idea."

The palace is surprisingly busy upon our late return. I notice the extra hands rushing about as I hand in my horse to the stables. The stablehands busy themselves with trimming the hedges and tidying up the gardens in a bid to make them presentable.

Two men follow behind Keelhan and me, dragging the prisoner after us as we enter the castle. Servants filter through the halls, skirting around me as I go, my stride purposeful as I manoeuvre through the corridors with Keelhan at my side. The boy's eyes are glossy with fear beneath the swelling and bruising across his face. He remains silent, his earlier bravado withering away the further we head into the palace.

I pass by the training room, I falter, noticing movement coming from within. I begin to slow, whilst staring toward the room. Keelhan slows, glancing at me with a furrowed brow. Curious, I peer around the door to where a couple of the chosen are sparring, the blonde one I immediately recognise as one of the girls who followed Nesryn to my doorway.

Keelhan clears his throat, his impatience evident as he watches me. "We haven't time for you to be gawking at females," he comments dryly.

I scowl, unhappy at being scolded away from watching the young women train, and returning to his side as he heads towards the king's quarters.

Barilius inspects us, leaning with his back on one arm of the chair, and his legs sprawled out across the opposite side as he rubs a hand across his mouth. The two soldiers shift nervously from foot to foot. The boy is frozen in fear. Only Keelhan and I are somewhat unfazed. We're in one of his many living spaces, furnished with dark wood and deep maroons and greens. I glance at the tapestries along the wall, all bloodied scenes of the Elven War, before flitting my eyes back to the king. His lips curl in displeasure and I sigh inwardly. Whatever happens now won't be pleasant.

"Why have you brought this traitor to me?" he asks finally, his eyes fixing on Keelhan.

"We understand that he is a messenger for the rebel group, Sire. He is a valuable asset if we wish to eradicate the problem," Keelhan explains.

King Barilius straightens in his chair, eying up the pair of soldiers and Keelhan, his eyes lingering on the captain as he waves his hand at them.

"Leave us," he orders.

After a moment of hesitation, Keelhan bows, the Aslitír following suit as they turn to leave. I move to follow when Barilius's eyes shift to me and he shakes his head once. I pause, looking after the others as they let go of the tethered boy and leave. He drops to his knees and I note his trembling hands as he cowers on the ground, his head bent low.

As soon as the door clicks shut behind them, Barilius's eyes lock onto mine, his brow knitting as he briefly takes in the boy and returns his gaze to me.

"Kill him."

I glance at the boy, his eyes glossy with fear as he dares to look up at me.

"Your Highness, he's just a child," I protest.

"A child who has made his ranks with the enemy," King Barilius snaps.

"Do we not need the information he holds?" I reason.

"I need nothing from the little shit, or his band of delusional extremists," he spits.

He gets to his feet and stares me down. Out of the corner of my eye, I see the boy flinch.

"When will you learn, Lysander, that the enemy can look like anyone? A man, a woman, even a foolish child," he sneers at the boy, who shrinks away from him.

"The members of this Righteous Hand group are no different. They are all equally guilty of treason and they need to be struck down. Even if that means that his blood is spilt," he continues, gesturing to the boy.

I want to say something but I know I can't. I swallow my frustration and a feeling of utter helplessness tugs at me. I bury it deep.

"He is of no use to me alive. Kill him."

I stiffen at the finality of his words. I shouldn't be surprised at the king's cruelty after all these years, yet it cuts through me. My gaze shifts to him, my lips set in a thin line as we lock eyes. When I don't move, he closes the gap, squaring up to me with eyes so cold they could be the eyes of Death himself.

"You dare defy me, boy?" he demands.

"He's a *child*," I argue through gritted teeth.

"Mercy is for the weak, soft-hearted *fools*," he spits.

All of a sudden, my head jerks back with a sudden force and I stagger back a few paces. My hand reaches for my throbbing jaw as I stare at Barilius in surprise. He drops his hand, his gaze unwavering.

"You will do as I command, boy. Or do you forget yourself?" he demands.

"Yes, Your Majesty." I say finally, swallowing my anger.

I right myself and step forward, inhaling a shaky breath.

I lift my hands, releasing the shadows from within. They writhe and twist through the air, hovering in wait for my next command. I baulk at the order, glancing wearily at the boy before me, who scrambles back in fear, watching me with terrified tears streaming down his filthy face.

"Kill the brat. Do it now!" the king bellows, his voice ringing loud in my ear.

My chest squeezes as I lift my hand to strike. I force myself to look into his eyes as I swing my hand down. My shadows move with sickening speed, meeting their target in seconds and splattering blood across the room.

NESRYN

CHAPTER FIFTEEN

I wake up to the sound of screaming.

My heart jolts in my chest and I scan the darkened room frantically. I hold my breath as I listen but the screaming has stopped. I let my breath loose and for a moment, I wonder if it had just been a figment of my imagination or even the remnants of a bad dream.

Something within me whispers it was more than that and I find myself slipping from the safety of my sheets and padding over to the door. As I cross the room, I realise that I'd fallen asleep in my training leathers and I find that I'm grateful for it. With a swift click, I unlock it and peer out into the corridor.

The hall is eerie and shrouded in shadow at this late hour. Each Chosen's room is closed, the girls behind each door still deep in slumber and undisturbed by whatever it is that I think I heard. I scrutinise the space and before curiosity gets the better of me, I quickly dip back inside my room to grab Stormtip, shoving the sheathed blade into the loop of my trousers as I leave the room again, pulling the door closed with a gentle click.

The shadows dissipate as the scattered orbs of elvynlight illuminate the panels of the walls and bathe the whole space in a soft blue hue. I keep close to the wall, my palms prickling with nervous sweat as I scope the empty space. I strain to listen as I turn the corner, nothing but silence filling the halls. I'm surprised to find that there are no Aslitír on patrol like the king said they would be.

'Where could they have all gone?'

As I turn to creep down yet another length of hallway, I hear muted footsteps. The hairs along my spine rise up and I press against the wall, inching towards the corner. I'm grateful for the six-foot sculpture hiding me from view as I peer through the bent arm of the stone soldier posed in mid-battle.

I step back, flush against the wall as a tall figure walks slowly into view. He stops several doors down from where I'm standing, and as he hovers by the door, I realise it's Lysan. I'm about to brush off my curiosity and make my way back to bed when something in me tells me to stay. Unease fills me as I watch him from a distance. Something about his demeanour is off. His saunter is gone and the playful smirk is non-existent. I expect him to take hold of the doorknob and leave me alone in the corridor, but he hesitates, his shoulders slumped in defeat. His mannerisms are so far from what I'm used to that it surprises me.

'He thinks he's alone.' I realise.

This picture is far from the upstanding image of King Barilius's Second, and his top Shadowcaster. His shaggy hair is dishevelled and dripping a thick liquid onto the floor. The sound is barely audible but in the silence, it lands with a thud as it hits the marble floor. As I look closer, I realise his hands are dripping as well, slick with something dark and wet that stains his skin.

His head lifts and he looks toward my hiding spot as if he sees me through the darkness, and for several moments I forget how to breathe. In the dim light, I see how his eyes are hollow, muted and dull, how his lips slope down into a frown. His chin beneath the spatter is bruised and beginning to swell and the front of his clothes are splattered with the same dripping liquid. My stomach drops.

Blood.

My body turns ice cold, the horror of what I'm seeing undoubtedly written all over my face. He changes before my eyes. Before, he was a high-ranking member of the court, weighed down by his troubles. But now, as he stands alone in the darkness, I see him for what he is. A feral beast after a successful kill.

I will my feet to move, but they refuse. Once again, the foreign sensation of power fills my gut with fearsome strength. I feel it rise up in anger at the sight of him. Despite its call to be freed, I fight against the primal urge and push it back down into the dark and it's forgotten once more.

'Whose blood have you spilt?' my mind screams at him.

"Who's there?" he calls, his voice gruff.

The sound kick starts my body into drive and before I know it, I'm running back along the hall, my feet carrying me swiftly and silently back to my room. I lock the door behind me, knowing it will serve little protection against his power. For some ridiculous reason, hearing the final click of the lock makes me feel better. Though it doesn't stop me from erratic breaths as I try to calm my breathing, to no avail.

I lean my back against the door as I slip silently to the floor. I stay this way until morn.

The rattling handle jolts me out of my daze and sends my heart racing as I scramble away from the door. My eyes are wide with fear and my breathing is uneven and shaky as I stare at the door.

"Lady Havenore, are you in there? Is everything alright?" the voice filters through.

I leap to my feet as I recognise Hesta's voice. I wince at the stiffness in my joints as I unlock the door and pull it open, tentatively peering around the door. There in the hall stands Hesta, Sarleigh and Perin, watching me with concern.

"Oh Nesryn, sweetheart, you look awful," Hesta gasps.

"Did you sleep poorly?" Perin asks beside her, her eyes scanning my face.

"Yes. Well, something like that," I mutter, my mind taking me back to Lysan's blood-spattered form.

I step back as they bustle into the room and Hesta disappears through the bathroom doors. Perin and Sarleigh turn to face me with determined eyes.

"We can't have you looking all pasty tonight. Perhaps a tonic to bring back some of your colour?" Perin suggests with a shy smile.

"A bath will help, but I'll go and have someone fetch one from the market," Sarleigh offers.

I nod, my exhaustion evident.

"We'll need to get you out of these," she notes, wrinkling her nose as she looks down at my leathers.

"They're comfortable," I reason.

"They look as though they need a good scrubbing," she retorts.

"Let's get you out of these and into a nice warm bath, I'm sure it'll make you feel ten times better," Perin steps in.

I nod as she presses a hand against my lower back and guides me towards the bathroom, leaving Sarleigh to busy herself with beauty tonics. Hesta straightens as we enter, holding her hand in front of her as she waits for me to undress. Steam and moisture swirl through the air, the warmth of the space relaxing me as I inhale the sweet scent of honeysuckle soap.

I lay back as they wash my hair and scrub away the dull ache from my bones. When I finally step out of the bathroom, I feel much less exhausted and a little more like myself. When I check the mirror, I can still see the deep bags under my eyes but Perin assures me that the tonic will help clear those in no time.

I sit patiently as she styles my curls into an intricate braid of multiple plaits drawn up into a master braid with curves across the middle of my head and stretched down my spine. I admire her work and thank her before slipping behind the screen to get changed into a fresh vaita.

Sarleigh returns with a tray of colourful glass bottles with pretty droplet-shaped lids by the time that I'm dressed. She sits me down and goes to work, picking up bottles and dabbing their contents onto my skin with concise but gentle fingers. When she finally steps back and encourages me to look at myself in the mirror, I'm stunned at the drastic change. My skin no longer looks ashen and puffy, instead, my colour has returned and the slight pink hue of my cheeks matches the colour of my lips. My eyes don't sting when I blink, the redness in them gone. I look fresh and vibrant just like the day I arrived.

"It looks wonderful, thank you," I tell her, placing a hand on hers as I smile.

"We'll apply them again tonight for the ball, perhaps, before we accentuate your beauty with some cosmetic powders."

"Perfect," I answer.

"Your dress should be arriving later this afternoon, the tailor's delivery girls will deliver it to your room for you," Hesta informs me.

"Then I shall return later to receive it," I reply, getting to my feet.

"Very well, Nesryn," she dips her head.

The three of them leave promptly after, leaving me alone once more. I watch myself in the mirror, contemplating joining the others in the dining hall. Something snags in my stomach at the thought.

'*Food can wait. There's something I need to do first.*'

I move down the hall, glancing towards each of the doors as I try to recall which one is Erryn's. It takes me several attempts but on the fourth door, I knock and enter into a darkened room with drawn curtains and the softest glow of elvynlight.

A figure lays on the bed and my heart lurches as I see the state that Erryn is in.

'*I got lucky,*' I realise as I look at the fragile girl laid on the sheets.

I step further into the room, my eyes trained on the slow rise and fall of her chest. In the dim light, I see the severity of her injuries and my jaw slackens in shock. She's dressed in nothing but her undergarments, though with her skin charred and swollen, she couldn't possibly wear anything more. There is a rawness that covers most of her olive skin and my eyes sting with tears for her. The blistering red patch snakes up her leg, across her stomach, up over her collarbone, and covers half of her face. The wound is crusted and extremely sore, though it has a dull shine to it. The kind that comes from a thick coating of ointment slathered on top of the burns.

Her face is what makes my mouth turn dry. Her eyelids are closed over her almond-shaped eyes. I feel a wrenching in my gut as I see that the left side is sealed shut to protect the more severe burns. Her lips are bent and twisted, the skin pulled down by her scarring. As I look her over, fearing worse, I realise that half of her hair has been singed off. Large clumps have broken off on her pillow, while the side that's still intact fans out in lengths of dead straight ebony.

'*She'll be permanently disfigured,*' a tiny voice tells me.

Guilt tugs at me as I stare at my fellow Chosen. I walk around the bed and seat myself in the small armchair beside it. I notice the bottles of pills and ointments on her bedside table and I wonder morbidly how often they're applied, how regularly her wounds must be cleaned and aired.

I realise that I haven't seen her handmaidens and as I glance around the dark, silent room, my heart breaks for her just that little bit more. No family or friends to crowd her bedside, no visitors to stay by her side to remind her she isn't by herself. She's alone.

"This is all my fault," I whisper, my voice breaking.

Tears begin to spill over my cheeks as I reach for her good hand, wrapping my fingers around it and squeezing gently.

"Oh Erryn, I'm so sorry," I say softly through the sobs.

After my visit to Erryn, I shuffle back down the corridors towards my room, thoughtful and quiet. I think of my uncle, of my home, and wonder what he would be doing right now. I wonder if he spars with Jarek now that I'm gone, or if he's ended his employment for that very same reason.

I miss Ragna and Ceryl and I miss my room, but most of all I miss knowing my role and where I stood.

Here, I'm just a number. A colour symbolising the Havenore family crest. Here, I only matter if I claim the title of Chosen. If I beat the others through the trials. Others that I've come to know and call my friends. I don't know whether I'm capable of pushing that all to one side just to win a prize of honour.

I think of Erryn and the life she now faces, branded with the failure of losing The Choosing, both on the outside and in. I pray that Vilkha will follow through on my request and send correspondence to her family soon.

I breathe out a long, defeated sigh as I continue on my way. My jumbled thoughts stick in my head with seemingly no way of untangling them. I think of the SunMoon ball that the king is hosting tonight, and I contemplate how the next trial will fit into these festivities.

The idea of meeting the king properly sends a nervous jolt rushing through me and I consider what it would be like, should I win as I had hoped to all that time ago. It feels as though an age has passed since then. I feel the weight of The Choosing, the decisions I would have to make, and now, the worry about what I would be giving up to win. I can't talk to the others when they're going through the same thing as me. If only Uncle Erathon were here, maybe then I'd have someone to talk to about it all.

"Nes!" a voice calls down the corridor.

I stop, pulled from my thoughts and turn to see Reverie rushing towards me. I wait for her to catch up, studying her face as she stops beside me.

"We missed you at lunch," she says, peering at me. "Is everything alright?" she asks, tilting her head to the side.

"I... I went to see Erryn," I mumble.

Ria straightens, her brows knitting together in concern as she purses her lips. I watch as she takes in what I've said, tucking her golden hair behind her ear and taking my hand.

"Come, you look troubled," she says, leading me towards the doors of her room. "You can tell me what's on your mind," she adds.

I smile gratefully at her and let her lead me through her doors, wondering if she knew how badly I needed to hear that.

It's much later when I finally make it back to my own room, feeling a hundred times lighter than before.

I step into the room and all the air leaves my lungs. My eyes widen at the gown across the room. I drink in the rich emerald fabric that fans out like rippling water, layer after layer. The sequined bodice shimmers in the light, beautifully crafted to cover my torso, whilst also showing a sliver of cleavage. I surmise that the upper section of my chest will be bare, the straps, fanning wide across to loop over the curve of my shoulders.

"Beautiful, isn't it?"

I yell, spinning on the spot and clutching my hand to my chest in a fist.

"Perin, you startled me!" I breathe, smiling weakly.

"My apologies, I came to get started," she replies.

"Are Hesta and Sarleigh not coming?" I ask, peering behind her at the door.

"Hesta has gone to collect your corset and shoes from the seamstress. Sarleigh is on her way with the powders for your face," she explains.

I nod, complying as she gestures for me to sit at the vanity. Perin quickly gets to work unbraiding my hair and letting the dark coils fall freely over my shoulders and down my back. She then slides two pear-shaped emerald droplets into my earlobes and steps back.

As she finishes, Hesta and Sarleigh arrive to rub various creams and powders on my forehead and cheeks before working on my eyes. I watch as she pulls out a small brush and a golden powder that glitters in the light.

"You must stay very still," Sarleigh warns as she opens the tiny pot with a careful hand.

I hold as still as I'm able to as the brush wanders across my lids with soft, even strokes until Sarleigh steps back and tells me to open my eyes. I'm met with her satisfied smile before Hesta cuts in and pulls me toward the screen, the half corset hanging from her other hand as she asks me to strip off.

I wince as she pulls in the ribbon, the fabric tightening around my waist as it cinches in. Finally, she ties it off and tucks the loose ribbon into the corset before giving me a wry look.

"You'll have to lose that," she says, her eyes dropping to the brassiere.

I let out a resigned sigh as I unclasp the back and cover my breasts with one arm whilst draping it over the top of the screen. Without a word, she disappears, returning with Perin and the dress. They help me climb into it before Perin fastens up the tiny green buttons along the back.

She walks around me holding a circlet of pale gold crafted into a multitude of linked antlers, embellished with a beautiful oval cut emerald in the centre of the headpiece. I lower my head as she places it atop my curls, securing it around my forehead.

"Take a look," she says with a proud smile.

I pick up my skirts and walk tentatively towards the mirror. Sarleigh gasps as her eyes fall on me and she too smiles widely.

The skirts swish around me as I stop in front of the mirror, my lips parting in surprise as I look at the stranger standing there. Her eyes are framed with gold dust making her green eyes pop. She looks like an empress, clad in rich green. Her skirts spread out around her in an impressive circle, and the corded straps curling across her smooth shoulders look like wild, living vines.

The golden circlet of stag antlers and emerald sparkles like a crown and I find myself speechless.

"A true belle of the ball, miss," Hesta says softly from behind me.

"Thank you, it all looks amazing," I say as I turn back to them all.

A knock at the door draws my attention to the two young women peeking through the door.

"Are you ready y—" Mas starts, her eyes widening as she takes me in.

"—Sweet goddess, look at you!" Ria cuts in, stepping into the room.

I take in her midnight blue gown, hugging her impressive figure and glistening with white jewels across the bottom and the long sleeves. Mas's gown is a floaty burnt orange shade, like the colour of the sunset in Sunwake, her skirts embedded with glittering rubies.

"You both look incredible," I breathe, staring at them both.

"We all do," Mas corrects me as they link arms with me and accompany me from the room.

Perin steps forward, handing me my mask and dips back to stand by Sarleigh.

"You girls have fun now… and good luck," Hesta calls after us.

Ria and Mas drive me towards the two Aslitír standing watch at the archway leading into the gardens. We hand the two guards our masks and they take them and bow their heads in unison as they give way for us to enter.

Full of excitement, we step into the gardens and I look around in awe.

The palace grounds are lit up and bustling with well dressed Aslitírs and The Chosen adorned in all their finery. There is the buzz of conversation and a sweet melody floating from the temporary stage where the band of musicians play. The moon is full and bright above, and bigger than I've ever seen it, with a yellow hue to its usual pearlescent white. The air is surprisingly warm, with a soft breeze that filters through the trees above. Lanterns are lit and hung about the branches above, giving out a warm light, and I find myself surprised at the common use of elvynlight here.

The hedges and grass have recently been trimmed, combining with the fresh smell of the nebiulas.

"I think I see Vena—and some of the others," Ria's eyes dart to us and she looks almost guilty as she pulls away. Her hair brushes my face as she unlinks her arm from mine and strides off.

"Is it just me, or did she add that last part on a little too quickly?" Mas asks, her amber earrings dangling to and fro from her small ears.

I follow Ria through the crowd before I smile and shrug.

"What's the deal with them anyway?" she mutters as we continue through the staring crowds.

"I think they were friends, or from the same town at least," I murmur back, recalling the carriage trip.

"Sounds... complicated," Mas says, her voice leaking the pity that we both feel seeing the way that Ria stares after Vena.

"I think it's best that we leave it up to them," I reply with a half-shrug.

We reach Ria and Vena soon enough and as I take in Vena, my breath hitches in awe.

Her dress is a glittering black that hugs her womanly figure. I can hardly tell where fabric becomes skin and I must admit that it's quite the illusion to behold. Her cheeks are dusted with a soft shimmer that catches in the light, making her look iridescent, adding to her beauty.

"You look beautiful, Vena," I admit, putting aside my differences to make an effort.

"Yes, I know," she answers, the chivalry lost on her.

Ria jabs her in the side and gives her a look. Vena rolls her eyes and stops to take me in properly, with a grimace that looks more disgruntled than cruel.

"Your dress is rather pretty too, I suppose," she offers. I don't miss the proud smile Ria offers her after this comment.

"Do we know when we'll be given our fourth envelope? Or even what the next trial could be?" Mas cuts in, and I sigh inwardly, grateful for the distraction.

"No, but I suspect it will be soon," Vena comments, her hardened gaze on my friend.

As we converse, three Aslitír draw near, egging one another on. Our attention shifts to them as the tallest of them steps towards Ria.

"May you do me the honour of joining me for a dance?" he asks, sweeping into a low bow and extending his hand.

I watch as Ria suppresses a smile and places her hand lightly in his.

The other two men step forward, extending their hands to Vena and Mas, while Ria is escorted across the gardens. Vena glances at the young man offering her his hand and walks away without a word, while Mas, bashful, takes the other's hand.

"I'll dance with you," I offer the crestfallen young man.

His smile returns as I take his hand and he leads me in the direction of the music.

As I stare across the dancefloor, I notice Lysan beneath the shade of the tree. He's dressed in a black suit and black shirt like a walking shadow. He's leaning in, speaking to a man of similar age with straight blond hair that skirts his shoulders. The blond one is dressed in the king's colours: black, gold and maroon. The brass buttons reflect the light of the lanterns above and I realise that they suit him well.

I watch them curiously as they talk quietly amongst themselves, hunched inward in a bid to keep their conversation private. Even from here, I can see their brows are furrowed in concentration and their lips move too fast for me to even attempt to guess at what they might be speaking about. The way their mouths move furiously and without pause makes me think that it must be something very important.

I inwardly scold myself for allowing my curiosity to get the better of me and turn away, picking up my skirts and walking towards a table full of beverages. The server stands to attention as I reach the table, his eyes lingering on my cleavage. I clear my throat and he starts, his eyes flicking to my face as his cheeks turn red and he offers me what's on the table.

I notice the bottles of red lined up and smile fondly at them as thoughts of my uncle surface in my mind.

"I'll take a glass of that please," I say, pointing to the closest bottle.

He nods and pours me a glass and hands it carefully to me, avoiding my gaze. His cheeks are still red. I turn around, scanning the dancefloor for the young man I left. When I don't see him in the crows, I look past the swirling figures and stop short when I meet Lysan's eye. He stares at me across the space, his expression solemn. I quickly realise that his blond friend is no longer beside him and my curiosity is tugged once more as I wonder what words they shared. I try not to shudder as the image of him soaked in blood resurfaces in my mind. As I turn to walk away I bump into someone and stumble, the glass in my hand tipping.

"Whoa steady there," a male voice warns.

The person rights me, the glass in my hand steadying as I peer up into bright blue eyes and a familiar face. The man who had been talking with Lysan across the gardens. I suddenly find myself void of words.

He runs a hand through his hair as he gives me a wide smile.

"Does the lady speak?" he asks playfully.

I snap out of my silence, heat prickling up my neck. I shift uncomfortably on the spot for a few moments before lifting my chin, levelling his gaze.

"My name is Nesryn, of the House of Havenore, my lord," I answer.

Recognition flashes in his eyes as he takes my free hand and pulls it to his lips.

"A baroness, how delightful. But I assure you, milady, I'm no lord," he says with a wink and a dazzling smile. "Please allow me to introduce myself. Keelhan Zander Collmore, Captain of the Aslitír," he announces with a dip of his head.

"A pleasure, Captain," I reply, dipping my own in response.

"The pleasure is all mine, Lady Havenore," he pauses, his eyes travelling the length of me before returning to my face with a widening smile. "You look beautiful tonight."

"Thank you," I reply, glancing down at my gown before taking a sip of my wine.

He then reaches into his jacket pocket and retrieves something white. I realise as he hands it to me that it's the envelope for the next trial. I look up at him in surprise.

"I believe this is for you then," he says finally, holding it out to me.

I half-turn, placing my glass on the table behind me, and take the envelope from him, quickly turning it over and breaking the seal on the back with one swift movement. I draw the paper out with anticipation, unfolding it and reading through the next trial in the form of yet another riddle.

> Upon the mark, the shadows tell,
> Here protection must be bought.
> Until the toll of midnight's bell,
> Sure and fleeting now be caught.

I read it again, my brows knitting together in confusion as I try to make sense of the rhyme in my hands.

"Is everything alright?" Keelhan asks.

"I'm not exactly sure," I answer, pulling my attention from the paper in my hands.

"Anything I can help with?" he offers, stepping closer.

I'm suddenly aware of how close our bodies are and I give him a small smile whilst shaking my head and folding the letter back inside the folds of the envelope. I grab my wine and take a large gulp.

"No, thank you, Captain," I say after swallowing.

"Then for now, you wouldn't mind honouring me with a dance, perhaps?" he holds out his hand.

I consider the trial and how little I understand of it and wonder how many of the others have read it. Out of the corner of my eye, I notice Chandra dancing with one of Keelhan's men, and around her Zariya and Lesya with two more Aslitír, swirling about the dancefloor.

Mas and Ria are nowhere to be seen. My eyes flit back to Keelhan and I try to ignore the part of me that screams to start deciphering the riddle. I tell myself that I have time as I take his hand.

"I suppose one dance won't hurt," I reply.

He smiles and leads me onto the dancefloor under the light of the moon. He holds me close to him as he steps in time to the music. I follow his steps to the rhythm as best as I can, my skirts swishing around me with our movements. I'm beginning to relax and enjoy myself when someone taps on Keelhan's shoulder and stops us mid-step.

"Mind if I cut in Keel?" Lysan says, sending a wink in my direction.

Before I even have time to scowl at him, he's whisked me away from Keelhan, leaving him watching after us with a surprised look plastered on his face. Lysan spins me away from the centre of the dancefloor, moving us around the edges as he steps in time to the melody.

"You look delicious tonight," he comments with another wink.

I choose to ignore him, though I feel the heat pooling in my cheeks. In such close proximity, he smells like the air and earth after rainfall, and it's enough to make me try and pull away from him.

"I hear you had quite the experience during your last trial. Tell me, was it intentional or are you really that foolish?" His cocky smile causes my blood to boil as he steps closer to me.

"Shut your mouth," I snap.

"Or what, you'll hurtle me across the room? Set me ablaze?" he suggests, raising a brow.

I scowl and try to leave but he holds my hands tightly in his, spinning us around the grassy dancefloor, and I notice how his shadows move with us. The surge of something foreign yet familiar rises to meet my anger.

"You should try to be more careful, destroying the competition is a fast way to gain enemies, unless you're into that lone wolf aesthetic like the Astalón girl," he tells me, his eyes moving across the gardens to where Vena stands alone.

"Vena's methods are unorthodox but they work," I point out.

"So you agree with them?" The amusement in his tone doesn't go unnoticed.

"I didn't say that," I glare at him. "Just because they work, doesn't mean I agree with them," I continue.

"That just makes you a hypocrite," he says plainly.

I look up at him, his seafoam eyes swirling with deep amusement, his raven hair falling across his forehead as he tilts his head. My eyes flit to the tendrils of darkness that swirl around us shrouding us in shadow as we waltz across the dancefloor and I shudder as I look away. I feel the concerned or fearful eyes of the other Chosen as we move past them hand in hand. I can sense their fear, recognising it as the very same emotion swirling around my stomach.

"At least I'm not a monster," I mutter.

"My shadows are hardly what I'd call monstrous," he scoffs, his eyes scanning over my head at the rest of the crowd.

"I wasn't talking about them," I murmur.

His body stills as he snaps to attention, his eyes on me. His expression is unreadable but I detect his anger in the ink trails moving around us.

"And what exactly would you know about monsters, Nesryn?" he asks, his words clipped.

I pull free of him, taking a step back as I watch him evenly, my chin raised. My anger ignites the dormant beast within but I refuse to give in to it. He says nothing and we stand this way for several moments as I quell the pull within me.

"I saw you last night, covered in blood," I admit. "Evidently, it wasn't your own," I surmise, looking him up and down.

A shadow falls over his eyes as he stares at me, his lips set in a thin line. "That was you."

A statement, not a question.

"Careful of what you choose to say next, Havenore," he warns.

"Or what, you'll slaughter me too?" I challenge.

CHAPTER SIXTEEN

Nesryn's eyes are icy and hostile, fuelling my growing irritation. I step back further, curling my hands into fists as I fight to contain my power and maintain a calm composure. The flicker of fear in her eyes as they flit to my hands then back to my face only increases my rage and I scowl.

"What I do, and how my powers are used, is no concern of yours. I answer to the king and the king alone," I snap.

"Yes, the king's dog, what a *fitting* title," she answers in a bitter tone.

"You will do well to remember who you're speaking to, I am still the king's Second," I warn her.

"So he sees it fit to have you kill without mercy?" she demands, the disgust in her eyes bright and fierce.

"Mercy is for the weak," I answer, repeating his words.

"I hardly believe that the king would stand for your methods," she pushes back.

"You have no idea what the king is like," I remark, laughing bitterly.

"I know enough. You thirst for blood, you're a murderer. People are right to be afraid of you," she says cooly, her eyes begging me to challenge her.

I cock my head to one side, the amusement easy to cover the simmering anger beneath. "Are you afraid of me, Nesryn?"

The question seems to take her back and she falters in her stride, suddenly void of words. I keep her under the protection of my shadows, aware of the next trial already in motion.

'*She needs to make it through this trial,*' I remind myself despite my faltering cool.

"I'm not afraid of the likes of you, *Shadowcaster*," she spits, venom in her words.

I feel myself glower at her and I watch as she visibly shrinks back, her frame looking even smaller in her sea of emerald skirts. Her fear only ignites my anger further.

"And yet you cower from me like a terrified *child*," I bite back.

As soon as the words leave my lips, the image of the boy floods my mind, the terrified look in his eyes, his trembling body and thundering heart falling forever silent. With that comes a wave of sickness. She stands straighter in defiance and annoyingly, I find myself impressed.

"You're a villain, a blight. I saw what you're capable of, you have no compassion, you haven't a heart," she spits.

"It's people like you who have made me into the monster you claim me to be," I say evenly.

Her visible disgust and fear fill me with a deep hatred that I cannot fathom, and without another word, I storm away from her.

Somewhere in the background, I hear Keelhan call out after me. I dismiss him without a second thought as I push past the guards, away from the festivities.

My shadows follow, writhing angrily behind me.

The stroke of twelve chimes rings through the palace as I move through the halls with wide strides, my hands curling tightly into whitened fists as I replay our interaction over and over in my head. I don't know where I'm headed as I walk, all I know is that I need a release and I need one soon.

I make it to the training room just in time to unleash my fury, hurling shadows at the mannequins lined up in a row, their fabric bodies crumpling to the floor in sliced up piles. I send my darkness outwards in a destructive path that not a single person is safe from.

Her words ring in my head as my hatred intensifies and the next shadows that come from me pour out of me like a tidal wave. I watch on as they destroy everything in their path. Years of gear, weapons and equipment crumble into piles of rubble and dust in my wake.

Blackened scorch marks stain the walls and the ceiling, the smell of the room now one of putrid darkness. I scour the room for another target but find none.

I release a ragged breath, as sweat beads at my temple. I can still feel the anger rolling off me in waves as the urge to destroy more of the room fills me. Darkness pours from my hands in tendrils, pooling at my feet and feeding on my fury.

'*You're a villain, a blight,*' the words ring in my head.

The boy's face returns, his lifeless eyes crying crimson tears. I try to brush it away, to force it to disappear, but there it remains until I release another wave of darkness and destruction, causing the very walls of the palace to shudder in my wake.

A throat clears from behind me and I draw my shadows back, whirling around with my arms raised, ready to strike. Melek flinches slightly but stands his ground. After several long moments, I drop my arms, the darkness dissipating around me.

"What do you want, *messenger*?" I snarl.

"The king demands your presence. A matter of *urgency*," he says, drawing out the last word.

I take a long, deep breath in and exhale through my nose with a huff as I stride towards him. Melek looks past me, his glossy eyes moving around the room behind me.

"I'll send word for the servants to clean it up in the morning."

"No," I growl, "Let them see what a monster is *truly* capable of," I sneer, before pushing past him in the direction of the tower.

CHAPTER SEVENTEEN

I stare after Lysan as he storms off, his rage palpable. Suddenly feeling exposed in the moonlight as the shadows follow their master, I step back under the shelter of the trees above. People stare in both directions and I dip my gaze, unable to bear their eyes on me. My heart pounds from the adrenaline coursing through me and the icy rage that I feel. The foreign entity inside me tries to force its way out. It's almost as though Lysan's presence rouses whatever is it from its slumber.

My breaths are short and shaky when I finally look back up, noticing Ria and Mas weaving through the crowd around the dancefloor towards me. Most dancers have left the space—Lesya and her partner, the only ones still swaying together in the centre beneath the moonlight. I watch them shift and turn to the music. Then, as the clock strikes twelve chimes, he unfurls her in a spin, the glow of moonlight iridescent on her gleeful face until suddenly, out of nowhere, a scream rips through the night and I realise it's coming from Lesya.

I watch on in frozen horror as her dance partner pulls away as she falls to the floor in anguish, the light of the SunMoon pouring over her. No one dares to step forwards, too fearful of what may become of them, but like me, I see the desperate need to reach her and help mirrored in their expressions. It's only as the last chime echoes into silence that the moon rays disappear into the darkness and release Lesya from their grip.

Her body slumps fully to the floor, her brown hair fanned out around her trembling form. I snap out of my frozen state and rush to her side beside the others. Seeing that no one else will, I turn her over. Some recoil as they note the unnatural purple hue of her once brown eyes, her lips moving slowly, though no sound comes out.

"Lesya," I call to her, holding her face in my hands.

She doesn't respond, completely unaware of everything around her. I glance in concern at the others fanned around me, the Aslitír stepping back to give us room. I recognise Keelhan among them, his face set in a grim expression, but he doesn't step forward. Anger blooms in my chest.

"Captain," I snap, drawing his attention.

"Y-yes," he replies, startled.

"Some *help*."

"I—yes of course," he stumbles, pushing past his men towards us.

He reaches down and gently lifts Lesya into his arms, determination set across his face as he strides towards the palace.

Murmurs begin to erupt around us as I scramble to my feet.

"The riddle, do you think that it meant…" Ovie trails off, unable to finish her question.

I glance over at her, then at the others, suddenly noting Chandra's absence as my eyes move through The Chosen. "I don't know, but she's one of us. We need to make sure she'll be ok," I say, looking at the others, daring them to challenge me.

"Go with her. We'll find a healer and meet you in her room," Vena speaks up, directing her words at me as she reaches for the two girls nearest to her, Zariya and Twyla.

I nod once and grab my skirts, kicking off my heeled shoes and rushing after Keelhan. Ovie, Ria and Mas follow closely behind.

I keep to the side of Keelhan, glancing anxiously at Lesya every so often. We reach her room and I push the door open, letting him carry her inside.

Her handmaidens are there and gasp in horror as their mistress is gently placed on the bed.

"A healer should be here soon," Ria tells them, as she pats one on the hand.

"I'll wait outside the door," Keelhan says as he nods to me, stepping back towards the door.

"What happened, did anyone see?" Ovie asks, glancing around at us as he leaves.

Mas slips a hand into a hidden pocket in the folds of her dress and pulls out the envelope, looking at us warily as she reads the letter aloud.

"Upon the mark, the shadows tell, here protection must be bought. Until the toll of midnight's bell, sure and fleeting now be caught." She repeats the words carefully, trying to find the meaning behind them. "Could it be that it was a part of the trial?" she asks.

"Possibly... I mean, it happened on the last chime of midnight," I say slowly.

"That can't be a coincidence," Ria murmurs.

"I don't like this, first Erryn and now Lesya. This isn't what I thought The Choosing would be," Ovie says.

"We'll wait for Vena and the others to return with the healer, and then we'll figure out what comes next," I step in, unwittingly recalling Lysan's warnings about the king.

I glance towards Lesya as Mas steps forward and reaches for her hand, running her thumb back and forth as she leans in and gently moves a strand of Lesya's hair out of her face. Her eyes swirl with a violet hue, her lips moving incoherently. I try to listen but no sound seems to emanate from her. My eyes move to the door as I quietly plead the others to hurry.

When the door finally opens I jump up from where I'm sitting. Across the room, Ovie stops her pacing and looks to the door, hopeful. The healer strides in with Vena and the others in tow. Keelhan glances in before pulling the door and shutting us all in without him.

"I came as quickly as I could," she says as she steps closer.

She stops short when she notes Lesya's form on the bed, her face falling as her eyes travel the length of the girl's body.

"Well, don't just stand there, help her," Vena snaps from behind her.

"I can't," the healer says, her face crestfallen as she steps closer, studying Lesya's face.

"How long has it been since she was affected?" she asks, her back to us.

I glance at the clock. "Just over an hour ago."

The healer heaves a shaky sigh and straightens, her expression grim. "Then I can't do anything for her."

"What do you mean?" Ovie demands, stepping closer.

"She's suffering from Lunar Fever," the healer explains, looking to all of us.

"But what—" Ovie starts.

"—It's a rare, but terrible sickness. And if not treated within the first half chime of the affliction, then the damage is permanent," she explains.

"What do you mean when you say *damage*?" Vena cuts in, eyeing the healer with a suspicious stare.

"The first stage is paralysis. When she regains movement, the hallucinations will start. Then her memories will fade and she will quickly lose her lucidity completely," she says, her tone grave.

"So... she's slowly going to go mad?" Vena says, her tone hard.

I bring a hand to my mouth in shock, my tear-filled eyes dropping to Lesya, still immobile on the bed.

"Oh Goddess," I choke.

"All I can do is try to keep her comfortable, but her family will need to be notified," she continues.

"Y-yes of course," Ria murmurs, her eyes wide and staring at nothing.

In the corner, I hear one of Lesya's handmaidens begin to sob openly. The rest of us stand around the room shocked into silence. No one wants to speak, but I force myself to look to the healer.

"Please do what you can. We will leave you to do your work, but please call on us if you need anything," I say, looking pointedly at the others.

As they begin to filter out of the room, I step closer to the healer, reaching up and removing my earrings one by one. My heart constricts as I look to Lesya one last time, handing the earrings to the healer.

"Your payment. Please do what you can for her," I say softly.

The healer's brow furrows as she takes the emerald droplets and nods curtly. I thank her again and join the others out in the corridor.

Keelhan searches my face as I pull the door shut behind me, while the others stand around waiting for someone to speak.

"Will she be alright?" he asks, glancing around at our pale, stricken faces.

I shake my head and look at him evenly. "No, she won't. She has Lunar Fever," I tell him.

He lets out a long breath and runs a hand through his hair. "Shit," he murmurs.

"What do we do now?" Ovie says breaking the spell over the others.

"We go to our rooms and regroup in the morning. It's late and I'm tired. We'll request an audience with His Majesty in the morning," Vena says matter-of-factly.

Keelhan purses his lips and I glimpse something like doubt in his eyes before it vanishes entirely.

"I will seek you out tomorrow, ladies," he cuts in, lowering into a bow before he spins on his heel and strides down the hall and out of sight.

There's a murmur of acceptance before we all start towards our rooms, our dresses swishing against the cold marble floors. No one speaks as one by one our doors click shut.

The morning comes all too soon and I awake groggily to someone shaking me.

I blink rapidly and open my eyes to see Sarleigh standing over me with a serious expression on her face. I bolt upright up, alert but not fully awake as she lets me go and steps back.

"What is it? What happened?" I demand as I pull myself free of the sheets tangled around my legs.

"I'm sorry for the rude awakening, miss, but we've been told that you have to be ready and in the courtyard as soon as possible," she explains.

'Could it be to do with Lesya and last night?' I wonder.

"Have you been told what for, Sarleigh?" I ask as she leads me towards the bathroom.

Hesta and Perin are already there, waiting. They look stressed, the worry lines on each of their faces clear above their knitted brows. I stop and fold my arms, my heart thumping in my chest as my unease grows.

"What is going on?" I demand.

All three women glance at each other, sharing a silent conversation as I stand before them. I cross my arms, waiting for an explanation.

"The king has summoned The Chosen. He wants to see all of you," Perin says, her eyes moving to me.

My arms slacken in surprise. I haven't seen the king since the day of the first riddle and I suddenly find myself wary of what his summoning is about, especially after the events of the evening before.

"I see," I say quietly. "Then we can't keep His Highness waiting," I say, taking off my nightgown and stepping into the steaming waters.

Vilkha leads me along the hall, collecting the others as we go. We all glance at each other with concerned expressions but no one says a word. I look around and frown as I realise Chandra is still missing from our numbers and I glance at the others who shrug in answer. As we walk past Lesya's room, all of us turn to stare at the door and I wonder what the others might be thinking.

The king's messenger leads us outside towards the courtyard. The sun is bright and I have to squint as my eyes adjust to the brightness. I notice how the decorations of last night's event have been removed and the gardens are now back to normal.

As we turn the corner, I see the king standing tall with a handful of the Aslitír beside him. Lysan and Keelhan stand directly on either side of him with faces of stone. My unease returns as we get closer and I notice how they're all standing in a line, obscuring something behind them. Vilkha has us step forwards in a line, then he steps quietly to one side.

"Good morning, my Chosen. I trust you enjoyed last night's festivities," the king booms.

Each one of us curtseys and I give a sidewards glance to Ria beside me, her expression grim.

'*The king doesn't know,*' I realise as we straighten.

"It has come to my attention that not all of you are aware that your role as Chosen is a sacred one. Some of you would dare to tarnish the title I have bestowed upon you and I find this to be an unforgivable insult."

We dare to glance at one another, confusion and fear etched on our faces as the king steps forwards.

"You're confused," he observes, peering at us with glowering eyes.

"Bring them out," he orders with a wave of his hand, turning to resume his space between his captain and his Second.

My heart stops in my chest as a pair of soldiers emerge from within the palace, dragging the soldier that I recognise from the ball, naked, and to my horror, Chandra.

I feel the collective gasp behind me as I follow her across the courtyard to where they're both dumped in front of the king. The clinking sound of chains alerts me to the shackles locked around both of their wrists and ankles and I feel sick as I watch her bare body tremble beneath the shadow of the king. I stare in muted shock at the mortified girl before dragging my eyes to Lysan in horror. He avoids my gaze, staring straight ahead and jutting his chin out as he purposefully ignores Chandra.

"This one here has tarnished the reputation our kingdom holds so highly. Has soiled her standing as my Chosen and as a noble in my court. She is *filth*," He glowers at her, and I flinch as he spits in her face.

She releases a sob, but quickly quietens as the king turns his attention to the soldier.

"And as for you, *scum*, you should know better!" he roars, releasing his temper.

The young man says nothing, his mouth set in a tight line as he looks down at the ground in shame. His hair falls forward over his forehead, limp and dishevelled. My gut twists as I look at them both in such a sorry state.

Silence spreads over the courtyard, the only sound to break it is the clinking of the metal shackles followed by the sound of the king's boots as he steps away from them with a scowl. My heart pounds heavily in my chest as I look between Chandra and the king's stony expression.

"An example will be made," he utters.

'Is this what Uncle Erathon meant when he told me King Barilius couldn't be trusted?' the small voice whispers in my head.

The deadly calm in his voice sends a chill down my spine and I watch Chandra turn to him with a look of pure terror. The tension in the air is thick and unwavering as King Barilius lifts his hand to beckon Keelhan forwards. He obeys immediately.

"Lift their arms," he orders.

Keelhan beckons to two of his men who grab Chandra and the young Aslitír's chains and drag them towards the far end of the courtyard. The sound of metal scraping against stone cuts through me and I try not to wince. Without a word, they haul the heavy chains through a pair of metal hoops embedded in the stonework with a bunch of grunts and huffs.

Both Chandra and the soldier are hoisted to their feet, their arms held above their heads, their bare bodies on display. I struggle with the image and shift my gaze back to the king as he summons Lysan.

"Flog them. The both of them," he tells him plainly.

"No—please no!" Chandra cries.

I can feel the unrest beside me as the other girls begin to fidget nervously. Lysan merely nods once and steps towards where the two are chained. I watch as he pulls his hands out from his pockets and inky tendrils begin to accumulate around him.

"Please," Chanda whimpers.

"Turn them around," Lysan orders, his voice gruff.

The soldiers do as ordered and roughly turn the two of them so that they're facing the wall. I can see from here the way Chandra's whole body shakes as she tries to stifle her sobs. I feel the sinking feeling in my stomach squeeze into a knot and I realise the depths of my pity for her.

Without so much as a warning, Lysan lifts his forearm and brings it down sharply to his side. His shadows obey and two of them lash out, striking the pair with a swift blow. Chandra cries out instantly as it connects with her back, the skin already blistering. The man grunts but squares his shoulders as he takes the punishment.

"Again," King Barilius commands.

The rest of us watch on in horror as the tendrils bow to their master without hesitation. The only thing that drowns out the sound of the blow as the shadows connect with skin is Chandra's screams and sobs.

"Again!"

I glance towards the others and take in their ashen expressions. Some grip each other's hands tightly, while others like Mas have silent tears streaming down their face. None of us can bear to watch or listen, but every time we look away the king's voice cuts through the torment ordering us to turn back and pay attention.

"Again," the king grunts.

With growing disgust for the king and his Second—even the Aslitírs and their captain—I watch Chandra's knees give in, her trembling body slumping after the sixth lash. Her cries fall silent as she collapses, the man beside her faltering too. My eyes travel across her back. Where there was once smooth porcelain skin, there is now a mess of blood and raw, blistering welts. The cuts are deep and criss-cross over her back in long strokes like some twisted child's game. If she survives this, there won't be a healer in all of Askrhea who will be able to fix the scarring.

"Again!" King Barilius orders.

This time Keelhan and the soldiers look at him with muted but surprised expressions. Even Lysan seems to hesitate before raising his hand.

"I said again!" he barks louder.

Lysan does as ordered and I swallow the bile rising in my throat as I watch the blood drip down their bodies. Chandra's limp body hangs from the shackles and the stripped soldier with his head hung low, his once clenched fists now hanging limply as the pain overwhelms him.

"And again," he says, his tone steeled.

As Lysan raises his arm once more, I find myself unable to withstand any more and my heart plummets.

"Enough!"

I blink, surprised at the sound of my own voice, loud and raw against the heavy silence. The king glances towards me before turning and slowly stepping closer until he's peering down at me with a sinister look in his dark eyes.

"You wish to take her place, girl?" His tone is loud enough for all to hear and equally as menacing.

Angry tears blur my vision as I hesitate. In the end, I shake my head. My fear of what he's capable of is too great.

"I didn't think so," he sneers.

"B-but if you carry on, you'll kill her," I choke out the words before I can think better of it.

The king glances at me, bored, before shifting his gaze to Lysan. I watch as the Shadowcaster dips his head in a quick nod with a bleakness in his eyes that surprises me.

"Fine. Bring her down," he orders with another wave of his hand before sending a meaningful glance my way.

He then turns to us, observing each of our faces, and stopping on mine for several seconds longer than the rest of the girls.

"Let this be a lesson to you all. You are The Chosen, you have a reputation to uphold, my reputation to uphold, and if you betray my kindness and trust like this *slut*, then know that the consequences of your actions will bring you the very same fate," he warns.

He turns back to the two of them, Chandra hanging limply from her shackled wrists, beside the trembling soldier, and we all watch as two of the Aslitír gently bring her down and carry her away.

The king sniffs as she's taken back into the palace, before glancing at the remaining guilty party.

"Ten more for the man who seeded her," he orders.

His command is met with gasps from me and the girls, and a troubled expression from Keelhan. The man's shoulders slump, as a quiet sob escapes his lips and my heart breaks for him. Lysan's face is void of emotion as he takes in the order. He hesitates for a second and I feel triumphant.

'*Surely he will refuse now?*'

Then Lysan calls his shadows to him and my smugness shatters into despair. No one dares to utter another word as the king marches away.

I hear him as he stops beside Vilkha, who nods solemnly before making his way towards us.

"Come girls," he says quietly, ushering us away from the barbaric show.

As we filter back through the doorway, I dare to glance over my shoulder just as Lysan raises his arm with the next strike, and as the crack sounds across the courtyard, the young man's screams erupt from deep within him, cutting through the dense silence.

LYSAN

CHAPTER EIGHTEEN

The thick silence that blankets my room is unwelcome and eerie after the piercing sounds of Chandra and Dorin's screams. I lean against the closed door and take a moment to collect myself, inhaling long breaths of air and expelling them slowly. I push away from the door and stride into my bathroom to splash cool water over my face. I gasp at the sharpness of the water, but it does nothing to soothe my being on edge. The king's orders ring in my head, swirling with the sounds of screams and Nesryn's firm plea.

As I close my eyes and splash my face with another handful of water, I picture her face in my mind. Her jutted out lip and furrowed brow over fearful eyes. I recall how she had squared her shoulders despite the tremble running through her, fists clenched as she had stood up to Barilius. The image sends a shiver down my spine; she now had his attention and that couldn't be a good thing.

I hold the basin and stare down at the water circling the drain, water droplets dripping down my face as Dorin resurfaces in my mind. I was grateful when he'd fallen unconscious from the pain. Despite Keelhan's expression and my wavering will, I had completed my orders with a heavy heart, though with so many Aslitír as witnesses, I had little choice in the matter.

Towelling my face dry, I step back into the room and stop, my fingers drumming against my thighs. I need a distraction. Deep down I want nothing more than to down a few fairly strong drinks and bury myself in someone long enough to forget today's events, and the night before as well.

The tower had been empty when I'd gone searching, and when I finally managed to pry the information of the king's whereabouts from two trembling servants, my mood had only soured further.

I strode towards the throne room and with a flick of my wrist, cast shadows ahead of me to throw open the heavy doors with an unnecessary flourish. I burst through the billows of dissipating shadow, my voice raised.

"And just what could be so urgent at this ho—" my voice died in my throat as I took in the scene before me.

I recognised Dorin straight away by the inch of tight strawberry coils atop his head, though his face was paler than I'd ever seen it, his brown eyes glassy with poorly-masked fear. The girl beside him clung to the clothes in her hands which she used to try and cover her naked body. Even from where I stood, I could see how hard she was trembling, and it wasn't from the cold.

My eyes moved to Barilius who lounged in his throne lazily and I could tell, despite his posture, that he was alert and furious. The glint in his eyes and the sharp look he'd given the two of them said enough. Two Aslitír stood beside him, witnesses to the scene that played out.

"Soldier, repeat your report so Lysander here is caught up to speed," his voice cut through the silence and echoed across the high walls.

"Yes, Your Majesty," said the man on the far left, straightening before he stepped forwards two paces.

"I was completing my rounds and noticed Dorin missing from his patrol route. On inspection, I discovered him with her," he said, his nose wrinkling in disgust as he surveyed the young woman distastefully.

"Balls deep, I think was the term you used, soldier," Barilius sniped and straightened in his chair.

I looked from Dorin to Chandra and back again, before I met the king's gaze.

"What is it you need from me, my king?" I asked, despite the sinking feeling I felt as the words left my mouth.

His mouth had twisted into a sinister smile that didn't meet the flash of fury in his eyes.

"The bitch is of no use to me now. They've made a mockery of me, so it's only right that I return their gesture with one of my own," he said as he got to his feet.

I dared to glance at them both again, my own anger ebbing away as I took in the way that Chandra held in her tears and bit her lip until she broke through the skin. Dorin on the other hand was motionless, but the twitch of his temple and his clenched fists said otherwise.

I watched on as Barilius strode casually down the steps, giving them a wide berth and a vengeful look before stopping several feet before me.

"Tomorrow morning, wake the other girls and bring them to the courtyard. I plan to make an example of these two," he stated, finally answering my question. "I'm sure you're itching to exercise those shadows of yours again," he added.

I tried to not show my disgust at his eagerness for bloodshed. I answered with a bored, half-shrug.

At this, a sob slipped from Chandra's lips and the king glared at her. I watched on as she looked to the floor, forcibly silencing her anguish.

"Get them out of my sight," he growled, kickstarting the two soldiers into action.

I watched on as they escorted them from the room and the king placed a hand on my shoulder.

"I expect you to be on form tomorrow," he told me.

"What about the captain, shouldn't he be here for this?" I questioned, only now noticing his absence.

Barilius's eyes clouded over and I held my breath as I waited for his response. But instead, he chose to say nothing and instead patted me one last time before striding away, leaving me alone in the deserted throne room.

I'm drawn from the memory as I think of Keelhan. I'd seen his face this morning, the look of blindsided shock behind the mask of collected calm as the king gave his order. With a resigned sigh, I realise what I need to do before anything else.

I wrinkle my nose in displeasure as I enter the soldiers' quarters, the heavy stench of musty balls, sweat, and booze hanging thick in the air, mingling with cigarette smoke. I'd been led here by my generally sound knowledge of Keelhan and his moods. One of Keelhan's men had been thrown under the bus—by his own

selfish choices—and the king blamed poor leadership. So…
Keelhan was back in his bad books, for now.

The Aslitír quarters are hidden away in the lower levels of the
castle, made up of long rooms full of the basic necessities for the
lower class soldiers. Any with rank would be found in their own
private rooms. As Captain, Keelhan enjoyed the same comforts
that I did on the floor above. That changed nothing for Keelhan
though as he spent most of his free time down here, surrounded
by his soldiers. It's a gesture of equality and the reason he's
always been well-liked. I'd always seen it as a humble act.

I move through the rows of beds, aware of the men's eyes on
me as I saunter past, hands in pockets. I feel the anger in the
room; word must have spread about this morning's flogging. I'm
fully aware that their anger is for me, but their rage is
misdirected. The further in I go, the stronger the smell is and I
can't help the grimace that flickers across my face. I scan the
room but my friend isn't here.

'Do these men ever bathe?'

I come to a stop midway along the walkway and heave a sigh,
turning to my right, where one of the soldiers, Hendrix, lounges
on his bed, lazily wiping down his boots.

"Where is he?" I ask him bluntly.

He glances at me with the same distrust and disgust they all
do, before pointing further through the jungle of doubled cots to
the far end of the room. I can just about see the top of Keelhan's
head through the bunks.

Without another word, I make my way towards where
Keelhan is sitting in a circle with a number of his men, playing a
game of cards with a lit cigarette in his hand. I stop and watch as
the smoke billows up into the air as he busies himself with the
game. He seems much more relaxed than earlier, with a carefree
smile on his lips as he engages in banter with the man opposite
him and places another card on the growing stack in the centre.

It all falls away when he notices me standing there. His eyes
darken as he draws the cigarette to his lips and pulls in a lengthy
drag, exhaling it in one large puff. As he gets to his feet, so do
two members of the Aslitír in his card game, and I watch,
stunned, as they step together, blocking his path to me. I laugh at
their attempt to delay the inevitable.

Keelhan steps forward and pushes past the soldiers, his arm
rearing back before his fist flies forwards and connects with the

side of my face with a loud crunch.

Some of the men cheer their captain on as I stumble back a few steps, rubbing my face as I lift my eyes to meet his. They burn with an anger that I haven't seen in a long time.

"Are you done?" I ask, straightening.

"Oh, I'm just getting warmed up," he glowers at me.

I can feel the buzz around us as men stop to watch, keen for some action. Looking at Keelhan, I can tell he's been waiting for this all day. Avoiding this conflict doesn't seem to be an option, but I try anyway.

"We don't have time for this, Keelhan," I answer through gritted teeth.

"Oh, there's time. You're not walking away from this," he argues.

"I was following direct orders, Keel, let it go," I say pointedly.

At this, a murmur ripples through the soldiers and they share looks with each other. I can sense the uncertainty spreading through the room as they all look towards Keelhan.

From where I'm standing it doesn't look promising. The fury emanating from him is palpable.

"Let. It. Go," I warn him.

"You'd like that, wouldn't you?" he spits, the venom in his tone igniting my anger.

I drop my shoulders and roll my neck, frowning as I meet his eye, prepared for the onslaught. I keep my face impassive as he rushes at me. I spread my fingers out wide and throw my arms forward. In seconds the shadows swirl out from behind me and launch forward, slicing through the air toward him. He's thrown across the room and I blink when he connects with the far wall with an almighty thud. He gasps for air, winded by the blow, but my shadows don't let up, pinning him firmly to the wall.

I glance at his men, a single brow raised in silent question. I wait for them to rise up to my challenge, to aid their captain, but all I receive are hateful glares. No one moves a muscle to help. They understand my role, but that doesn't mean they have to like it. I stride toward Keelhan, watching as he writhes beneath the pressure of the inky darkness.

"Your soldier fucked a Chosen and was stupid enough to get caught," I tell him.

He glares at me, chin jutted out. "Maybe you should focus on the rumours spreading around about the palace and *I'll* be the one to deal with my men."

"You don't like it? Then stop throwing your tantrum and take it up with the king," I finish, anger clear in my voice.

'*What rumours?*' I wonder.

I save the thought for later and lean closer, my eyes never leaving his.

"We may be friends, Keelhan, but you will remember your place," I tell him under my breath.

The fight in him falters and he releases an angry shaken breath as I pull away. With another flick of my wrist, the tendrils release him and draw back to my side. Keelhan lands on his feet with a heavy thunk and shoots me one last dirty look before he pushes past me, roughly knocking my shoulder with his and storming off.

I turn my head to watch him leave before my eyes fall back on the soldiers. They turn to me instantly, some with vicious scowls, others with undiluted hatred, and some even with fear.

"Who here has heard these so-called rumours?" I demand.

Silence ensues, but I wait, my eyes scouring the faces of those who stare back through knitted brows. After a drawn-out silence, my patience begins to wear thin and I clench my fist as I wait for one of them to speak up. I quickly realise that none of them will. I breathe heavily through my nose and let my shadows swallow me as they look on in surprise. Then I disappear from their sight.

"Rumours about the palace, eh?" I mutter to myself as I traverse the halls.

I hide my eagerness to know more. I have to tread carefully if I'm going to interrogate servants. News will spread and people will stop keeping their silence, or worse, the king will find out.

The halls are surprisingly quiet as I make my way through the long corridors and back to my room for my coin pouch. I turn the corner, not paying attention as I collide with someone. We both stumble back and I look up, angry, only to find the feeling dissipating as a young woman stands in front of me. The Chosen girl, Zariya. She looks at me guiltily and it sparks my suspicion.

"Apologies, my lord," she mumbles, her eyes focused on the floor.

"Aren't you meant to be in your room?" I ask, my head tilted and a single brow raised.

I watch on as her brow knits together in confusion and she hesitates before shaking her head. The jet black braids sway with her movements. Suddenly, I'm reminded of the ways that my shadows move.

"Our next trial was postponed. Some of the girls were a little… traumatised after this morning," she says with a wince as she dares to meet my eye.

As I think back to the show that the king put on, the part that I played in it. I'm not surprised in the least.

'*You're a villain,*' Nesryn's cold, bitter voice resonates through my mind.

I shake my head the slightest bit to rid my mind of her and focus my attention back on Zariya, whose dark eyes watch me warily.

"It's getting late," I comment, turning to leave.

"So, is it true?" she asks.

"Is what true?" I ask, glancing back at her.

"That there are haters of the crown in the palace?" she presses.

I find my interest suddenly piqued.

'*So* that's *the rumour,*' I realise.

I compose myself quickly before I face her.

"How did you come to know of this rumour?"

"People have been talking since…" she trails off and glances at me fearfully.

"Well?" I press.

"Since the spectacle this morning," she says quietly.

"I see…" I trail off, reliving the moment strike after strike and trying not to shudder.

"They're saying someone tried to divert the attention from themselves and placed Chandra in the spotlight," she continues, fiddling with her hands.

"Divert attention from what?" I ask, my eyes watching her long fingers as she clasps and unclasps them, her palms slick with sweat.

"No one seems to know. That or they won't tell… my lord," she replies with a slight shrug.

"Well, I suggest you head back to your room. It's late," I point out, motioning for her to leave.

"Y-yes, my lord," she answers before scurrying off.

I wait until I hear the sound of a door opening and closing shut, feeling satisfied. Just as I'm about to move away, I hear a door open further down the hall and before the person can see me, I immediately surround myself in shadow like a walking camouflage. The door closes with a soft, almost inaudible click before a figure appears in the hallway. Her eyes shift warily as she looks around, clearly afraid of being spotted. I remain where I am, knowing with slight confidence that she won't see me. As she moves closer, I frown at the servant's clothes she's wearing just as I recognise her as another of The Chosen girls.

'The Drullanon girl,' I observe. *'What was her name again? Twyla, that was it.'*

I hide in the safe confines of my shadows, silently watching as Twyla glances around tensely, moving quickly and quietly with an alertness that has me curious about her intentions.

Eventually, she sneaks along the corridor and slips around the corner and out of sight.

I think back to what the boy said: *'You'll never stop us, we're everywhere and more join every day. In every tavern, inn, every nook and cranny.'*

I step forwards with a newfound purpose.

"Now where-oh-where are *you* going?" I wonder aloud as I follow after her.

CHAPTER NINETEEN

The rest of the morning goes by in tense silence after Vilkha leads us back to our rooms, informing us en route that the king has ordered that our trial will be delayed for a short while. None of the girls speak after what we saw, but I'm sure that we're all thinking the same thing. The king is dangerous. Far more so than any of us imagined.

The realisation twists my stomach into tightly-wound knots and I suddenly miss my uncle very much. His personal views on the king are beginning to make sense to me now, and I wish he'd have warned me of this. I think of Stormtip and realise that in his way, he did. I just didn't listen. Despite my growing fear of King Barilius, all I can think about is Lysan's shadows cutting through Chandra's skin and the immense pity that overwhelms me. I can't help but wonder what will happen to her now that she's been so publicly shamed and punished.

I study Maskia whose eyes are trained on the lengthy carpet. I take note of how pale she is before glancing at each of the others, inspecting them one by one. Their faces are as ashen as they were in the courtyard and I wonder vaguely if I look the same. Even Vena is uneasy.

One by one, we're ushered back into the confines of our rooms. Our numbers diminish and I'm taken aback as I realise that that's exactly what The Choosing is. Finally, when it's just myself and Vilkha, we come to my door. He gestures towards it and I step forward and then stop, turning my attention to the sullen-looking messenger.

"What will happen to her?" I dare to ask.

He gives me a pitying look. "The trials are now over for her. She will return home stripped of her title and her honour, as per the king's order."

My jaw drops. There is so much that I wish to say, but I think better of it and swallow my angry words.

"When is the next trial?" I ask instead.

"It's been postponed to tomorrow afternoon, my lady," he answers. "Your clothes will be delivered to your room by tomorrow morning."

"Clothes?" I question, tilting my head.

"Your next trial requires more physical activity. It was recommended that you each have suitable attire for it," he answers.

"I see," I murmur.

"I urge you to get some rest, Lady Havenore. I will have food delivered to your rooms at once," he says, sweeping into a low bow before walking away.

I move to my door, my hand hovering over the handle. I can't bring myself to go in, my mind too full. Instead, I walk back down the hall, heading in the direction of the training room.

I stop in the doorway, my mouth agape. The entire room is completely destroyed.

The floor is cut in two with jagged lines running across the floor and reaching high up the wall. Loose stone, wood and rubble litter the floor, along with multiple pieces of training equipment, sliced into pieces.

Black marks stain the ceiling and walls around the deep cuts through the room and it quickly dawns on me who is responsible. My unease deepens as my eyes travel the room, my mouth set in a grim line.

'How much more destruction is that man capable of?' I wonder.

"Oh my lady, has no one told you? That room is currently off-limits," a voice cuts through the silence, startling me.

I turn to see a servant scurrying toward me and I step back from the doorway warily. She sends me an apologetic smile and lets out a short sigh.

"My apologies, Lady Nesryn, I don't want to disappoint you but Master Lysan has left it in quite a state after he last used it," she explains quickly.

"I can see that," I mutter, my eyes sliding from her to the mess through the doorway in front of me.

"Another room will be set up in the meantime. Would you like me to show you where?" she continues, gesturing the way she came.

"Oh, no that won't be necessary. Thank you," I reply.

"Alright then, my lady. Well if that is all, I'll be on my way," she replies.

"Y-yes of course," I reply with a shake of my head.

I step to the side and let her rush around me, watching as she curries off along the hall and disappears around the corner. When she's out of sight, I remain standing in the doorway of the destroyed room for several more moments, peering at the jagged cuts and thinking of how wild they are, compared to the precise cuts he made along Chandra's back. A shiver runs through me at the thought of what he's capable of and I can't help but wonder if berating him only made me more of a target.

My mind travels to Erryn and Lesya and my nervousness grows stronger as I consider them both. I wonder if the king planned all of this or whether it's all just some huge coincidence. Though after this morning, I'm beginning to believe the latter option less and less.

With a heavy sigh, I turn and leave, making my way back the way I came.

I stop outside Lesya's door first, surprisingly nervous. It feels like an age since the events of last night, but the chaos of it is clear in my mind, and I wonder what fragile state she is in, if anyone has even thought to see her as I have.

I take a breath, bracing myself as I lift my hand and rap my knuckles against the door. The sound echoes along the hall and I step back, waiting patiently for an answer. Several moments pass and nothing happens, so I step forward and knock again, watching as two handmaidens, a blonde and a brunette, leave Mas's room, heads bent as they whisper amongst themselves.

"Do you think it's true?" one whispers to the other.

"A spy in the palace? Pretty unlikely if you ask me," the brunette replies.

"A lot seems to have slipped past the king recently," the blonde one continues.

"It's how he has come to The Choosing."

"Those poor girls," the brunette sighs with a shake of her head.

They continue their conversation but as they move further and further away, it becomes impossible to hear what they're saying.

'Spies in the palace?'

I don't need to wonder why there would be. I've seen a deadlier side to the king and his Choosing, but the idea of spies in the palace still makes me feel uneasy. With spies comes trouble.

"Focus on the task at hand," I murmur to myself as I turn back to the door.

This time I don't bother to knock and simply turn the handle, pushing against the door and swinging it open. As I step into the room my eyes widen in surprise and I stop short. My heart begins to hammer in my chest as my disbelieving eyes scour the room.

The curtains are drawn and the room has been freshly cleaned. New sheets blanket the bed, while neatly-arranged cushions have been plumped and placed at the head of the bed. The quilt is smooth and looks as though no one has slept in it. The chair that had been placed by the side of the bed has been moved back to the far corner of the room. The vanity table is empty of perfume bottles and jewellery. There is no evidence of anyone having stayed in here, but more worryingly, Lesya is gone.

My breathing is slightly erratic as I rush across the room and into the bathroom, but find it equally as empty.

"Where is she?" I ask no one.

Nothing in this room hints at her staying here the night before, bedridden and gravely ill. It's as if all signs of her existence have been completely erased and it sends my already fraught nerves into turmoil. I rush about the room in a frenzy as my mind flicks through the many possibilities until I come to a complete stop as a thought dawns on me. Without a word, I run out of the room and head across the hall, straight for Erryn's room. I don't bother knocking and just barge right in, surprising Erryn's handmaidens as I stumble through the door.

"Oh my!" one of them cries as she gets to her feet.

"Is she here? Is Erryn here?" I rush through my words.

"Of course she is," says the one standing in front of Erryn's bed.

"Are you alright, my lady? You look like you've seen a ghost," the other adds after a moment of silence.

Before I'm able to answer, she steps to the side to reveal Erryn's charred face, staring at me. The reality of what I'd done hits me hard again as I look at the girl lying in bed, wrapped head to toe in bandages.

I can see the pain that shines through her right eye, the swelling and rawness disfiguring the left side of her face.

'*Because of you,*' a small voice echoes in my head.

The guilt and relief I feel at seeing her safe in her room cause tears to fill the corners of my eyes. I rush forwards and drop to my knees at the side of her bed.

"I don't think that's—" the handmaiden behind me starts.

"—Hush Ritta, let her be," the other tuts from across the bed.

I gently take Erryn's hand between my own and lift my gaze to meet hers.

"I'm so sorry, Erryn," I choke on my words as a tear slips down my face.

"I didn't mean for this to happen, I never—" The lump in my throat cuts off my words.

"—It's alright... accident," she responds slowly. Her voice is raspy and crackles but her words ease the guilt ever so slightly.

I gently pat her hand and with a tight nod, I release it and get to my feet, wiping away the stray tear on my cheek.

"Lady Havenore, Lady Drulfeard needs her rest. You may come visit her another time," the handmaiden advises.

I nod and turn away, stopping sharply at the door as I remember what brought me into here in the first place. I half-turn and look at each of the maids.

"Lesya, across the corridor, where is she?" I ask.

The two of them share a concerned look but say nothing.

My suspicion grows as I look at each of them pointedly.

"If you know something, speak now. What happened to her?" I press.

"We don't know my lady, there's been not a peep out of that room all day," Ritta answers.

"She's very sick with Lunar Fever, surely you must have seen, *heard* something?" I reply incredulously.

"I'm sorry, my lady," the other maiden answers with a sad shake of her head.

I let out a shaky breath and drop my gaze to the floor in defeat. I don't bother to speak as I turn on my heels and leave the room, closing the door firmly behind me and resting my back against it as I rub a hand over my face. My eyes move to the slightly ajar door in front of me, leading into Lesya's barren room, and my unease doubles. I waste no time and stride across the hall to knock on Maskia's door.

She opens it almost immediately, her face falling when she notices my expression.

"Mas, I need your help. Lesya's gone," I explain.

Her eyes flit past me to the open door along the corridor and her expression shifts to one of determination.

"Let's go," she answers, pulling the door closed behind her.

It's late when I finally make it back to my room. Maskia and I scoured the palace in search of Lesya, but no one could tell us where she'd disappeared to, or why her room was now empty of all of her belongings. We'd even bumped into the captain, but Keelhan had been too busy scowling and nursing a bottle of aged brandy to be of any help. I notice the food placed by the small table and chair in the corner of the room. Judging by the limp vegetables, it's been sitting there for quite some time. I don't have an appetite regardless and I turn away from it, noticing the new clothes folded neatly and placed at the foot of my bed.

Thinking that writing a letter to my uncle will help lift my mood, I move toward the vanity and collect the paper and quill from the left-hand drawer, placing it on the table in front of me. I stare at the empty page, willing myself to write something, but I continue to sit there with the quill hovering an inch above the page.

'*Can I really tell him the truth*?" I question.

I think of everything that's happened so far; the potion disaster, the ball, the king's punishment of Chandra, and I place my quill down.

'*What disaster awaits us in the next trial?*' I muse.

The next thought resurfaces after days of being pushed to the back of my mind, but I can't deny my fear any longer as it swirls around and around my head.

'Will I even survive The Choosing?'

Leaning back in my chair, I try to shove the thought away, but to no avail. With a defeated sigh, I push away from the desk and move back to my door, heading towards Ria's room.

I grab the handle, not thinking twice about it as I push down and enter the room. My eyes widen as I see Ria and Vena entwined in the centre of the room. For the first time, I notice Vena's hair is a mess of thick, tight coils, spanning her head in a beautiful silver afro. I notice one of her hands is behind Ria's neck, bunching her blonde tresses in a fist. Ria's porcelain hands move quickly about Vena's body, sliding hungrily over her smooth curves.

I stare wide-eyed and gawking at the two of them, unsure where to look but also unable to look away as they kiss deeply, utterly enthralled by one another and completely unaware of my presence. I feel heat creeping up my neck and burning my cheeks as my eyes flit to where Vena's hand slips between Ria's legs as a moan escapes her mouth. I choke as I quickly come to my senses, inadvertently alerting them to my presence.

They both freeze in shock and stare at me, horrified. I back out of the door and shut it with a quick slam, surprising myself when I release the handle and realise how tightly I'd been gripping it. I let out a shaky breath as I hear shuffling behind the door, and I sprint back to my room.

As soon as I shut my own door behind me with a solid click, a laugh of disbelief bubbles out of me. I bring my hand to my lips, staring ahead at nothing while my mind whirs. All those secretive looks, all of Ria's excuses to dip off to goddess-knows-where. Now it all made sense.

The rushed knock at my door causes me to yelp in surprise and jump away from it with a start. I open it a fraction to find a dishevelled and wary looking Ria peering at me through the gap.

"About what you saw," she starts as soon as my door opens.

"Look Ria, it's none of my business," I reply with a shrug, holding my hands up.

She shifts on her feet but doesn't move away from the door. I sigh in defeat and step to one side, allowing her in. With a grateful glance, she steps into the room and turns to me.

"Are you going to tell the Shadowcaster?" she asks, her tone nervous.

"By Ciel no. I don't even want to *think* about what he would do with that information," I mutter, hurt that she would even think that of me.

We pause and I think of all that's occurred over the past few weeks. I think of Erryn, Lesya and Chandra. I contemplate the horrors we've witnessed and the fear we've all shared and despite inwardly telling myself I wouldn't, my tongue slips loose.

"What will you do if the king chooses you? What do you think will happen then?" I demand.

"I—I don't know," She falters, glancing at the floor as her cheeks begin to colour.

"I mean hell Ria, that's why we're all here. He could choose you," I reason.

"He might choose you," her voice is quiet as she says it, knowing her argument is irrelevant.

I sigh and run a hand over my face.

"I just think you need to be more careful, Ria. This Choosing is proving to be more dangerous with each passing day and if you and Vena got caught—" I stop short, breathing out a short stifled breath.

"You're my friend, and honestly, I've come to love you." I pause, offering her a reassuring smile. "I just don't want you getting hurt like the others."

"I know, I'll—we'll try," she replies, placing a reassuring hand on my shoulder.

"I know I shouldn't be surprised, but cold and calculating Vena? Really?" I comment with a wry smile.

"Vena is sweet once you peel back the layers of hostility," she reasons with a small, secretive smile.

"Vena seems to have a tendency to only look out for number one," I argue.

"She'd never betray us like that, she does care, Nes. In her own way," Ria disputes.

"And what if it's a case of you or her? What if you're discovered and she has to choose?" I press.

"It won't come to that," Ria answers crisply.

"I hope to the goddesses that it doesn't, because Vena isn't the one that'll have your head."

"Point taken," she answers with a sigh.

She turns back towards the door but hesitates as she opens it. "I know you don't trust her, but Vena is on our side, Nes. She's one of us, and right now we need to all stick together."

Before I can agree, she's slipped through the door.

CHAPTER TWENTY

I follow Twyla through the palace and through the kitchen towards the servants' portal. My curiosity deepens when she somehow manages to slip past the servants and through the portal, completely unnoticed. I continue to camouflage myself within my shadows; servants gossip and the king's Shadowcaster being here would certainly be something to talk about.

In mere moments I've shadowfolded, landing in a darkened alley across from the landing point. Despite her drawn-up hood and plain clothes, I recognise her immediately. She glances around, before pulling her hood down further and darting down the street. She blends into the crowd effortlessly and I find myself having to shadowfold across the roofs of the surrounding buildings to get a clear view of her.

I'm intrigued as she heads towards the lower levels of the city and away from the busier streets still teeming with people.

We move on from the clean streets and well-dressed people to the smell of rotting vegetables and stale urine which fills my nostrils and leaves a dank taste in my mouth. She becomes more confident as we reach the slums of the city, careless almost. People litter the street, sleeping rough on street corners and I watch on as she stands straighter, no longer looking over her shoulder. She weaves through the back alleys and darkened streets towards a seedy-looking tavern that I recognise from my youth.

"The Crooked Spade," I murmur in amusement, a memory of Keelhan and I stumbling out from its doors drunk as lords.

I recall how Keelhan in his drunken stupor had tripped over the corner of his cloak and had been sent sprawling into a cluster of Aslitír. This had been before he'd even joined their ranks and become their captain. We'd both been beaten black and blue that night. A half-smile tugs at my lips at the memory.

I drop down into the alley below and step into the mouth of the street, watching silently as Twyla strides purposefully inside.

'*Perhaps the rumours are true,*' I think to myself.

I wait patiently for her to disappear through the doorway before I make my move. The tavern is a modest-looking place despite its surroundings and holds the rooms above for board. It's rare around here for there to be an unoccupied space in the lower levels, but it comes in handy as I peer towards the slim walkway that bends around the back of the tavern. I waste no time and shadowfold one final time to the back of the building, in between two large bins full of rubbish and broken glass.

A young boy comes out with a large black sack and I see how he struggles and fights with the bag the whole way down the steps and to the bins on either side of me. He's a scrawny thing and reminds me of the messenger boy from Talló. The thought sends a cool chill down my spine.

He turns his back and begins a feeble attempt at hoisting the bag over the lid. I see my opportunity and slip past him, and into the tavern. Even from down here, I can hear the commotion of drunken folk, clinking glasses, and flirtatious barmaids. I keep my back pressed to the wall as I enter. I creep towards the open door at the end and find that the staircase is empty as I make my way to the top. I peer around the corner and the tavern is as dark and dingy as I recall. The tables are heaving with people. Clusters of men and women chat loudly to one another across the tables, their drinks sloshing in their glasses.

I spot Twyla immediately, as she weaves through the room towards me. She pulls her hood down revealing a curtain of brown hair and almond-shaped, hazel eyes that scan the room suspiciously before continuing. I step back and melt into the shadows enough to be invisible to the naked eye, watching as Twyla walks through the doorway and climbs the stairs two at a time.

'*Someone seems to be in a hurry,*' I observe.

Once she's cleared the first flight, I follow after her, keeping my footsteps light. Despite the safety of my shadows concealing me, my hand hovers over the hilt of my dagger. The stairs lead me to the first level and I peer around the corner just in time to see Twyla reach the end of the corridor and lean forwards, knocking in a strange rhythm against the fourth door on the left side.

I make a mental note of it as someone lets her in and she disappears into the room, the door shutting quickly behind her. My eyes travel along the wall to the adjoining room and I furrow my brow in concentration, sneaking inside.

To my surprise, I'm not alone and I stumble back as I come face to face with an older man who reeks of whiskey and vomit. He cries out in surprise, stumbling back several steps into the side of the small cot. I quickly put him in a chokehold to silence him, squeezing until his scrabbling arms go limp. I lay him down carefully on the cot, unconscious but breathing, and straighten my clothing, letting my shadows melt away.

'*He won't be bothering anyone for a while,*' I think as something on the wall grabs my attention.

In our scuffle, the small picture frame hanging on the wall has fallen, revealing a tiny crack in the plaster. I press my face to the wall and squint through the small hole, pleased to find that I can see the adjoining room after all—however, limited it may be.

I recognise Twyla sitting on the cot against the far wall. A small table has been pulled into the middle of the room and from what I can see, it's covered with maps and papers and held down with an encrusted dagger. A man sits beside her, but I'm only able to see half of his face. I can tell there are more people in the room but they're just out of my eye line.

"Things aren't looking good," Twyla says gravely.

"What's going on? You were meant to send word three days ago," a female voice says.

"Things have been happening at the palace that has changed things," Twyla replies with a solemn gaze.

A pause.

"How so?"

"There's been trouble with The Chosen," Twyla answers, glancing at the man beside her.

'*I'll say,*' I think to myself.

"I knew it!" the man beside her exclaims, an excitement in him that hadn't been there moments before.

"It's just like you said, Row, the girls can't be shipped off to nobles and royals across the continent. You've spoken to half of the people Barilius has claimed to have sent these women," Twyla continues.

"So what are you saying, Twyla?" Row questions.

Twyla pauses and glances down at the table as if trying to work out how to say it.

"I'm saying that once those girls go through those doors, they aren't supposed to come back out."

I frown at her words, thoughts of Loísia creeping into my head. I try my best to shake them and concentrate on the conversation going on in the other room, but despite my best efforts, her unseeing hazel eyes stay with me.

"This is all just hearsay, where's the proof?"

Another voice steps in, this time it belongs to an older man. Familiarity tugs at me as I hear his voice, but since I can't place it immediately, I brush it aside, determined to catch the rest of their conversation.

"Yeah, Freckles, tell us you got summing at least," the man beside her asks as he bumps shoulders with her.

She rolls her eyes at him and as her eyes move across the room to the familiar man's voice. There is some rummaging and shuffling as Twyla digs around in her pocket and pulls something out. I try to get a good look as she unfolds the corners of what looks to be a handkerchief, but all I can make out is a small collection of greyish looking shards covered in soot and ash. A ring and something else glistens in the light amidst the strange items.

A tenseness seems to fall over the room and I wonder what this so-called discovery means to this small band of people.

"Twyla, what is this?" Row breathes, stepping forward.

"These fragments of bone are all that's left of Rohana Duhrannes and Mallon Vythierre," she says with a grave expression.

"What?" The man beside her squawks.

I recoil from the wall, my eyes scanning the floor as I try to make sense of what I've just heard. I shake my head in disbelief.

'*They were sent home. I saw the carriages leave through the portal myself,*' I tell myself as I think back to the morning their carriages were piled with their belongings.

'*But were they in the carriages, Lysan? Did you check?*' a tiny voice asks me.

"Shit…" I murmur, bringing a hand to my face and rubbing my chin in aggravation.

'*Barilius has some explaining to do,*' I consider as my promise to Loísia rings in my head.

"By Ciel…" Row breathes. "But how?" he asks. I quickly press my ear to the wall.

Twyla gives a half-shrug, her eyes dark as they lift to meet his.

"They refused to partake in the trial. They were told they'd be going home, only it seems they never left the palace walls."

"But the king slipped up, he showed his true colours and the girls are wising up now. They're getting suspicious." Twyla says knowingly.

I peer through in time to see Twyla fold the supposed bones out of sight once more.

"Keep up the good work, Twyla, we're gettin' so close," the young man beside her grins.

Twyla doesn't return the sentiment and drops her gaze to the floor, seemingly hesitant.

"What is it?" Row speaks up.

"I'm not so sure we're doing the right thing. Leaving those girls to fend for themselves… at this rate, there'll be none left," she says, looking at them with concern.

"We won't let it come to that. For now, just keep your eyes and ears open and stay close to the Havenore girl. We need her alive," the second man says.

Twyla glances between the man and Row, and I can only assume they've shared a knowing glance from the distasteful expression on their informant's face.

'*Nesryn?*'

"Nesryn? Why?" she asks, her brow knitted.

"All will be explained in time. Now you need to get back before they realise that you're missing," Row tells her as she ushers her towards the door and out of sight.

I step back from the hole and stare at the ground once more as I try to process all that I've heard. A part of me wants nothing more than to rush straight back to the palace and demand answers from the king, but I know that despite my anger, that isn't a well thought out choice. I simmer in anger, anger at the king and his deceit, and the bitter anger at myself for letting two more innocent girls die.

"I'm sorry, Lou. I'm trying," I say to the darkened room.

I unclench my fists as I hear the other three members leave the room. I wait until their footsteps have disappeared down the hall before I shadowfold to the roof. The air is welcomingly cold after the stuffiness of the drunkard's room and I'm grateful for it as it clears my head and narrows my focus.

From here, I can see Twyla pull her hood up and scuttle up the street back towards the higher levels of the city. Next, is the young man that I recognise from sitting beside her, his red hair glinting under the light of the lamp as he dips down the opposite street. Then, one after the other, the last two step out from within The Crooked Spade, a red-haired woman and a black man.

I can't see much of their faces from where I am, but I watch them as they draw their own hoods over their heads and slip away out of sight. Something niggles at me as I think of the black man. The way that he holds himself and the sound of his voice in the room is oddly familiar to me.

"Who are you people?" I wonder aloud, staring at the empty street.

My eyes travel to the speck in the distance that is Twyla. She's almost out of sight as she climbs the steep hill back towards the peak of the city.

'She can wait,' I tell myself as I shift my weight and shadowfold into the alley beside the tavern.

I peer out to check that the coast is clear but I roll my shoulders back nonetheless, as I shroud myself in shadow and step out into the darkened street. Several yards ahead, I catch a glimpse of auburn hair and my mouth curls into a devilish smile as I begin to follow.

CHAPTER TWENTYONE

The morning of the next trial arrives and I'm awake before the sun has risen above the horizon.

I draw myself up, rubbing a hand across my face, blinking away the blurriness from my eyes, my mind and body exhausted from the constant tossing and turning. My thoughts are jumbled and I've long given up on trying to manage them throughout the long night. The letter addressed to my uncle, which I'd begun writing in the wee hours of the morning, lays half-finished on the table, the quill laying across the page, staining the corner with droplets of black ink.

My balcony doors are wide open, the sheer curtains billowing from the cool morning breeze. I watch and listen, content in my silence as I mentally prepare for the next task. I had heard from Melek late last night that the event had been pushed forwards due to the growing restlessness spreading throughout the castle. I sit up in bed and flinch at the feeling of dampened sheets, only to pull back the covers and find them stained red. I release a frustrated sigh and climb out of bed, ripping away the sheets from the bed and bundling them up in a pile beside the door.

I bathe and dress quickly, combing out my hair long before Hesta, Sarleigh and Perin arrive in my room. They blink in surprise when they walk in to find me dressed and waiting.

"Good morning, Nesryn," Perin says brightly.

"Good morning, ladies," I answer with a soft smile.

Sarleigh glances down at my custom wrap-around tunic and stretchy cotton trousers, accompanied by soft black shoes with rubber soles. Just as my vaita does, the ensemble matches my family's crest. The fit is both flattering and comfortable, freeing up my movement for more of a physical trial. I'm grateful for the base colour of black and I shift uncomfortably in my seat as I try to subtly adjust the folded cloth in my undergarments.

Perin however glances at the bed in disarray and moves to fix it without a word.

"Are you so eager for your trial? It doesn't yet start for another five chimes," Hesta comments with a chuckle, stepping further into the room.

"I was informed that our trial time had changed. It now begins at nine chimes," I blink, confused.

Hesta stops short and glances at the others, sharing a look before her attention shifts to the clock hanging on the wall.

"Oh, goddess. Sarleigh, see to it that her hair is braided tightly. We don't want it getting in her way."

"I'll make sure the kitchen knows of the changed plans," Hesta continues, making her way to the door.

I watch as she hesitates before the door, cocking her head at the bundled sheets. She glances back at me with a small smile of understanding and despite the heat climbing my neck, I smile back.

"I'll see to these," she says to my relief as she bends down to bundle them up into her small arms.

I watch on as she leaves me with Perin and Sarleigh who quietly tend to my hair, looping the strands into tight braids that follow the shape of my head and continue down my back. It doesn't take long to finish the two braids and I sit twisting my head back and forth as I admire them in the mirror.

"Thank you," I smile.

"Do you want us to tie it higher up for you?"

"No, that won't be necessary," I answer, getting to my feet.

I watch as Perin glances between the clock and me with a wary look on her face.

"You'd better hurry on after Hesta if you want to make it in time for breakfast," she tells me.

The dining hall is silent save for the sound of clinking cutlery as the handful of girls dotted about the table busy themselves with their meals. Twyla and Ovie look up to meet my gaze as I stride through the door, but their attention quickly returns to their meals. Only Ria and Mas smile and beckon me closer.

I move further into the room, seating myself across from the girls. I take in their matching attire, the same wrap-around tunic and cotton trousers as mine, their family colours bright and vibrant against their paler complexions.

"Does anyone know why things have been hurried along?" Mas asks quietly, her own braid falling over her shoulder as she leans in.

I shrug as I reach for the steaming pot of molten chocolate and pour myself a cup whilst adding two mint leaves. "I thought maybe one of you might have known."

"I overheard some of the staff mentioning how some of them were preparing the gardens for us," Twyla comments from across the table.

Our attention shifts as we turn towards her, my eyes meeting hers over the rim of my cup. She too has her hair braided and twisted into an oval-shaped knot on the top of her head. The look gives her an edge, accentuating her almond-shaped eyes and the smattering of freckles across her nose and under her eyes.

"What do you suppose the challenge is?" Ria asks her.

"Whatever it is, we need to be cautious," Vena cuts in.

I blink in surprise and turn to her. Her dark eyes are on me for a moment longer before they scan the faces of the others around the table. The others fall silent as Vena draws in their attention and the tension is felt across the table.

"Whatever this next trial is, it will have an element of danger. Keep sharp," she warns.

"Someone will still be eliminated," Ovie comments.

"Eliminated, not seriously injured," Vena snaps, giving Ovie a dark look.

"Or worse," Ria murmurs.

As if on cue, Melek steps into the doorway just as the clock chimes nine times, ringing out across the dining hall. He takes in each of us as our conversation dies down.

"It's time," he announces.

We're led outside into the gardens and past the courtyard where I notice splatters of Chandra's and the Aslitír's blood now dried and staining the soft grey stones, and I force myself to look away as a wave of nausea washes over me. We pass the tall hedges and move through the section of gardens where the SunMoon ball had taken place. We stop after the stables, where the space opens up into a wider area of trees and beautifully carved statues. There are several fountains scattered about, separated by low hedges and tall trellises of colourful roses and honeysuckle.

The warm breeze filters through the trees, wafting the smell through the air. I'm admiring the space when Melek stops in front of me and hands me an envelope. He continues down the line, passing each girl their own envelope before he steps back.

"You have until sundown to complete your next task. I shall come and find you then. Good luck," he tells us, before walking through us and back towards the palace.

I glance at the others who already seem to be busy opening their envelopes. The uneasy feeling in my stomach settles slightly as I rip through the paper and pull out the card within.

> Words of stories left unsaid,
> Tear away fate's outer shell.
> The beast within cannot be fed,
> Deep inside thy Sunwake well.

"What could that even mean?' I wonder, frowning at the words.

I dare to sneak a glimpse at the others lined up beside me and I find myself relieved to find several of them wearing the same expression as me. Vena, determined, is the first to break away and strides with purpose deeper into the gardens and disappears from view. Next is Maskia, then Zariya. Twyla and Ovie move off together, leaving just Ria last. Ria turns to me and gives me a reassuring smile.

"Luck be with you," she utters before she too leaves.

I take a breath and read through the riddle one last time before I move after her.

'*Let the trial begin,*' I think grimly to myself.

I move further into the gardens, losing track of the girls as they split up, venturing off in search of the answer. I examine the paper in my hand, following the narrow slate path through the shrubbery, still unsure of the riddle and its meaning.

"The beast within?" I wonder aloud, furrowing my brow.

"What in Asteria's name does that mean…" I trail off as I turn the corner.

Looking up, I notice that the little path has led me into a smaller section of the garden, filled with flowers of vibrant red, burnt orange and bright yellow, all with hints of gold. To my far left, is a cluster of young trees with deep and rich coloured bark, their branches reaching out across the sky, offering cool shade from the harsh rays.

In the centre of the garden is a beautiful onyx sculpture of a woman looking up towards the branches. Her face is serene and one hand holds the shawl draped around her tightly, while the other is held out as if to catch the falling leaves from above. The scene is beautiful and I stand and stare at the craftsmanship for several moments before shaking my head and stepping further into the garden, eyes alert.

As I explore, however, I come across nothing but budding perennials and trumpet vines amongst dahlias as I move furtively around the statue searching in every direction.

"Nothing," I mutter as I move towards the arch leading out of the space.

As I round the corner, I collide with someone and stumble back, drawing my fists up to cover my face in a fighting stance. My eyes meet Twyla's as she rights herself and furrows her brow at me, her lips pinched.

"Look where you're going," she snaps, barging past me.

I drop my fists and roll my eyes, ignoring the comment before continuing on. Glancing over my shoulder at her, I notice her do the same, only this time her expression is one of curiosity. She disappears in a flash. I notice Ovie and Vena rush ahead of me, dipping through the gaps in the shrubs, and following the many weaving paths clearly designed to disorient. Despite seeing them run around the gardens, I keep my pace slow and steady as I follow the path through another arch of flowers and into another private garden.

I stop short, my eyes widening at the layout before me. If the last garden was vibrant and colourful, this one is the complete opposite. White frills and white roses fill the flower beds around the space. The sculpture is made of marble so white that it glows in the light of the sun. This one is carved into the shape of a girl on the floor with flowing skirts curling around her in a wide circle. As I walk around the statue to take a glimpse at her face, I lean in to see the snowflakes delicately carved to look like they've landed on her skin. I inspect the statue carefully, my eyes travelling between the detailing and the flowers surrounding it. Suddenly, an idea begins to take root.

"If this one symbolises Snowhold and the other Barrenfall... then there must be others which symbolise Warmwell and Sunwake," I murmur.

'*The seasons,*' I realise.

I pull out the paper and read the last line out loud.

"Deep inside thy Sunwake well. *Oh!* The answer is at the Sunwake sculpture," I murmur as I work it out.

I speed walk around the woman covered in snowflakes and make my way through the archway and back to the main path. I spot movement through the hedges and break out into a run, rushing through the maze in search of what I'm looking for. I'm weaving through the trellises and heading towards the other side of the gardens when I hear an earth-shattering scream and judder to a stop, my heart pounding in my chest. I follow the sound, surmising that it's coming from within the Sunwake garden. Snapping out of my frozen posture, I run as fast as I can towards the sound. Ahead of me, Vena comes to an abrupt stop all of a sudden as she hears it too. She hesitates as if debating something, before turning and running away from the tormented screams.

I furrow my brow, anger rising within me.

'*Coward,*' the thought burns brightly in my head and I continue towards the sound.

I speed through the archway and grind to a halt before the sculpture, taking in the smooth curves and intricate details of the piece, a woman made of white marble with streaks of gold running through it. She's surrounded by sunflowers and yellow roses, their scent potent in the still air, filling my nostrils with their perfume and causing my eyes to water slightly. I walk hastily around her, immediately noticing the gravel path leading through the tall hedges and beyond to what looks to be a tiny grove.

The screaming has stopped, but it isn't long before I begin to hear the whimpers and the sound of shifting soil. I could swear it sounds like someone is being dragged.

"*Help,*" the voice pleads.

I sprint down the path to the grove and skid to a stop on the gravel when I see the well. A hand bursts into view from inside and grabs the wall. I snap out of it and rush over to help them. Before I have a good hold on them, a huge flurry of colour shoots from the well with an almighty whoosh, throwing me backwards and landing me unceremoniously on my backside.

The ground shakes slightly as something lands, stopping only a few feet before me, casting me in its shadow. I look up and my heart pounds faster in my chest, from fear or wonder, I can't tell. I take in the auburn feathers and the large black eyes peering down at me, reflecting my conflicted expression.

"A phoenix," I breathe, my voice and body trembling.

It cocks its head to the side, blocking my view as I try to look past it at the girl groaning as she hauls herself up and over the edge of the well. She lifts her hand, feeble shadows creeping across the floor and trembling before dissipating as her hand drops.

'A *Shadowcaster*?' I realise in disbelief.

The phoenix hears her and shifts around, stretching its neck in a territorial fashion, and opening its wings and beating them in a threatening way. I don't have time to think about my next move, my body takes over as I scramble to my feet and dart around the phoenix as it snaps at me. I stop in front of my fellow Chosen and turn to face the creature before it can attack her. I splay my arms wide, my expression a mixture of terror and defiance as I roar, asserting my dominance as I hold my ground.

The beast lowers its wings and its feathers flatten as it observes me, seemingly interested. It looks as though it's alight from the way the sun hits its golden and burning orange feathers, like a burning sunset. It's a breathtaking sight, seeing such a rare and beautiful creature up close like this. I'm sure that I'd feel honoured to be in its presence if I wasn't so terrified.

I watch as it peers at the girl at my feet and looks back at me, assessing its next move. As I scramble to work out what I should do, I remember what my tutor had taught me as a child and take a shaky breath.

"Vá cirya'mé," I say loud and clear.

'*You* will not *pass me*,' I reiterate to myself.

The bird draws its head back, tilting it to the side as it watches me with unblinking eyes. I hold my breath, afraid that my command will go ignored. Then, as if the phoenix has finally understood, it takes a step back and stops, holding as still as the statues in the garden.

When I'm confident that it won't try to attack us, I slowly drop my arms and reach into my pocket for the paper. It watches me closely, its black eyes blinking as it keeps its attention on me. I know that if I can keep it distracted for long enough we may just be able to survive this.

"Tana'mé aquet mecin?" I ask, gingerly holding out my riddle.

'Please show me the answer,' I plead.

The phoenix watches me for what feels like several long moments before it reaches around its body and plucks a single feather with its beak. I watch in tense silence as its head swivels around its body and it lowers the large feather into my hands.

My hands drop at the weight of it and I brace my legs to keep my balance. Up close, the feather is the length of my arm and a stunning, vibrant mix of red and orange with hints of shimmering gold.

I look up at the creature before swooping into a low bow.

"Hanta me'amma Ruinè-Willin. Thank you for this gift," I speak clearly as I straighten.

It bows back and soars into the sky, shifting as it twirls and shrinks, diving straight down into the well. As it does so, the large feather in my hands mimics the action, shrinking down to a more manageable size and I slip it into my sleeve. My knees give out as soon as it's out of sight and I heave a sob as I turn to the girl curled up behind me.

A broken noise escapes my lips as I take in the sorry sight of the young woman before me. I recognise her instantly as Zariya but her face is a tangled mess of clawed open skin and clotting blood. Her dark skin is pale and ashen from blood loss and shock, but I'm grateful to hear her shaky breaths nonetheless. My stomach turns as I take in the fleshy mess that was once her eyes and I realise that there's no way that she'll be able to see again.

"Oh, Zariya," I breathe, my hands shaking as I gently reach for her.

She flinches, whimpering in fear and pain as I pull her arm over my shoulders and wrap my free hand around her back.

"I-It knew. It knew what I was," she manages through hiccuped breaths.

Before I can answer, I hear the others running towards us. Maskia is the first through the trellis of yellowed daisies and skids to a halt when she sees Zariya, horror masking her face. Ovie and Twyla are next, followed by Ria, then Vena, the latter slips through the crowd of girls and stops short as she meets my eye.

As soon as I see her, a red mist clouds my vision and I'm up on my feet, leaving Zariya and storming towards Vena. She hesitates and attempts to step back amongst the others, but I push past them. Some are smart enough to give us room as I shove Vena backwards.

"What happened to being cautious? What happened to looking out for one another?" I demand, spit flying from my lips.

Vena moves to shove me back, but I dodge her and throw a punch aimed at her jaw. She is too quick and blocks it, though the force of it causes her to lose her footing and stumble back several steps.

"You're a fucking coward," I yell.

I throw another punch and this time it connects with her chest and sends her staggering back. She clutches her chest as she glares at me. This time when she looks at me there is a fury in her eyes and she strides forward twisting her body to throw a punch at me.

'*Good, fight me you hypocritical bitch,*' I think.

She surprises me with a kick, but I grab her foot and fling it back. I follow after, throwing punch after punch before she dodges my onslaught and kicks me in the ribs. I feel myself fly backwards for several seconds before I land heavily, my back crashing into the hedge, breaking and snapping twigs.

"Stop!" Ria cries as she steps forward, trying to step between us.

"Move," Vena orders her, shoving her aside as we run at each other.

In moments we're a tangle of fists and jabs, moving through the garden in a violent dance. Vena throws in the occasional spinning kick which I quickly learn to block. Just as I feel my body begin to ache, the foreign feeling within me stirs. The sensation is unfamiliar, yet a part of me welcomes it. I feel it grow within me, filling me until it collides with the invisible wall inside me, just out of my reach.

In my frustration, I lash out with a push kick, my foot connecting squarely with Vena's ribs and sending her soaring into the back of the sculpture. She tries to get up but her knees buckle and she slips back down, winded. We glare at each other across the space with heavy, laboured breaths but neither of us moves. Some of the others, I realise, have followed us across the gardens and stand watching us with an equal amount of eagerness and wariness.

With my anger receding, I spit a mouthful of blood onto the grass. I walk over to where Vena is sprawled against the base of the large marble sculpture. I look down at her disdainfully.

"What you did was disgusting. No matter the standing, she needed our help and you abandoned her in her time of need. These trials are becoming lethal and we need to look out for each other."

I turn to the others, looking each of them in the eye as I wipe away the blood running down my chin. I catch Ria's eye and watch as she frowns at me, anger rippling off her.

"We may not have to like each other but we're being picked off one at a time. We're playing a dangerous game. Are we really going to just stand by and let them take us out one by one?" I demand.

"She's right, we need to make a stand," Twyla utters, stepping forward.

"We still have to complete the trial and collect the token," Vena cuts in, getting to her feet.

"I have your token right here," I say, drawing the phoenix feather from my sleeve and holding it in her face.

I ignore the gasps, my eyes trained on Vena's.

"Now, are you going to mean what you say? Or shall we expect more betrayal from you?" I ask cooly.

She blinks and I hide my surprise when she nods, and glances toward Ria before casting her eyes down.

There is no one to greet us in the courtyard, so we move as one into the palace, Zariya barely conscious, her arms slewn across mine and Vena's shoulders. Our progress is slow but as we turn into the hall, I spot Melek, walking towards us from the other end. He slows, momentarily stunned by the sight of us, before reaching us in a few strides.

He opens his mouth to speak but I hold out a closed fist—much to his confusion—and open my hand, one finger at a time until my palm faces the sky. His eyes widen at the feather in the centre.

"You will accept this token as all of ours and you will send for a healer. No more blood will be spilt today," I tell him with a steely gaze.

He blinks, surprised, before his gaze shifts from the feather to me. "That isn't what the king instruct—"

He stops abruptly as his eyes fall on Zariya and her mangled eye sockets. I notice with grim satisfaction that he's turning a pale shade of green, but I don't let that stop me. I glance at Ovie who quickly swaps with me, Zariya groaning as her body shifts under the new support. I inch closer until I'm only centimetres away from Melek's face and I have his full attention once again.

"Another Chosen has fallen during this trial. More blood has been spilt. Your king will accept this or he will have no Chosen to compete," I tell him bluntly.

I breathe a sigh of relief as a yell of agreement erupts behind me.

LYSAN

CHAPTER TWENTYTWO

My eyelids feel like sandpaper against my eyes as I climb the steps towards my room. In my thirst for knowledge, I'd lost track of the hours slipping by and daylight had arrived all too soon, along with the realisation that I was too far out and too tired to waste any energy on shadowfolding back to the castle.

I barely pay any mind to the commotion I hear as I enter the hall, the sound muffled and distant to my ears, as though I'm submerged in a body of water. I had followed Twyla's friend until dawn had broken over the horizon and I realised how long I'd been gone. It had been a pointless pursuit and I had nothing but the same sliver of information that I'd gotten from the tavern.

'*I need my bed,*' I think for at least the hundredth time this morning.

I stop abruptly when I see The Chosen in a cluster, three of them ahead of the rest, the middle girl's arms draped over the shoulders of the other two as they support her. As I get closer, I hear the argument between Melek and Nesryn.

"You will accept this as all of ours. No more blood will be spilt." Nesryn announces.

"That isn't what the king instruct—" Melek replies, stopping short.

His voice is strong and even until he looks at the girl hoisted between the others and falters, the beads of sweat on his brow announcing his discomfort.

I watch as Nesryn glances at another of The Chosen. The Montallet girl snaps to attention and takes over supporting the girl, Zariya. My stomach tightens as I hear the groan that escapes her as Ovie slips into position, pulling her arm over her shoulders and standing there waiting as Nesryn steps closer to Melek, until she's right in his face.

I don't hear the next words, but as curiosity draws me nearer, Melek catches my eye and begins to stumble over his words. Nesryn's attention swiftly falls on me and I'm surprised by the fury in her green eyes.

"What is the problem here?" I manage, pulling my eyes away from Nesryn and turning to Melek.

Before Melek can open his mouth, Nesryn strides up to me, holding out a phoenix feather tightly between her fingers. There is swelling around her eye and her lip is split, blood crusting around the wound. I barely have time to process her sorry state before she's in my face.

"This token will serve as passage for the seven of us into the next trial," she demands.

"Nesryn... Zariya won't be able to—" Vena starts.

"—Shut up," Nesryn snaps over her shoulder.

To my surprise, Vena does, her bruised lips turned into a thin line as she heaves a frustrated sigh and looks to the floor.

When I look at the girl she's holding up, I stop short, my eyes scouring the girl's face... or rather what's left of it.

Slick blood coats the unmarked portions of skin but the tear marks across her eyes are what snags me and I feel my fists clench as I look at her ravaged face. There are sections where I can see the bone, gleaming white through the ripped tissue and bloody flesh.

'*This is what happens when you aren't here. This is what happens when you don't keep your promise,*' I chide myself, Loísia's voice echoing in my mind.

"Has anyone sent for a damn healer? By the goddess, Melek, be useful for once and get help," I order him over Nesryn's head.

He skitters on his feet and rushes away surprisingly fast for a man his age, and one in heavy robes.

I turn my attention away from him and look down at Nesryn, aware that my expression is dark and angry, though from the anger rolling off her and the way her spring-coloured eyes burn bright with it, she doesn't shrink away. In fact, she doesn't budge. I snatch the feather from her hands and turn it around in my own, drawing my eyes from hers to examine it. I purse my lips in fake contemplation before I let my shadows creep up over it, consuming it completely and shadowfold it away, making it disappear before their very eyes.

"What the hell did you just—" she starts, some of the others gasping behind her.

"—Nevermind what I did. Your demands have been met. The six of you will continue with your trials," I inform her.

"I said seven," she argues through gritted teeth.

I lean down so that my face is level with hers. "If you want your little friend to fend for herself, be my guest. It'll be rather tricky with no eyes and half a face though."

My face veers violently to the right as her hand whips out and slaps me hard across the cheek. I blink away my surprise and try to reign in my anger as I slowly turn back to face her, my expression dark and sombre once again.

"I wouldn't try that again if I were you," I growl, standing to my full height and releasing a handful of shadows that twist and writhe around me.

She recoils, a mixture of fear and anger in her eyes as she looks me in the eye for several more moments. She glances at the others and nods once. They hesitate, looking between me and her.

"Take her to her room, make sure she's comfortable," she tells them tiredly.

When they finally start moving and are far enough away, Nesryn turns back to me, her brow knitted as she surveys me for several moments.

"I know the king has done something with Lesya. What will happen to her?" she asks bluntly.

'Lesya? The Raviffete girl?'

When I say nothing she sighs and shakes her head, her eyes growing cold and bitter.

"If anything happens to Zariya, and if I find out that you or the king have hurt Lesya too—"

"—Is that a threat, Nesryn?" I cut in.

Something in her demeanour shifts and I watch as she battles with herself before letting out a shaky breath and meeting my eye.

"Yes. It is," she says plainly.

She doesn't wait for me to answer before turning away and following after the others.

I watch her for a moment, following her steps as she distances herself from me, the niggling question hovering on my lips slipping free.

"Why do you care what happens to them?"

My question is answered by a deathly silence, though her footsteps falter. Her braids sway as she looks up from the floor and she stares straight ahead for a moment before glancing at me over her shoulder.

"Because they're one of us," she answers simply and walks away.

As the words leave her lips, I feel my heart slow as I'm taken back ten years, to the same corridor, but to a different girl. One with golden hair, half-pointed ears and eyes of everlasting blue. Her voice had echoed down the hall with that very same answer.

Despite my obvious absence over the last day and night, Barilius is exuberant when I answer his summons. He gestures me into his study impatiently but with an eagerness that has me wary as I follow after him. He is restless, pacing through his shelves of vials, picking up one and scrutinising it before placing it back on the shelf and moving away to the next. The whole thing has me wondering what has him all worked up.

Across the room his cauldron bubbles and emits a light steam that filters across the room and out of the small window, left slightly ajar. The space is messy and unkempt and I question how many nights the king has been holed up in here, preparing for the final day of The Choosing.

He points to the stool at the side of his desk and I hesitate, looking at him sideways.

"Sit, Lysander," he orders.

When I don't, his demeanour shifts and his molten eyes fade into a dark glare. The sneer that comes with it seems natural after so many years of being on the receiving end of it.

"I think I'll stand, my king," I answer, tilting my head.

"You'll do as I say, boy," he growls.

I flinch at his use of boy, a name he hasn't used in quite some time. I decide not to disobey further and stride forward, sitting on the stool as he goes back to picking vials from the shelves. I say nothing as he drops several ingredients into the cauldron, the contents hissing and gurgling as the ingredients are added.

I note how he stands by the black candle with its forever burning flame. I watch in amazement as he scribbles something on a piece of parchment and brings it to the flame. In seconds it catches alight and with a black puff of smoke, it evaporates before my widening eyes.

"What was that?" the words leave my lips before I have the sense to keep them to myself.

King Barilius whirls around with wild eyes. "Nothing you need to worry yourself with."

"Then is there a reason you called for me, my king?" I ask, eager to be free from his scrutiny.

"You've been quite busy, haven't you?" he says, lowering the vial in his hand, his eyes trained on me.

"Busy?"

"Tell me why my informants are telling me that my Shadowcaster likes to sneak out into the night. *Without* seeking the permission of his king?" he asks.

His voice is eerily calm but I recognise the sheet of jagged ice beneath. I realise my answer must be carefully thought out. I straighten in my seat and meet his eye.

"I was following up on a rumour spreading around about the palace," I answer.

Barilius steps closer, his happy mood gone. He searches my face for hints of a lie, but finds none.

His hair sways as he seats himself across from me, the vial twisting between his fingertips as he regards me.

"What. Rumours?" he demands through clenched teeth.

"Members of The Righteous Hand. Spotted in the city," I answer, the lie easily slipping from my lips.

Barilius scowls and pushes the chair back as he stands, resuming his pacing back and forth across the small strip of floor.

"Righteous Hands? Pah, fools would be more precise," he growls, squeezing the vial tightly in his grasp.

He looks at me and gestures frantically with his hand. "Well, go on, report!"

"Nothing to report, Your Highness. A childish whisper which led to nothing but a waste of my time," I lie.

He bristles, staring through me for several long moments before he comes back to himself and blinks me back into focus. His grip loosens on the vial and he nods, thoughtful.

"Find who started this treasonous lie. I want their tongue," he orders me.

I nod once. "It will be done, my king."

He shifts his stance and opens his mouth to speak, but before he can, I quickly divert the conversation, steering it away from me as I lift a hand and shadowfold the phoenix feather into the space between my fingertips.

His breath hitches and the vial is forgotten. It falls to the floor with a loud clink and rolls away beneath one of the shelves. He steps closer, muttering to himself as he snatches the feather from my grasp and strides back over to the cauldron. He tilts his head to the left, falling silent as he reads through the large open book at the side of the cauldron, before continuing on with his muttering as he drops the feather in.

There is a flash as orange sparks fly from the cauldron, fading as they float through the air. My eyes follow them one by one as they blink out of existence.

"How many survived?" King Barilius asks.

"All of them, though Zariya Gladdreiys caught the beast's claw," I answer, standing.

"Only one plume?" Barilius demands over his shoulder.

'Remember your promise,' I tell myself, as I think of the deal struck with Nesryn.

"Of the many to retrieve it, this was the first," I lie.

"Who?"

"Nesryn Havenore," I answer after a moment's pause.

"Ah, Erathon's girl," Barilius nods slowly as if in approval.

"From what I hear that girl is rather outspoken when the opportunity arises," he continues.

"Yes, Your Highness," I reply.

"She has caught my good graces today, as well as my interest. See to it that a close eye is kept on her for the remaining trials. I have a good feeling about that one," he orders me, lazily dismissing me with a wave of his hand.

"As you wish, my king," I answer.

My stomach drops as I bow, hiding the unease on my face.

NESRYN

CHAPTER TWENTYTHREE

Sleep comes in fitful bursts through the night, my sheets twisted around my legs as nightmares plague me.

Twisted images of the phoenix and Zariya; her face clawed beyond recognition, the splashes of blood dripping to the floor echo through my brain. Then Lesya, glowing under the light of the full SunMoon, her beautiful face twisting and contorting into a horrifying grin. Her bouts of laughter are unending and haunting while tears slip free from her terrified eyes and slide along her cheeks.

Finally, Erryn. Her screams pierce me as she writhes within the black flames. I fight my body to go to her, but I remain frozen, only to watch as her skin blisters and breaks, the heat from the flames causing the blood to evaporate instantly. Horrified, I can do nothing but stand and watch as she falls to her knees and her voice breaks and falters beneath the crackling flames.

I wake with a jolt and the remnants of a gurgled cry on my lips. Sweat leaves a sheen on my skin and gathers in beads at my brow. A few loose coils stick to the slick skin as I suck in uneven bursts of air. My eyes travel around the empty room, from the chair and small table in the far corner to the vanity and the curtains swaying from the slight breeze on the balcony.

"Just a nightmare," I mutter.

I rub a hand across my face and climb out from my bed, grateful to find the sheets still white this time. I pad across the room into the bathroom, jumping back in surprise as I see Perin shutting off the water.

"Sorry, miss. I didn't mean to startle you," she apologises, getting to her feet.

"It's rather early for you to be here, isn't it?" I ask with a gentle smile.

She dips her head and I notice a small blush creeping up her neck. A slip of dark hair falls free from her bonnet and I watch as she twists it back into place before meeting my eyes.

"You've been waking so early that... well... I thought you could use a nice warm soak to help ease you," she answers. "I've added some extra tonics into the water to help with the bruising," she adds, peering at my battered face.

"Thank you, Perin," I tell her, grateful for the gesture.

"The others will come in a short while, I'll let you bathe in privacy," she says. With that, she leaves.

The room is warm and enticing, clouds of moisture hang in the air. The water smells citrusy and sweet and I undress quickly and step into the warm waters. My movements send tiny waves rippling across the surface and clusters of bubbles stick to my shoulders as I immerse myself. As I lie there, I think of home, the scent of the orchards and the narrow halls. I think of my shelves of books and my uncle's company. The thought of him tugs at my heart and I submerge myself further into the warm waters around me.

"I miss you," I whisper to no one, tears pricking at the corners of my eyes.

The others are already standing outside in the courtyard when I arrive. The sky is bright and the air is warm despite the breeze shifting through the air. Vena glances over at me, the swelling across her face more visible than the bruising. We keep eye contact for several moments before she looks away. I consider it a triumph. Ria is standing next to her and her eyes fall on my face.

Ovie stands beside Twyla and Maskia, the three of them talking amongst themselves, though I'm not close enough to pick out anything. Tiredness tugs at me, but I shake it away, focusing on reserving what energy I have for the task ahead.

As I venture closer, I see Ria say something to Vena before wandering over to me, tugging on the ties of her wrap-around tunic. Maskia catches my eye as I pass her, and she steps away from them and over to me, her blonde ponytail swishing back and forth with her movements. She has the widest grin on her face.

"Look at the state of you," she chortles.

Ria gives her a pointed look and she quickly muffles her chiding.

"Looks worse than it is," I tell her, my eyes travelling over to Ria.

She looks at me with an unimpressed expression before shaking her head. "As long as you're both ok."

I shrug. "I'm fine."

"Good, because I'm about to wipe the floor with your arse," she answers with a wry grin.

I frown in confusion before she hands me an envelope. I take it slowly and rip open the seal to read the letter within.

> When the cousins meet the clock,
> To know the tongue one must be taught.
> Count the full and deadly knock,
> All for one and one for naught.

As I look up, I notice Vilkha and Keelhan striding through the archway towards us. I notice Keelhan's shoulder-length hair is tied up into a makeshift bun, his usual attire of the Aslitír's maroon and gold uniform gone, replaced with dark brown leathers. The change suits him and I can't help but note how broad and muscular he seems to be.

"Look lively girls," he calls as he stops several feet away.

I follow after the others and stop on the outside of the group hovering near Keelhan. He takes each of us in, counting heads before he's satisfied and nods abruptly.

"Your next challenge falls into the category of combat. If you haven't already worked that out from Vilkha's fancy poetry," he says loudly, a smirk pulling at his lips as he glances at Vilkha.

"So very amusing, Captain," the messenger murmurs, his hands flattening a crease in his maroon robes.

"You will follow me to the training arena. My men have it all set up for you," he says, turning away.

We follow him across the courtyard and around to the side of the palace. I'm already wondering what type of combat test we have to partake in when my eyes fall on the high walls of the arena. I notice with slight surprise the two soldiers posted on either side of the entrance, armed and staring straight ahead.

It's only as we near that they acknowledge their captain and allow us to pass through. The others murmur around me as we follow the arch overhead. The stone path gives way to dry, barren earth. There are lines drawn across the space with white chalk, faded from the sun. The high walls circle around us and at the far side of the arena, hanging against the wall, are numerous weapons of different sizes and styles. My eyes are drawn to the curved sword hanging on the left side of the display, the metal glinting in the sun.

'*I'll choose you,*' I decide.

"Now listen up," Keelhan calls out to us.

My head snaps towards the sound of his voice and I wander over to him, the others doing the same. He draws his blade from its sheath and looks out over all of us, twisting it in his hands.

I can sense the anticipation of the others, the eagerness to prove themselves. Despite myself, I feel it too.

"The trial is simple enough, the first to draw blood will be the winner and will fight against the others who have won, and so on and so forth until there are but two left. We will then choose your final weapon for you. The one to lose in the final round of combat will stand down as Chosen and return home," he says clearly.

I look around at the others, who in turn do the same, concern laced across their features. Out of the corner of my eye, I spot Vena watching me across the space with a determined gleam in her eyes.

"As there are an even number of you, you'll be sectioned into pairs. Who will be the first among you to step into the ring?" Keelhan continues.

Silence befalls the group, but it's quickly filled with murmured voices as my hand shoots straight up, Vena's too.

"I will," we say in unison.

A grim smile creeps across the captain's face as his eyes meet Vena's, then mine. "Very well."

He and Vilkha part as he gestures to the far wall decorated with a multitude of weapons, each blade sharpened with deadly precision.

"Choose your weapon," he instructs, his voice booming across the space.

Before I can even make a move, Vena's already rushing towards the curved blade that had caught my eye. I mentally curse and rush forward, but it's too late, her hands are already wrapped around its hilt as she admires the steel greedily.

She looks up at me as I come closer, a small triumphant smirk on her lips and I can't help the scowl that surfaces.

"Better luck next time," she says airily as she walks away.

I grumble beneath my breath before turning back to search for a different weapon. As my eyes scour the wall, I spy a set of twin swords. They're at least several inches shorter than Vena's blade, though the curved shape marks them immediately as Elven. The gold woven into the hilts and along the blades gleam bright, fashioned into the shape of a sun and a crescent moon. Something stirs within me at the sight of them and I don't realise that I'm holding my breath until I have my fingers wrapped around the hilts tightly and I release it in a huff. I'm surprised how little they weigh.

"Are you going to keep screwing around or are we going to get on with this?" Vena calls from behind me.

The sensation in my gut strengthens and I tighten my grip on the hilts as I heave a frustrated sigh. I spin around and lock eyes with her before striding forwards.

"Remember, the first to draw blood—" Keelhan begins.

"—Yes, we know pretty boy," Vena cuts in, our eyes locked as she poises for my attack.

I hear Keelhan mutter something before pairing up the others, but I shut out the drone of his voice as I circle with Vena. She moves first, sprinting towards me, blade raised. I lift my left blade to meet it, blocking its path with a long clang that echoes across the arena. I swipe with my right blade, but she draws back and readies herself to strike again. From where I'm standing, I can see the determined gleam in her eyes, the concentration on her face, and the firm set of her jaw before she runs at me again. I swerve this time, spinning away from her steel and coming back around with an attack of my own.

I slam down hard with my right blade, the steel cutting through the air and juddering to a stop with her block. I can feel the surge within as I'm filled with an energy I can't explain. Despite the temptation to tap into it, something within me prevents it and it stays locked behind the wall as we spar. As Vena attacks again, her foot flies out to trip me but I see it just in time. In her momentary distraction, I manage to push her back and knock the sword from her hand. We watch together as it flies across the space and lands in a dusty heap several feet away.

We glance at each other for a split second before she lunges towards her weapon and I throw down my own and lunge for her. We land in a scrambled heap, dust flying everywhere as we fight. When the dust clears, she's on the ground beneath me, my arm raised and poised to hit her again. I stop when I notice the blood trickling from her nose and drop my arm.

"Done," I yell hoarsely across the space to the sidelines where Keelhan and Vilkha are observing us.

I get to my feet with a groan and dust myself off before reaching out and holding out my hand to her. She glares up at me and wipes the blood away with the back of her hand, swatting my hand away as she scrambles to her feet and stalks off.

Over the next hour, we spar off in pairs until we're whittled down to two: Maskia and me. A layer of sweat dampens my clothes and the adrenaline courses through me, keeping the tiredness away.

I wipe away the beads of sweat saturating my forehead as I stand in the centre of the arena across from Maskia. Strands of her golden hair stick to her flushed face, her ocean blue eyes sharp and fierce with determination as we watch each other across the space.

"Lower your chosen weapons!" Keelhan calls.

I watch Mas for a moment who smirks and drops her weapon to the ground, the metal clattering into the dust. When Keelhan clears his throat, I know he's waiting for me.

I glance towards him as his eyes meet mine. The slight wind blows strands of his shoulder-length hair across his face before he draws his hand back through it and turns to one of his Aslitír.

I watch as he motions to the soldier and I spin the swords in my hands once before slamming the pointed ends into the earth, the hilts wobbling.

The soldier steps into the space between us, a wooden box in his hands. He opens it to reveal velvet cushioning, and on it, lay two sharpened blades of what looks like solid gold, each with a ruby handle wrapped in lines of gold. They look as beautiful as they do deadly.

I look at Maskia, who returns my gaze before reaching for the closest of the two daggers. I follow suit, grasping the hilt in my hand as Keelhan clears his throat.

"You will spar, the first to carve a cross on their opponent will be deemed the winner," he explains.

With a silent nod, I turn back to Mas, assessing me from across the space. Around us, another soldier draws a large circle around us, the white chalk arena stark against the dusty earth.

Determination clouding Mas's face, her aqua eyes darkening as she grips her blade tightly in her right hand.

I shift, and position myself ready for an attack, gripping the blade in my hand fiercely. My heart pounds in my ears as the adrenaline kicks in, and I narrow my eyes, feeling ready.

"Begin," Keelhan calls.

Maskia's first attack is deathly fast and catches me off guard. I feel the air caress my face as I swerve back from her swipe at me, blinking in surprise. A knowing smirk tugs at her lips and I pinch mine together, adamant not to underestimate her again.

She inches towards me again, but this time I'm ready for her and I dive under her arm, moving behind her and kicking her backside, causing her to stumble forwards. The others giggle and whisper in hushed tones as Maskia glares at me over her shoulder. She spins on her heels just as I launch into a sudden attack, the dust flying out beneath my feet as I swing the blade at her. She weaves around me with incredible speed before returning my onslaught with one of her own.

We move with a fluidity and speed that causes the world around us to blur as we continue in a rhythm of meeting one another's attack.

I feel myself begin to tire as we continue on this path, and I notice from the slowness of her swipes that she feels the same.

"You need to work on your stance if you're to ever get a shot at the upper hand," Jarek's voice filters into my mind.

As she moves to swipe again, I shift, remembering the long arduous lessons with Jarek. The way he'd kick me into position, twisting my body, and shifting my legs and arms until my body remembered the stances with the smallest remark from him.

'*Time to shift it up,*' I tell myself.

In the time that it takes for Maskia to launch herself into another frontal attack, I've shifted the blade from my right hand into my left and twisted my body into a fighting position that I imagine Jarek would be proud of.

I slice through the air, the swing of my arm wide as she jumps back. Her ponytail swings out, catching the blade and a section, several inches long, falls to the floor. We pull apart, both of us watching the hair fall before meeting each other's gaze. Something in our fight has shifted; a deadly calm has settled over me. Her change of demeanour is evident as her eyes narrow. A bead of sweat crawls down her temple as silence envelopes us, the air wrought with tension.

Then, it snaps and she suddenly lunges forward, a war cry flying from her lips while the blade in her hand swipes in a figure of eight. She moves in on me with cat-like precision and I find myself impressed with her form. I evade her, running towards her attack and sliding across the arena on my knees, arching backwards under the swing of her dagger.

I hear the gasps and cries behind me, but I block them out as I hone in on Maskia, jumping to my feet and marching towards her just as she spins. I land a foot in the centre of her ribs and shove her back whilst bringing my blade diagonally down, then upward across her cheek, hoping the tip has nicked her skin as she's sent sprawling backwards.

I heave shallow breaths as she stumbles backwards and falls precariously onto her backside, dust flying around her, the dagger somehow still in her hand.

I stalk forwards when Keelhan's voice stops me in my tracks.

"Wait!"

I watch as he steps forward, his hair falling over his shoulders to his chest as he strides towards Maskia. I follow him, peering hesitantly over his shoulder at my flustered friend. Across her cheek is a small cross, welling with blood.

A pang of guilt wells in my chest at the sight of it.

"Well, it may be small but it meets the requirements all the same. We have a winner," Keelhan announces, straightening as he takes Maskia's dagger.

He turns and grabs my wrist in his hand. Without warning he lifts it into the air, only dropping it as the small unison of cheers die down.

"Congratulations," he says, meeting my eye as he holds out his hand.

"Thank you," I answer, handing him the dagger and quickly moving past him.

I look down to Maskia who in turn meets my gaze with one of resignation. Holding out my hands to her, I give her an apologetic smile which is met with a genuine smile back as she takes my hand and I hoist her back to her feet.

"You fought well," she admits.

"As did you," I reply.

"But let's not do this again for a while. I prefer being on the other side of a blade," she continues, bringing her fingertips to her bloodied cheek, smearing the thick liquid.

"Yeah," I chuckle, bumping shoulders with her as we join the others.

"And did it have to be the face?" she asks playfully, pulling a face.

At this, I throw my head back and laugh.

Keelhan leads us back to the courtyard where Vilkha is left in charge of escorting us back to our rooms to prepare for dinner.

The exhaustion has slowly crept up on me and after spending the entire afternoon in a dusty arena under the fierce sun, I find myself welcoming a well-deserved soak in my scented bath.

The group is quiet as we move through the hallways after the messenger, the sounds of our footsteps bouncing across the high walls and ceilings as we walk in single file back to our rooms when one of the girls behind me suddenly breaks the silence as we turn onto our corridor.

"Oh," Mas breathes behind me.

I hear a dull thud, followed by several gasps and Ria's cry cuts through them. My eyes widen at the sight of Maskia crumpled in a heap on the floor.

I rush back to her immediately, dropping to my knees beside Ria who's already pulled her into her lap, brushing the loose hair away from her face.

"What happened?" one of the girls asks over my shoulder.

"Is she alright?" asks another.

But I barely register them, the sounds muffled as I frantically search Maskia's face. It's drained of colour, the cuts on her cheek flecked with dried blood, and her eyes glassy as they lift to meet mine, her breathing laboured.

"I don't feel so well," she manages.

I move a hand to her forehead, feeling the heat pouring from it, and look to Ria with growing fear.

"She's burning up," I say quietly.

I run the back of my finger across the unmarked side of her face as my mind tries to come up with an explanation.

I look at Ria with fear closing around my heart and squeezing my chest. Wordlessly, she lifts her face to Vilkha who is now standing behind me, gaze icy and hostile.

"Send for the healer, and report to your king. Tell him another Chosen has fallen."

CHAPTER TWENTYFOUR

My breaths are heavy and uneven as I bury myself in the woman beneath me, her body wrapped around my own and her nails digging into my back. I block out the sharper angles of Gracie's face, imagining them softer as I close my eyes and see *her* behind the darkness, like a beacon of light beckoning me to her. The moans that slip free from her lips tug me away from her image, ruining the fantasy momentarily, until I draw it back together. Until it's just Loísia, only her.

'*Loísia*' my mind reverberates with her. Her smile, her voice, her body.

I see her, feel her body beneath mine and my body speeds up, thrusting faster, harder. But then the words come back, tearing my vision apart.

"They're one of us."

It's *her* lips moving, *her* imploring eyes. But it's Nesryn's voice that comes out.

I pull myself free of the girl beneath me and lay back on the bed, panting with effort as she slides her leg over me and runs a hand across my sweat-slickened chest. I glance distractedly at the top of her blonde head with a furrowed brow, moving to stroke it whilst blocking out the fact that it's two shades too dark.

When I feel her hand reach down and begin to play with me, her soft caramel eyes reaching up to search mine, the fantasy is shattered and I push her away, sitting upright as I reach for my trousers. I feel the bed shift as she lifts herself up onto her elbow.

"You're leaving?"

"I am," I answer over my shoulder.

"Your time isn't up, my lord. Was it something I did?" she surmises.

I laugh bitterly and shake my head, before running a hand down my face. I shift on the edge of the bed and look at her. She's young and pretty enough to catch a man's eye. But her bright brown eyes aren't Loísia's frosted blue. Her blonde waves which curl around her bare breasts are too mousey. And despite the urge for connection, for physical touch, my heart just isn't in it. My thoughts are too scattered for me to find the release I crave.

"I'm no lord, Gracie. You know that," I tell her. "And no, you're not the issue here, so I'll take my leave," I continue as I get to my feet and reach for my tunic.

"Then here," she says softly, reaching around me towards the small table beside the bed.

I watch as she grabs a handful of coins from where I placed them and leans across the bed towards me, the buckles stacked along her flattened palm. My eyes move from her hand to her serious face, and I tilt my head to one side, perplexed.

"You overpaid," she states matter-of-factly.

I reach out, and fold her fingers over her payment, shaking my head once.

"No. I didn't."

Without another word, I grab my leather holster and loop it around my hips, my sword slapping against my leg as I tighten the straps. I glance at Gracie once more, my eyes travelling over her ample body one last time before I head for the door.

The palace is surprisingly thriving with life when I return, the dusk creeping into the warm evening. Maids bustle about cleaning the rooms of The Chosen, and pairs of Aslitír patrol the corridors as I slip past into the kitchens.

The sweet aroma of fresh pastries and bread wafts through the air, causing my mouth to water and I try to remember the last time that I ate. I pass the workers, some of which eye me warily as I saunter through and collect a fresh pastry from the pile cooling on the counter.

The first bite is warm and rich, the smooth custard centre melting on my tongue as I savour it. My stomach growls in appreciation as I head back towards my room. As I turn the corner, I stop short, the mouthful of pastry turning to tasteless mush in my mouth and I swallow it with a shudder.

Ahead of me, hanging around the door to my room, is Keelhan, with a troubled yet faraway expression on his face. I'm immediately taken back to the last time that I saw him, the anger that controlled his features and the sharpened tongue that unleashed his fury.

These kinds of things were normally water under the bridge, but this time was different. He'd overstepped the mark. We rarely fought like this and unease tugs at me with surprising strength. I remain where I am, carefully reading his stance and the way that he keeps shifting from one foot to the other with an impatience I've never seen in him before. He's uncomfortable. I wonder how long he's been standing there waiting.

I'm not in the mood to talk and I have no desire to hear what he has to say. As I turn to walk away, a new destination in mind, he looks up, noticing me.

"Lysan," he calls, pushing away from the wall.

Irritated, I roll my eyes and turn away to walk back the way I came. I hear his rushed footsteps as he runs to catch up with me.

"Dammit, Lysan, we need to talk," he shouts after me.

"I think you said enough the last time I came to find you," I reply over my shoulder.

I hear his step falter for a moment before he resumes his quick pace.

"This isn't—" he starts.

"—I'm not in the mood, *Keelhan*, now isn't the time."

"But we have a problem—it's about the girls!" he calls, the irritation in his voice clearer.

"Figure it out," I growl dismissively.

Before he can answer, I shadowfold out of his sight.

The catacombs are cool and welcoming as I sit beside her makeshift headstone.

"Aflora livitus," I conjure quietly, watching as the purple petals begin to float down to land on the mound of earth.

I lay a hand on the disturbed earth and release a long sigh. "I'm trying, Loísia, but my promise is falling through," I say softly.

My voice echoes along the cavern walls as I sit beside her stone, thinking of the words we'd shared all that time ago.

We'd been in bed, laying together under the sheets, skin to skin when she'd turned to me with her wide blue eyes watching mine. I felt her run her fingers along my jaw, sending my head into a spin.

"He shouldn't be allowed to do this to us, Lys," she sighed.

"It isn't fair," I'd agreed.

"What happens when there's none of us left? What happens if I—"

"—Don't speak like that," I murmured to her, cupping her face in my hand.

Her frost blue eyes met mine, searching as though they held the answers to all her fears, all her troubles.

I wish they had.

Then before I can stop it, the memory switches and my body freezes.

I can hear the screams that tear through the air, the writhing shadows that had erupted from me as I held her in my arms. Her body trembled in my grasp, blood streaking down from the corners of her mouth along her chin and from her nostrils, as her faded blue eyes looked up at me.

"The others... like me," she struggled, her voice raspy and gurgling with blood.

She choked on her cry and she lifted her shaking hand to wipe a stray tear from my face and smiled weakly at me before her face turned serious and bleak once more.

"Save them, Lysander. Do it... do it for me, I beg of you," she pleaded, her teeth stained red behind her wobbling lip.

"I will, Loísia, I will. You have my word," I'd promised, holding her tighter.

"Thank—" she started, stopping suddenly with a wet cough.

I watched on helplessly as she spluttered and choked on her own blood before a breathy sigh left her lips and her chest remained motionless. I watched her face frantically as those everlasting blue eyes I'd come to adore faded into a muted, glassy colour.

"No... no, no, no no," I stumbled, my hand shaking as I wiped the blood away from her pale face.

"Loísia, please," I begged through gritted teeth, her image blurring as hot tears filled my eyes.

When no answer came, I'd buried my head in her chest, my tears wetting her skin where I should've felt her heart beating. But it hadn't. She was gone.

And a roar of anguish poured from me as my shadows encircled us in an impenetrable cocoon of darkness.

I blink myself back into the room, clearing my swollen throat and sniffing as I roughly wipe away the tears I feel running down my cheeks.

"I'm trying, Loísia, but what can I really do?" I ask her.

When my question is met with nothing but silence, my heart squeezes in my chest and I pull my hand back, turning my face away from her grave.

The gardens are welcomingly quiet as I find myself wandering through the hedges, grateful for the night. I'm unsure what drove me to walk through the gardens alone, but surprisingly, it helps more than drinking ale or bedding Gracie ever could.

I shove my hands deep into my pockets and stare ahead along the pathway lit by the full moon and the stars above. My head is a cloud of jumbled thoughts that I can't seem to untangle. It only sours my mood further as more memories of Loísia tug at my heart and strengthen my guilt.

I follow the trail that she used to take through the winding maze of hedges towards the sculpture of Snowhold. As I step through the archway I stop short, freezing on the spot.

The moonlight blankets the space before me, causing the white roses and frill flowers to glow as if dipped in starlight themselves. The marble sculpture of the young woman, with her legs wrapped to one side beneath her flowing skirts, is iridescent, the detailed snowflakes carved atop her cheeks, mesmerising. It stops me in awe every time, taking me back to my bittersweet memories. But tonight, that isn't why I stop. Beneath the shadow of the sculpture sits a young woman on her knees. Her dark curls are loose and free, blowing ever so slightly in the light evening breeze. Her shoulders are slumped and her back hunched, shifting every so often as a sniffle breaks the serenity of the setting around her.

As I step through the archway into the space, my shoes clipping against the stone slabs beneath my feet, her body stiffens and she gasps and spins around, those familiar green eyes watching me. Her lashes cluster together and glossy streaks cut along her tear-stained face. I can still see the bruising around her eye and healing lip and the new cuts and bruising just beginning to appear. I watch her curiously, surprised by her presence and intrigued by what has her in such a sorry state.

Her eyes narrow defensively as she realises who I am. She turns back to face the sculpture, her body now rigid as she looks up at the Snowhold statue's marble face.

"What do you want?" she demands.

I move closer, only stopping when I'm standing beside her at the foot of the sculpture. After a moment, I glance down at her, a part of me irritated at the disturbance of my own thoughts and peaceful evening, until I see the fresh tears slipping down her golden cheeks.

"I came for my own peace of mind," I tell her, keeping my gaze trained on her. "Even us monsters enjoy a quiet stroll once in a while," I add, tearing my gaze away and finding myself focusing on one of the carved snowflakes.

Silence fills the air around us as we share the space, neither of us willing to speak. I can't seem to untangle myself from the thoughts of Loísia and the words Nesryn mimicked in the hall a couple of days ago.

"Something's happened," she admits, her voice cracking.

I blink in surprise as it pulls me away from my thoughts and I slowly lower my gaze to her face. She stares ahead, tears glistening in the light as they fall freely down her face, but she doesn't wipe them away. I decide not to speak, surprised at her sudden need to share her thoughts.

"Maskia's dead," she says, her voice thick as a sob wracks her frame.

The surprise hits me first, followed by an immediate sense of betrayal and guilt.

'You're failing at your promise,' Loísia's voice berates me.

'Could this be what Keelhan was trying to tell me before?' I wonder silently, suddenly angry at myself for not hearing him out.

"What? The Lockport girl... How?" I demand, my brow furrowed.

She looks up at me with glassy eyes of spring green catching the moonlight. Her bottom lip trembles as she fights through her emotions.

"It was me," she admits the guilt in her voice stuns me to silence.

Before I can find my voice, she continues on, dropping her gaze as she speaks. "Our trial was in the arena, w-we had to cut a cross into our opponent's skin and... well..." she trails off, unable to continue.

"Lady Lockport was your opponent," I surmise.

She nods, sniffing as she wipes a stray tear with the back of her hand.

"She collapsed on the way in, the healer told us she'd been poisoned. I-I can only think of the blade I cut her with. I killed her. I killed my friend," she sobs.

I watch her as she breaks down, her body wracked with stifled sobs as she covers her face with her hands, releasing her anguish into them. Unease settles around me as I watch her in silence, unsure what to do.

'*One of us,*' her voice filters through my mind once more.

"Nesryn—" I start, tentatively reaching for her.

She turns and recoils from me, fear and pain coating her features. Before I can utter another word, she scrambles to her feet and rushes away, her coiled curls flying out behind her as she disappears out of sight. I remain where I am, listening after her footsteps as she flees the gardens and heads back towards the palace. A heaviness settles over me, followed by a surge of anger. Without warning, my fist flies towards the marble sculpture, shadows swirling around my fist as it collides with the marble and an almighty crack cuts through the night. I slowly pull back to see the giant split in the young woman's side, tendrils of shadow still wavering around the crack before fading away.

Then, out of the silence, I hear the sound of muted footsteps rushing through the gardens and quickly shroud myself in shadow. I glimpse Twyla as she rushes past the archway and further into the gardens, my curiosity piqued.

Without another word, I slip out of my hiding spot, letting the shadows fall away, and follow after her, pushing all thoughts of Loísia and Nesryn to one side.

'*What other secrets are you hiding, Lady Drullanon?*'

CHAPTER TWENTYFIVE

My head feels heavy the next morning and I feel nauseous from the hours of crying I'd done once I'd returned from my walk in the gardens. I think back to my outburst in front of Lysan and feel ashamed of myself, angry at allowing him to witness my moment of weakness. When Perin, Hesta and Sarleigh arrive with news of the next trial being held at dusk, I quickly dismiss them from their duties and climb back into bed, alone with my thoughts. Guilt twists my stomach into knots, causing the nausea to worsen as I dip in and out of fitful sleep, plagued with nightmares.

At noon, there is a gentle knock and before I can send them away, Ria's and Vena's faces appear through the slim gap in the door. I sit up, propping my back against the head of the bed as they make their way in, shutting the door behind themselves with a soft click. I watch on in silence as Ria walks over to the bed and takes a seat on the edge, close to me. The skin around her eyes looks red and puffy, the warm colour of her grey-blue eyes dull and glassy from crying. Her nose is pink and her blonde hair, separated into twin braids, is tousled and slept-in.

Vena seats herself in the chair across the room, watching us silently. Her sombre look doesn't hide the tiredness in her eyes, or the lines set across her brow. And for the first time ever her sleek silver hair is dragged up into an uneven twisted bun, with wispy strands escaping at every angle. Her lips are pulled down into a slight frown but I can sense her curiosity in her lingering stare.

"We came to see how you were doing," Ria explains as she reaches for me.

I let her, my eyes travelling to our intertwined hands, surprised at how tightly we hold on to one another. New tears prick in my eyes from staring too long without blinking and I draw in a long breath, releasing it in a shuddered sigh.

"We've lost another Chosen. And it's all my fault," I say simply.

"Oh Nes, it isn't your fault. Tell her, Vee," Ria replies, turning to give Vena a pointed look.

Vena shifts uncomfortably in her seat, but as she opens her mouth to speak, I shake my head, silencing her as I look at each of them in turn.

"I've gone over it again and again in my mind, there is nothing out of the ordinary. There is nothing that could've poisoned her except that blade," I tell them.

"You can't know that for sure," Ria reasons.

"Alright, supposing we go with your theory," Vena cuts in, leaning on her elbows on her thighs as her eyes meet each of ours. "Who's to say it was only your dagger that was poisoned?" she continues.

Ria glances between us and shrugs at me. "She has a point, Nes."

"Maybe, both of them were poisoned, but it took making the cut for it to enter your bloodstream. And Maskia never marked you once with her blade," Vena points out.

"But that doesn't matter, because I marked *her*," I argue, my voice breaking as I look away, curling my hands into fists.

"Maskia's death is not on you," Ria tells me harshly, pulling my face back around to meet hers.

"It's on all of us," Vena adds, slumping back in her chair.

"The five of us that are left," Ria mutters as she climbs into bed beside me and rests her head against my shoulder.

I watch her silently, holding her gaze across the space.

"And you're right. No more rivalries, we *survive* the trials together, we find a way out *together*," she continues.

"Together," I agree with a slight nod, content with our truce.

Melek is the one to collect us when the time comes for our next trial. We dress once again in our wrap-around tunics and stretchy cotton trousers, with the black soles to match, before we leave our rooms. Only this time, I make sure to have Stormtip concealed beneath my clothing.

As we're led out single file across the courtyard, I glance up at the sky. The air is surprisingly warm as I look out at the watercolour yellows, rich peaches and vibrant pinks and oranges that make up the dusky sky. Dark grey clouds break up the image as little tiny flecks of starlight begin to poke through.

Ahead, the archway leading into the gardens looks strangely out of place, the iron gateway full of swirling mist and streaks of starlight that I recognise instantly as a portal.

"Where do you think it leads?" Ria murmurs to the rest of us as we stand before it in a short line.

"I don't know, but wherever it does, it can't be good," Ovie mutters in response.

Melek stands before the portal and pulls out a single envelope before glancing at each of us in turn.

"Your next trial lies through the portal behind me, but before you each step through, here is the accompanying riddle," he explains, drawing out the letter and clearing his throat.

> "Retrace the footprints, here to hell,
> Over land and under dock.
> Tear away fate's outer shell,
> Enter by the crimson lock."

He lowers the letter and stands to one side, allowing us passage through the waiting portal. He looks to each of us one last time, his gaze lingering before he gestures for us to step through. Vena glances at the rest of us, a single brow raised before she runs towards the portal and disappears through with a single ripple.

Ria looks at me, reaching over and squeezing my hand before she follows after Vena. Twyla goes next, then Ovie, until I'm the last left. Melek watches me from where he's standing and I take a deep breath, suddenly grateful for the weight of Stormtip as I pick up speed and jump through the portal, the fizzle of magic scattering pins and needles across my bare skin as I'm hurtled through to the other side.

I land with a roll, ending on my knees before slowly getting to my feet. The world sways left and right for a few moments as I gather my bearings. My ears pop as I start to focus on the here and now. I feel the others around me as I begin to take in our surroundings and I stop short as I turn around to see dark, looming hedges that climb high through the gloom and into the grey skies above.

The air is heavy and darkening around us, all signs of the dusk skies gone. There is moisture in the air, curling around my ankles as visible particles of mist. I dare to look ahead at the ominous dark hedges and unease grows in my stomach as I glance at the others who share the same worried expressions.

For several long moments, no one dares to speak, each of us staring at the darkened maze ahead of us and shifting nervously on the spot. Ovie leans forward as she glances at each of us in turn and she clears her throat.

"Any idea what we're meant to be doing?"

"Well, he said: retrace the footprints here to hell, over land and under dock, tear away fate's outer shell, enter by the crimson lock," Vena speaks up, repeating the riddle.

"It's rather vague," I admit with a shrug.

"What the hell is a crimson lock?" Ria cuts in.

"Whatever the case, our goal is somewhere in there," Twyla gestures to the maze.

I inch closer, curious about the endless walls of green and reach out and touch it, searching for a gap or small opening. A sigh whispers along the length of it, the ground trembles slightly underfoot, and I gasp in surprise as the hedges suddenly pull apart, creating a doorway wide enough for me to step through into the maze.

I spin around, my shocked expression matching those of the others. Determination replaces my surprise as I think of Mas. No one else is going to die. We would win this together no matter what. I look to the others in solemn silence, meeting their eyes as I jerk my chin towards the entrance.

They move forwards, one by one, the leafy walls shuddering as the magic comes alive. The hedges open into five separate doorways, one for each of us until the ground finally stills. I take a deep breath and glance at the others one last time before turning to face my doorway and stepping through, the gaps snaking closed behind me, locking me in the maze.

The silence is palpable and the ground thick with unearthly mist as I stalk through the twisting paths, moving deeper into the maze. My breaths are shallow, the blood in my ears pumping as I round another bend, Stormtip clutched tightly in my grasp. I try to listen out for any of the others, but I hear nothing and see no one as I move on. The hedges are too high and unstable to even attempt to climb, and so I quash the idea almost immediately despite my eagerness to find the others.

My unease causes that strange power in me to rise to the surface, momentarily distracting me as I try to fight it back down. As I round another corner, I come to an abrupt stop, my eyes trained on the crossroads ahead. The path forks into three alternate paths; one to the left, one to the right and one straight ahead.

But it's what is in the centre that makes me pause.

Stacked in a pile are weapons. Swords, daggers, an axe, and even a bow and quiver full of steel arrows. I let out a wary breath, dropping my arm, sheathing Stormtip as I sneak forwards, my eyes darting to each of the paths as I stop before the pile.

'*Why would this be here?*' I wonder.

I steal another glance at each direction, trying to peer through the mist and gloom. I strain my ears, only to be met with the ongoing silence. A shiver runs down my spine as I remain standing, an eerie sense of being watched washing over me as I stare at the pile once again.

'*What is it that I need to protect myself from?*' I contemplate.

The ground begins to tremble and the wind picks up, howling through the maze. My heart picks up and I act on instinct, lunging forward and grabbing the hilt of the closest sword. The blade shimmers as I pull it free from the pile and as soon as I do, the ground trembles harder and the pile vanishes from sight.

As the ground settles, I blink and let out a shaky breath as I watch each route, waiting for something, anything to come stalking towards me. When nothing appears for several moments, I relax, my shoulders dropping as my attention shifts to the sword. It's a simple enough weapon, made for use, not for looks. The hilt is sturdy and wrapped in a leathery fabric for better grip, and the blade is curved and deathly sharp. Content with my choice—not that I could change it, even if I wanted to —I take a step forward, eager to carry on when I hear a noise behind me. I freeze, my stomach dropping as I slowly turn around.

The hedge at the end ripples as a giant paw appears, then another, dropping to the ground with echoing thuds. My eyes widen as the creature emerges from the maze's walls, its glowing purple eyes finding me and locking onto me with a deep, rumbling growl. My breath hitches as the creature ventures from the shadows and my jaw drops as I take in its swirling coat. Beneath the black is something *other*, entire galaxies and clusters of stars swimming beneath the dark shape of the puma. Its eyes glow with power and its fangs gleam gold as it growls.

'*That's no ordinary puma*,' I realise.

It crouches back, belly low to the floor, ready to spring and attack as it lets out an unearthly roar.

'*RUN!*' my mind yells.

And in the split second that it takes for the beast to move, I tear through the hedged path, whipping up a trail of mist behind me and skidding around corners. I slam into the leafy walls in my desperation to get away. By the sound of the yowls and the heavy thud of paws, I can tell without daring to glance behind me that the creature isn't far behind.

The air comes alive with sound as I run, the chaotic sound of the others' panicked screams echoing through the air and clouding my judgement. My own sense of panic claws at me as I pump my arms faster. Despite the adrenaline coursing through me, I feel myself tiring, my legs slowing and I know that I'll need to face the beast, sooner rather than later.

Ahead of me, I see another crossroads and I quickly conjure up a plan, hoping and praying that it works. I throw myself into running as fast as I can before turning right at the last minute and colliding headfirst with someone.

I open my eyes to meet a pair of onyx ones as Vena stares at me, panic-stricken. I scramble to my feet, grabbing my fallen sword with one hand and helping her up with the other. She moves to speak but I cut her off with a shake of my head.

"No time," I huff before I turn just in time to see the puma round the corner and leap.

Without thinking, I shove her to one side and throw out my sword in a wild jab, catching the beast along its side. Black shimmering liquid oozes from the creature and spills out across the dusty path as it roars in pain.

As it turns for a second attempt, another creature appears at the end of the way and my mouth goes dry.

The creature is a stunning mixture of swirling blues and whites with a bird's head and a wicked, curved beak. Its neck is long and thick, and its four legs end in rubbery feet with talons so deadly that the phoenix's were child's play in comparison. Its long, feathered tail is covered in colourful plumes that draw the mist left and right.

"What the—" I breathe, stunned.

"Let's *go*," Vena shouts and she grabs me and drags me with her.

I let her pull me back to the crossroads and around to the right, spinning and running after her when she eventually lets me go.

"What the *hell* was that?" I cry.

"A peacock griffin!" she shouts over her shoulder.

"*What*?" I cry in dismay as I follow closely after her.

We round the next corner and she skids to a halt, drawing me against the hedges as we breathe heavily, catching our breaths.

"Don't you see?" she hisses between gulps of air.

I look at her, waiting for her to finish, my heart hammering in my chest as I gulp down mouthfuls of air to soothe my burning lungs. Her dark eyes meet mine, a sliver of her silver hair slipping over her forehead as she looks at me somberly.

"They've pitted us against our mascots," she finishes.

A roar interrupts us and suddenly we're back to running, now at each other's side as we make our way through the depths of the maze.

"I've tried cutting through the walls and forcing my way through, there's no way out," Vena calls to me, shaking her head.

"We have to get to the centre, it's our only choice. There has got to be a way out of here," I answer.

"The crimson lock. Maybe it's our ticket out of here," Vena recalls, giving me a meaningful look.

I nod in her direction as another scream rips through the air. Behind us, I can hear the puma and peacock griffin on our tail and I pray that we are able to maintain the gap between us for as long as we need to.

As we pass through another cross in the path, someone blurs in front of me, colliding straight into Vena and throwing them along the left path. Despite my urge to maintain our advantage, I skid to a stop and round the corner, stumbling straight into the heap of limbs and bodies that make up Vena and Ria.

They groan as they untangle themselves and get to their feet, and I catch a glimpse of something bright orange through the greenery, and my heart picks up pace.

"Ria... Vena..." I call to them in warning.

"Go! We're behind you," Ria yells, kickstarting me into a run.

I hear the yowl of the puma closing in as I fly through the maze, delving deeper and deeper with each twisting turn, praying that my body carries me fast enough. I hear the girls behind me, their heavy breaths matching mine as we follow the weaving path.

My heart falters as I round the next turn, the hedges opening up into a clearing. My stomach drops as dread claws at me, the panic rising in my throat as I realise that I've led us to a dead end. I look around and my hope reignites when I notice a stone archway in the far corner, the keystone reads 'Beauty and Divinity.'

"There!" I point out.

"That's my family motto," Vena announces as we rush towards it.

We glance at each other in mutual understanding. When Vena glances at Ria, she nods towards the archway. Vena steadies her breath and steps forwards, tentatively reaching out her hand.

Nothing happens.

"We're missing something. It's not activating," Vena says.

We hear the sounds of our creatures getting closer, and further afield, another scream fades into the mist.

"We're running out of time. There's nowhere to go," I announce, my mouth dry.

"Shit!" Vena barks, running a hand over her hair.

She paces back and forth as Ria looks at me with an ashen face. She holds out her sword, her hand trembling ever so slightly. "Then we face what's to come, together."

I let out a shaky breath and slowly hold my sword out to match Ria's stance. "Together," I nod.

Ria's lips lift in a ghost of a smile before she turns her gaze, her eyes glassy. I follow Ria's focus to Vena, who is watching us silently. With a sigh, she steps forward, holding out her weapon.

"If this is it, if this is… the end…" she falters as the sound of our mascots close in. "Then it has been an honour competing against you," she manages, holding our gazes.

The moment is interrupted by the arrival of the three beasts: my puma, Vena's peacock griffin, and Ria's bull. We eye them warily, shifting into defensive stances as they make their way into the clearing, each of their luminous eyes set on their target.

I draw out Stormtip with my free hand, my eyes trained on the beast ahead, an intense silence filling the air as each of us size up our opponent. Adrenaline pumps through my veins in anticipation of what is to come. I try to focus on what Jarek had taught me over the years, but only Uncle Erathon's words filter through me now.

'Hear the unheard, see the unseen, and endure.'

"It's been an honour, girls," I mutter as my grip tightens on the hilts of my blades, my eyes locked on to the beast's.

"*No.* No blood but theirs will be spilt today," Ria vows, the anger in her voice rippling through the air.

I'm unsure who moves first but all of a sudden I'm in the middle of the chaos. Claws and deadly fangs come flying at me as the puma attacks, and I quickly block the move with a swift swing of my sword, jabbing the beast with my dagger into its chest. Its roar cuts through me, my ears ringing from the reverberation. This time, I'm disoriented when it swipes again, its claws finding their mark and ripping through my clothes and skin from the top of my right shoulder and along my chest and breasts.

The pained scream that leaves me is cut short by the excruciating sting of my open wounds. The shock takes hold of me before I can block it out. The air squeezes from my lungs and I stumble back. I look down to see my front already covered in blood and the battlecries on either side of me are drowned out by the pulse thudding in my ears. I swing wildly at the creature, but it evades me easily. I'm slow and weakened and losing blood fast. I'm knocked from the side by Ria's bull as it charges her, sending me spinning into the hedge, my eyes rolling back into my head as I try to regain my bearings.

When I manage to open my eyes, the world is no longer spinning. I have little time for relief as I notice with growing dread that my puma is readying itself for its final blow. I scramble to my feet when something out of the corner of my eye catches my attention.

I turn to see Vena battling the peacock griffin, her hair now a mixture of silver and red, her eyes alive with determination. Then, too late, I notice the creature swing out its claw and my strangled cry of warning does nothing but distract Vena from her fight.

The talons have pierced her chest before she can react and her eyes widen in surprise as the peacock griffin lifts her into the air and tosses her across the space. There is a sickening crunch as her body collides with the stone archway before she crumples to the floor like a broken ragdoll.

"No, no, no, no, no," I mumble, my voice foreign to my own ears.

A strangled scream comes from my left as I realise Ria has seen it too and something within me twists. I watch in horror as she drops her weapon and rushes to Vena's side, her face hidden from view.

The peacock griffin gives a final triumphant squawk and leaves the maze as Ria's bull moves to charge my unsuspecting friend and my gaze flits between the bull and my puma to Ria in panic. But Ria is a mess, completely unaware that her mascot is about to strike her dead beside her lover.

As my attention moves back to the glowing eyes of my mascot, its hearty growl rumbling through me as it pounces, something within me snaps. I feel the foreign sensation fill me, fighting against its cage, pushing against my mental barriers until the force of it gets the better of me and the barriers dissolve away into nothing. In my anger, I give in to the power. In the moment, all I know is pain and vengeance.

"Enough," I scream, my throat raw as I throw my hands out.

Light explodes all around me, filling the clearing with blinding white light and as quickly as I throw my arms out, I pull them back in, sheltering my eyes. It dissipates as quickly as it came, the darkness flooding back almost instantly, and the foreign sensation settling once more. When I'm brave enough to open my eyes, the beasts who had been about to kill us are in pieces, strewn across the grass. Where there should be blood, inky pools of black ooze and shimmering gold lay. I'm surprised to find myself steady on my feet when I step forwards and I find that the pain is gone. I look down in amazement at the ripped fabric across my chest to see the healed, albeit pink, skin showing.

Ria's broken sobs pull me from examining my injury and I rush over to Ria's side. Vena lies unnaturally still in Ria's bloody arms. The girl's onyx eyes are vacant and dull. Her rich skin is already turning grey as it loses its radiant sheen. Blood carpets the ground around them both, trickling towards the stone archway.

I look on as the blood touches the stone, watching bitterly as the words etched into the keystone begin to glow and the portal thrums to life. Anger coils in my stomach as I swirl my tongue against the roof of my mouth, the copper smell of blood filling my lungs.

"Ria... I—I'm sorry, but she's gone," I choke.

If she hears me, she shows no sign of it as she holds her lifeless love tightly to her. Her pain is evident but I see that it's the shock that has her locked in place, unable to let go.

A strange feeling climbs up my spine and I glance around, the eerie feeling of being watched renewed. I don't want to stand here any longer than we have to, my growing dread becoming claustrophobic, as though the hedges are closing in on us. I see a flash of something in my peripheral vision and I turn to see a piece of the Zouvsa bull laying limply on the grass. I watch it for a long moment and see a small spark fly from it. My breath hitches and I turn back to Ria still on her knees, swaying.

"Ria let her go," my tone is harsher than I'd like it to be, but we don't have time.

She ignores me and rocks back and forth with Vena's slumped body in her arms, her sobs becoming louder, as she wails in her grief.

"Reverie, dammit, you have to let her go!" I say through gritted teeth at my heartbroken friend.

As I glance at the pieces once more, I spot another spark and I realise that we need to move.

Without another warning, I grab Ria under her arms and tug her away with all my might. Gradually, with another pained moan, and a grunt of effort from me, she releases her and I stumble back with my friend in my arms.

Across the clearing, I notice the body of the fallen bull and puma, piecing themselves back together, the magic that created it replenishing its life, piece by piece. Nausea washes over me. I waste no time in grabbing our weapons and pushing her ahead of me towards the maze, pulling her up when she stumbles.

"Go now!" I yell, pushing her forward through the winding path.

She turns back, and a strangled cry escapes her lips as she looks past me. "No—I can't leave her!"

"You have to! Those things are coming back," I shake my head roughly and push her forward again when she slows.

"Find your gate. It only needs your blood to open. Get the hell out now!" I scream after her.

I watch as she stumbles into a run, her tears still pouring down her cheeks and guilt tugs at me until she's out of sight.

I turn back to the clearing with every intention to push Vena's body through the portal to the other side.

'You're one of us. I won't leave you here,' I think to myself as her face surfaces in my mind.

I clutch Stormtip tightly in my hand as I prepare for what's around the corner, unsure how long it will take for the creatures to regenerate. I round the corner back into the clearing and see the glowing portal, now vacant of magic.

I backtrack to where Ria had released Vena, bypassing the creatures as confusion takes root. I realise I'm not alone when I discover drag marks through the grass, as though someone had clawed the soil. My stomach drops as I notice blood smeared in the other direction towards the hedges. I follow the marks with my eyes and look up, a shiver tingling across the nape of my neck.

Tendrils of darkened shadow swirl around the space, collecting around Vena's lifeless, broken body. They whip about wildly, like a flagpole caught in a vicious storm. This is a different kind of magic. A darker magic. As the whorls of inky blackness whip through the air, there is an urgency in me that tells me to run, and not from the dangers growing behind me. Something calls for me to stay for just a little longer.

I pick out the figure in the eye of the hurricane, engulfed in darkness. A man, clad in black and silver, with piercing eyes of seafoam blue, looks up from dragging Vena's body, wide with surprise. Suspicion immediately fills me as I take in the scene before me. Why would he be here? Where was he planning to take her?

The fragile bloom of trust that I didn't know had been growing within me, wilts and dies in my chest at the sight of him, replaced with burning rage and icy realisation that tastes like frost and ash on my tongue.

'*You have no allies here,*' a bitter voice whispers in my head.

We stand frozen, facing one another for a second more before he vanishes from sight, taking Vena's body with him, his shadows coiling in on him and themselves until I'm alone. I give in to the voice and turn, weaving around the half-restored creatures, and run with all my might through the maze.

The roar that erupts through the silence is too far away for me to worry about as I fly deep into the maze, the blood pumping in my ears and my fury hurtling me on.

I slice the sharp edge of Stormtip across my palm as I find my way into another clearing with the familiar words '*honour and valour*' etched into the keystone. I stride forwards with newfound energy, slapping my bloodied palm against the stone archway and watching as the magic within it hums to life. I step through as the image of what I've seen in this maze burns its mark into my soul.

The king's choosing is no longer my only concern. He doesn't act alone. And as the magic fizzes across my skin and I'm transported back to the palace grounds, I know only this:

Lysan cannot be trusted.

Lysan is a liar.

Lysan is the enemy.

LYSAN

CHAPTER TWENTYSIX

'She saw me.'

I pace back and forth in my room as I consider what this means, consider my next move in the days to come.

'She saw me and I froze like a fucking fool. I'm so weak.'

All this time trying to find a way in, trying to keep my promise to Loísia, wasted with one foolish move. I slam my fist against the wall, my shadows coiling around my knuckles and following the cracks spreading up the wall. As I pull away, they disappear into the darkness.

'Barilius won't be pleased when he discovers that the girl can see through shadows,' I consider. *'Either that or his interest in her will grow,'* I add, my mood souring further.

But how had she seen past my shields? No one could, not unless...

I think back over the times I'd spent in her presence, of all the times she could have accidentally shown me glimpses of any power, any proof that she was like me. I shake the thought away when I come up empty-handed.

"She would have to be as powerful as me to hide in plain sight, and even then Barilius would have noticed the moment he laid eyes on her," I tell myself.

I think back to the maze and my orders to follow the girls in. I knew it was to be enchanted as a part of the trial, but I hadn't realised what the enchantment was until I came across the beasts and my blood had run cold. When I'd finally come across Nesryn, Reverie and Vena, their creatures had been ripped apart by goddess-knows-what and Vena had been lost.

The look on Nesryn's face when our eyes had met stays with me even now, cutting through me as fiercely as it had done then.

She shouldn't have been able to see me, and yet she had. I knew she had.

"*Fuck!*" I growl.

I slam my fist into the wall again in anger, this time smearing blood as the cracks climb higher up the wall. My temple twitches from the pressure of my clenched jaw and shadows coil around the edges of my vision.

I shake my hand once as the pain ebbs through my knuckles as I compose myself, breathing in slowly as I straighten my tunic and smooth back my hair. Determination and anger run through me as my gaze turns towards the door.

"What in the hell was that?" I demand as I burst into the room.

Barilius doesn't even acknowledge me as I stride into his private dining room, his gaze focused on cutting the lump of charred meat on his plate. My anger simmers within me as I stop at the other end of the long table, my power aching for a release that I refuse to give in to.

After several long moments of cutlery clicking together, I watch as he sets them down and lifts his head to watch me. His dark hair is twisted back into a ponytail with a golden clasp holding it back.

"You'll have to explain, boy. I'm in no mood for your guessing games," he drawls.

"The ball, then the phoenix, the deathmatch, and now *this*?" I demand, slamming my hand against the table.

The sound echoes through the space as his eyes burn brightly with silent rage.

"Yes?"

"It's barbaric," I tell him through gritted teeth.

I watch Barilius as he picks at his nail beds, his boredom fuelling my frustration more.

"It's wasteful but necessary," he says, not looking at me.

I slam my hands down against the table, shadows pouring from them and twisting in the air.

"How is any of this necessary? The Chosen are falling one by one, their bloodstains these halls and you deem it *necessary*?" I shout in disbelief.

The air seems to leave the room as the king slowly gets to his feet, his anger palpable. My own anger fizzles out, replaced with sudden unease. The shadows curling around my hands fade into nothing and I feel my heart falter as the tension in the room rises.

"You dare to question my authority?" he asks softly, though the tone is as sharp as ice. "Remember who you stand before, who you have pledged your loyalty to," he continues as he rounds the table.

I straighten, angling my body to face him.

"Need I remind you of the last time you dared to do so, boy?" he says as he comes to a halt in front of me, his fiery eyes challenging me.

Before I can stop myself, my mind takes me back to the dank, barred room several levels below. The echo of scuttling rats and dripping water rings in my ears until the grinding sound of heavy metal fills my head and sends a jolt of dread through me. I subconsciously reach for my neck, as if the dimming collar is still locked in place, rubbing against my throat.

"No… my king," I say, slowly lowering my hand to my side, swallowing the words I wish to say.

"Question me again and I will strip away more than just your dignity," he says plainly, but I hear the edge to his voice.

It's a warning he won't let me forget.

The room is tense and quiet, the workers silently shuffling about the room, clearing away the king's meal, while Barilius's gaze remains locked with mine. His voice is a harsh sound against the silence when he speaks again.

"Melek," he calls.

"Yes, Sire," the messenger answers, scuttling out from a dark corner and into view. He stands patiently, waiting for the king to speak.

"Notify The Chosen that there will be no more trials for the time being. I want them well-rested," he orders.

Dread coils in my stomach but I keep my face unreadable, the king's eyes still on me as he speaks.

"And you, boy. You will inform them that I plan for them to join me for dinner in three days' time."

My mind runs wild with possibilities as I move through the palace, contemplating what the king's plan could be for the last few girls.

'*What is he planning*?'

I'm so caught up with my own thoughts as I round the corner that the punch to my gut takes me by surprise, winding me as I stumble back. I look up to meet green eyes alive with a mixture of anger and pain. I notice the sunken shadows beneath them as I fall still, suddenly frozen on the spot.

Her braided hair is caked with dust and spattered blood, and her face is no better, the flaking crusts of blood across her cheeks hard to ignore. Her clothing is ripped in places, nicks and scratches visible beneath, raw and fresh.

"Where is she? What have you done with her?" The rawness of her voice tells me of the hurt behind the anger as her arm swings out towards me.

"Nesryn I—" I start, unsure of what to say as I think of the freshly dug grave deep in the catacombs.

I dodge her attacks effortlessly, her swings, though wild and erratic, are teeming with rage, slowing her speed and altering the precision of her blows. I don't have to watch her fight me to see that the earlier trial has exhausted her, that her body is running purely on adrenaline and anger.

"You *knew*. This whole time you fucking *knew* what it meant to be Chosen. You knew our fates and you did nothing," she yells at me, her eyes now wet with angry tears.

Frustration and guilt fill my chest with a sense of powerlessness that makes me snap. Her truth is like ice in my veins and before I can stop myself, I lash out, shadows swirling around me, lifting her and flinging her across the hall, pinning her writhing body against the wall.

I glide towards her, my mouth set in a snarl as I take in her glare, her snarling lips as she fights against her bonds.

"How many of us have you watched suffer? How many of us have you watched die at the hands of your king?" she spits, and I turn my head, wiping the saliva from my chin.

Loísia's face appears in my mind's eye, the pleading look in her eyes changing to one of resentment and bitterness. Her promise burns holes in my fury until I have nothing left but the bitter hollow words that Nesryn had thrown at me during the SunMoon ball.

'You're a villain, a blight.'

My shadows waver and disperse with my anger and she drops to her feet with a thud that echoes along the empty hall.

"Nesryn, there's something—" I start, unsure of where my tongue is leading me.

There is the sound of steel cutting through the air and I suddenly feel the cool metal of her blade against my throat, my words lingering and dying under its tip.

"I'll kill you for what you've done," her words are coated in ice.

Despite the emptiness in my chest, a smirk appears on my lips as I meet her fiery gaze. "Maybe one day, princess, but not today."

Before she can open her mouth, I shadowfold out of her grip.

It's late by the time I eventually leave The Velvet Feather, my tunic ruffled and only half-tucked into my trousers. My head is foggy after the many hours spent in Gracie's bed ingesting heavy ales and having my fill of her. As I stumble into the street, I run a hand through my hair as it flops down over my forehead, the sweat from my brow having melted away the lotion I use to slick it back.

Nesryn and Loísia's words blur into one as I make the journey home, and by the time I've reached the doors to the palace, I know what I need to do.

The room is dark and quiet as I shadowfold into the furthest corner. Across the way is the four-poster bed. In it, my target.

I don't bother with discretion, stepping into the dim light and clearing my throat. Almost instantly, I watch Twyla bolt upright, quickly drawing a small dagger from under her pillow and pointing it towards me, her chest heaving with erratic breaths.

"There's no need for that," I tell her, folding my arms.

She says nothing, refusing to lower her blade.

"I come unarmed," I continue, unfolding my arms and holding out my hands.

"That doesn't mean *shit*, Shadowcaster. I know who and what you are," she answers, the disgust in her voice evident.

"And I know who *you* are, little spy," I reply, narrowing my eyes as a smile creeps along my lips.

Her arm slackens and her eyes gloss over with newfound fear.

"Though I've quite enjoyed joining you on some of your little adventures, all good things must come to an end. So don't try to move against me, little pigeon, because this knowledge will find its way to the king. You'll be dead within the hour, and that *would* be a shame," I reply.

"What..? Y-you're not going to kill me?" her brow knits together in confusion.

"Now, why on earth would I want to do that?" I ask, tilting my head to one side.

"I could think of plenty of reasons, though I'm sure you of all people don't need one. You thirst for blood as much as your twisted king does," she sneers.

"My business doesn't concern the king, but it has everything to do with you," I reply, watching as she flinches under the sheets.

I step into the pale moonlight that filters through the curtain. She watches me warily and I notice with slight amusement how her hand trembles as she holds out her weapon.

'*That little trinket won't save you from me,*' the thought echoes in my mind.

"No... No, I'm not going to kill you," I drawl, giving her the impression that I'm thinking aloud. I watch as she visibly relaxes, just slightly.

"Because you're going to help me with something," I finish, the corner of my mouth lifting into a smirk.

NESRYN

CHAPTER TWENTYSEVEN

The promise I'd made rings hollow in my ears as I stride the hall, my earlier anger now a void of emptiness since Lysan slipped away like sand through my fingers.

I move along the halls with purpose, my nerves twisting knots in my stomach as I make it to Ria's door. Unsure of what I may be walking into, I try my best in the next few seconds to prepare myself. I pause when I realise I expected to hear her sobs through the door, but instead, I hear deathly silence. I take a breath and reach for the handle, not bothering to knock before walking into the room.

I glance around the room and blink in surprise when I find it seemingly empty and neat. It's dark and cold, like a shadowed husk. I'm not prepared for the eerie silence that greets me either. It's only when I hear a shuddered breath from across the room that I realise I'm not alone.

"Ria?" I say slowly.

I drop my shoulders and cross the room, passing the first bedpost and peering around the side of the bed to find Ria's familiar form huddled up in a ball. Her hair is a tangled mess of bloodied braids and her face is pale, blotchy, and tear-stained. I notice grimly how much of her is covered with blood and I can't help but wonder how much of it belongs to Vena.

I lower myself down beside her, my body protesting as I move. The floor is hard beneath me, the cold of the stone seeping up through the thick rug and into my bones. I brush shoulders with my friend, scooting closer to her.

"She's gone," she says, her voice thick from crying.

The numbness in her voice has me lost for words and I slide an arm around her shoulders, squeezing them. Silence envelopes us as I try to find something to say, but nothing comes to mind.

"Ria I—" tears prick in my eyes as I start.

I look at her as I blink away the tears, taking in the muck and grime caking her face. The blood has soaked into her clothes and stains her hands, curled up in her lap.

"Let's get you cleaned up," I tell her softly.

She lets me help her to her feet and lead her into the bathroom. She sits wordlessly in the corner, perched on the toilet seat as I move about the room, lighting the candles and running the bath for her, pouring in an array of sweet lotions and salts as I've seen my handmaidens do with my baths.

When it's ready, I strip down to my undergarments before she silently lets me peel her own clothes away from her trembling body. In the dim light, I see the scratches and bruises across her body and I make a mental note to seek the healer for her special tonics. I lead her to the sunken bath, the hot water rippling as we step into it. I sit her down and get to work untangling her braids and washing out the blood and dirt. I wash her skin as she stares blankly at the wall, shadows from the candlelight dancing across her face.

When she's finally clean and dry, I rummage through the drawers, pulling out a pair of cotton trousers and a matching long-sleeved shirt. My breath hitches as I note the rich blue and white colours, recognising them instantly as the colours of the Astalón House.

"Those are Vena's," Ria's voice cuts through the silence, her voice still raw.

I start at the sound, bunching the clothing up in my hands as I turn towards her, noting her eyes fixed on them. She reaches a shaking hand out for them, her eyes glossing over.

"I'll wear them," she tells me.

I don't argue and hand them over to her to dress herself. She does so quickly, wrapping her arms around herself once she's done. I gently lead her back to the four-poster bed, lifting the quilt for her to slip beneath. I turn to leave when I hear her move.

"Please don't leave," she whispers.

I give her a small smile and nod, turning back towards her. She shuffles over and I climb under the quilt with her. We sit like this for several minutes before her breath hitches.

"I can't believe she's gone, Nes," she whispers into the darkness.

"I know, Ria, I know," I answer, gently patting her hand.

Her body begins to tremble, shaking beside me as sobs begin to wrack her body once more. The sound of her heart breaking tugs at my own. I can't bear to see her face crumpled in pain. I slip my arms around her as she buries her face in my chest, a low moan escaping her through her tears. The sound of her grief is overwhelming as I try with all my wavering strength to hold the broken pieces of her together.

I stay with Ria until she's fallen into a deep sleep before I put the rest of the clothes back on and slip away, shutting the door with a soft click behind me.

My clothes are grimy and bloodied but I don't return to my room, deciding instead to walk the halls in a feeble attempt to clear my head. The night is inky black outside the window and I can't help but feel surprised. It feels as though days have gone by when only a number of hours has passed. Exhaustion tugs at me but my head is too full and my heart too fraught with emotion to attempt to sleep.

I let my feet lead me along unfamiliar corridors and down zigzagging steps towards the lower levels of the palace. Rows upon rows of simple wooden doors run the length of the narrow hall, and I let myself wonder whose rooms these doors belong to. As I come to the end of the hall, I come to an open door that leads to another flight of stairs, heading deeper into the belly of the palace. I'm aware that I probably shouldn't be down here as I hover at the lip of the first step, but despite my better judgement, I continue on, my soft soles padding against the cold stone.

The deeper I go, the damper the walls and stone steps become. Mould and mildew climb the arched walls and clog the air with a noticeable aroma. I scrunch my nose up in distaste until I come to a stop at the base of the stairs. Torches hooked on the wall light up the long, dank corridor. Barred cell doors line the opposite side and rat droppings and muck litters the cold stone floors. As the stench of old urine fills my nostrils and turns my stomach, I turn to leave. My attention snaps back to the cell doors as a soft singing voice filters through the gloom.

I creep forward, lured by the soft voice, familiarity niggling at me. The first three cells are empty but the voice grows ever louder with each door I pass. As I reach the fifth door, I falter, tripping over my own feet and stumbling closer.

"Lesya?" I cry in dismay, my voice reverberating along the damp walls.

The bedraggled girl sits against the far wall, her body trembling and covered in filth. Her brown hair is a tangled mess atop her head. To my dismay, I realise that she's still wearing the gown from the SunMoon ball, the corset hanging loose as her body has wasted away. Her hands are red with cold and there are sores around her wrists. The long chains shackle her to the far wall, bolted to the stone. Her cheeks are sunken when she looks at me, her purple eyes too bright, glossy from the Lunar Fever gripping her body.

A gasp cuts through the space and I realise that it came from me. My hurting heart is ripped wide open all over again as I realise how long she has been down here, left to rot in a cell.

"Lesya... what have they done to you?" I breathe in disbelief.

She giggles in response before continuing the same melody as before. Her head sways this way and that with the melody, the words muddled nonsense. I step closer, my hands gripping the bars as I search frantically for a way in.

I'm still searching when I hear the clipping sound of boots against stone. I freeze, looking around for somewhere to hide and coming up blank, my heart beginning to pound heavily in my chest.

"Oh, Lesya... I hope you're ready for me, sweetheart," a man slurs.

I'm filled with a sick feeling as his words reach me, and by the way he slurs his words, he's evidently drunk. Knowing there is nowhere for me to go, I can only stand and wait for the man to find me, readying myself with an excuse.

When he finally makes it towards us, I take note of his uniform. He's an Aslitír. My unease grows as I watch him stumble towards us, his blonde hair flopping over his forehead, his eyes glazed from drink. A smirk pulls his lips upwards as he wags a finger at me.

"You shouldn't be down here, missy. Tut, tut," he berates in a teasing voice.

"I realise that now, I'm sorry. Release Lesya and we'll head back to our rooms without a fuss," I tell him.

He shakes his head slowly, his smirk growing into a smile that sends a prickling unease through me. As he moves a step closer, I take a slow step back.

"We both know that isn't going to happen now, is it darling?" he replies, his blue eyes flashing with malice.

I glance behind me only to see a dead end and he chuckles as he edges even closer.

"Oh, scared little fawn, let's have some fun. The king doesn't have to know," he says, reaching for me.

"I'm a Chosen, you know you can't touch me. You can't touch any of us," I warn him, shifting into a defensive stance.

Something changes in his expression, his eyes darkening as his demeanour suddenly changes and he lunges for me. Panic threatens to suck me under but I focus on Jarek's words drilled into my head. I dodge his hands and pull my elbow back, thrusting my fist up into his nose.

The Aslitír chokes out a pained cry and stumbles back holding his face as blood begins to stream from his nose.

"You little *bitch*!"

He wipes away the excess blood, his eyes enraged as he roars and rushes to me. I try to dodge him but this time he's prepared. He's surprisingly fast as he counters my swerve and grabs my arm.

We grapple as he drags me towards him. I try to scream for help when his hand roughly grabs my braids and slams my head against the stone. Stars burst into my vision with a wave of nausea as the room begins to spin. I stumble in my disoriented state, his feet knocking mine out from underneath me and I fall hard onto my back. Knocking the wind from my lungs.

I scramble for Stormtip and realise in horror that it's not there as another wave of nausea rolls over me.

'*I must have left it in Ria's room.*'

The panic I'd been fighting now swallows me whole as I feel him flip me over onto my front.

The floor is ice cold and wet against my cheek as he rips down my trousers and climbs on top of me. A panicked whimper escapes my lips as I'm filled with utter terror and helplessness. I try to fight him off, but I have no more fight left in me as he pins me down and slams my head against the floor, sending me into another spiral of spinning stars as he forces his way into me. I cry out at the pain as he moves, a numbness spreading through my chest as his rhythm speeds up, the weight of him sickening. Tears slide down my face as I stare into the stars clouding my vision, while the haunting sound of Lesya's eerie melody filters through the darkness.

I wake up in my bed, groggy and disoriented, with a vague memory of dragging myself back to my room once I was alone. Holding my head as I sit up, my head screams at me, an exceedingly large, well-formed lump on the left side of my head beneath the top of my braid. I look to the mound of filthy clothes on the floor across the room, and quickly look away.

A choked sob escapes me as my mind is flooded with images of last night; memories I want erasing. Pain throbs across my body in aching waves and my heart constricts in my chest as I feel the panic envelop me. The feeling of shame and disgust has me writhing in my own skin. The numbness that comes next is worse and I just manage to make it into the bathroom before I empty the contents of my stomach over and over, until my throat is raw and tears stream down my cheeks in ragged lines. I try to squeeze my eyes shut and block it out, pushing away the memory of his rough hands and impatient fingers. Instead of welcoming darkness, I'm greeted with his face and his bright blue, glossy eyes, and his face the picture of greed. I can still smell the stench of ale on his breath. The thought makes me queasy and I'm back on my knees, heaving up bile. My arms tremble as I hold myself up, my emotions a rolling wave threatening to drag me under with each memory that resurfaces. Each one is another moment that I'm forced to relive what the bastard did to me.

I pad back to the bed, wincing from the pain between my legs. I hear footsteps approaching as I try to fight the sickness that overwhelms me. I look up as my door opens and Lysan meanders in.

"I'm here to inform you that the king has invited you to dine with him in three—" he stops.

The clipping of his boots against the marble floor comes to a sudden stop, his nose wrinkling at the stench of vomit as his seafoam blue eyes find me. I shrink back, my heart pounding erratically in my chest as I hold a hand up to stop him from coming any further. I dare to glance up at him through the curls that have fallen in my face. His expression falters for a split second as he takes me in.

Minutes go by and he says nothing. I try to fight the trembling but my body betrays me. When he steps closer, my blind panic resurfaces and I scramble back in the bed, kicking the sheets back. I press myself against the wall. I watch him with wide eyes as his own grow dark, his mouth set in a tight line.

"This is a far cry from the death threats you hurled at me yesterday," he breathes, the usual dryness gone from his voice.

My heart stops in my chest as I follow his eyes to the white sheet stained with blood. The breath is knocked out of me as I stare at the stain, tears pricking in my eyes as I continue to tremble.

"What's this—" he starts, moving towards me again.

I drop my head in shame. "Don't! Don't come any closer," I blurt in a breathless whisper.

He doesn't stop and moves around the bed and reaches for me. When I draw away, his eyes flash with irritation and a blast of shadow comes flying towards me. The scream that escapes me is drowned out by the shadow as I'm ripped from the safety of my bed and dumped in front of him at the foot of it. The shadows pull away from me, my vision clearing as I begin to hyperventilate. They hover around my frame as they cut through the air like ink in water. I look up to a seething Lysan who stands over me, his eyes holding deadly storms.

"You *stupid* girl! Have you not learnt from the last bitch who whored herself out to the Aslitír?" His voice is calm but there is an icy rage simmering beneath the surface.

"I-I," I stammer, the lump in my throat growing larger as I think of the soldier, his weight pinning me down.

He reaches for me and I throw my arms up, the sleeves of my nightgown slipping down to reveal purple and yellow bruising around my wrists. We both look at the same time, and something changes in his demeanour, reflecting in the tendrils of shadow around us as they pause in the air.

"I see," he says carefully, slowly straightening. "Who?"

The lump grows as the memories fill my head. I feel him hovering over me, but I'm in my own head, the tears threatening to spill over my face. I feel the anger and the shame threatening to swallow me whole and something in me breaks.

"Nesryn, *who*? " he growls, snapping me from the thoughts.

He reaches for me suddenly and I snap out of it, recoiling from his touch. The darkness writhes in his seafoam eyes and he grabs me and pulls me to my feet. His rough touch refuels my queasiness and I claw at him.

"Who Nesryn?" His voice is harsh as he demands the information.

"Aslitír. In the cells," I manage.

"What the fuck were you—oh never mind," he starts.

"She was there. Lesya… he—" I start, sucking in a breath as the memories replay in my head.

He finally releases me but my tunnel vision only intensifies as I reach for the hilt strapped to his hips. He hesitates for a split second as I pull it free and hold it toward him before my panic rises and I try to turn it on myself, wanting an end to this feeling, this pain.

His darkness is on me before the blade can meet its mark and he reaches for me once again, the rage rolling off him in terrifying waves as he wrestles the blade from my grasp, the metal clanging against the stone as it clatters to the floor.

'*This is the truth of him,*' my mind warns me.

He holds my chin tight in his grasp as I try to escape, his touch is sickening.

"Please, end it. Make it end," I beg.

"Oh no, *Princess*. You don't get the easy way out, you lost that choice when you handed yourself over to Barilius so willingly," he spits, the venom of his words snaring me.

"You will not die today, or the days after," he tells me, his fury a living thing writhing around us and casting us both in its shadow.

I watch as my own horror is mirrored in his darkened eyes. I have to stare back at myself through his eyes for several agonising seconds before he finally lets go of me. He snatches his dagger from the floor and steps away, and with each inch of distance, I feel as though I'm no longer completely blinded by fear.

Lysan withdraws his shadows, light leaking back into the room with such force that I find myself squinting from the brightness. He stands there as though he intends to say something, but immediately, he seems to think better of it. After an eternity of silence, he finally turns towards the door, stopping just before it.

"No more death in these trials, not on my watch," he mutters, and I wonder if I'd heard him right.

Before I can work up the nerve to question him, he leaves. I don't realise that I'm holding my breath until the door clicks shut behind him, my composure disappearing into nothing as the anguish of the past few days washes over me again. The ache of missing my uncle rips the rest of me apart.

It's only when Lysan's steps seem to fade away down the hall that the tears that I had been holding back flow freely down my face.

CHAPTER TWENTYEIGHT

A low guttural moan emanates from behind Nesryn's door. I listen silently to her painful sobs, fighting the sudden urge to burst through the door and obliterate the pain within. I'd seen the look in those spring-green eyes of hers, not dead, but worse. I'm reminded all too much of the promise I'd made. The promise I'd failed again and again to keep. No more.

"Aslitír. In the cells."

"What the fuck was she doing down there in the first place?" I wonder aloud.

As I turn, I see one of her handmaidens scurrying up the corridor. She starts when she sees me, dropping into a curtsey. I dismiss the gesture and wave my hand for her to stand.

"Lady Havenore is to have no visitors today. I want her cleaned up and the healer sent in. No one else, is that understood?" I tell her.

"Yes m'lord," she answers.

I nod once and wave her away, watching as she hurries back the way she came. My mind travels back to Nesryn, comparing the girl I saw last night to the girl she is this morning and anger simmers within me.

I forget about informing the rest of the girls. A new job slips into my mind. Containing my anger as best I can, I make my way towards the lower levels and the soldiers' quarters.

The room is busier than I expected at this hour, and I try to recall the switchover times in my head but I come up blank. The soldiers who see me stare suspiciously as I stalk past them. My eyes scour the room as I search for Keelhan, meeting several pairs of eyes as I come to an abrupt stop in the middle of the walkway. I turn to the closest man with a frown.

"Keelhan. Where is he?" I demand.

The man shrugs. "I don't know, but he's not here."

"Helpful," I mutter.

"Last I heard he was cutting training short to relieve Olin from duty," someone says from behind me.

I swivel around. "How long ago was this?"

"Not long, a half chime, maybe," he answers with a shrug, his hand on the hilt of his sword.

"I heard he got into a bit of a scrap. The man could never hold his drink," someone pitches in.

Alarm bells ring in my head as I turn towards the voice. The man perches on the end of one of the cots. He watches me with the same wary eyes as the others as my attention is wholly on him.

"From what I hear, Keelhan's benched him," he continues.

"What post?" I demand, my gut telling me I already know the answer.

"Dungeons," the soldier replies.

Before I can hear any more, I shadowfold.

I appear in the lower levels, the hall quiet save for footsteps coming my way. I turn in their direction, knowing they've come from the usual route into the dungeons. The man wears his uniform scruffily, his blonde hair tousled and hanging limply over his forehead. His blue eyes are drowned out by the purple and yellow bruising running under his eyes and across the bridge of his crooked, swollen nose.

The rage within me roars to life once again as I realise Nesryn didn't go down without a fight. My anger is a living entity, twisting and writhing within me, begging to be set free.

He looks up from the floor as he notices me moving towards him. His eyes narrow slightly in distrust.

"You were on shift last night, weren't you, soldier?" I query.

"What's it to you?" he demands gruffly. He clenches his fists.

"As your king's Second, it's my business to know," I counter.

I watch as his face pales, his step faltering and it takes everything within me not to tear him apart there and then. I waste no more time and close the rest of the gap between us and throw a punch. I feel the satisfying crunch as my knuckles collide with his cheekbone.

Before he can recover, I grab him and shadowfold into the closest room.

We stumble into the empty space and I quickly right myself, watching him do the same with twin flames of fury in my eyes.

"You ignorant, prick! She needed to remain unspoiled. What will the king want with her now? What do you think he'll do when he discovers his soldiers are too ripe with greed to guard his Chosen and are too busy fucking them?" I growl with anger.

He baulks at me, his jaw-dropping as I watch the colour drain from his bruised face. I glare at him as his eyes flick to the shadows slipping free around me.

"What will you do?" he asks, taking a step back.

My snaking shadows answer the question for him.

"You touched her against her will, against the king's will," I say, tutting as I shake my head slowly.

"No, I wouldn't! Whatever she told you, she's lying!" he pleads, scrambling up against the wall.

"The only liar I've come across is you," I retaliate, my inky tendrils growing around me as I stretch my power.

"She did that, didn't she?" I say, gesturing towards his nose. "Nasty break, must've hurt. She must have been defending more than herself," I observe dryly, cocking my head to one side.

I watch him as he lifts a hand towards his face, halting in mid-air as his eyes meet mine. They flash with understanding.

"What has she told you?" he asks quietly.

"Enough. But then, I've always been good at reading between the lines," I answer as my shadows rear up.

"I didn't! I didn't touch them!" his tone hints at the panic he feels.

"This deceit will be your last," I glower, my tone dark as my shadows rush in to meet their victim.

The rhythmic sound of dripping is interrupted by a heavy banging against the door. I blink as I mentally come back into the room. I take in the red walls, the blood dripping from the ceiling, and what is left of the former Aslitir. As the banging continues, I stare at the remains slumped against the wall in front of me, feeling absolutely nothing as I pull my shadows away from barricading the door.

I turn to see Keelhan fall into the room, his mouth agape as he sees the remains of his man on the floor.

"Lysan... what the hell have you done?" Keelhan's face is ashen as his eyes travel across the blood-spattered room.

"He took something that wasn't his," I tell him plainly, a dark edge to my tone.

"What in Asteria's name did he take to merit this?" he asks gesturing to our surroundings.

"He made claim to The Chosen," I inform him, sending him a dark look.

"What?" Keelhan breathes in disbelief.

I watch as he stares at what is left of the soldier, his brows knitting together as his mouth sets in a thin line.

"How?" he asks, cutting through the silence.

I meet his eyes, unwilling to dignify his question with an answer.

"Surely not," he says in disbelief.

When I don't look away, he shakes his head in disgust.

"Shit..." he runs a hand over his stubbled chin.

"Lys, the king will have your head for this," he says after some time.

"Barilius would have punished them both. I simply punished the guilty party."

He lets out a sigh and turns on his heel. "Leave this, I'll deal with your fuck-up later. There's something you're going to want to see," he says, leaving the room.

I follow after him wordlessly, letting him lead me down into the cells and stopping in front of a cell holding a familiar face. Surprise pours through me like ice water as I take in Lesya Raviffete shackled to the wall, muttering and giggling to herself.

When she looks up at us, I flinch, immediately noting the purple hue of her eyes. I look over at Keelhan who meets my gaze with a wary look of his own.

"The king's order," he explains, answering my silent query.

My surprise is replaced with a burning anger as I take in the poor girl, visibly deep in the clutches of Lunar Fever, sitting in her own filth and muck. Nesryn filters into my mind as I suddenly understand.

"Now is not the time to wage wars with Barilius," Keelhan warns, reading my expression.

"Maybe not," I say evenly, my eyes trained on Lesya.

"*Lysan*," Keelhan warns me, his tone grave. "Don't be foolish! We are coming so close to the end of this, don't rile the king. His good graces will only last so long," he continues.

"This has to end, Keelhan!" I bite back, jabbing a finger at the unhinged young woman behind the cell door.

"I don't like it either, Lysan, but it is the will of our *king*. Stay out of his way, don't encourage his wrath," he says, almost pleadingly.

I step forward, my eyes flashing with the fury set deep in my bones. He levels my gaze but doesn't back away from me as I approach him, leaving only centimetres between us.

"Don't dictate me, *Captain*. Remember your place," I warn him.

"Why don't you remember *your* place, Lysander? I could very easily have you removed from the palace until you get your head screwed on properly," he counters.

I send him a dark smile in response. "You'll have to catch me first."

"Dammit Lys—" he curses as I shadowfold.

A plan forms in my head as I realise with a grim smile that it's well overdue.

NESRYN

Chapter TwentyNine

The day passes by, unnoticed by me after Lysan leaves. At first, the flashes come back in pieces, scattered across the day, despite my attempts to block them out. Perin, Sarleigh and Hesta join me eventually, bringing with them a healer as per the Shadowcaster's request.

"You will not die today, or the days after."

His words resonate through me, causing me to shudder.

My handmaidens busy themselves around me, removing my clothes from the floor and the soiled sheets on my bed without a single word. I vaguely see their concerned glances and the way that they step on eggshells around me. The numbness has taken root in me, outweighing the pain.

I watch blankly as the three of them bustle into the washroom. I can hear the vague sound of running water and the tinkling of vials as the healer sorts through her bag of remedies.

"Take this first, my dear," she says, holding out a tiny vial of golden-looking liquid.

"What is it?" I ask warily.

"It's a tonic. To prevent pregnancy," she whispers, leaning in close. "I understand you may be in need of it, my lady."

The lump in the back of my throat grows from embarrassment and shame, but I take it from her and swallow, shaking my head free of the barrage of thoughts that threaten to drown me.

"You'll need something for the pain and the visible marks too," she mutters, taking the small glass back and glancing between me and the contents of her bag.

I look away for a moment, wondering if I should feel self-conscious, but I don't. I feel empty.

Out of the corner of my eye, I see her reach out to me with a small corked vial, its contents an iridescent blue.

"This should help," she explains, wiggling the bottle.

Gingerly, I take it from her and pull the cork free. Without a word, I bring the vial to my lips and swallow it. The liquid is sweet and tingly as it glides down my throat.

The pins and needles spread from my lips to the rest of my body in no time, the cuts, bruises, aches and pains all disappearing one by one. I watch on, as the brushing around my wrists slowly disappear, as though they had never been there, but the weight of what caused it remains like a bitter aftertaste that I can't shake. The healer takes the empty vial back, returning it to her bag with a clink.

"And something a little stronger for the mind," she considers aloud, meeting my vacant state with a scrutinising eye. "Pharopedil Elixir. Take two drops of this each day. It will help your mind heal," the healer tells me gently.

My eyes flit to her hand and the triangular-shaped bottle in her grasp. Behind the glass is a greyish liquid that takes on a golden hue when swirled.

"This bottle should last you until two moons' time. Should you need more, simply send for me, my lady," she says in earnest, handing me the bottle with a pitying look.

I take in the soft wrinkles around her wise eyes and the gentle kindness in her deep brown orbs. I draw the bottle close, studying the gold as it hits the light.

"I must warn you that there is powerful magic in this elixir. You must only take what I've suggested, my lady," she tells me, studying me.

"Two drops only," I repeat, my voice distant to my ears.

She blinks in surprise but recovers quickly with a smile and nods in agreement.

"I wish you luck and health, my lady. I will see myself out," she tells me, sweeping into a curtsey before turning and leaving, her brown bag clicking with each step.

Moments later, Perin pops her head out of the washroom, informing me that my bath is ready. I look at her as my stomach balls up into a mess of knots. I set the bottle down on the vanity and slowly get to my feet.

Perin waits patiently by the door, but as I take a step forwards, I turn back to the bottle on the table. After a moment of internal debate, I let out a shuddering sigh and twist off the rubbery top to discover it's attached to a glass pipette. I pinch the rubber top, watching as the glass tube sucks in some of the Pharopedil, the grey and gold twisting around the narrow tube. I squeeze two droplets onto my tongue and swallow, twisting the pipette back into place.

There is a dull tingling in my throat and I wait for it to course through me as the last tonic had. I feel nothing as the tingling feeling in my throat fades away.

I walk to the tub, undressing and moving into the water as quickly as possible. The women approach me, soaps and sponges in hand, and I feel an irrational panic rising in my chest. The revulsion at the idea of being touched has nausea hurtling through me.

"No!" I choke out, holding up my shaking hand.

The handmaidens pause, sharing a concerned look as they shift at the edge of the sunken bath. My eyes flit warily between the women, my panicked breaths coming shallow and fast. With my heart still hammering in my chest, I lower my hand back into the water, the billowing steam wafting through the air.

"I'm sorry, I-I just don't want to be touched. Co-could you wait in the next room for me... please?" I say.

Sarleigh and Perin look to Hesta, waiting for her answer. The eldest woman nods once, a mixture of pity and understanding glittering in her eyes.

"We'll be just outside if you need us, milady," she says, ushering the other two towards the door.

I watch, heart hammering, as she follows them out, sliding the door behind her with a quiet swoosh.

When I'm finally alone, I let out a shuddering breath and sink into the hot water, submerging myself beneath the surface in the hope that it will wash away the past several days from my memory.

For the first time in a while, I feel a sense of weightlessness wash over me.

When I finally force myself from the bath, the water is cold and my skin is wrinkled like a prune. I reach for the towel they left and wrap it around myself as I reach for the door.

As soon as the swoosh of the door sounds, all three women stand to attention, peering at me in anticipation.

"How are you feeling?" Perin asks, a tentative smile on her lips.

"Better," I answer, my smile strained.

I look at the fresh sheets on the bed, wanting nothing more than to slip between them and sleep for an eternity. To forget about everything in the velvety darkness of sleep. Hesta's gaze follows mine before she gives each of the others a meaningful glance.

"Miss, before we take our leave, the king's messenger has been with news."

My attention snaps to her, the hollowness in my stomach igniting with vengeful anger.

"What news has he?" I ask.

"The king has cancelled the following trials and instead invites you to take rest over the next few days. He invites each of you to dine with him in three nights' time," she relays.

Surprise registers on my face, my anger replaced with confusion. My face must show the turmoil I feel because Hesta smiles at me reassuringly, her hands clasping gently in front of her.

"If I may, I believe his majesty plans to choose his Chosen on this night," she adds.

I consider the possibility of his choosing me and I see my chance to get close to the king. My skin breaks out in goosebumps at the thought of physical touch, but I force it down momentarily, the taste of vengeance too sweet on my tongue.

"Thank you, that will be all," I say quietly, gripping the towel as I look up from the floor.

"There are fresh clothes in your chest, and hot soup and fresh bread over there on your table. I've sent for tea. It'll be brought up in a little while," Sarleigh chimes in.

"Thank you, ladies," I reply.

"We will await your summons, miss," Hesta says, dipping into a curtsey.

I wait for them to leave the room before I quickly dress and towel my hair dry, twisting it up into a bun as I move towards the bed. I stare at the steaming bowl of vegetables and meat, my stomach turning at the thought of food.

Instead, I reach for the bottle of elixir again, swigging a mouthful rather than bothering with the pipette. Finally, I climb into the warm cocoon of the soft mattress and thick blankets, burying myself deep within its safe folds.

The days fly by, though I barely notice. Food is brought and left, taken away untouched. My handmaidens arrive, only to be dismissed, and I spend my hours sleeping fitfully, nightmares plaguing my dreams and jolting me awake in cold sweats. They send me rushing to the bathroom at all hours of the night, vomiting acid and bile as violent tremors wrack my body.

As time goes on I find myself taking more than the required dose of the elixir, welcoming the tingling sensation of the magic and the floaty feeling that keeps the flashbacks at bay, easing the revulsion of physical touch. The empty bottles begin to pile up in the bottom of my clothes chest, hidden beneath folds of fabric.

On the third day as I stare up at the canopy, a knock comes, followed by Ria's face appearing through the gap. I sit up in bed, my eyes following her as she steps into the room, leaning against the door until it clicks shut behind her. I watch her from where I sit, taking in the bags beneath her eyes and the sag in her shoulders. Her face is pale and drawn, her eyes look dull and tired as she looks across the space to me. She still wears Vena's clothes, the blue and white cotton looser on her than it would have been on her love.

"I thought you may have come back… the other night," she says, tilting her head.

Her voice cuts through the silence and I realise all of a sudden that I welcome her company. I think of the night I left her asleep, a lump forming in my throat as I push the memories away, locking them in a mental box where his bright blue eyes can't find me.

"I'm sorry. I wish I had," I answer, my voice croaky as I fiddle with my hands.

"You left this in my room. I had no idea you even carried a weapon," she says, pulling Stormtip out from behind her.

I watch as she twists it around in her fingers, studying it. An ache swells in my chest as I look at it, grateful to see it again.

"It was a gift from my uncle," I answer.

She looks up from the blade and walks over to the bed, perching on the edge and handing me it back. I take it gratefully, twisting it around in my own hands, taking in all its little features.

"Has something happened? When I tried to come find you, I was told you weren't seeing visitors," she says, tentatively taking a step forwards.

I open my mouth to explain but I shut it, surprised that she had been told that. My mind travels back to Lysan's visit and I put two and two together. Ria watches me, her eyes now laced with concern as she takes in my appearance.

"You don't look so great," she says gently.

I bark out a laugh, the sound strange in my ears. "You don't look so hot either," I retort.

She smiles and dips her head, but when she returns my gaze, the smile is gone and the pain she feels radiates through her. Tears prick her eyes, and I can only watch on as she blinks them away.

"We're not talking about me though, are we?" she says finally.

I flinch as she climbs further onto the bed, moving closer towards me. My heart flutters with muted panic, still under the influence of the elixir. My wary eyes meet hers and she pauses, her brow knitting together as she reads my body language. She slumps into a sitting position, her lips pursed.

"Nes, what is going on?" she asks bluntly.

Before I can even open my mouth to speak, she's talking again.

"You've been off-limits for days, guards stationed outside of your room. From what I hear, you're not eating and you won't let a soul near you," she continues.

'*Guards stationed outside*?' I think, surprised that I hadn't known.

She drops her head, her hands trembling as she reaches out and places her palm over the top of my hand. Her hand remains on mine and I stare at it, waiting for my skin to crawl from the touch, for the bile to climb my throat, but nothing happens.

"Chosen. Mas, Vee… our *friends*, they're dying around us at a speed that I—and goddess now Erryn's gone too, it's just us four left, Nes. I can't lose you too," she chokes out, tears streaming down her cheeks when she finally looks at me.

'*Erryn's dead*?'

Guilt drowns out the shock and I feel my vision blur.

"I found Lesya," the words are out before I can think.

"What?" Ria splutters, her teary eyes widening.

"Down in the lower levels, in one of the cells. I found her shackled, singing to herself," I continue.

"Fuck…" Ria breathes, her jaw slack.

"One of the Aslitír caught me down there," I continue, my heart beginning to pick up speed as my lip trembles.

Without meaning to, I squeeze my legs together beneath the quilt, pulling my hand from hers and clutching it tightly in my lap as I take in a shuddering breath. Ria watches me closely, her eyes widening in horror.

"Oh, Nes. *No*," she breathes quietly.

It's enough to undo me all over again, and as I fall apart, Ria's reaction is immediate as she reaches for me, wrapping her arms around my shaking frame. She holds me as the hot tears come fast and heavy, as the memories of what was done to me plague my mind. My breaths come in hiccups as she smoothes down my hair, and I try to focus on the steady rhythm of her heart.

"We'll get through this together," her voice rises above the hiccuped sobs as the pain in my chest eases.

As I sit up, she gently wipes away my tears, her own face just as tear-stained. I do the same as we smile tentatively at one another. She continues to look at me and it takes me a few moments to realise she's waiting for my response.

"Y-yes. T-together," I manage.

I stare at my reflection, the tingling buzz of magic fizzing against my lips as the magical tonic begins to kick in. The black halterneck dress is one of my own, the fabric glittering around my neck. The front is shaped like a diamond, the material curving along the sides of my breasts to wrap around the middle of my back. The skirts begin at my waist and flow freely to the floor.

The evening has crept in quickly, the hour of our meal with the king fast approaching. Having dismissed Perin, Hesta and Sarleigh, Ria had announced we would be preparing for tonight ourselves. Despite the handmaidens' wariness at first, they had eventually agreed, leaving us to our own devices after informing us that one of the messengers would collect us when the time comes.

Despite my ease with Ria, I still take the healer's Pharopedil, swallowing a large mouthful. The elixir tingles against my tongue and I swallow it quickly before she notices. I slip the bottle into a hidden pocket of my dress before she looks my way. My simmering anger at the king and his treacherous Second is overshadowed by the single, unforgivable act of the Aslitír.

Ria comes up behind me in a fitted gown of royal blue, the sleeves and chest embossed with glittering silver beads that continue along the hem of the dress, where the skirt flares. She wears her hair freely, the blonde tresses traipsing down her back, with one side pinned back with matching silver clips. I watch her through the reflection in the mirror as she fixes my hair into a nest of curls atop my head, leaving a few to fall freely and frame my face. She pins it in place and steps back proudly to admire her work.

"That should do it. After all, we want to look the part," she says.

"We don't want to arouse any more suspicion," I agree as I meet her eyes through the mirror.

"You have it?" she asks, glancing at my skirts.

I nod, the feel of Stormtip strapped to my thigh giving me a sense of reassurance. I take a breath, my thoughts weighing heavily on my mind as I turn around to face her, my expression serious.

"What happens if tonight he picks a Chosen? What do we do?" I ask.

Ria's grey-blue eyes meet mine with a hardness that catches me off guard. "I don't know, but we'll be ready."

I nod, my lips set in a thin line as I ground myself through the feeling of weightlessness from the elixir.

Vilkha collects us at eight chimes, leading us along the hallway with Twyla and Ovie. They seem as quiet and withdrawn as Ria and I. We walk through the east wing and across the main halls of the palace. Instead of our usual dining room, Vilkha escorts us along the main corridor and through into the ballroom, where an elaborate set up of food and wine greets us. I hear the others gasp and mutter in surprise as they take in the large room. Tables have been laid out in a horseshoe formation, adorned with steaming plates of mouthwatering food and large jugs of red wine. The hall is decorated with pink blossoms and beautiful orbs of elvynlight which float about the room over our heads. The whole set-up is breathtaking and I find myself staring in awe.

Vilkha clears his throat. "Presenting to His Highness, King Barilius Saurhen, First of His Name: Lady Twyla Drullanon, Lady Ovie Montallet, Lady Reverie Zouvsa; and finally, Lady Nesryn Havenore," he announces.

As we step into the room, my eyes fall on the centre of the horseshoe. In a tall seat of twisting gold, and sat there in all his finery, is the king himself. A wave of shock hits me as my eyes fall on his face, the surrealness of his presence unnerves all of us as we shift on our feet, dropping into a wave of curtsies.

"Good evening, ladies. Congratulations on making it to the final stretch of this season's Choosing. I must say, I am impressed with how well you've all done thus far," he says as he gets to his feet, his hands flat on the table as his amber eyes appraise each of us in turn, returning to me as they move back along the line.

"Thank you, Your Majesty," Ovie says, dipping her head.

He seems to ignore the comment and straightens where he stands, his eyes finding me again. Several strands of dark hair fall over his shoulder, the silver of his clothes glinting in the light as he shifts, opening his arms wide.

"Please, sit. Eat, drink. Let us toast to your success," he says, beckoning us to the tables.

'What of those who have lost their lives to succeed in your death trials?' I think to myself as I follow after the others.

We seat ourselves on the opposite side of the table, where King Barilius can easily see us as he lowers himself into his own chair, leaning back as he watches us with intrigue. A few servants begin plating up the food, while others pour us goblets of crimson wine.

"Please, enjoy," the king offers, his smile wide and showing too much of his teeth. The sudden image of a wolf appears in my mind.

The clatter of silverware begins to echo through the large space when the king snaps his fingers. At the sound, music begins to gently play, filling the room with a beautiful melody that travels through the air. I focus on it as I stare warily at the food on my plate, my stomach twisting at the thought of eating anything.

I peer at Ria, but her head is down, her attention on her plate as the fork in her hand moves morsels around the dinnerware. I reach for the goblet instead, bringing it to my lips, noting the king's gaze resting on me until his eyes are hidden behind the view of my cup. The rich heavy taste of wine hits my tongue as I inhale the fumes and swallow. I'm grateful for the kick at the back of my throat as the liquid warms my stomach. I do my best to pay attention to the small talk flitting across the dining table as the king makes conversation with the others and I note that the interest that he shows in his body language doesn't reach his eyes. He speaks with Ovie, discussing some political matter relating to the whispers of a small rebellion to the west.

'*I hardly blame them for rebelling when they have a man as murderous as Barilius on the throne,*' I think to myself as I take another long sip.

As I lower my cup, I notice King Barilius's attention has shifted to me once again and I pause, my hand hovering in the air.

"You seem rather quiet, Lady Havenore. Lost your appetite, have you?" he comments, his gaze dipping to my untouched plate.

"No, not at all your grace. I simply got caught up in the atmosphere and your excellent taste in wine," I lie, quickly saving myself.

His lip twitches before he smiles, the gesture not reaching his eyes. "Perhaps we could work up an appetite with a short stroll?"

In a split second of panic, the warm welcoming taste of wine sours in my mouth. I glance to the others before meeting the king's eye across the table. Placing my drink down as steadily as I can, I swallow, choosing my next words carefully.

"It would be an honour, Your Majesty, but would this not disrupt the rest of your guests?"

"I hope you ladies are able to entertain yourselves for a short while, while I escort Lady Havenore?" he queries, his eyes never leaving mine.

A murmur of agreement moves through the table as each of the girls answer him. As he gets to his feet and moves around the table, I glance fearfully at Ria, whose pinched face mirrors mine. I do my best to smooth my expression as King Barilius stops beside me, holding out his hand.

'Stay calm and smile,' I tell myself.

I peer up at him through my lashes and put on a tentative smile, as I reach for his arm. I get to my feet, my dress swishing around my legs, the feel of Stormtip at my thigh reassuring as he leads me towards the double doors.

"Enjoy the food, girls. Lady Havenore and I won't be long," he calls over his shoulder, his gaze locked on mine.

As we walk away, my pulse thumps in my throat, making it hard to swallow. Despite my best efforts to remain collected and calm, I can't help but feel like prey holding hands with the deadliest predator.

King Barilius leads me through the palace corridors, my hand resting in the crook of his arm. As we walk leisurely beside one another, I bite the inside of my cheek, my skin crawling at the touch. I do my best to focus on my anger rather than the fear and disgust that threatens to unravel me. A pair of Aslitír soldiers follow behind us at a distance, causing a bout of distress to run through me. I find myself warily glancing at their eyes every so often, but not recognising either of them. Despite this, their presence brings me no comfort.

"It's not often I get the pleasure of such beautiful company or a peaceful stroll," he tells me as we walk.

"I imagine Your Highness has little time for his own leisure," I reply, doing my best to glance at him every so often.

"You would be right. Kingdoms seldom reign themselves," he answers, a flash of something dark passing in his eyes.

I open my mouth to reply but the moon catches my eye through the arched window over his shoulder and words evade me. His brow knits together as I let go of him, relief coating me as wonder draws me closer to the window. I study the pink hue coating the moon, the craters a deeper reddish tinge in a sky of deep, darkening blue.

"Ah, I see the BloodMoon has begun its ascent. It should be at its highest point later tonight," King Barilius comments as he stands beside me.

It takes all of my willpower not to shudder as his arm brushes mine. I bite down on my cheek, this time breaking the skin, my tongue immediately tasting the warm coppery flavour of blood.

"It's breathtaking," I manage.

"There is a place in the palace that will have the most picturesque view of it. Come, I will show you," he says, grabbing my hand with a ferocity that fills me with nausea.

Despite the strong urge to snatch my hand away, I let it remain in his, following after him through the palace halls. We make our way through the west wing into a section of the palace that I no longer recognise. I try not to let the panic swarm me as I begin to lose track of the turns we make, to wonder how much time has passed. The king pushes on fervently, only slowing when we reach the footwell of a winding stone staircase. Unease settles in my chest as he glances over me to the Aslitír behind us. They slow to a stop as soon as they notice his meaningful glance.

"This way," he says, turning to me.

He releases my hand and gestures to the stairs. I glance at the soldiers who are stationed on either side of the stone archway. I then look at the king, who nods once, excitement shining in his eyes. Warily, I move towards the steps, following them up and around until I reach the heavy wood and iron door at the top, noting the golden knocker; a demon with three horns sprouting from its forehead.

Feeling ill at ease, I avoid looking at it again, instead, twisting the doorknob pushing it open with a loud creak, and stepping into the lit room.

The room itself is deceiving. It's much bigger than what I assumed when climbing the steps up the tower. But that isn't what sends an icy chill through me as I look around me.

Shelves circle the room, stacked full of different shaped bottles of strange liquids and numerous vials of off-colour powders. Dusty books litter the rest of the spaces—on shelves, the floor, and even against the tiny window above the desk where several black half-melted candles stand, burning purple flames. Across the room, a pinkish light pours down from several openings in the roof, shining onto an altar of solid, polished black stone. To its right stands a claw-footed cauldron of iron.

I realise too late this is a room of dark magic, and as I turn to confront the king, a sudden burst of pain erupts from the back of my head and I crumple into the awaiting darkness.

I wake up with a pounding ache pulsating through my skull. I wince as I try to sit up. Panic courses through me in waves when I open my eyes to see the light of the BloodMoon pouring over me and I struggle against the bonds tying me down. A panicked whimper escapes me as I look up at the pair of amber eyes watching me intently.

"So glad you could join me for this special occasion," King Barilius taunts.

"What are you doing? Let me go!" I shout, tugging at my wrists.

I scream, throwing my body left and right as I try to scramble free, but to no avail.

"Scream, you little bitch. No one will hear your cries," he laughs.

King Barilius's face twists into a vicious sneer as he steps around the altar, an open book balancing in one hand as he regards me. His hair falls over his shoulders as he leans towards me and I pull away in fear.

He steps back and barks a laugh. "Oh no, girl. You're not going *anywhere*. I've waited long enough for this, so lie back and enjoy the show," his eyes gleam with malice as he moves away.

"What do you mean? What do you want from me?" I scream, fighting my bonds.

He returns moments later with a dagger the shade of blood as a wide smile tugs at his lips. "Your life," he answers.

He moves swiftly, slicing it across my palms and the soft soles of my feet as I cry out. Blood wells from the cuts and I strain to look as the blood runs off my hands and onto the black stone, moving in an unnatural line across the flat surface. The stone heats beneath me, creating patterns that I can't decipher as another sob erupts from me. He puts the knife down, collecting a dark bottle and returning to my side.

"I've always found it interesting how much easier it is to administer this spell with a female host. Their life source always seems to last longer than men," he comments airily.

"Life source?" I demand, fear clouding my mind.

"Shh, hush now, here comes the tricky part," he says, his voice taking on a slightly delirious tone as he throws a handful of black liquid over me.

I retch at the smell as he moves away, setting the bottle down, and returning his attention to the book, one hand reaching up to the moon above as he reads out the incantation.

"Until the toll of midnight's bell, I offer up your dying name, hark the BloodMoon's shadow tell, of shadows life and darkness gain," he chants, his voice growing louder with each word.

The air around me grows heavier as I feel an unnatural pull in me. I choke on a gasp as I feel the blood drawn from my wounds, my fear escalating to a new level as I watch my blood lift into the air, floating above me, rippling like a ribbon in the moonlight.

My vision begins to blur as I feel my life fading away from me. Suddenly, a jolt of electricity runs through me and the sound of a whip cracking cuts through the air as the magic dissipates and gravity pulls my blood back, splashing across me as I'm bathed in my own blood.

A roar erupts from across the room where the king stands. He slams the book shut, glaring at me with a rage that fills me with icy dread.

"You whore!" he bellows, tossing the book aside.

"Please," I manage, the weakness deep set in my bones.

"You impure piece of filth! I will have your worthless life for this!" he yells as he grabs the blade once more and rushes towards me.

A scream erupts from my lips as my stomach gutters and I squeeze my eyes shut. I'm bracing myself for the pain when the king curses and I open my eyes to see him hurtling backwards into the wall with a gruesome crunch. Bright golden light explodes from me, pouring into every dark corner of the room. It burns through my bonds, through the cracks in the walls and drowns out any hint of the BloodMoon's pink light.

I feel my body pushing through the weakness and blood loss until the blinding glow dies. A hollow feeling fills my chest as I lay there, afraid yet accepting. I look to the sky, seeing nothing but a fading glow and hearing the low hum of power. Finally, darkness shrouds me and I welcome it with open arms as it pulls me under.

LYSAN

CHAPTER THIRTY

The horses are restless as I wait with them, their neighing and whinnying dismissed as my thoughts turn elsewhere. I remove the king's colours from their saddles, ripping off the royal crest to avoid rousing suspicion. The unease of what I'm about to do has me grinding my teeth and wincing at the shooting pain along my jaw.

I shift my shoulders, the Aslitír uniform a tad too tight for my frame as I try to keep my head down. Luckily, there are few people around to see me as I lead the horses through the gardens, tying them loosely to the trees near the courtyard, in view of the door.

'*I hope she knows what she's doing,*' I think to myself as my eyes linger on the entrance to the palace.

Despite myself, I glance at the rising BloodMoon, taking in the deep pink hue and the curvature of the craters visible on such a clear night. The stars glisten around its circumference, seemingly brighter besides the red moon and the deep, rich blues of the sky.

I had shadowfolded into Twyla's room the moment I'd stepped away from Keelhan, finding the young woman casually whittling one of the bedposts, a bored expression on her face.

"I was wondering when you'd show your face again," she commented dryly.

"We need to get you and the other girls out of here on the night of the BloodMoon," I told her.

"I could've told you that," she'd sniped.

I pulled out an iron key from behind me, having swiped it from under Keelhan's nose. Twyla's brow knitted together as she regarded the key, her almond eyes lifting to meet my gaze as she waited for me to explain.

"This key unlocks the cells below the palace. When the time comes, you will need to free your friend," I told her.

"What friend?" she'd asked.

"Lesya Raviffete."

The girl's eyes had widened in shock before darkening with anger. I'd noticed how her grip around the hilt of the weapon tightened. I'd thought back to Lesya then, her purple eyes and fractured mind rotting away in that dark, dank cell.

"What the fuck is wrong with that man," I heard her mutter beneath her breath.

Without a word, I held the key out for her. She watched me with a wary expression, twisting the hilt of her blade in her hand before she'd reached out and grabbed it from me.

"The rest of the plan will go ahead as normal," I'd told her.

"You said you'd signal me when it's time. What's the signal?" I added, recalling our last conversation.

She'd broken into an impish grin then, her eyes dark and secretive. "Oh, don't you worry, you'll know it when you see it."

As I'd turned, calling upon my shadows, she'd called out to me. I stopped and turned back to her, meeting her curious gaze, her head tilted to one side as she'd studied me.

"Why are you doing this? How do I know you won't betray us to your king?" she asked.

I met her gaze as Loísia's voice filtered into my mind.

'Stop this Lys, promise me you'll end this bloodshed, promise me you'll save the others who come after me.'

"I gave my word, that is all you need to know," I answered.

I turned away then, stepping towards the door as my shadows reared around me. "The BloodMoon rises in three days. I will uphold my part, but you must be ready."

And with that, I had swept from the room shrouded in shadow.

I'm torn from my thoughts as a sudden blinding flash of light illuminates the night. I shield my eyes. For some reason, it spooks the horses, who break free and gallop away before I can stop them. When I lower my arm, I look up to see the sky to see it as bright as day.

Shock and awe freeze me to the spot, words failing me as I follow it to its source: the tower. I feel my power drawn to it.

The brightness pours out of the windows of the tower until all of a sudden it dies out, the night flooding in once more. I blink away the black spots from my vision, alarm bells now ringing in my head.

I look in the direction of the fleeing horses and scowl. I have no choice but to leave them. Twyla won't be happy, but there are more pressing matters to deal with.

"*Shit*," I mutter, breaking into a run, drawing the darkness to me in swirling tendrils as I shadowfold into the palace.

I'm vaguely aware of the servants zipping past my line of view as I tear through the palace, heart thrumming in my chest at the sudden exertion. For the millionth time, I curse the wards set up around the tower, forbidding me to shadowfold inside. I look ahead as I run, turning down another corridor and colliding with someone. *Hard.*

I'm momentarily winded as I right myself and prepare to face the person I've crashed into, only to discover it's Twyla. Her eyes are erratic for a moment, her ebony hair pinned up, stray strands falling loose around her face as she straightens too. My eyes travel across her body, taking in the gown of emerald silk. I look from the small bust visible between the slips of fabric stretching over her chest to the tight waist and loose flowing skirts.

"Pretty," I comment.

"Now is *not* the time for your bullshit," she scowls, lifting her dress to resheath the tiny blade I hadn't noticed in her hand.

"What is it? That wasn't you signalling?" I ask, faltering at her expression.

"What?—No, of course not," she snaps, shaking her head.

"But we need to go. *Now*. I've rounded up the girls and sent them for Lesya, but there's one problem," she continues.

"What?" I ask, sensing that I already know.

Twyla huffs out a breath and steps closer.

"Barilius has Nesryn," she says.

I blink once, twice. Icy fingers stroke the length of my spine as I stare unseeing at Twyla. My mind is already in the tower. I glance around, aware of how exposed we are and step towards her, grabbing her arm and shadowfolding into the closest empty room.

"What the hell are you playing at, Shadowcaster?" Twyla demands as she brings the cold metal of her weapon to my throat.

I throw her away from me with a flick of my wrist, the darkness swirling around my hand.

"Now is not the time for your fucking trust issues," my tone is harsh.

Her fighting stance falters as I give her a hard stare.

"Horses are no longer an option. We'll rendezvous at the Snowhold sculpture. Tell the others to hide and wait for me there. There's a secret passage, you'll be undetected and it'll take you far away from here," I tell her.

Twyla steps forward, nodding once as she registers the information.

"No one is to know that I've helped you. Understood?" I demand.

"No one," she answers.

"If you breathe so much as a word to anyone, I'll make sure Barilius preps a spike for your head beside mine," I taunt.

She scowls but heaves a breath through her nose as she nods, her eyes serious.

"Then I have your word. When you leave this room, turn left and it'll take you back to the main corridor," I tell her, turning on my heel.

"Wait, where are you going?" she calls after me.

"I know where he's taken her. I'll get her, you worry about the others," I tell her, sprinting in the direction of the tower.

I climb the tower steps, two at a time until I reach the top. Taking a deep breath, I shroud myself in shadow and step through the door. The smell of blood and magic hits me immediately.

'If that light wasn't Twyla then what the hell caused it?' I wonder.

Even as I think it, my shadows begin to sing, their whispered voices answering a call I've not sensed in a long time. My eyes travel the space, searching as I take in Barilius's crumpled form to the right, unconscious and slumped against the wall. Swallowing the nervous lump in my throat, my eyes travel to the body laying on the black stone.

My blood runs cold as I take in Nesryn's unmoving form, fearing the worst. My powers draw me closer, as though the call is coming from her. She looks so small atop the altar, the bonds spreading her arms and legs, her glittering dress fanning out around her. I take note of her blood forming intricate patterns across the rest of the space, fizzing with golden hues of magic. My eyes move to the cuts on her feet and the angry-looking wounds across her palms.

'It couldn't have come from her... could it?' I consider the sensation settling into my bones as I look down at her.

As I take in the blood pooled around her it strikes a chord within me. Despite my better judgement, my mind takes me back to the moment in her room, her eyes frantic and afraid. I think of the pain radiating from her, the suffering she'd endured. The memory ignites my anger, burning away the ice in my veins.

"No. No more," I growl, glaring in the direction of Barilius.

I look down at her pale face and I feel myself begin to panic, the thought of another life wasted tormenting me. Just as guilt begins to claw at my stomach, I see her eyelids flutter.

'Thank the goddess,' I think to myself, pulling her into my arms.

I look down at her as I shift her in my arms, making sure she's secure as her head rests against my shoulder. I pause as her eyes open, noting the faded green hue before they close once again.

Taking one last look around at the king, I notice him beginning to shift and realise I need to hurry. I quickly call on my shadows, whisking us both away from the tower.

I land in the darkened tunnels, panting with effort as sweat begins to bead on my brow. I hold Nesryn tightly to me as I stumble in the darkness. Although memory serves me well in the catacombs, I'm aware of how little time we have.

"Sílya'Kalya," I recite the Elven spell, casting it into the darkness.

Almost instantaneously a glowing orb forms ahead of me and I inhale deeply as I look ahead and break into a run. I speed down the narrow tunnels, Nesryn tight in my arms, her legs bouncing with the movement. I glance at her pallid face as she rolls in and out of consciousness.

Memory takes over as I head towards the gardens. I grit my teeth as I prepare to shadowfold, exhaustion clawing at me as the orb blinks out of existence with us.

I appear above ground, the cool air welcome as I move through the hedges. I pant with effort as I search the path for Twyla, the shrill sound of an alarm blares from the palace. I falter, glancing over my shoulder and scowling at the sound, knowing that it can only mean one thing.

My legs carry me quickly towards the Snowhold statue when Twyla suddenly appears from the shrubs.

"The Aslitír have been alerted. We don't have much time," she tells me, her eyes drifting to Nesryn.

"I know that," I snap.

"Fuck," she breathes, helping me lower her beside the statue. "What happened to her?"

"The king almost succeeded," I answer, rounding the statue.

"Where are the others?" I ask, glancing at Twyla.

She nods her head towards another of the sculptures. "Over there, hidden," she replies.

"Lesya wasn't the only one down there, you know," she adds gravely.

My eyes dart towards her sombre face.

"Zariya and Chandra too," she says.

"Great. So, the whole gang is back together," I comment dryly.

"Not exactly. We got Zariya out. She's in a bad way though," she comments.

"Chandra?" I ask, wariness pooling in my chest.

She shakes her head and the wariness turns to frustration. Another tally to add to the list. I glance to the place where Twyla had said they were hidden and let out a heavy breath.

"They won't see you, not from there," she reassures me.

I nod, gritting my teeth as I summon my power again, straining against the exhaustion. The shadows draw to me and I wrap them around the statue, using them to push the Snowhold woman forward. Beneath her is an iron hatch that comes into view, which I instruct Twyla to lift. She does so quickly, grunting with effort.

"That's your way out. Follow it southeast, it'll bring you to the outskirts of the city," I tell her. "No matter what, don't stop, don't look back. Keep going," I tell her harshly, drilling in the point.

She nods and rushes for the others as I step back, melting into the shadows. I watch as Twyla leads them to the hole. Reverie gasps at the sight of Nesryn before a hard look washes across her face and she bends down, pulling her friend onto her back and carefully climbing down into the darkness. One by one, they follow until Twyla is the last above ground.

"Thank you," she says in earnest as I step out towards her.

She offers me a reluctant smile and steps down to follow the others, but I stop her. She hesitates, her eyes widening in surprise as I hand her my blade.

"Make it look convincing," I tell her, bracing myself.

Blood oozes from my wounds as I reach into myself, drawing upon the last ounces of strength I have left. Groaning with effort as I summon the darkness, the shadows pull the statue back over the iron hatch as though it had never moved at all.

I stumble away from the gardens, moving through the hedges and out towards the palace, taking in shallow ragged breaths. My powers are depleted, my body is weak, and exhaustion threatens to swallow me as I make it to the doors leading into the palace.

Holding my hand against the deepest of my wounds, blood seeps through my fingertips at the base of my ribs. My body suddenly wracks with a fit of coughing and I spit blood.

'Maybe a bit too convincing,' I think to myself.

I dare to think of the girls on the road to their freedom and a satisfied smile tugs at my lips. A handful of soldiers storm towards me, led by Keelhan.

"I did it, Loísia. I kept my promise," I mutter to the air.

I pull in a ragged breath as my knees buckle. The last thing that I see is Keelhan's concerned face before the velvety void of darkness pulls me under.

MAPMAKER

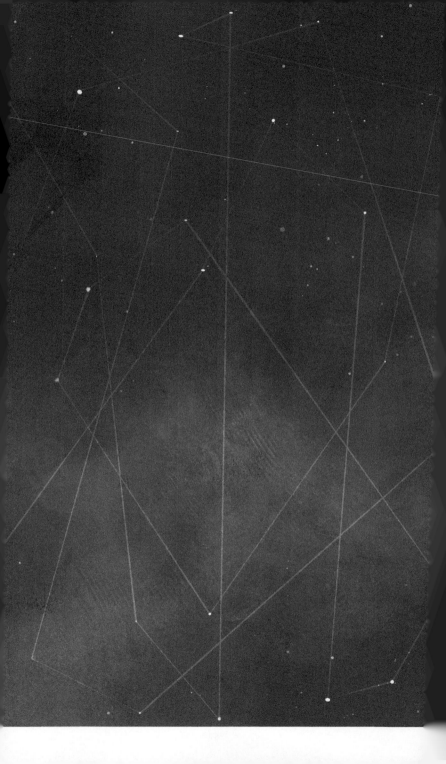

CHAPTER ThirtyOne

I wake up screaming, my throat raw as I launch myself upright, blinking and disoriented by the gloomy room. I'm shivering with cold sweat, sucking in uneven breaths as panic rises in my chest. My throat burns as bile fights its way back up. A dim glow coats the room and as I begin to catch my breath, I follow the light with my eyes. My breath hitches as I follow it down to the bunched up sheets in my hand, noting the slight smell of burning.

I recoil, dropping the sheets and staring at my open palms as I try to stop the light flowing from them. The power surges and swells as I fight against it, trying to draw it back inside. I close my eyes, releasing a long wobbly breath as I reach for the tether to the power.

After several long moments of the light flashing and dimming in my palms, I manage to quell it and it fizzles out completely, swamping me in endless darkness. I climb out of the bed and turn on the light, the cold glow bathing the room. I look back at the two large holes burned into the sheets, the edges covered in embers. Noticing the charred pieces of bandage on the bed, a defeated escapes me as I look at the damage. I sit on the edge of the bed and run my hands across my face.

I'm not at the palace.

I'm not a Chosen.

I'm safe, for now.

I repeat these three facts in my head as I look around me for the hundredth time before drawing out the bottle hidden beneath my pillow. I glance at the dwindling liquid before taking a mouthful and slipping the bottle back into its hiding place. I've lost track of how many days have slipped by since the tower. I've lost count of how many times I've woken tangled in burnt sheets, slick with sweat. I've lost count of how many days I've been holed up in this room, alone with nothing but my muddled thoughts and an elixir that I'm running low on.

The room is a box room, filled with only basic amenities: a bed, a wardrobe, a desk, and an adjoining bathroom. There are no windows, just white-washed walls on all sides and one door to go in and out. Not that I've been let out yet.

From the other side of the door, I hear a key turn in the lock and I straighten. Twyla steps into the room, her dark eyes flitting towards the damaged sheets before she meets my gaze. In her hands is a tray of steaming stew and a small roll beside a glass of water. My stomach growls at the sight of it, the smell wafting towards me. Silently, she walks over to the desk and places the tray down gently beside Stormtip before spinning on her heels.

"Will you tell me where I am?" I ask her, repeating my daily question.

As always she sighs. "You're somewhere safe, Nesryn."

I get to my feet and close the gap. Twyla's expression remains passive as I stop in front of her, meeting her gaze.

"Will you please just tell me what's going on?" I demand, frustration leaking into my voice.

"Look, I can't tell you yet. But I have brought a visitor," she explains as she walks past me, stopping at the door.

My intrigue piques at this as I turn, my eyes following her across the room. She sends me a slight smile that doesn't reach her eyes.

"I wish I could tell you more, Nesryn, especially after all you've been through. But I'm just following orders, and she's made it clear that it isn't time for you to meet her yet. Not until you've regained your strength. So I need you to be patient for just a little longer," she explains.

"Who—wait—" I call after her.

She's left before I can utter another word and I falter as a familiar face enters the room, clicking the door shut behind him.

He stands tall, just as he always has, his locks tied up into a ponytail. His chin is thick with facial hair which has grown substantially since that last time I saw him, making him seem older. His dark eyes are the same, warm and familiar.

"Hello, Nix," his voice rumbles, thick with emotion.

A whimper bubbles up in my throat, escaping me before I can hold back. Tears of relief brim in my eyes as I rush towards his open arms, crashing into him and wrapping my arms around him. I bury my face in his chest and inhale the scent of cedar and the ocean as his arms slip around me.

His familiar embrace is warm and welcome, and for a split second, I relish it. Then in my mind's eye, I see the flash of blue eyes and the stench of ale. The panic sets in before I can prepare myself, my skin crawling from the closeness and my chest seizes as I push away from him, recoiling from his touch as he watches me, the pain in his eyes palpable.

"I-I'm sorry. Goddess knows I've missed you, but I can't-I just can't," the words tumble from my lips between hiccuped breaths.

I step back, bumping against the desk, my hands finding the edge and gripping on as tightly as I can in an attempt to ground myself.

"I understand, I can't imagine what you've gone through," he manages, his eyes never straying from me as he moves to the bed.

I watch as his attention shifts to the two holes in my bedsheets. Shame creeps over me as I watch his reaction, waiting for a look of disgust or horror. Instead, I'm surprised to find grim resignation on his face.

"I heard there had been an incident at the palace, one connected to Starweavers. I just had no idea it was you," my uncle says.

I stare down at my hands, the truth laid out before me. "Starweaver," I repeat in disbelief.

"It's a gift, a tremendous talent," he reasons.

"A talent that I have no control over," I frown, thinking back to the many times I had fought with the power coiled within me and no idea how to handle it.

"I'm sure that will come with time, Nix," he says gently.

When I look up at him, his expression is strained. "I wish there was more time. There is so much I need to say to you," he sighs.

I open my mouth to reply and I feel my eyes glossing over as I think of how I had wished to be back at his side, wished for his advice, the comfort and safety of him when I had been deep within The Choosing.

"I missed you," I murmur.

He looks at me then, his eyes full of love and warmth. "I'm so grateful to see you here. I was so afraid—" he chokes.

"—I'm here, I survived," I say, reassuring him as much as myself.

"Barilius has kept us in the dark about The Choosing for too long, now we finally hold the upper hand," he cuts in, his fists clenched.

"The king is a tyrant," I spit.

"There are rumours flying around that one of his own helped you escape," Uncle Erathon gives me a questioning look and I can't help but notice the suspicious glint in his eye.

"I don't know what they have to gain by helping us, whoever they are," I reply, trying to recall the face of the person who carried me from certain death.

"They may prove to be a crucial ally," Uncle Erathon reasons, tilting his head.

"An ally for *who* exactly?" I demand pacing back and forth.

My uncle watches me carefully and I can tell that he's weighing out his options. Whether to give me an answer or to keep me in the dark. Something within me snaps.

"I'm sick of secrets, I'm sick of deceit, of the wool being pulled over my eyes. I'm *done* being kept in the dark, Uncle," I bite.

His attention falls to my clenched hands, the bright glow of my power reflecting in the dark pools of his eyes. His mouth is set in a thin line before he sighs, defeated.

Hope sparks in my chest and my power draws back into me, surprising us both as the glow disappears. I stare at my scarred palms, speechless. He takes a deep breath in and nods matter-of-factly.

"I think it's time you met Rowena."

Uncle Erathon leads me down narrow corridors with low ceilings. Not a single person passes us on our way and it leaves me with an eerie feeling, making me glad I snuck Stormtip out of its hiding place and sheathed it safely beneath my clothes. The empty halls of the palace creep into my mind unbidden and I shiver. The space feels compact and I find myself glad that I'm not claustrophobic as the path becomes narrower and the walls tilt inwards ever so slightly. The walls are plain and mud-coloured, interrupted only by shabby wooden doors every few yards. The air, albeit musty, smells like the sea and I wonder briefly how close we are to water.

Finally, as we round another bend, the corridor widens and a few stray people wander past. I watch them curiously: a dark-haired woman, a raven-haired young man whose almond eyes drift towards me after nodding at my uncle; and finally another young man with bright auburn hair. My eyes follow him as we cross paths, taking in his broad arms weighted down with scraps of metal and pieces of machinery. His warm brown eyes meet mine for a split second as we pass each other and when I glance back over my shoulder, his impish grin widens and he winks at me. I turn my head back around quickly, feeling a blush creep up my neck while I stare determinedly at the back of Uncle Erathon's head.

He slows as we arrive at a pair of large double metal doors. He glances over his shoulder at me before throwing both doors open and stepping through. I don't know what I was expecting, but it certainly wasn't a cluster of people huddled around a large table in the middle of a rather spacious room. Nerves bite at me as I step into the room after my uncle.

There are six of them in total, three women and three men. They snap their heads up in unison, momentarily distracted from whatever they were studying on the table between them. One of the women, in particular, holds an heir of authority as she looks at me. Her dark eyes narrow as she eyes me, and a strand of her bright red hair falls to frame her face, curling down towards her chin as the corner of her lips tug up slightly. The top section is tied back, tumbling over her shoulders and down her back. Beside her, one of the young men watches me curiously, his tousled blond hair falls across his forehead, complimenting his hazel eyes. I move along the line of unfamiliar faces until I stop at the third woman, a gasp escaping my mouth. My eyes widen as Twyla stares out at me amongst the group of strangers, her surprise mirroring mine.

"What in the goddesses name is this?" I demand, swerving around to Uncle Erathon.

"Nesryn, look, there is a lot that you don't understand yet," Twyla starts to reason.

Her gaze moves to my uncle and her eyes narrow as she looks to him, her expression grim. "I was told she wasn't ready."

I frown and turn to look back at my uncle, frustration seeping into me as he looks past me to my prior competitor. "I'll decide when she's ready."

"How about no one decides for me?" I cut in, glaring at them both.

I march towards Twyla as my anger flares. "What I want to know is where the hell you've brought me and why."

She pulls back as I approach her, a flicker of fear in her eyes, her unease evident. As I get closer, the fear fades, replaced by steely determination. She takes a deliberate step towards me as her brow knits together.

"I had orders and I followed them. I regret nothing. You and the others are safe, and that bastard Barilius didn't get what he wanted," she snaps.

'*The others!*' I yell, thinking of poor Ria stuck somewhere in this twisting labyrinth.

"We are a group who seek to challenge the current king. We don't follow his ways or methods of running our kingdom, Nix," Uncle Erathon cuts in.

I glance towards him as gestures to the people in front of us. "I have brought you before just a handful of our members. But the one I wanted you to meet tonight is one of our leaders. Rowena."

'*So, this is the rebel group,*' I realise, recalling some mention of them in the palace.

"Well then, now that we've got the reunions out of the way…" an impatient voice cuts in.

I look past Twyla to where the red-headed woman now stands, leaning casually against the table, her arms folded across her chest.

"What our fearless and oh-so-modest ring leader means is that we want you to join us. You have valuable information on the king that we could use, and we can offer you the chance at revenge for your fallen comrades," she continues.

'*Ring leader?*' I turn in shock to meet my uncle's eye, but he refuses to look at me.

Shock and understanding hit me at once and I find myself reeling. I consider all my uncle's political views from over the years, the odd absences, and the less than enthusiastic attitude towards the king and The Choosing. I'm so stunned that I forget what she said.

"It's your choice," Rowena shrugs. "You can continue with your worthless life, or you can become someone who matters."

That gets my attention.

"Because what I've gone through, what I and others have suffered within those walls clearly doesn't," I spit back.

"May matter to you, but you see, girl, our cause matters plenty more than that," she states.

Anger spikes within me. "If you're trying to scare me, it's not working," I tell her through clenched teeth.

"Oh?"

"You're just pissing me off," I finish.

"I don't care about one person's feelings. We're on the verge of war here, girl, and I need to know which side you stand on. His or ours," she counters.

"*Row*," Uncle Erathon warns.

"Oh come on, Thorn, you know what's at stake here! If the girl can't take it she should run back to the palace to play princess," Rowena retorts.

The anger in my chest spikes and my powers burst to life. My arm whips out without warning, the light pouring freely from my palm and twisting into a long tendril that flies towards the redhead. I make it move to my will, wrapping it around her and throwing her against the nearest wall. Those around us cry out and clear the space, but I ignore them, my attention trained on the woman in my grasp.

"I have watched friends die needlessly, I have been attacked, beaten, tortured by trials I had no control over and shackled to a fucking altar as a sacrifice for whatever demons Barilius worships," I tell her, my anger and power rising with each word that leaves my lips.

I press Stormtip to her cheek, my furious gaze boring into hers. "Insult me again, and the next breath you take will be your last,"

"Bit of a hothead, aren't you?" she observes, seemingly unfazed by the cold steel digging into her.

"Just like her father," she continues, directing the comment this time to my uncle.

Shock cools my temper and the firm grip I'd had on my power slips, the light fizzling and fading as I step back. I try to read her face, my brow furrowed, but I've never been any good at reading strangers. I turn around, only to find my uncle already watching me with a wary look. I narrow my eyes, turning back to her.

"What do you know about my father?"

"Plenty," she replies, glancing knowingly at my uncle.

My gaze snaps back to him. "What the fuck is she talking about? Talk," I snap, pulling the blade away from her cheek.

"You've got some bite to you, haven't you? I like that," Rowena purrs, wiping the blood from her chin and glancing at it.

"Rowena that's *enough*," my uncle looks at her, his expression darkening as they hold each other's stare.

"Fine, Thorn. You win. But I hope you know what you're doing," she says dryly.

Rowena's scrutinising gaze darts back to me, along with five other pairs of curious eyes. I want to shrink back, feeling suddenly unsure of myself as I realise how little I really know about everything.

Silence ensues as she folds her arms across her chest and studies me with a thoughtful expression. As I think of my friends somewhere in this strange place, and all of the truths that have come to light, her expression shifts and changes into something like resignation. She unfolds her arms and half-heartedly gestures around us.

"Nesryn Havenore, welcome to The Righteous Hand."

CHAPTER THIRTYTWO

The rats haven't bothered me yet today.

I wonder if I'll wake up to their sharp bites tonight, if I'll manage to keep the pesky little bastards at bay, or whether I'll collapse into yet another fitful sleep plagued with nightmarish horrors.

The stench of mould and mildew is distasteful but I've grown used to it. It's the icy cold that causes my body to protest, seizing up my joints to the point of pain. The cell is small and cramped, with black mould rotting away the walls, and no window to keep my mind busy. Time is endless in here, and the lack of elvynlight keeps me from deciphering the time; each day blends seamlessly into the next when you're kept in perpetual night.

I sit in the far corner of the tiny space, my back pressed up against the moist wall. I try to move as little as possible, but with every breath, a tight pull of burning pain seeps into my bones from the fever wracking my body. Daring to lift my shirt, I examine the now filthy bandages wrapped around my middle. Blood and pus seep through the strips of cloth, the smell is enough to turn my stomach. I don't let myself think about what will happen if the wound isn't treated soon.

The groan of the cell door draws me from my feverish thoughts. I squint as a light shines in my face, blinking as a silhouette comes into view. I strain my neck to avoid the light, trying to get a better look at the visitor, to no avail. The metal collar slices into my neck and I jump as it pinches my skin like a vice. I shift my weight to release the pressure off my back. It screams in protest as I tip my head back and sit up straight. Heavy boots clip against the wet stone as black spots blur the edges of my vision. For the first time since I was thrown in here,

I dare to wonder what awaits me when I inevitably face the king. I fight the shudder that rattles through me as I refrain from brushing my fingers against the collar.

I look up at my visitor, my vision hazy but clear enough to pick out those familiar eyes.

Keelhan.

His lips are set in a thin line as he studies me for several moments, his arms folded across his chest.

"Lysander Pyremear, you have an audience with the king,"

"Oh, we're using full names now are we, *Keelhan*?" I comment wryly.

I attempt to get to my feet, using the wall to support me. My limbs are heavy and stiff from the lack of use. I feel hollow and alien without the strength of my shadows, without my magic. I hiss through my teeth as the wounds on my back reopen from the movement, my pride fading as the pain resurfaces. My knees buckle and I drop back to the floor, my wrists jarring on impact with the icy stone. I swallow my temper as I hear some guards snicker under their breath behind their captain. They know that I can't do anything while wearing this collar and they're revelling in it.

The amusement is gone from my eyes when I look up at his men, my stare unflinchingly cold. Their smiles fade instantly. Keelhan clears his throat and they snap to attention as he gives them a hard look. I watch as he slowly kneels on one knee and regards me with solemn eyes and a pitying smile.

"I will help you until we reach the doors of the throne room," he informs me.

Anger bubbles within me, a reaction to my sense of pride. I want to tell him I can make it alone, that I don't need his help, but my body is weak and I have no magic to aid me until this wretched collar is removed. I swallow my words and my throat bobs, brushing against the metal. I fight the urge to shudder. I won't give him the satisfaction of seeing me struggle more than I have to. Him or his men.

"Lys... you know that when we reach—" Keelhan continues, his voice low and his eyes shifting uncomfortably.

I meet his eyes with a sharp look. "I know," I cut in.

'*I will show no weakness in his presence, never again.*' I vow to myself.

Holding my head higher, determination settles in my chest. "Take me to him."

The trip from the dungeons is long and rough, even with Keelhan's aid. My eyes ache at the brightness after the long days of darkness, the strain of the light causes a pounding sensation behind my skull.

Everything seems bigger, the corridors wider, the walls higher than before—though maybe it's because I've been cooped up in a box for countless days. My back throbs with pain, the heat of it burning through my skin and into my chest. I can sense the amusement of Keelhan's men flanking us, and I know it has always brought them great pleasure to watch a Shadowcaster suffer.

We turn the corner and Keelhan stops before the large doors. He drops my arms and I sway as I try to keep myself upright. I'm so tired, I feel in my very bones, but I manage to remain standing.

I pause there, letting time slip by as I wait for the Aslitír to open the doors for me, but they don't. Anger and frustration fight to creep through the nonchalant mask I've so carefully crafted. I glance back over my shoulder at the one on my right.

"Don't insult me. Open the doors," I order them.

I feel their hesitance. But even in my current state, I still hold greater power than they ever could. Ranks be damned.

"Do as he says," Keelhan barks, furrowing his brow.

The men stride forwards, pulling open the heavy doors with grunts and strains until there is enough space for both of us to walk through into the throne room, side by side. I inhale once as I prepare myself to face the king again. I wonder idly what this latest disappointment will cause me.

Across the empty hall, Barilius sits on his throne as he usually does, his body slumped backwards in a seemingly leisurely manner. Yet another part of his deception. He holds an envelope in his hand and dangles it carelessly above the lone candle at his side. I expect the slow-burning of the paper to snap him out of his relaxed posture, but to my surprise, he doesn't move a muscle. I blink in surprise as the flame turns from orange to black and the envelope vanishes into the flame. Thinking myself to be delirious, I look to the floor and back to the candle again. The candle has returned to its normal colour, and I wonder if I'd seen it change at all. As I step closer, I see the sharp gleam of his eyes and the anger rolls off him in waves.

Somehow, I manage to drop down to one knee without groaning, bowing my head before him. "My king."

"It would seem I didn't leave you down there long enough if you're still standing," Barilius sneers as I manage to straighten.

I watch as he strokes his beard, his ringed fingers pulling it to a point, the picture of careful contemplation. His amber eyes flash and he stands suddenly, prowling along the strip of carpet towards me, stopping a mere few feet away.

"Tell me, boy, how did my Chosen escape their guards, my men, *and* my most powerful Shadowcaster?" he asks, finally breaking the silence.

"They must've had help, my king," I answer, meeting his gaze.

"And who do you suppose did that?" he snipes, glaring at me.

I swallow. "Spies hidden within the palace. These girls knew how to best me and my powers. I only just managed to stop them from harming you. I lost them in the gardens after I followed them there. They must have had information on where to go, and how to do it undetected," the lie is well-rehearsed and comes easily.

King Barilius's brow raises as he studies me. It's nothing he hasn't heard before in my earlier interrogations, only this time, his rage is not at the forefront of this questioning.

"Rebels?" he questions.

"They've been causing issues in Tralló for months. Who's to say they haven't been using that as a distraction to somehow infiltrate the palace," I reason.

"I fear Lysander may be right. These rebels are smart, Your Highness, and their numbers are amassing as we speak. I have no doubt that they are the culprits here, they must have found a way to smuggle The Chosen out," Keelhan cuts in.

Barilius's gaze moves from me to his captain as his expression darkens with rage. "Rebels who have been allowed to escape my Aslitír! Tell me, *Captain*, do I need to make an example of you too? Do I need to have Lysander clean up your mess *again*?"

Keelhan's eyes flicker to mine briefly in understanding. I fight against the memory of the messenger boy and how his blood clung to my skin. Bile rises up in my throat.

'*People are right to be afraid of you,*' Nesryn's voice taunts.

"No, my king," Keelhan says finally. "I will do everything in my power to detain these rebels and bring back your Chosen few," he continues, dropping into a bow.

"I don't want you to *detain* any of them. They have mocked my power by stealing from me. No, Captain, I want them killed on sight. Every single treasonous bastard," he spits.

I glance at Keelhan's frozen face as he digests his orders. He swallows once, then nods slowly, the picture of obedience. But I can see from how his eyes have darkened that this will plague him later.

"Yes... my king."

"And the Chosen?" I dare to ask.

Barilius turns back to face me, a cruel smile twisting his lips as his eyes dance with a sadistic fury that sends my heart skittering in my chest. "I'm going to make an example of them."

As much as I'm tempted to see Keelhan's reaction, I don't look at him again, even when Barilius dismisses him with an impatient flick of his wrist. Instead, I keep my eyes trained on Barilius as he watches me back. There's no way I'm letting my guard down around him now. He steps closer, his smile slipping into more of a grimace as he catches a whiff of me.

He takes a step back, flattening his tunic as if he can wipe away the filth off from me. His eyes flicker to my neck. "Let your time in that cell resonate with you."

Before I can utter a word, he grunts and reaches for my neck, his eyes levelling with mine.

"Do not sabotage yourself, boy. Your place at my side will remain for now, but my patience will only spare your fuck-ups for so long," he warns.

"Yes. Thank you, my king," I answer.

With the next movement of his fingers, the magic binding the collar to me seeps away, and I feel the sigh of relief run through me as my own magic returns. He lowers his hands, pulling it away with him as we hold each other's stare.

The hollow feeling disappears as my powers flood through me once more. My heart picks up speed as I feel my power revitalise me. I fight the urge to use my shadows, to work them after so long without, but I hold back, remembering whose presence I'm in.

"If I find that you have anything to do with this, anything at all, I will strip you away to nothing," he tells me.

Before I can open my mouth, he dismisses me. He walks back to the throne, turning the collar over in his hands like an unspoken warning.

NESRYN

CHAPTER THIRTYTHREE

Twyla is the one who returns me to my room and I find myself disappointed as I think of my uncle's feeble excuse for leaving me. I'm quiet as I follow her back through the winding corridors, my head muddled and filled with questions. The effects of the elixir have long since left me and all I want is to down the last mouthful and sleep dreamlessly.

"All this time... Why did he never say anything?" I ask.

Twyla glances distractedly back at me as she walks. "Erathon knows how vital our cause is. Perhaps he was protecting you as much as he did us? I'm sure he'll come find you to explain once he's done back there."

"Where are the others? Where are my friends?" I press.

Twyla heaves a sigh as we stop by an open archway. She leans against the wall as she meets my eye.

"They're being questioned right now. You'll be reunited with them soon enough, Nesryn. Just try to be patient for a little longer," she answers, her condescending tone making me bristle.

My frustration grows and I scowl in silence. Twyla's eyes flit down to my clenched fists, her almond eyes narrowing.

"You may want to ease off the abilities for now. No one is out to get you, and we can't be having a Starweaver temper tantrum, now can we?"

I blink, the glow in my hands fizzling out. "What did you call me?"

"It's what you are, isn't it?" she answers with a shrug.

"I don't know what I am, but I can't be," I argue in disbelief.

She then moves to the side and gestures for me to go into the room beyond the archway. My chest squeezes as I take in the room that's definitely way bigger than the one that I left.

"This isn't my room," I state.

"I know. You're here to see Yvaine. She'll be asking you some questions and helping you manage your powers," she explains.

"I told you, I can't be a Starweaver—" I begin, only to be cut short as she lifts a hand to silence me.

She juts her chin towards the room and after another moment of watching her, I do. As I look around the room, I take in the heavy smell of potions cooking and aged books. The space is much larger than the tiny dent in the wall that is my room. Not a single space is left empty. The wide gaps between the shelves are filled with glass bottles, each one holding a unique ingredient for a magical potion. The other spaces are filled with thick leather-bound books, the spines turned out just so, the alphabetical order on full display.

A low table stands to the right, handfuls of open maps and pieces of parchment sprawled across it, lit with an orb of hovering elvynlight. And to the left is a low chest of drawers beside a closed door. There are a few personal touches displayed on the drawers, but otherwise, it's the plainer half of the room.

Twyla brushes past me into the room. "Yvie!" she calls.

"Come on in, I'll be right there," a voice calls back.

Twyla turns back to me and encourages me closer with a smirk. "Don't worry, she doesn't bite."

As I inch closer, I hear someone rummaging through the shelves further back and try to peer around Twyla, but whoever is there is too far back for me to see. Twyla gestures for me to sit on the only chair in the room but the rummaging stops and Yvie appears from behind the shelves.

I don't know what I expected—maybe someone standoffish like Twyla—but I know I didn't expect the young woman before me. Her porcelain face is framed with lengths of rich brown hair that falls just over her shoulders, and wide, clouded blue eyes. A sprinkle of freckles are scattered over her nose and beneath her bottom lashes, and her small mouth curls into a wide, welcoming smile as her eyes fall on me.

She is petite but shapely, I notice, as she manoeuvres herself around the shelves towards us. I glance at the chair she sits in, noticing how it's decorated brightly, like an extension of herself as she wheels herself closer to us. A strange sensation ripples through me as I look at her, my powers ignite within me, somehow drawn to her despite me managing to hold back.

I swallow my questions as she reaches us, though more emerge as Twyla leans forward, bending to plant a quick kiss on her lips. Heat rises up my neck as I quickly look away, scrambling to find anything more interesting than the two women.

"You can go now," the girl says to Twyla, smirking.

"Well then, Nesryn, I'll leave you in Yvie's capable hands," she tells me.

I watch as she backs towards the door, winking at Yvaine as she does. "I'll swing by later. Good luck!"

With one last flourish, she's gone. And I'm left alone with Yvaine.

Silence fills the air for several long moments as I take the seat that Twyla pointed to and face her.

Her smile returns as she meets my gaze. "Well Nesryn, it's nice to meet you. Yvaine Cregore, at your service." She holds out an ink-splattered hand.

Tentatively I reach out, sucking in a breath as I shake her hand. I draw my hand back quickly before the crawling starts. If it bothers her, she doesn't say.

"I know this is a lot, especially after everything you've been through, but I need to question you like the others. Then we can get to the fun part," she says.

"The fun part?" I query.

Yvaine smiles wryly at me as she lifts her hand. Bright sparks fly from it, twirling through the air in front of her before fading into nothing as she shuts her fist. I stare at her, wide-eyed and open-mouthed.

"You're a Starweaver," I breathe finally.

"Just like you," she points out.

I shake my head as I look down at my open palms. "I don't know what I am, but I can't be. These powers revealed themselves through the trials."

"Yes, well, we know about those. Barbaric man…" she tuts, her eyes darkening.

"Nesryn, in the girls' briefings they mentioned the king took you somewhere, but none of them could tell us where," she speaks slowly, almost warily.

I'm suddenly transported back to that room, full of bottles and potions. The memory of the cool stone against my back, the restraints rubbing against my wrists and ankles. I feel my heart thumping in my chest.

"We'd gone for a stroll, and Barilius… he mentioned the BloodMoon. The next thing I remember is waking up in that tower," I reply, my voice quiet as I meet her eyes.

"What else do you remember?" she asks.

I think of the way he'd sliced his blade across my hands and feet, how he'd sneered and chanted the words that haunt my dreams.

'Until the toll of midnight's bell, I offer up your dying name, hark the BloodMoon's shadow tell, of shadows life and darkness gain.'

"He told me he wanted my life source. I-I think he was practising forbidden magic, *dark* magic. And I don't think it was the first time either," I tell her.

"I would tend to agree. That palace is a breeding ground for evil intent," she murmurs, her expression worrisome.

"It didn't work though, the spell went wrong somehow. But I know if it wasn't for the light, I wouldn't be alive right now," I continue.

"That was you," she answers.

"What was me?" I ask, glancing back toward her.

"The light, it came from you. You were defending yourself," she explains, searching my face. "You must have wielded it with enough force that it drained your strength faster than you could draw it back. It would explain your weakened state when you arrived," she says to herself, deep in thought.

"But I didn't mean to do anything," I argue.

"Hold out your hand," she says with a soft smile.

I do as she asks, watching as light ignites her fingertips and extends into the air in long wisps. I feel my own power come to life within me as I mimic Yvaine. I become giddy almost as the light from my hand swirls into the air. The twin beams of light spin around one another before colliding with a jolt, the glow brightening and then dissipating into nothing. I let out a shuddering breath, feeling lighter than before.

"You felt it when you walked through that door, just as I did. We are the same, Nesryn," she says.

"But I never had these powers before the trials," I frown.

"Starweavers are born, not made, Nesryn," she reasons.

"But I'm telling you, I didn't have them before. They appeared after the trial where I got the spell wrong," I recall, remembering the moment I'd been flung across the room.

"What spell?" Yvaine asks, leaning forward.

"It was an unbinding spell, to open a locked box," I tell her. "Only it didn't so much unlock the box, it just—" I lean back in my chair, my eyes widening in realisation.

"—It unlocked you," Yvaine finishes.

She turns her chair and wheels closer to me, a pensive expression on her face. "It seems to me that a dampening spell was placed on you, probably as a child. And when you cast this unbinding spell in the trial, you freed yourself from your invisible chains."

I think of the way the power feels within me, how familiar yet strange. I wonder why I'd never felt incomplete without them if I really did have them from the moment I came into the world.

"But why would anyone want to hide my powers?" I ask, staring down at my hands in disbelief.

Yvaine shrugs, letting out a heavy breath. "That isn't an answer I'd be able to help you with, I'm afraid,"

Disappointment tugs at me, but I try to swallow the bitter feeling as Yvaine draws my attention back to her. She gives me another warm smile and this time I can't help returning it.

"But I can help you learn to use your powers," she adds.

I nod shyly, a bloom of hope unfurling within me for the first time in a long time.

'I will not be helpless. I will not be the victim.'

"Going back to Barilius, in the tower… Do you remember who helped you? If you drained yourself you wouldn't have been able to get yourself out, Starweaver or not," she says.

I think back to the moment after the darkness, the moment I knew I wasn't alone. I close my eyes as I recall my bonds being cut and someone lifting me into their arms. I remember fading in and out as I was carried through the palace, into the cool night air.

I remember opening my eyes and looking at them, their face had been a blur, but I had seen it before my descent into darkness once more.

The more I try to focus on their face, the more it slips away from me and I scowl as I open my eyes in frustration.

"I wasn't alone, but I can't tell you who helped me, I'm sorry," I answer in defeat. "But whoever it was, they saved my life."

Yvaine's questions continue on for a while longer before, eventually, she stops.

I fiddle with Stormtip's hilt as I find myself craving an escape from it all, the questions and the memories that haunt me. As I glance back towards the rows of bottles lined up along the shelves, I think of the elixir that the healer had given me and before I know what I'm doing, the words slip from my lips.

"Pharopedil?" Yvaine frowns, following my gaze to the potions behind her. "Yes I have some in supply, did you need it?" she asks.

"It helps… with the nightmares and the flashbacks. A healer at the castle gave me some after a few of the ordeals…" I explain, feeling the heat of my embarrassment crawl up my neck.

She smiles in understanding and swivels around, stretching up to reach the shelves. She plucks one of the closest bottles, a diamond-shaped bottle in a brilliant shade of deep blue. She returns to the table and holds it out to me. I take it and pull the cork free, peering inside at the familiar greyish liquid with its golden hue.

"I trust you know how powerful it is? How to use it responsibly?" she comments, her cloudy blue eyes analysing me.

I swallow the uncomfortable lump in my throat and nod, whilst slipping it into the pocket of my borrowed clothes. I look up to find her watching me thoughtfully.

"I'll have someone send some more appropriate clothes to your room," she observes.

I look down at the oversized tunic and baggy trousers, my lips drawing up into a half-smile. Oversized or not, anything is better than the king's vaitas or the black gown he was willing to kill me in. I shudder at the thought, the memory of his amber eyes and his cruel smile too raw for me to bear.

"If that's all, then I'd like to go back to my room now," I tell her as I stand, the thought of that small box room suddenly welcoming.

She nods once with a tight smile and I turn to make my leave. I pull in a lungful of air which I release in one shaky breath when Yvaine calls out my name. I turn back, searching her troubled face.

"I know Row and the others haven't given you much choice in joining our cause, they assume you want revenge for what has happened to you and your friends—"

"—They would be right," I cut in, clenching my fists.

"Well, revenge isn't what The Righteous Hand stands for, but we're a family here and we take care of our own. The king has taken something from each of us, and what we're doing here is important for the future of our kingdom," she continues.

"I'm no longer naive enough to believe that the king's intentions are good. I see him for what he is: a tyrant. I know what we're up against. The question is, do you?"

She sighs. "What I'm trying to say is, when you were a Chosen, you never had a choice. But here with us, you have a choice, you will *always* have a choice."

I feel the anger fizzle away at her kindness. "Thank you, Yvaine."

"My friends call me Yvie" she replies, cocking her head to one side as her smile returns.

"Nes," I smile in return.

"Noted," she nods, her smile faltering as she looks up at me again.

"But Nesryn—Nes. If you do join our cause, you need to be prepared for everything this life will throw at you. Row, especially, will push you for information. You'll need to be ready to fight if need be. You need to decide if you will let your choices break you or define you."

Yvie's words stay with me as I wander down the length of corridor, trying to find my way back to my room, her directions quickly forgotten. I pull out the blue bottle as I walk, again ignoring the pipette and swallowing a mouthful instead. The magic fizzes as it runs down my throat, spreading through me quickly. I sigh with satisfaction as the worries and haunting memories melt away, and for the first time in days, my mind is clear.

I wander aimlessly, a carefree smile on my lips. I feel the tiredness in my bones but it doesn't bother me nearly as much as it did before. Although I know I'm lost, there is a spring in my step and a vague sense of adventure coursing through me as I round the corner, colliding straight into someone.

I sprawl back against the wall behind me, blinking in surprise as I see a familiar pair of hazel eyes. I get to my feet as he rights himself and sends me a dazzling smile. I can't help but notice how straight his teeth are as I lean against the wall to steady myself.

"Sorry about that, didn't see you," the man says, his accent crisp.

My eyes widen as I study his face, wagging a pointed finger at him as I recognise him. "You're the man from earlier, the one in the hall beside Rowena," I state.

"Well spotted," he chuckles and shakes his head slightly, his tousled blonde hair swaying with the subtle movement. "And you're Nesryn," he adds, his eyes travelling over me.

"Actually I'm lost," I reply with a sheepish smile.

He barks out a round of laughter, causing my lips to tug up at the sides. I feel light and airy as I stand there, the tingle of the elixir going to my head. When his laughter dies down, he crosses his arms and leans casually against the bend, studying me with an amused smile.

"I must say, you're not quite what I expected," he tells me, a dimple appearing in his cheek.

"And what exactly were you expecting?" I ask, curiosity getting the better of me.

His smile deepens, causing the dimple to become more pronounced. I fight the urge to stare at it, focusing instead on his next words as he pulls away from the wall.

"You know what, I'm not sure. But whatever it was, it was far less interesting," he says, turning on his heel. "Come on, I'll show you back. I think I know which room is yours," he calls over his shoulder.

I waste no time following, hurrying quickly after the intriguing man. We walk and talk through the maze of winding corridors until he stops in a vaguely familiar hall beside the closest door.

"Well, we have arrived," he states with a smirk, folding his hands over his chest.

I twist the handle and push the door open, pleasantly surprised to find that it is my room.

"Thank you," I beam.

"Pleasure is all mine. It's an honour to meet the daughter of our founders," he replies with a wink.

"Founders?" I grin, thinking he's telling some joke that I'm not getting. I tilt my head slightly and he dips his head as he smiles, half a dimple appearing.

I wait for his amusement to subside so he can explain. I lean against the door to my room when he finally lifts his head.

"Anwyn Eliffire and Faolán Havenore. They were the ones who started The Righteous Hand, who created all of this," he explains, gesturing to everything around us.

My smile slips and my head starts to spin.

He looks at me then, with curious eyes, his brows knitting together. "Didn't you know?"

CHAPTER THIRTYFOUR

"It's over," I breathe as I manage to shut the door behind me.

I lean my body against the door, my earlier strength waning. Looking around my room, I see nothing out of place and I'm grateful that it's been left undisturbed. After so many days of being cramped in a dingy cell, it feels strange to have so much room to move around in, so much clean air to inhale. I notice the stifling scent of my grimy skin then. I hobble over to the washroom and turn on the tap, watching the hot water rise with anticipation. After a moment's hesitation, I drop in some healing remedies and watch as they swirl in the rippling water.

With strenuous effort, I peel the clothes from my body and dump them on the floor, making a mental note to dispose of them properly later. I hiss as the hot water reaches my back, the open wounds stinging against the heat. Once I'm fully submerged, I manage to relax my shoulders, letting the water soak through the layers of grime and filth etched into my skin. The stinging soon subsides into a rhythmic throb as the remedies begin to work their magic. I breathe in a lungful of air and slip beneath the surface, water filling my ears and drowning out the silence with a low roar of pumping blood. I let myself feel weightless as I run my hands across my face, finally allowing myself to replay that night over in my head.

When I finally break the surface, there are stars floating around my vision. I think of The Chosen, and of their escape. I don't dare to wonder what will happen now, what the king will order me to do to The Righteous Hand rebels. My stomach turns at the thought.

I lean back in the bath, resting my head against it as my eyes flutter shut.

I'm floating in an endless sea, then I'm not.

My surroundings sharpen and I'm in the depths of the maze, the swirling mist at my feet, and the endless night above. My legs move of their own accord and as I look ahead, I see a glimpse of white disappearing around the corner. Curiosity gets the better of me and I follow, peering around the corner as I reach it.

This time, my heart stops, and my mouth dries at the sight of her.

She turns back towards me, clad in a beautiful shimmering gown of pearlescent white, the top of it hugging her petite frame and stretching along the lengths of her porcelain arms. Her eyes meet mine and I'm taken back by how bright their blue hue is, like a clear sky on a frosty Snowhold morning. Her dewy skin has a breathtaking glow to it but my eyes are drawn to her lips. They curve into a secretive smile that sends a flutter through me as she brushes her platinum waves over her shoulder.

"Loísia," I breathe. In that moment, her name is the answer to everything.

Her giggle drifts towards me as she turns and picks up speed, her skirts floating out behind her as she runs through the maze. I give chase, calling out to her as I do, but she only laughs, the sound echoing through the high hedges. I practically fly down the winding path after her, my feet barely touching the ground. We break away from the maze and suddenly a tower looms ahead of us. I falter in my run, losing momentum as I stare up at the statue, only to look back down just to see Loísia disappear through the entrance.

"No, wait!" I shout after her, but she's already out of sight.

I refuse to give in to defeat. I rush up the swirling staircase two at a time. Her tinkling laughter disappears further up the winding steps and when I finally reach the large wooden door, I throw it open so hard that it judders on its hinges. I spot her almost immediately. She's facing away from me, her long blonde hair swaying against the small of her back. Her hands hang limply at her sides, her body angled towards the altar of black stone.

My stomach twists at the sight of it.

"Lou?" I call warily, my voice no more than a whisper.

As my hand touches her shoulder and I spin her around, her eyes are no longer blue, her skin no longer pale and glowing. Instead, I'm met with eyes of spring and soft tawny skin. Coils of rich brown shape her face, falling over her shoulders and springing at her back.

"You can't save us, not in the end," Nesryn's voice is haunting.

I take a step back, shock dulling my senses as she moves a step closer.

"You aren't a hero," she continues, her expression neutral.

"But I did save you. Barilius can't hurt you, you're free of him," I argue, though I know deep down that it wasn't enough.

"We'll never be free of him," she replies.

I open my mouth to speak, but no words come.

"You'll watch me die, just like you did with her. Because you're the enemy," she continues.

"No!" I yell. "I made a promise!"

"You're a monster just like him, Lysan. You cannot save, you only destroy," she says as she stops in front of me, her angry eyes boring into mine.

I wake up with a jolt, sending rough waves rippling across the surface. The water is stone cold, my skin prickling as I climb out. I regret giving in to the tiredness as the pain in my joints comes back anew with the frigid air.

I try to shake the remnants of the dream from my mind but her words linger there, rooted in my mind. Any thoughts I had of visiting the catacombs are immediately dismissed as images of Loísia and Nesryn fly around my head. I curse under my breath as I try to get a hold of myself. I glance at the neatly-made bed, quickly deciding against sleep. There's no point in trying when I'm too unnerved by the thought of reliving the same dream so soon after. Instead, I rub some salve on my wounds and dress quickly. My stomach rumbles and I know I should eat, especially in my weakened state. But it's not food that will ease my troubled mind right now.

Somehow, I end up in The Crooked Spade, a large stein of ale in my hand.

I can feel the hateful stares of some of the other customers, but I ignore them, too wrapped up in my own thoughts to give a shit about dirty looks from judgmental fools.

I watch the amber liquid bubble behind the glass, contemplating Barilius and his brutality.

"If you keep glaring at it like that it'll grow bitter," a voice pipes up.

I glance up to find Keelhan standing over my table.

"How'd you find me?" I ask, my gaze returning to the drink in my hand.

"You aren't that hard to find," he says breezily, taking the seat across from me.

"Or you followed me," I cut back, looking at him over the rim of the glass.

Keelhan pauses at the accusation, meeting my eyes for only a moment before he signals for one of the barmaids. I scowl but say nothing, bringing the stein to my lips and welcoming the slow burn of alcohol as the liquid moves down my throat.

When Keelhan has handed the woman a few buckles, she gives him a glass overflowing with ale. I watch the froth drip over the side as she places it down in front of him and leaves. He takes a long swing before setting it down again. He looks furtively over his shoulder before he settles back, meeting my gaze across the table.

"You really need to stop pissing off Barilius. Whatever you're trying to do here is risky, Lysan," he mutters.

"I didn't realise it was any of your fucking business," I snipe, taking another swig.

"Of course it's my fucking business. You really expect me to believe you lost those girls in the gardens?" he argues.

I stare him down and say nothing.

He leans in now, dropping his voice. "You've as good as guaranteed their deaths."

"No!" I snap, slamming my hand against the table.

The noise gains us several pairs of eyes, but I ignore them as I glare furiously at Keelhan.

He flinches away from me slightly, surprised at my outburst.

"*Barilius* guaranteed them that. Don't fucking pin that on me, Keel," I warn him.

"You know something, Lysan, something that will get you into more trouble with him when it comes to light," he surmises, frowning at me.

"Or maybe he's just become too reckless and power-hungry. Have you even considered that?" I retort. "Six women have died because of him, Keelhan. *Six*. And that doesn't include the four he left for dead," I continue, my blood beginning to boil.

"I know," he replies, his grip tightening on his drink.

"*You know*," I repeat mockingly, slumping back in my seat.

I let out a bitter laugh, shaking my head as I lift my eyes to meet his, a dark expression on my face.

"Just like you knew what that bastard soldier was doing down in those cells," I comment, my voice eerily calm.

Keelhan's face slackens in shock before his face reddens with indignation, his blue eyes raging storms as he gets to his feet, looming over me.

"My oath is to the crown, that is what I serve, and that means I serve Barilius. You forget yourself, Shadowcaster," his voice is like sheet ice.

"It would seem you have lost all sense of morality in your years of servitude, *Captain*," I retort, unfazed by his anger.

"We are brothers bonded by our oath to Barilius. I know who I serve. You would do right to remember the same. Or do we have a traitor in our midst?" he asks, no doubt an attempt to ridicule me.

"I know who I serve, Captain. But don't mistake my serving him for me agreeing with his methods," I point out.

"You're playing with fire, kid," he spits, his temper getting the better of him.

"And you're forgetting who you're talking to," I warn him, letting my shadows snake into view.

"We may both serve the crown, Keelhan, make no mistake. But your oath is not simply to the bearer of the crown, it is also to the people it governs. And you have failed them," I continue, my eyes still trained on his. "We both have."

He glares at me before slamming his drink down and storming out of the tavern. I draw in the darkness and turn my attention back to my drink, intending to down the rest of it and make a quick exit.

"It's not safe to talk here," a voice utters from across the room. "Meet me at the inn south of here."

The familiarity of the voice tugs at me and I'm taken back to the night I'd followed Twyla here. To the little room somewhere above me where I'd listened through the wall to Twyla and her three companions.

I lower my glass in an attempt to avoid rousing suspicion, my eyes wandering across the room in search of the voice. I find him almost immediately: a young man with a bulky build and bright auburn hair, a lighter shade of it running across his jawline and chin in an attempt at a beard.

He makes his way towards the door, alone. Whoever he'd been talking to must have left through an alternate exit, I decide. I watch the red-headed man leave, my interest piqued.

When he's far enough away, I get to my feet, dropping a few buckles on the table that clink against the empty glass as they land. Then, I roll my shoulders back and follow after the unsuspecting man.

CHAPTER THIRTYFIVE

"You need to concentrate, Nes," Yvie's voice filters through.

I scrunch my eyes shut more, trying to block out her voice, to block out everything but the feel of the light between my fingertips. My body thrums with power as the light flows through me and I reach out, imagining myself shaping the glow into beautiful, bright tendrils.

"That's it, Nesryn, you're doing it!" Yvie's excited voice cuts through my concentration.

Just like that, my control is lost. I open my eyes to see the light dissipate into nothing. Frustration pours out of me as I smack my fist against the table, causing Yvie to start.

"Damn it," I hiss through my teeth.

"It's ok, it's only early days, you'll get the hang of it eventually," she reassures me, placing a hand on mine.

"No, I won't. I can't get this right, I've still not seen any of my friends, my uncle is nowhere to be found and—" I stop short, heaving a frustrated sigh.

I turn to meet Yvie's gaze. "It's been two weeks."

Her expression changes to one of sympathy as she holds my gaze, her hand unmoving from mine. She seems to be having some sort of internal struggle as she looks at me, hesitant. I wait for her to say the same thing that she's been saying to me all week: *be patient.*

To my surprise, she says something I wasn't expecting.

"I think they're just waiting on your decision," she offers.

I blink and turn away, staring at the far wall as I contemplate her words.

"You'd be an incredible asset to us, Nes. You aren't alone in your hatred for Barilius, The Righteous Hand have a plan. A plan that you could be a vital part of if you join us," she explains, leaning in closer.

"Vital? How?" I ask.

"You were Chosen, you've been within those walls and come back out," she explains.

She looks at me with her wide eyes and an odd feeling begins to settle over me.

"You girls are the only ones to have ever made it out alive. Do you not realise how rare that is?"

My ears ring as I try to make sense of her words. Shock numbs me as I think back to my time in the palace. Every moment where I might have sensed something was off. Every death, every danger, to my very last moments of consciousness high up in the king's tower.

I consider the previous Choosing, and the lack of word from the palace after it had finished. No news, no girls, no final Chosen. Just months of silence and eerie mystery surrounding the most core tradition of our kingdom.

'*How was it never questioned before now?*'

"We were never meant to come back out," I breathe.

"That's our theory," Yvie answers.

"He was going to pick us off one by one until only the strongest was left, the most resilient," I continue.

"But for what gain? That's what we can't understand," she sighs, leaning back.

'*He was going to sacrifice you,*' a little voice in my head murmurs.

"And this is why our cause needs you, Nesryn. All of you," Yvie says, levelling my gaze.

"I don't know how I can be so vital. I want him to pay, really I do, but I can barely control these powers I have…" I trail off, staring at my open palms.

'*I can barely make it through the day without the flashbacks, the fear,*' I think.

"I know you've been through a lot, and I know it's a lot to take in, we all do. But if we don't stop him, more girls—like your friends—will die," she reasons, tilting her head.

I stay silent.

She lets out a breath before reaching for a piece of parchment and quill. I watch as she scribbles directions on it before handing it to me.

"If you still aren't convinced then I can't force you, but I do think you should speak to Wylan Ginemoux," she explains as I glance down at the map in my hands.

"Wylan?" I repeat.

"If anyone can vouch for our cause, it's him."

I walk the corridors, glancing down at the map in my hand as Yvie's words run through my head.

As I reach my supposed destination, I draw in a long breath and rap my knuckles against the wooden door. I hear the quick shuffling and fervent voices and I'm suddenly aware of interrupting something. I debate knocking again and telling them not to bother, that I'll come back later. I blink in surprise when the door suddenly opens and I'm met with a semi-dressed man with trousers that sit a little too low on his hips. I try to keep my eyes away from his very bare, very muscular torso, but they betray me several times as I feel heat rising up my neck and warming my cheeks. I try to focus on his face, noting his amused smirk and the way his eyes glint as he takes me in. His dark, almond-shaped eyes and olive skin remind me of Twyla and I wonder silently if they're related. His dark, shoulder-length hair reminds me of silk as he tucks it behind his ear.

"Can I help you?" he asks, his voice surprisingly deep.

"O-oh yes. I'm looking for Wylan Ginemoux," I explain, holding up my scrap of parchment in explanation.

The man draws back, a flash of surprise on his face that disappears as quickly as it came. His lips twitch as he tilts his head, analysing me. I shuffle on the spot, finding the silence uncomfortable.

"Are you Wylan?" I ask tentatively.

He chuckles, shaking his head once as he opens the door wider, allowing me to see further into the room.

"No, the name's Maz. But if you're looking for him then you've come to the right place," he says, his lips curving into a smirk.

"Hey, future king, you have a visitor," he calls over his shoulder.

'*Future king?*' I wonder as my eyes fall on the blond man dressing further back.

"It's you!" I cry in surprise.

He looks up with widened eyes as his gaze meets mine. A grin appears immediately as he straightens, his blond hair falling into his eyes.

"Nesryn, to what do I owe the pleasure?" he asks, striding forwards as he buttons his shirt.

I glance at Maz, unsure, before looking back at Wylan and scrunching the parchment up.

"Well, I was wondering if I could come in… unless it's a bad time?" I reply, unable to meet Maz's eye.

"Maz, stop playing guard and let her in," he says, waving a hand towards him. "And maybe put on a shirt, you can see the poor girl is mortified. Besides, it's rather distracting," Wylan continues, winking at Maz as he saunters past.

Maz studies me closer as I step into the room, and I quickly avert my gaze, scowling as he chuckles and disappears behind an adjoining door.

"Don't mind him, he's harmless," Wylan assures me.

He gestures for me to sit on the small plush sofa against the far wall. I take the opportunity to look around the room. The space is at least triple the size of my room, furnished with two chests, a double bed towards the back of the room, and the seating area I find myself settled into.

There are two doors adjoining the room, one of them is shut, and the other looks like a washroom from what I can see around Maz.

Wylan joins me, sitting across from me, his expression curious as he waits patiently for me to speak.

"Sorry if I interrupted," I blurt, earning a hearty laugh from Wylan.

"Don't you worry your pretty little head about that. Now, you said you came to see me," he replies.

"I know you all—The Righteous Hand—want to recruit me, and I know now, thanks to you, that it was my parents who created this group," I start.

He nods.

"But what's the end goal? Why does my decision hold so much weight? I may have been a Chosen, but my powers are unpredictable—*I'm* unpredictable," I explain, only daring to look at him when I've uttered the last word.

"Nesryn, it's because of who you are that we want you to join. It's your birthright as the daughter of two of the people who built this very organisation from the ground up," Wylan explains. "However, some of us also feel that you are a rare asset, one that we are in great need of," he continues.

"Some of you... like you?" I ask.

A ghost of a smile appears on his face before he nods. "I understand that the weight of this turmoil rests heavily on your shoulders and I know what that weight feels like."

"I don't understand," I frown.

"As you know, The Righteous Hand wishes to remove Barilius from the Akhozian throne," he explains.

"They want the king gone," I agree.

"They don't just want him gone, Nesryn, they want the rightful heir to rule Akhozia. The one who will put an end to The Choosing and the bloodshed once and for all," he continues, his expression growing serious as he leans his elbows on his knees.

My eyes widen as Maz's teasing words ring in my ears.

'Future king.'

"They want you to rule, to take Barilius's place," I breathe.

He nods once, his expression hard to read as his hazel eyes darken.

"I wasn't convinced at first either. I had no idea that the blood in my veins was royal blood. And I'm no fool either, Nesryn. Barilius is a powerful and dangerous foe. But a decades' long wrong must be righted, the blood crown must fall and I must be the one to do it," he tells me. "This is my legacy, just as yours is honouring your parents by following in their footsteps. You could finish what they started."

He speaks with such passion, such sincerity, that I find myself wanting to believe him.

"What if I'm not like them? What if I'm not strong enough?" I whisper, feeling a tear slip down my cheek from frustration.

"Nesryn, you have walked into the beast's den and escaped with your life still in your hands. Few able to boast about such an accomplishment," he points out. "You also threw Rowena across a room with incredible power," he adds.

I scoff. "I lost my temper," I argue.

"That doesn't matter. Considering I heard you haven't used them until recently, you showed incredible resilience and ability.

That is someone that I want with me," he watches me with awe.

"If I agree... there's no turning back. I'm afraid," I admit with a shaky laugh.

"Fear is human, Nesryn. It wouldn't be worth the risk if what we are doing didn't make us afraid," he reasons.

I nod as his words sink in.

"And you aren't the only one who is afraid, we all are. But we have something Barilius doesn't," he adds.

"What's that?"

Light returns to his eyes, along with just a hint of a smirk. "We have what he wants. We have you."

Time has crept by, unbeknownst to me, but I find myself unable to leave. Maz, now fully clothed, brings over tea and three cups which he pours out before joining Wylan on his loveseat, the leather crunching underneath his weight. I look at the raven-haired man, whose attention is focused on Wylan and curiosity gets the better of me.

"How did you both join the re—The Righteous Hand?" I ask across the table as I lean forwards to take the steaming cup in front of me.

"The rebellion?" he grins. "My father was a mercenary until he married my mother. My family heard whispers of a band of people willing to fight the bastard king. My older sister was in the last Choosing, when she didn't come back, we felt there was no alternative. My sister deserves justice," Maz explains, staring at the liquid in his cup.

"I'm so sorry," I manage.

Maz shrugs, but I notice how his eyes dull slightly, how Wylan gently places his hand over his, steadying the tremor.

I look to Wylan, waiting for his story. He sighs, defeated.

"I never actually went looking for The Righteous Hand, I had never even heard of them until that day," Wylan says, his eyes not leaving Maz.

"Until what day?" I ask, clearing my throat and looking away, embarrassed by the intensity of their eyes on each other.

"The day their search ended. The day Row and the others found me—"

An insistent rapping on the door interrupts the conversation and a girl bursts into the room without warning. I jolt in surprise as she scrunches up her freckled face as soon as she sees the two men sitting together.

"Ugh, get a room," she scowls, before pouting.

"We kinda did, you just keep barging in," Maz retorts dryly, not bothering to look at her as he takes a sip from his cup.

I snort with laughter, almost choking on my tea. Wylan draws his hand back from Maz's as he turns to face me again. I see his shoulders relax as he shakes his head.

"Nesryn, allow me to introduce my delightful sister, Drya," he explains with a sweeping gesture.

"A pleasure, Drya," I say.

Her eyes widen to saucers as she stops and stares at me.

Her hair is like the beginnings of a burning sunset, glowing like an orange halo around her rounded, freckled face. Her eyes are similar to Wylan's in shape only, where his are a smooth hazel, hers are a soft mossy green. I can tell they're related, but only if I really look. At first glance, they look nothing alike. But when I consider their mannerisms, their matching dimples and their heart-shaped faces, the resemblance becomes uncanny.

After several moments of her staring at me like I'd killed someone, Wylan barks out a laugh and turns to me, his dimple appearing as his eyes glimmer with amusement.

"Well, that's a first. Whatever enchantment you're using, Nesryn, make sure you give it to me later. I've never seen her so quiet!"

I dip my head, hiding the smirk on my face as Wylan's sister finally snaps out of her stupor. Her expression changes completely as she fixes me in place with a bright, dazzling smile.

"You're Nesryn! Reverie has told me so much about you," she tells me excitedly, spinning on her heel and waving someone closer.

As Drya turns to face the door, a familiar face appears in the doorway, knocking the air from my lungs. I forget about everyone else in the room as she steps inside, stopping beside Drya. Her grey-blue eyes search the room until they stop on me. I watch her lips part as surprise gives way to joy and her eyes gloss over with tears.

"Nes," my name is a whisper on her breath.

"Ria," I choke in reply, scrambling to my feet.

I'm already halfway towards her before she moves. We collide into one another as my tears flow freely. I wrap my arms around her, feeling the welcoming solidness of hers around me. Broken sobs escape my lips despite my effort to keep them in. Relief floods through me as I embrace my friend, the loneliness I'd felt since my arrival melting away as we stand there, unwilling to let each other go.

"They wouldn't let me see you," she explains in a rush, pulling away and placing her hands on either side of my face.

"They wouldn't let me either," I reply, doing the same.

"I'm so glad you're ok," she says, her lips wobbling into a smile.

I laugh with happiness, a stray tear slipping down my cheek before Ria wipes it away with her thumb. I stop short as a thought comes to mind.

"The others?" I ask, searching her face.

She nods as we step apart. "They're here, and they're alright —for the most part."

I finally remember the others watching us and I feel my cheeks warm. I look at Maz, who to my surprise, gives me a small smile. All of a sudden, Maz's attention shifts to the doorway behind us.

"I was wondering where you'd gotten to."

I whirl around to see my uncle in the doorway, his eyes travelling over each of us and ending on me. His smile doesn't reach his eyes and my stomach flutters with nerves.

"I'm sorry to steal her away from you all, but there are things that my niece and I must discuss," he explains.

"Of course," Wylan nods, suddenly beside me.

"A pleasure, again, Nesryn," he says to me with a wink.

"Likewise," I answer, giving him a smile before smiling at Maz too.

I hear Drya mumble something behind me, but my attention shifts to Ria as she pulls me in for another hug.

"I'll come find you later," she whispers as she lets go of me.

I nod before she turns and walks past my uncle and disappears through the doorway.

The walk back to my room is quiet, the conversation stilted as I follow him along the halls.

My room is quiet and dark when we arrive, and as elvynlight fills the room, Uncle Erathon closes the door behind us. I can't help but feel cramped in here after my visit to Wylan.

Uncle Erathon sits at my desk and I perch on the edge of my bed, the silence between us stifling enough for me to speak up.

"Earlier. Why did that woman—Rowena—call you Thorn?" I glance over at him.

He watches me quietly. I can see he's debating how to answer which does nothing to ease the wariness building in my chest.

"It's my name. Or it was, many lifetimes ago," he answers finally.

I nod once and look away, remembering the first conversation I had with Wylan, and all the questions I hadn't asked him.

"I found out recently that this band of rebels, this group, was created by my parents. Why did you never tell me that this was a part of their legacy?"

He blinks once, unfazed by the question. "Their greatest legacy was always you, Nix."

"What else have you been keeping from me?" I snap.

I turn away, fiddling with my fingers as I try to keep my abilities under control.

"Nix I—" he starts.

"—No, Uncle. No more lies, or secrets, or half-truths," I demand, getting to my feet.

He sighs and nods. "Your father was a Starweaver."

The information knocks the breath out of me and I stare down wide-eyed at my trembling hands.

"Then... these gifts came from him?" I ask, already knowing the answer.

"The unbinding spell," I murmur to myself, my fingers curling in on themselves. "Yvie said someone must have bound my powers as a child, that—" I falter as I look to my uncle, whose expression is one of guilt and shame.

"It was you," I breathe in disbelief. "You *knew*? You knew about these gifts—my gifts—and you *hid* them from me!" My voice comes out as a guttural growl and I fight to keep myself in check.

"I did it to protect you, to keep you safe. If the king knew about your gifts—"

"—These powers could have kept me safe! They could have saved my friends' lives in that wretched king's trials! I wouldn't have been so fucking powerless—" I draw in a sharp breath as the memory of him resurfaces and I recoil in disgust.

Tears wet my eyes and anger floods my chest as I stare at my uncle, my only family, who does nothing but look helplessly at me.

"Get out."

"Nix," he pleads.

I shut my eyes, feeling a heavy tear slide down my cheek. "I said, get the fuck out."

I keep my eyes shut, listening to his shuffling footsteps as he makes his way to the door. I hear the groan of the hinges as it opens and closes, followed by the click of the latch. When I finally open my eyes again, I'm alone.

My emotions threaten to drown me as I stand alone in the sea of silence. The walls around me seem to close in tight. I rummage around the side of my bed, finding the half-full bottle of elixir right where I left it. Without a second thought, I pull the cork free and gulp down a handful of swigs before slumping down on the bed, the effects washing over my body.

I hear the door click open and someone enters, but I'm too delirious to care, too busy staring at the low ceiling and enjoying the warm buzz behind my eyes. I only realise it's Ria as she steps into view and her fuzzy outline sharpens.

"What the hell is this?" she demands, snatching the small glass bottle from my limp hand.

"Pharo—Par-pedal Elixir," I manage, giggling as I stumble over my words.

I watch as she lifts the bottle to the light, showing the last dribbles of liquid at the bottom. She drops her arm down and glares at me in disbelief, tears pricking in her eyes. I know I should feel bad, or guilty or something. But I don't. Instead, I feel nothing, nothing but a glorious weightless feeling that I crave, that I *need*. A light in the never-ending darkness that plagues me.

"Are you out of your fucking mind? How much of this have you taken?" she demands, her rage palpable.

I manage a shrug, another giggle escaping me as her face contorts with frustration and something else.

"How long?" her voice is eerily calm as she holds the bottle out towards me.

"A month, maybe a little more," I reply, fighting the gormless smile threatening to spread across my face.

"By the goddess, Nesryn. Are you crazy? You could've killed yourself!" she snaps, her voice breaking.

She climbs onto the bed beside me, slapping my face with both hands. I'm too deep in the haze of elixir to fully absorb her words.

"No more, do you hear me? Not one drop more!" she says climbing off me and reaching for the door, locking it from the inside.

"What are you doing?" I ask, my voice slurring as I try to prop myself up on my elbows.

"Waiting it out. I don't care how long it takes. Hours, days, months. Makes no fucking difference to me," she tells me as she flops down into the chair by my desk.

"What?" I blink, her words beginning to sink in.

"You heard me. We are staying in this room until every last drop is out of you," she says, shaking the bottle in front of me.

The realisation sinks in and I sit up. I watch her hand as she lets go of the bottle but it's too late. I hear myself cry out *no*, but the bottle falls to the floor before I can reach it. Ria's foot comes down hard, smashing the bottle to pieces, and I watch in horror as the last drops of Pharopedil Elixir fade into the floor in a small damp puddle.

I look up at Ria, watching me with a piercing stare that makes me want to back down, but I don't.

"I needed that!" my voice sounds empty.

She drops to her knees beside me with a mixture of anger and tears in her grey-blue eyes, her lashes stuck together by her tears. Tears that I hadn't realised were falling down her face until now.

"What you *need* are your friends. Not some bloody potion," she argues.

"But—"

"—No Nesryn! I lived that hell too, I suffered and bled like you, I—I lost people too," she yells, her voice breaking.

I watch her face as it contorts with emotion and I remain silent as she reigns it in with one shuddering breath. Then, she grabs my face in her hands and searches my eyes.

"No matter what, we promised we would do this together, we would *survive* together, and goddess above, I meant it," she says, her voice raw. "So we will get through this. Together. You can hate me all you want, Nesryn Havenore, but that was the deal," she continues, a sharpness in her gaze now.

Eventually, I nod, repeating the most important word of the vow we'd made to each other.

"Together."

CHAPTER THIRTYSIX

The night creeps in unsuspectingly as I follow after the red-headed man.

Despite the late hour, the streets are still full of life, people bustling home from a hard day's work, weary workers making their way to the closest tavern for a soothing ale. Not wanting to be recognised, I pull my collar up and keep my head down as best I can, hoping it's enough to slip past undetected.

I don't dare to shroud myself, even with my powers restored. I'm not strong enough to keep up the illusion for long. I make sure to keep a safe distance between me and the man I'm following, trying to keep tabs on him through the crowds.

Smells of street food waft past my nose as the sellers call out their offers from their stalls. My mouth waters at the delicious scents, but I ignore my growling stomach, knowing it can wait a little longer. I make a mental note to come back through this way once I'm done. This mysterious meeting sounds too intriguing to miss. The further out of the city centre we go, the fewer people there are for me to blend in with. So I stick to the shadows, moving between buildings when the man checks behind him before continuing on his way. I notice how he keeps to the darker alleys and darker paths leading towards the outskirts of the city, towards the farmers' fields.

My target becomes less wary of being tracked the quieter that the streets become. I notice with amusement how his awareness slips and his cocky bravado comes out as he strolls towards the dilapidated inn at the end of the road. I take in its creaky sign swinging in the wind, the curling paint barely legible, especially in the darkness.

Elvynlight glows in the glass canisters along the first floor walls, illuminating the path beneath them.

'*Unusual*,' I think to myself. '*Farmers and lowlifes don't tend to be magic users.*'

I sneak towards the inn, hiding in the shadows of a building several yards away as I watch my target glance around for unwanted eyes. Seemingly satisfied, he makes his way inside, the door bouncing back against the frame behind him. A minute after, I slip across to the inn and scale the wall up to the first rickety-looking balcony. I glance through the grimy window, peering into the darkness to see the young man climbing the stairs up to the next level and disappearing along the hall. I waste no time climbing from balcony to balcony around the side of the building, my rigorous training spanning years coming into good use.

When I reach the other side, I crouch down at the edge of the balcony, making sure to steer clear of the glowing elvynlight. I strain my hearing, breathing in as shallow breaths as possible, as the door to the room opens and closes quickly. I press my back into the wall, shrouded by the climbing ivy and the darkness of night, grateful for the clouds above blocking the moon's glow.

"I have news for you, news from the castle," a voice gloats.

My ears prick at this. '*A spy?*' I consider, amused and intrigued.

"Spill, old man," the redhead says, his voice muffled through the wall.

I frown and look around for a better spot to sit and listen, glancing up towards the roof. I climb it, straining with effort and trying not to wince as I reach the top, noticing a small sunroof with a triumphant smirk. Silently, I pad over to the tiles and crouch low, tilting my head towards the glass below me.

"The king has released the Shadowcaster," the other voice says.

"Shit," the young man grumbles.

"He's yet to earn back the king's good graces," the older man offers.

"Just give him time. That man is not to be toyed with, good graces or not. He'll weasel his way back in with the king in no time. We'll have to be vigilant, he's slippier than a sea snake," the redhead argues.

'*Probably much more than you give me credit for,*' I think with a smirk, as I glance down at the top of his head.

"And what news have you at headquarters?" the elder man asks.

"We're keeping a low profile. Barilius will be looking for those girls and they're in no shape to be moved yet. But the tides are shifting in our favour," he tells him, excitement in his voice.

"You mean the true heir, is he—" the excitement is clear in the elder man's voice.

"—Quiet, old man. Not here," the younger man reprimands, cutting his sentence short.

A jolt runs through me as I contemplate what this means.

'*The true heir. Could this be the same one Barilius believes dead?*' I consider.

"What does this mean for the kingdom, for Barilius?" I murmur, my heart picking up speed.

'*If The Righteous Hand plan on removing the crown, it'll mean civil war,*' a little voice in my head whispers.

"For now, all you need to know is that the true heir is in our midst and he has joined our ranks. Our next move is in Madmire," the younger man says, a determination in his voice that stirs the unease within me.

"*Madmire? What could these rebels need so far east?*" I wonder.

"And one other thing," he continues.

I snap back to the conversation below. The wind picks up around me, making it harder for me to hear. I lean in closer to the window, placing my ear against the glass.

"Twyla won't say who helped her that night. See if you can discover who it was. Anyone daring to cross Barilius is worth The Righteous Hand keeping an eye on them," he says.

A shiver runs down my spine as I draw in my strength and shadowfold.

Barilius is in his tower, his back turned to me as I stride into the room. Sweat beads on my brow and I try to calm my panting before he turns, knowing it had been a bad idea to shadowfold so far from the palace. I can feel the strain in my body, though I refuse to let him see that as I step further into the room.

He stands by a candle burning a black flame and I think back to the one in the throne room, my curiosity reignited. He quickly turns, shielding it from view as he scowls at me, his mouth twisting into an unpleasant sneer.

"You better have a damn good reason for bursting in here unannounced, boy."

I grind my teeth, unclenching my fists slowly. For a split second, I wonder if I should tell him all I've heard, though I decide it's not worth the risk of him finding out the truth—or the punishment I'd receive.

"I come with news, my king," I answer, sweeping into a low bow.

"News that couldn't have waited until tomorrow?" he retorts, cracking his knuckles as he steps closer.

"The rebels have been grouping, Your Highness. They have plans."

I feel him pause, noting the contemplative expression on his face as his sneer turns sombre. He looks back at me, his amber eyes searching my face, and I feel my pulse quicken.

"Tell me what you know," he says, waving me forwards.

"We were right, my king. There are spies within the palace," I confirm.

"Ungrateful fools, I will see their blood spilt where they stand!" he hisses as he storms across the room and then back, his dark eyes alight with bloodlust and greed. "What else have you learned?" he demands, stopping right in front of me.

'The true heir is in our midst.'

The young rebel's voice echoes in my mind as I consider my options and what I'm willing to share. Unease grows within me as I realise how dangerous the game has become. How deadly keeping a single promise has made my position beside the king. For the first time, my judgement seems clouded, the good and bad are mixed with blood, and I find myself unsure of what I've gotten myself into.

I look to the king, keeping my expression carefully blank as I swallow the knowledge of the true heir. Now is not the time for talk of another beneath the crown. Now is the time to play it smart, to understand both sides. After all, I might need that information later.

"They will convene to the east."

"For what? What is in the east that is of use to them?" he demands, flexing his fingers, a wild look in his eye.

"That's all I know," I answer with a shrug.

I know there is no turning back now.

CHAPTER THIRTYSEVEN

One day blends into the next as I remain locked in the tiny room with Ria. My body aches with need, burning hot and cold with fever and spouts of cold sweats. My head pounds at my temples and the pins and needles that wrack my body make my skin so sensitive to touch that I am barely able to stand the feel of the sheets beneath me as I lie there. Even the comforting caresses that Ria attempts to give me are unbearable.

Images flash through my mind when I dare to sleep, haunting my dreams and leaving me screaming and launching myself awake. Dead eyes of the fallen Chosen, Lysan bloodied and sneering at me, with his snaking shadows swirling protectively around him; the Aslitír on top of me, his weight crushing me and squeezing the air from my lungs. The nightmares feel never-ending, tormenting me even as I lay awake in the dark. Ria's body pressed against mine on the small single bed is a comfort—though even that feels too much at times. I find myself crawling into the washroom to soak away the horrors in privacy.

I stay there for hours, letting my mind run on as I lay there numb, the hot water already cooling. I lay there until Ria comes to find me and pulls me, trembling, from the cold bathwater and back to bed. She only leaves long enough to bring us food and drink that remains untouched by me for the first few days; I'm unable to stomach even the thought of eating.

Ria offers words of encouragement despite my sullen and snappy attitude towards her. She tells me of the freedom we can enjoy once this is all over, and despite the hollowness still dwelling within me, I let her hope. The lightness in her voice is the first thing in days that makes me feel something other than discomfort and pain.

It takes seven days for me to finally emerge from the tunnel, for my body to recover.

On the eighth day, Ria wakes and sits up beside me, blinking away the sleep from her weary eyes, her braid a tangled mess. She searches my face as I give her a weary smile, the remnants of last night's dream lingering in my mind.

"How are you feeling?" she asks tentatively.

"Like if you don't let me out of this room in the next hour, I'm literally going to be climbing the walls," I reply dryly.

Ria stares at me wide-eyed for a moment before she breaks out into laughter.

The sound is welcome to my ears, momentarily lifting the darkness shrouding me. I watch her, unable to fight the smile creeping across my face.

When her laughter dies down she looks at me, her grey-blue eyes still sparkling as she reaches for my hand and squeezes it. The smile that stays on her face is warm and familiar, and I find myself feeling guilty at the way I've treated her over the past few days, realising how grateful I really am for her.

"I suppose we could stretch our legs," she says airly.

It's the best thing I've heard in days.

"They'll be officially recruiting the newest members in a few days. I heard there's a feast," Ria tells me as we amble down the narrow corridors.

I glance sideways at her, noting the hopeful tone in her voice.

"You want to join the cause," I surmise.

"I want to do *something*, I want to fight back, Nes. Otherwise, all of her pain and suffering was for nothing," she says, her gaze on the floor.

I falter at her words, staring at her as she carries on several steps before stopping and turning back towards me. I see the tears in her eyes and the way she fights to hold them back.

"Vena's death wasn't for nothing, Maskia's death wasn't for nothing. We won't let any of their lives be lost for nothing, Ria,"

I tell her, my voice steadier than my hands.

"I want to honour their memory, Nes," she says quietly, her voice breaking.

"So do I," I agree, my thoughts straying to the Shadowcaster dragging Vena's body through the maze.

"Will you join with me?" she asks.

There's no denying the hopeful glint in her eye.

"I hardly see any alternative. Barilius must pay for the lives that he stole," I reply, a sharp edge to my voice. "Besides… it's my parents' *legacy*." I think of my uncle's secrets then and I feel a flash of irritation.

"No."

I look up in surprise as she turns and strides back to me. I hadn't realised I'd even stopped.

"Don't mistake your sense of duty for your parents' legacy," she says, reaching for me. "Your parents believed in a cause enough to bring to life all that you see around you. Their legacy isn't what they left behind, it's what they've instilled in here, in you," she says, pointing gently to my heart.

The knot that had formed in my stomach loosens as a lump forms in my throat. I swallow it back, blinking my tears away as I nod once, her words making me feel heavy and light all at once as we carry on through the halls. We say nothing for several moments and I welcome the silence, my head clear for the moment. As luck would have it, my stomach growls, causing a bout of laughter to erupt from my friend.

"We'll have some food soon, I promise. But first, there is something I want to show you," she says.

Perplexed, I tilt my head, giving her a look of confusion. She sends me a secretive smile and grabs my hand, pulling me along the corridor. We run together, our hair flying out behind us as I let her lead me through the base, twisting and veering around corners, laughing as we almost collide with unsuspecting walkers.

"Ria, where are you taking me?" I call out to her.

She laughs as she looks over her shoulder at me. "You'll see!"

Eventually, we round another corner and stop before a pair of open doors. I peer through, noticing a mess hall containing rows upon rows of long wooden tables and benches. I stop short when I see them all huddled together at one of the tables. They look up at Ria and I as we step into the room. Ria turns to me, letting go of my hand and smiling warmly at me as I step past her.

Ovie stands first, a wide grin splayed across her face and her caramel eyes sparkling as she looks at me. As she moves aside, Zariya turns in her seat and smiles, the top half of her face wrought with angry scars. Her eyes unseeing. But she's here, and she's alive.

I rush forward as Ovie meets me and embraces me. The discomfort of her touch is there, but I manage, too grateful to see her to push her away. As she lets go, Zariya reaches out for my hand and squeezes it, facing me.

"I'm here because of you." For a second, I think it's an accusation until she squeezes my hand gently. "Thank you," she tells me, the emotion and sincerity in her voice causing a lump in my throat as I squeeze her hand back.

"Lesya would be here too, but they're still seeing her in the medical bay. They haven't yet found a way to help her," Ovie pipes in as Ria joins us.

I turn to her in surprise, my breath hitching at the news. "She's here?"

Ria nods but her eyes darken, leaving me unsure how to react. A shiver runs down my spine as I picture her down in that cell alone, with him, and what she would have had to go through, probably for days. I find myself hoping that Lesya's mind is too broken to remember her ordeal. In some ways, it would be a blessing.

I shake my head free of the image and glance over at Twyla who remains seated. She smirks and salutes me. "Nice to have you back with us."

"Good to be back," I grin.

Hours later, we're still sitting around the table, our bellies full of delicious broth and fresh rolls, courtesy of Twyla and her access to the kitchens. I feel better after having eaten and more alert than I've been in weeks, surrounded by friends.

I sit quietly, listening to each of them as they relay their weeks after our escape. I'm grateful for the small sense of normality and eager to take in their words. Zariya is speaking when Ria mentions a vigil for the fallen girls and the others nod solemnly.

"Now, we aren't allowed above ground, not yet. It just isn't safe by all accounts," Ria tells me.

"We're underground?" I reply, my brows raised in surprise as I look up at the low ceiling. I suppose it made sense.

"Best place for us right now," Twyla answers from across the table.

"The leaders," Ria continues, "they've agreed we can have a vigil to remember the girls we lost."

My chest feels heavy as I take in her pained expression. I understand her pain.

"I want to say goodbye, Nes, I want to send her off with dignity," she states.

"Then we will, all of us. Together."

Despite the arrangements being very last minute, the hall is heaving with faces. Some I recognise, most I don't, and for the umpteenth time today, I find myself reeling at the number of people here, and how I've hardly seen a soul since I arrived.

The atmosphere is fraught with tension, those around me hovering with bated breath. Everyone has a crimson candle in their hand in preparation for the event. On the table in the centre, are the names of those we lost. Most of the people here have come clad in red, like the girls and I. The colour of death.

A heaviness settles over the room as to my surprise, my uncle steps forwards. He looks striking with his red tunic belted into maroon leathers. I haven't seen him in days, not since I sent him away. My stomach squeezes as I recall the moment. He stands before everyone, his dreads swinging as he looks across the room, holding his candle tightly in his hand, the glowing flame flickering with his movements. The little murmurs of conversation about the room die out as his gaze demands silence.

"We are here on behalf of the survivors from the palace. You may know them as The Chosen, but I refuse to name them as such. They and their friends suffered at the hands of the blood crown, and today we will remember and honour them as they should have been," he declares, his voice reverberating across the room.

He holds out an arm towards where the five of us stand, huddled together, and he invites Ria to join him. She glances back at me with teary eyes before she draws in a trembling breath and stands beside him, holding her candle tightly in her hand. At his side, she looks smaller, paler and meeker than I've ever seen her. All signs of a breaking heart, and I wish for nothing more than to help her heal. Maybe this will be the start of her journey.

"Their names are important, their identities, who they were and who they strived to be. Not all of you knew them, but I speak for all of us when I say that we are grateful for your being here," she says, her voice wobbling.

"Ve-Vena A-Astalón," Ria starts, her voice breaking.

I lift my chin and join her side, holding her free hand tightly in mine. "Maskia Lockport."

"Erryn Drulfeard. Chandra Roquenet," Ovie speaks up as she joins us.

"Mallon Vythierre," Zariya says beside her.

"Rohanna Duhrannes," Twyla finishes, the last to join us.

Uncle Erathon lights Ria's candle and she follows suit, lighting mine before I continue on the train. Around us, candles are lit and held above people's heads until there is a sea of flickering flames surrounding us. We join in, lifting our candles to the air in unison.

"We will hear the unheard, see the unseen, and endure even in the darkness. They will carry on through us, and we will do them proud," Uncle Erathon calls out.

"Hear the unheard, see the unseen, and endure," the crowd repeats in unison.

I stand there, pride and sadness battling within me as I find Wylan's steady gaze through the crowds. A sense of belonging hums through me as I realise I had always been a part of The Righteous Hand, I just hadn't known until fate intervened. He nods at me once and I smile in understanding, slowly closing my eyes as a tear falls down my cheek.

In my mind, I see them. The girls stand together smiling and I see the gratefulness in their expressions, their torment now over. I see each of them in their house colours before they transform into the beasts on their family crests. Pain and love swell in my chest and I feel my power expand further than me, stretching and twisting, taking on a life of its own.

I hear the girls gasping and open my eyes to a flood of brilliant light.

One by one, six animals appear before us: a peacock, a swan, a hare, a horse, a fox, and a wolf.

I watch on in shock as the shapes glimmer and glow before fading into nothing, turning to Ria and the others to find them already staring at me wide-eyed.

I feel my power draw back into myself and I blink, looking at the shocked faces of the crowd surrounding us. Surprise and shock pool within me as I realise it had been me. I'd been the one to bring them to life.

CHAPTER THIRTYEIGHT

Shadows writhe through the air above my head as I lie there, wielding them with the tiniest flick of my wrist. They dance above my head, causing the candles to flicker on the chandelier. The naked figure beside me sleeps, her breaths slow and even. I glance over at Gracie, taking in the mousey curls framing her face, noting how much softer her face appears in sleep. I feel an ache in the pit of my stomach as I watch her, drinking in the curve of her hip and thigh that disappears tauntingly beneath the sheet. I feel myself harden, craving the distraction of her. I shift my arm beneath my head with a sigh as I decide against waking her, for the time being. I turn my attention back to the ceiling and continue to manipulate the shadows above, watching them glide through the air.

As the days slip by into weeks, I find myself frequenting The Velvet Feather more and more with each unsuccessful evening of information-seeking. Despite my numerous attempts to discover more about The Righteous Hand, I continue to come up empty-handed. I make countless visits to the rickety inn at the edge of the city and the tavern deep in the run-down alleys. I discover nothing. My temper has begun to fray and it shows.

Gracie says nothing now when I find myself lured to her bed, even when I stay for hours after, lying quietly beside her as she sleeps. I am just a means of collecting buckles, after all.

I know the king will expect news from me soon, but with no news to share and with Keelhan giving me the silent treatment, I find myself content to lounge around here for some time. As I contemplate what I'll do next, I feel Gracie shift beside me, her hand slipping beneath the sheet and reaching out towards me. I feel my core heat as her delicate fingers wrap themselves around me and begin to gently move up and down, coaxing, teasing.

My shadows dissipate into the air as I get caught in her molten caramel gaze. A stray curl falls across her face as she watches me, her bottom lip caught between her teeth.

"I sense my lord could use some more attention," she murmurs across the mattress.

I keep my gaze steady but there is no denying the way that I harden at her offer.

A lazy smirk blankets my face and I watch her cheeks burn under my stare.

"What did you have in mind?" I ask, desire lacing my casual tone.

She gives me a seductive smile as she shimmies down the bed, disappearing beneath the quilted blanket. I feel her hands as they move across my upper thighs and reach greedily for my length. In the next heartbeat, I feel the soft graze of her tongue and I groan in pleasure, soaking up the feel of her lips, her tongue and then, her wet, hot mouth. I fight the urge to thrust, letting her pin me down with her body, letting her take control for the moment. She moves in a steady rhythm, her tongue flicking against my hardened shaft as she changes up the speed.

My hands move of their own will, slipping beneath the blanket and getting tangled in her hair. Closing my eyes, I let the sensation of pleasure ripple through me, the feel of her around me suddenly all I need. The graze of her teeth against my skin causes me to release a hiss of pleasure, and without thinking I apply pressure to her head, guiding her movements as the satisfaction of control fills me. Her movements quicken and a breathy moan slips from my lips as I throb with intense desire. The urge to ravage her overwhelms me, to delve into the fantasy of envisioning Loísia, is too great for me to fight. In the next movement, I've ripped the blankets off of us both and pulled her to me. Grabbing the curve of her hips, I thrust into her deeply, a breathy chuckle leaving me as she cries out with sudden pleasure.

My hands guide her as she moves her hips, pleasure rolling over me in waves as my eyes roll back and I slip into the burning embers of desire.

The king's summons arrive sooner than expected, and with an added surprise.

There is an impatient banging at the door when I find myself on the cusp of climax, Gracie's movements slowing above me as she warily turns her attention to the door.

"I'm *busy!*" I snap, desperate to find release.

When the banging persists, a frustrated growl escapes me and I pull myself free of Gracie, not bothering to grab any clothes as I stride purposefully towards the door. I rip the door open to find Keelhan on the other side. His brows lift slightly at the sight of me but I don't give a shit.

I notice how he wears his armour, his helmet balanced in the crook of his arm as he stands there. Sensing his discomfort, I hold the door wider in an attempt to unsettle him further.

"Are you deaf or stupid? I said I'm busy."

His eyes snap back to mine, a grim expression plastered across his face. "You think I want to be here? I have more important things to do than to go chasing after you every five minutes," he snipes back.

"I'd like to see you tell that to the king," I bite back.

"You can tell him for me when you see him. He demands your presence," Keelhan retorts, holding out a folded piece of parchment.

"Goddess help me, of *course*, he does," I say, swiping the letter from him.

"You may want to put some clothes on and follow me," Keelhan says with disdain.

I scowl at his tone.

"I'll come when I'm ready, now fuck off," I snipe, slamming the door in his face.

The room is dark and dingier than my last visit. Empty potion bottles litter the floor amongst ripped-up parchment with incoherent scribbles on. I wrinkle my nose at the smell coating the room. It's an odd mixture of burning and dark magic, stifling the air and overpowering my nose. By the looks of things, Barilius has been busy.

As I move further into the room, I hear the whisper of paper between fingers. I watch as Barilius scours through the open book, reading through the pages fervently as he mutters incoherent babble beneath his breath. He seems... unhinged. He grabs hold of a bottle and pulls the cork free with his teeth before returning to the scripture. In the next moment, he pours half the contents of the bottle into the cauldron and mumbles some incantation that results in a plume of black smoke erupting into the air. I watch with pursed lips as the smoke glimmers and glitters in the candlelight and my unease deepens.

I clear my throat and step forwards, making myself known. If Barilius is aware I'm here, he doesn't show it, his attention fully immersed in his magical efforts.

"My king?"

I watch him stiffen at the sound of my voice, his hunched back straightening as he turns towards me. His amber eyes are piercing and suddenly alert as I meet his gaze. I swallow.

"Lysander."

There is no edge to his voice, my name a simple statement. I don't know whether that's a good thing or a bad thing as I bow. He remains tight-lipped and silent as he watches me straighten.

When he simply continues to stare, I begin to think that Keelhan pulled me away for his own reasons.

"You summoned me, Sire," I say by means of explanation.

"I did and you're late," he says blandly, staring at something behind me.

I turn and follow him with my gaze as he stands in front of his unkempt desk and begins rifling through the stacks of papers and rolled-up parchment.

"What do you need of me, Your Highness?" I press after a length of silence.

"I need you to gather these for me," he says distractedly, handing me a bit of crumpled paper.

Tentatively I reach for it, eyeing the names scribbled in ink. A knot of dread forms in my stomach as I read through them.

"I don't understand. These are the names of the noblewomen," I say, looking up from the page.

"How observant," Barilius comments dryly, his attention still elsewhere as he moves back to the book and cauldron.

I falter as I notice the candle, lit with a black flame beside the book. A sinister feeling washes over me as I draw my attention back to the king.

"You want me to see if they're related to the rebel organisation?" I ask, lifting the parchment into the air.

"No, boy. The rebels are already in hand. The captain has his orders. These are yours," he says, pointing dismissively at the list in my hand.

"These women…" I trail off as I read through the list once more. "They're to be collected, then?"

Barilius turns, his eyes ablaze with fury, his lips twisted into a sinister smile as he steps towards me. "They may have eluded me once, but there is still time, and *this* time I will have what I seek."

Understanding blooms within me, quickly followed by an unrelenting dread that pools in my stomach and turns it ice cold.

"Prepare yourself, Lysander, you leave in two days. The second Choosing will be upon us in seven days' time!"

I charge along the corridors with newfound purpose, scanning the halls as I go.

My mind runs a mile a minute as I consider Barilius's plans, trying to figure out why he is so desperate for a second Choosing.

I find myself in the mood to break something as I realise I'm right back where I started, my efforts to help The Chosen null and void. Glancing at the paper again, I read through the six names sprawled there and huff as I make a beeline for the library.

'Barilius has lost his fucking mind.'

I lift my arms upon entering the library, my shadows snaking free and slamming the open doors shut behind me, barricading it from the inside. I stand in the centre of the space, my eyes travelling the shelves as I try to think of a plan. Something, *anything* that may delay more unnecessary bloodshed.

'There has *to be a way to help them,'* I reason.

I scrunch my eyes shut, pinching the bridge of my nose as I contemplate, clawing at my brain for ideas. Frustration begins to leak out of me as I push myself for an answer. I can't seek help from Keelhan, he's already on his way to rid the king of the rebel forces.

My eyes spring open. The rebels.

"There isn't enough time for me to send a physical message, but perhaps…" I trail off as an idea sparks in my mind.

I scour the shelves as I search for a particular volume. I feel a swell of satisfaction when I find it hidden in the back corner amongst some older books, the edges dusty from disuse. I open the worn leather, my eyes scanning the pages for the spell. I skim through the page that I need before I slam it shut with one hand.

"I think this calls for a trip to the shadow market," I murmur, memorising the ingredients and shadowfolding away.

CHAPTER THIRTYNINE

My room is a welcome sight after hours of rigorous magical training. I'm grateful for the few moments of peace I'll get before I attend the meeting the leaders have called for the surviving Chosen girls. They want us to make our choice, and if we so choose, to pledge our loyalties to The Righteous Hand.

Like the others, I've made my choice.

I let out a sigh as I close the door behind me. I don't bother lighting the room with candles, instead, I conjure a small ball of twisting light that follows me closely about the room. My own version of elvynlight. Though long and somewhat tedious at times, my lessons with Yvie are coming along well and I'm learning how to control my Starweaving abilities. I feel the well of power within me and take comfort in the knowledge of my strength. The thing that keeps the darkness from overwhelming me. That, and Ria's ever-watchful eye. I twist the taps for the bath on full and fill it with liquid soap and sweet-smelling lotions. When the bath is full, I quickly strip down and climb in, relishing the heat as the bubbles ripple across the surface. I release a contented sigh, closing my eyes as I soak away the stresses of the day. Before I know it, I'm slipping away as reality shifts into the realm of dreams.

I'm back on the stone altar, weak and exhausted, my powers extinguished from overuse. The world spins and the details are hazed as I'm freed from my bonds and a pair of strong arms lift me into an embrace. The man's chest feels hard against me, the rippling muscle taut with tension. I want to close my eyes, to sleep away the pain ebbing beneath the bone-shattering tiredness clutching at me, but somehow I glance up. I only manage to see the sharp lines of his jaw before the darkness tugs me under. In the next moment, I'm jostled awake by his movements. He's running and the world blurs by too fast for me to notice anything. My head smacks against his collarbone and I lift my heavy eyes to his face once more. I see his face this time but the details are hazy.

As the next wave of darkness tugs at me, I try to fight it, to get a better glimpse of the man saving my life, but my lids feel too heavy and I slip back under the velvety darkness. When I come round again, I'm still in the arms of my saviour being carried towards safety and I realise that I feel safe with this man. I want to memorise his face, so I can thank him when I wake, but I tumble back into the familiar darkness.

The next time I open my eyes, the cool air of the night washes across my face. The scent of nebiulas fills the air and I realise we're in the gardens, fleeing the palace. Behind us the great building looms menacingly, ready to crash down on top of us and swallow us whole. For a split second, I imagine our bodies entombed in the rubble until his voice rumbles through his chest and fills my ears.

It sounds as though we're beneath the water's surface as he speaks, the words thick and hard to understand. Weak, and fighting another wave of unconsciousness, I try to look up at him one last time, only to find him already looking down at me as he holds me tightly to his chest. His lips move but I don't hear the words he says; my eyes are focused on the pair of seafoam blue eyes watching me.

Something within me snaps, like a jolt of electricity, as the rest of his face comes into sharper view. His raven hair falls across his forehead and his full lips move though I still can't hear a word.

"*Lysan*?" I breathe in disbelief.

And as the word leaves my lips, the dream shatters around me, leaving me in complete darkness.

In the next moment, I'm standing alone with nothing but a thin slip on, my feet bare. As I look around I see nothing, and as I step through the large mass of space, I know that it's an endless expanse.

The ground shifts beneath my feet and I frown as I look down at it. The dark surface moves subtly, soft ripples break across the surface, becoming tiny waves with each movement I make. When I lift my foot, it's dry. Puzzled, I lower my foot and look around once more, searching for anything, anyone.

Just as I'm about to conjure light to guide me through the darkness, I notice something to my left. I squint, but it's just too far away for me to see properly. My confidence grows as I head towards it. Wariness turns into curiosity, into a need to know, to understand what I'd seen only moments before. The need for answers drives me into a run. My hair flies out behind me in chocolate whips and my feet land heavily, yet without a sound, as I push my body to its limits. My heart thrums in my chest, though I'm not sure if it's from running or the growing anticipation expanding in my stomach. The *something* comes into view as I get closer and I realise that the thing is a figure. I run faster, desperate to get to them before they disappear.

I skid to a stop when I finally recognise the outline of the person before me. He stands there as though waiting, unmoving, with his eyes closed as if in concentration. My curiosity gutters into hostility as I try to reach for my power, eager to feel the security of its warmth blazing between my fingertips.

"*You*," my voice echoes through the space. I flinch at the sound, unexpected in this silent place.

At this, Lysan opens his eyes and they lock onto me. A flash of surprise flickers there for a second before vanishing. The corner of his mouth tilts upwards as he takes in my face, the smile deepening as his eyes roam over the rest of me. Anger and embarrassment burn my face as I glare at him, recalling the many acts of brutality he and his king unleashed upon me and the rest of The Chosen.

"I'm going to kill you," the vow comes easily as I reach within myself for the light.

At this, he steps forwards, shaking his head as his mouth moves. I narrow my eyes at him, wondering what this new trickery is when I notice his steps slow. I lunge for him, hurling tendrils of light at him, only to watch him bat them away like they are nothing. An angry cry escapes me as I try again, only for him to do the same again. I notice his gaze, how he seems to implore me to listen. I stay in a defensive stance, confusion fanning the flames of my anger.

He tries to speak again, only for a single word to come through, echoing across the expanse.

"King?" I repeat, my tone sharp.

He falters and tries to speak again, only this time, I hear nothing. I begin to see his patience waning. He meets my gaze, distrust oozing from me as we stand yards apart, a sea of swirling darkness separating us. I want to get closer, to rip his lying heart from his chest but he shifts his stance, his brow knitting together in concentration as he stares across the vast space between us.

I watch in growing horror as he calls upon his shadows, sending them flying out towards me. My reactions are too slow and before I can call on my own magic in defence, his shadows pull back, swirling through the air between us in odd zig-zagging patterns. Then I notice the split in the darkness in the wake of one of his tendrils. Something new—or rather, something old—ebbs and pulses with a magical aura.

I step back with growing shock as I watch his tendrils carve through the air, slicing letters into the space. The flames glow a bright hue of purple as his shadows move through the air. I draw in a sharp intake of breath as I follow the letters, reading them aloud.

"Danger is coming."

I dare to look through the purple flames towards Lysan who remains where he's standing, as still as stone, though I can sense the tug of exhaustion in the lines running across his face, and the beads of sweat on his brow. He stares at me silently with a grave expression across his sharp features. The flicker of the flames reflect in his sea sprayed eyes before his shadows consume him and I'm left entirely alone.

I'm launched awake, drawing in ragged breaths as the cool water sloshes over the edge of the bath. A sense of urgency claws at me as I swing my legs around and climb out, the water running down my skin and pooling at my feet. Though my skin prickles from the cold, I'm grateful for the feel of solid ground beneath my feet, grounding me as I try to make sense of my thoughts.

"Lysan saved me?" I whisper to no one, recalling the first part of the strange dream.

The words feel wrong on my tongue, but the memories linger, no longer dreamlike, but real. As solid as the ground beneath my feet.

"But that can't be possible…" I trail off, turning to stare at my reflection in the mirror. "He wouldn't have… *would he*?"

My mind blares the message now burned into my brain.

'Danger is coming.'

I hurry into my bedroom and before I can think twice, I shrug on some clothes, twist my damp curls into a knot on the top of my head, and sprint out of the door.

I bang my fists relentlessly on Twyla's door.

I shift on my feet, drawing my hand away as I listen for movement on the other side before my impatience has me banging on the door again.

"Yeah, yeah, I heard you," Twyla grumbles as she opens the door.

She stops short, pausing as she takes me in, noticing the expression on my face. "Nesryn," she says in surprise.

I take in her black, strapped crop top and the matching low cotton trousers she wears, her toned stomach bare except for a hint of a tattoo that disappears beneath the band of her trousers. Her hair hangs dead straight over her shoulders, the jet black shade gleaming in the light.

"We need to talk. It's urgent," I tell her, glancing along the stretch of hall behind me.

I notice her glance behind her into her room before she turns back and shrugs, though her eyes are alert and I sense her wary curiosity.

As she steps back, I weave past her into her room.

I stop in the middle of the room before I turn back to face her, a hard look etched onto my face.

"I need to know who helped us escape the palace."

CHAPTER FORTY

I blink back into the present, feeling a little off-kilter after floating through the dreamer's expanse. The room is dark, the night having crept in with a predator's stealth. I think of Nesryn and the surprise at seeing her there. It wasn't meant to be her.

"Fuck," I murmur as I run a hand across my face.

I can only hope she understood the message, though the flash of hostility in her eyes told me all I needed to know. I look down at the open book before me, re-reading the same passage for at least the tenth time before I consider attempting the spell again. I dismiss the thought entirely, knowing that I will most likely reach Nesryn again.

I slam the book shut in defeat and get to my feet, my inked shadows blowing out the candles at a wave of my hand. The darkness that follows is thick and heavy, blanketing everything around me. I conjure elvynlight and follow closely behind the dim blue glow as it floats deeper into the winding tunnels.

A cool breeze flows through the catacombs as I make my way along the narrow, uneven path. Somewhere far off, an echoing drip of water sounds as I inhale the familiar damp scent.

I reach the graves in little time, stopping beside Loísia's stone and pausing in silence. I look at the others in turn, mentally naming them as the anger within me grows. Each one stokes the fire in me even more. I pull the list that the king had given me out of my pocket and read through the six names scrawled across the parchment. My shadows writhe around me, eager to be set free, to destroy.

"It was supposed to be over!" I growl.

I look towards Loísia's grave once more and my anger dissipates as I fall to my knees. I think of my promise, of her imploring eyes as the vow fell easily from my mouth. Bitterness coils into a ball in my stomach. Dropping my head in shame, I place my palm over the mound of earth.

"The king won't stop until he has what he wants," I tell her, my voice bouncing off the moisture-slicken walls. "But what is it he wanted from you, Lou?" I murmur. "What was he going to do to Nesryn?"

Spurred on by the doubts and questions swirling through my head, I quickly get to my feet and head back towards the library entrance.

"I have two days, Lou, two days to get to the bottom of this and warn them before it's too late."

My footsteps echo as I pick up the pace, determination taking root.

NESRYN

CHAPTER FORTYONE

Twyla stands in front of her closed door, her expression unreadable. I'm briefly disgruntled to find her room is also much bigger than mine, furnished with dark furniture and rich red fabrics.

"Are you going to tell me or are we just going to stand around here all day?" I cut through the silence, pulling my attention from the surrounding room.

"I can't tell you," she says eventually, rubbing the back of her neck.

"Can't or won't?" I retort, my patience wearing thin already.

I watch her as she walks over to her four-poster bed and perches on the end. She stares at the patterned rug beneath her bare feet, clasping her hands together. She sighs and drags a hand down her face before lifting her gaze to mine.

"You're not going to drop this, are you?" she asks wearily.

"It was the Shadowcaster, wasn't it?" I demand.

The tension in the room thickens as I note the slight widening of her eyes. It's the smallest gesture, but I note it all the same.

"Lysan saved me from the tower, then helped us escape, *didn't* he?" I press, stepping in front of her.

"How did you—" she starts, but I wave her off.

"—I remembered," I say curtly.

"I see," she says, with a tight nod, not meeting my eye.

"Why?"

"Why did I trust him? I couldn't tell you, Nesryn, I was just focused on getting us out of there alive," she answers with a dismissive shrug. But when I look into her eyes I see a sharpness there that wasn't there before.

"He's dangerous. If he chose to help, it's an angle he's trying to play, can't you see that?" I argue.

"Don't you think I already fucking know that? I've been doing this a hell of a lot longer than you have, Nesryn. Don't try to lecture me," she snaps, getting to her feet.

I press my lips together in anger as we stare each other down across the space. The tension is palpable, until Twyla breaks the connection, returning to her perch on the bed, her brow knitted in evident frustration.

"What's with all of this anyway, why come to me now?" she asks, her tone irritable.

Now that the answer is on the tip of my tongue, I reconsider sharing the information. I dismiss the doubt quickly. This is too important to keep to myself.

"He spoke with me—or at least tried to," I explain.

Twyla's attention snaps to me faster than I anticipate, her dark eyes watching me distrustfully.

"How? When?"

"Just now, through my dreams. It's why I came right here," I answer, cringing as I hear my own words.

"Are you sure, Nesryn?" she says, pushing away from the bed and closing the space between us.

She stops in front of me, her doubtful gaze scrutinising me. I'm flustered all of a sudden and I draw in a long calming breath as I think back to the dream and the message burning brightly in purple flame. I wonder if I am crazy, if I made it all up. But that didn't seem right. I know what I saw and it was more than just a dream.

"Yes. The full message didn't come through, though. I think he tried to say more but whatever magic he used wasn't strong enough," I tell her.

"What was the message?" she asks quickly.

"It was a warning. He said danger is coming," I tell her with a furrowed brow.

Her brow knits together as she rubs a hand across her face and drops it back down to her side. I watch her as she begins to pace the room, ignoring me for several moments before she stops and returns to where I'm standing.

"We need to tell Row and your uncle about this, but I want to make *absolutely* sure that this isn't some kind of trick before we start including others in on this, Nesryn," she explains.

"Alright," I answer with a quick nod.

"No one knows who helped us that night. So this will have to stay between us for now," she tells me with a hard look.

"Yvie—?" I start, but Twyla cuts me off.

"Not even Yvie, no," she answers with a shake of her head.

"We have a meeting with the others soon, so don't mention a word of this. I mean it, Nesryn, this stays between us."

I hesitate for only a moment before I nod in agreement.

"But we'll meet tonight... We'll use our own communication spell," she says, nodding to herself and ushering me from the room. "Come back tonight and remember, tell no one."

The door shuts in my face with an abrupt click, leaving me little choice but to head back to my room.

The meeting is busier than I expected.

The room is new to me and it seems rather stifling for the twelve people that are standing around the huge square table, littered with maps and curling parchment. Lanterns protrude from the closed-in walls, illuminating the space and casting an eerie glow as the shadows flicker on the walls.

By now, I recognise most of those standing around the table, some talking amongst themselves, others reading the sprawled out maps as I stand there, silent. Uncle Erathon, Rowena, Twyla, Yvaine, Maz and Wylan stand around discussing tactics and next steps that I don't really understand. It suits me just fine since they don't ask me to contribute. Ria stands beside me, her shoulders brushing mine. She remains as silent as me. I glance at the four faces that I don't recognise. A woman flanked by two men, and a third man who manoeuvres through the room to where Twyla stands beside Yvie.

I watch, mildly suspicious, as Wylan converses with the woman. She's dressed in thick, buckled leathers from the northeast and I wonder if she belongs to one of the Drúk clans; tribes of people hailing from the northeast of the peninsula, bordering on Frostmire Peak. She's of average build with coppery blonde hair and a fringe, the rest is braided back over her head and reaches past her shoulder blades. Her hair is styled to show off her half-pointed ears.

'*She's a mixed-blood,*' I realise.

A splash of cool surprise washes over me as I take in the soft peaks of her ears, amazed that she's brave enough to display them fully after the Elven War. Especially after what was left of the Elven hordes retreated across the frozen desert, across the waters to the Elvyn Isles. It was a war that had scarred our lands and killed hundreds of thousands of good men and women. It had come as no surprise when their magic and language was quickly restricted by the surviving rulers of the seven nations.

I can't hear anything that she says over the rest of the conversations filtering about the room, but her face is stony. Whatever she's speaking about must be serious because Wylan seems troubled.

"I think he's taken," Ria murmurs into my ear, her tone teasing.

I blink and turn to her, giving her a sheepish smile. "Was I staring?"

"Like a hawk," she grins.

"I guess I'm just curious," I shrug.

"About?" she asks, turning back to me.

"What's going to happen now," I answer quietly.

As if on cue, Uncle Erathon calls for silence in the room and beckons everyone closer to the table. The bustle of the room settles as the conversations die down into silence. All eyes fall to my uncle, whose own gaze travels around the table, a muscle feathering in his jaw when his eyes land on me.

"Welcome all, we are here tonight with some new faces and some old. I just wish it were under more promising circumstances," he begins. "It has come to our attention that the king will be sending a number of his troops into Talló within days. Sources say he wants to weed us out of our advantageous position. We may have no choice but to retreat until the all-clear is given."

There is a small grumble among the crowd but no one protests as my uncle commands the room. His eyes move to the young man standing between Yvie and Twyla. His tanned, freckled face stands out amongst the two girls, his auburn hair burning brightly beneath the flickering light.

"Jaeg, tell me you have good news for me," Uncle Erathon says, a tired note in his tone.

"We've made progress, but we're nowhere close to completing the project in time for the assault, when it comes," the young man informs us with a shake of his head.

"This is our closest base to the palace, we can't just give that up now! We're so close to infiltrating," Yvie pitches in, her hand gesturing to the table.

"I have contacts and more men lying in wait. I can call upon them for aid, should you need it," the mixed-blooded woman states. Her voice is heavy with an accent that I can't place.

"Thank you, Farren. We need all the help we can get," Uncle Erathon answers.

Rowena steps in, her attention on Yvaine.

"This isn't ideal, I know, Yvie, but Thorn's right. Besides, despite our spies, we have so little information about the layout of the palace."

"We were in the palace, we can help map out the level that we had access to," Ria speaks up, blushing as all eyes swivel to her.

"Thank you, Reverie, but while Twyla's intel helped us a great deal, sadly it will only take us so far. We'd still potentially be going in blind," Rowena explains.

"No, you won't," I say, breaking my silence.

I falter for a moment as the attention shifts to me, but I swallow my nerves and step closer to the table.

"Care to explain?" Wylan speaks up, gesturing to the maps laid out before us all.

I look at him, the small smile on my lips widening as an idea sparks in my mind. "Happily, Wylan. With all the years of my uncle teaching me how to memorise my surroundings, I've come to fancy myself as quite the cartographer," I say, glancing towards where my uncle stands, watching me. "Though perhaps it would be best if I just show you," I continue, turning back to Wylan.

I inhale a deep breath and close my eyes, reaching for the well of power within me. It comes easier now, answering my call immediately. All those lessons with Yvie have proven more than helpful and the fraction of doubt I have melts away as I tap into my power, encouraging it to flow through me.

No one speaks as I widen my senses, reaching out with my mind to the palace. It hadn't taken long for me to wonder what my mind was capable of, how far I could stretch my thoughts and memories. It had taken an equally short amount of time to find the books I had needed to research these methods through Yvaine's extensive library.

I recall the high tower, the gardens, the long halls and winding corridors, the levels of rooms, and the winding stairs. I feel the panic rise within me as I lead myself down, my hands wobbling for a moment.

I feel Ria's hand on my shoulder followed by a gentle squeeze, and I feel the tight band of panic loosen slightly. I push on, focusing on the memories that cling to me, mapping out each level as sharply as I remember it, shaping it from the light until it holds its form. I tune out the gasps and murmurs around me and when I reach the final room, I open my eyes to see the marvel I've created. It's an identical match.

The palace hovers inches above the table before us and I hold on to the tether that keeps it all together. I try to recall the recent lessons with Yvie, and as if she hears my thoughts, I see her tear her eyes away from the glowing map to give me a nod of approval. I hold the palace tentatively with the strands of light, setting it down carefully on the table. When I'm confident that all the layers are in place, I draw back slowly and cut the tether connecting it to the rest of my power.

As I gingerly lower my hands, I watch with a pounding heart as it wobbles for a moment, the structure threatening to collapse. I let out a short exhale of relief when it stays in one piece.

"Astounding," Wylan murmurs as he and Rowena lean closer to study the map.

I look past the 3D map to my uncle who watches me from across the table. He doesn't speak but I see the emotion swimming in his dark eyes and a pang of hurt blooms in my chest as I recall the lies and the deceit. Though deep down, I know that I can't avoid him forever, despite a part of me wanting to.

"This is incredible, Nesryn," Rowena finally speaks, her curls bouncing as she turns to face me. "Do you think you could replicate this?"

"As many times as you need me to," I answer.

"This will give us the edge we need," Rowena says. Her voice travels the room, but her eyes remain trained on my uncle.

"This only solves one issue. What about the Aslitír?" Yvie says, her attention on Rowena.

"Do we know how many he's sending?" Wylan asks.

Farren steps forwards, her hazel eyes flashing with determination as she places a hand on the table. "I can call in my men and have them set up a perimeter. No Aslitír would be brave enough to trifle with Drúk mercenaries."

"It may just be enough to drive them off," Wylan nods. "Erathon?"

"Or hold them at bay while we work on a better strategy to overpower them," Maz cuts in, finally speaking up.

"We appreciate any help you can provide, Farren, thank you," Uncle Erathon dips his head to the young woman.

A small smile touches her lips before it's gone all too suddenly. She pulls her arm up, her clenched fist smacking against her chest once before she and the two men with her leave the room. I notice the way her eyes linger on me for several moments before she and her two companions march out of the room.

"Girls," Rowena speaks up, calling both mine and Ria's attention.

"You may leave us for now. We will find you when we need you," she finishes, before slipping back into conversation with Twyla, Jaeg and Yvie.

"We've not really done much," Ria whispers to me as we head towards the door.

"I'm sure we'll be needed at some point, if there really is going to be a small army of Aslitír coming our way," I answer as we make our way into the corridor.

She's about to reply when I hear scuffling behind us.

"Nesryn, wait!" Wylan calls out after me.

Ria stops ahead of me and turns back, glancing between Wylan and me with a curious expression.

"You go, I'll catch up with you," I reassure her.

As she leaves, I turn to Wylan and Maz. Maz holds back, leaning against the wall as Wylan stops in front of me with a lopsided smile.

"That was incredible back there, you really held your own," he commends me.

"Thank you, my weaving has become much better since my lessons with Yvie." Several moments pass and he doesn't say a word. "What is it you wanted?"

The smile on Wylan's face slips and he gestures for us to walk. I walk alongside him, peering curiously at his pensive expression as we amble along the corridor.

"There is something that I've been wanting to ask you, ever since you decided to join our cause," he says.

I blink in surprise, glancing back at Maz who gives me a ghost of a smile, his dark eyes glinting with understanding. Confused, I turn back to Wylan with a raised brow.

"Dark times are coming, Nesryn, and I'll need as many on my side as I can get," Wylan explains, a hopeful glint in his eye. "Will you align yourself with me, become my right hand when the time comes?" he asks as we come to a standstill.

"I-I don't know what to say, Wylan. I'm honoured," I answer, surprise making my voice higher than usual.

"I see no one better suited to the task. Despite the little time we've had to get to know one another, there is no one I would trust more in this role," he explains, reaching out to squeeze my hand.

"But what about Farren? She seems rather capable. Or Maz?" I ask, glancing back at the raven-haired man hovering in the background.

"No thanks, I'm good with the role I already play," Maz cuts in, sending a flirtatious wink in Wylan's direction.

"While she is an enormous asset to us, and a dear friend, Farren has her own destiny to fulfil. But she knows she will always have a space on my court," Wylan speaks up, drawing my attention back to him.

"Will you give me some time to think about it?" I ask, reeling from his proposal.

"Of course, take whatever time you need. You know where to find me when you have an answer," he says, backing away with a smile.

I watch as he and Maz walk back to the meeting room, the enormity of his question weighing on my shoulders.

CHAPTER FORTYTWO

I wait until I know that Barilius will be busy elsewhere in the castle before I decide to make my move. Shrouding myself in shadow, I move swiftly and silently up the winding stairs. When I reach the final step, I shadowfold past the door, leaving it untouched. I hold my breath, expecting a repelling enchantment to take hold as I land in the room, but after I release the breath I'd been holding, something dawns on me.

No one within these walls would dare enter this tower without both the king's permission and presence. No one but me.

The anger coursing through me fuels me further and I move deeper into the room, all hesitation gone. The stale fragrance of magic use causes my nose to wrinkle and I notice several open vials and jars lined up along the stone altar beside the now-cooled cauldron. I look at them one by one, trying to decide what concoction Barilius may have been cooking up, noting the dying embers beneath the belly of the iron beast. Losing interest, I move towards the stand where the king's thick leather spellbook is propped up. I notice how the front cover glimmers ever so slightly as I analyse it with sceptical eyes.

'*A glamour,*' I realise.

"What are you hiding, Barilius?" I wonder aloud.

Casually, I pull open the book, flicking through the worn, crinkled pages until something compels me to stop. I let the front of the book fall back against the stand, the cover hitting it with a muffled thud.

"*Nexum Edhellen,*" I read aloud. "A communication spell," I breathe, stepping closer as I devour the page.

My lips part in surprise as I read through the spell and its requirements. It's nothing like the one I'd found in the library, this one was stronger. Much stronger.

"This may just work," I realise.

I straighten, glancing around the room and spotting a spare piece of parchment and quill. I grab them and return to the book, my gaze flitting between the spell and my scribbles as I copy it down. As I finish, a small triumphant smile spreads across my lips as I stuff it away in my pocket. As I reach out to close the book, the hairs on the back of my neck stand on edge. A strange hissing and sizzling noise cuts through the thick silence.

I spin around, half-shrouded in shadow when my eyes catch sight of blackened flames coming from the other wall, by the end of the bookshelves. Wary, yet curious, I gingerly step towards the origin of the sound, peering into the gloom to see a hexagonal pedestal of wood with clasps of iron holding the frame firmly together. The pedestal is weathered, but still stands tall in its corner of the room and I wonder why I've never noticed it until now. Splashes of dried red wax from the five candles atop it cling to the wooden surface in uneven clumps, looking a little too much like clotted blood. The flames die down as I get closer and I notice with piquing interest how a scrap of parchment suddenly appears in the centre, swaying gently on an invisible breeze that keeps it suspended in the air.

The candles continue to burn, the black flames eerie and unnerving as I move my gaze past them to the floating piece of parchment at the centre of the five flames.

The blooded moon is coming into alignment.

Be ready or be undone.

- The Black Orchid

"The Black Orchid?" I murmur under my breath.

"Could this be related to Barilius's second Choosing?" I wonder to myself, running a hand across my mouth.

'I've never heard him mention a black orchid before,' I think, my brow knitting together.

I stare at the paper, rereading the words as I try to make sense of them and coming up blank as I'm filled with more questions than answers.

"Focus, Shadowcaster. You came here for information," I remind myself, turning away from the strange message floating on its pedestal.

I move toward the desk again, this time, rummaging through the scrolls and poorly-kept parchment, searching for anything that will lead me to answers about The Choosing. I'm about to reach for the drawers when I hear footsteps echoing up the stone steps outside the door.

Not willing to risk being caught, I shadowfold away, back to the safety of my room.

I'm not in my room long before a hard banging rattles my door. Compartmentalising the things I've just seen and learnt, I walk towards the door, sculpting my face into a mask of calm indifference. Before I can reach it, however, Keelhan barges into the room, sauntering past me as he eyes the disorganised space. He paces about my room, searching for anything abnormal, only to come up empty-handed. I lean against the doorframe with my arms folded, one brow raised as his attention finally falls on me.

"Not up to any more of your little schemes?" he asks snidely.

"Schemes?" I repeat, the corner of my mouth curving upward.

"Come off it, Lys. I've not forgotten our quaint little chat in the tavern," he snipes back.

"Oh, come on now you're still not over our little squabble?" I answer mockingly. "Or has something else riled you up?"

Keelhan glances away while shaking his head, muttering what I expect are obscenities beneath his breath. When he finally looks at me, there is a tiredness in his eyes that wasn't there before.

"Lysan, I'm in no mood. I came to tell you we leave at dawn. From what I've heard around the palace, you're too busy galavanting about. Like you don't have shit to be done," states, the edge to his voice returning.

"Is there a reason for this flying visit or do you plan on lecturing me to death?" I counter.

"You should be preparing for The Choosing. Barilius is relying on us both," Keelhan argues.

"What do you think all my *gallivanting*, as you so eloquently put it, is for?" I ask, my tone taunting.

A flash of frustration appears in his eyes and I watch as the colour of them darken as his brow knits together. He signals for the two men at my door to step away as he strides back towards them, he turns back to me mid-step. We continue our staredown long enough for me to find it slightly amusing.

"No more games, Lysan. We're leaving for Tralló at dawn. We each have our assignments and you'd better be ready for yours," he warns me, the anger in his eyes waning. "Barilius won't have any more delays or continue to tolerate your fuck-ups," he says, glancing at where the collar had been fastened around my neck.

He's out of the door before I can summon a response and I begin to realise that we are mere pawns in the king's hands, the parts we must play in his deadly game of power and control. One that will only end in more bloodshed.

NESRYN

CHAPTER FORTY-THREE

The hour is late, easily well past twelve chimes when I find myself outside Twyla's door. I made sure that I wasn't followed, glancing along the empty halls for any unwanted eyes before I rap my knuckles gently against the door, only for her to open it at the third knock.

I blink in surprise at her promptness, until I find my eyes drawn past her, over her shoulder to the set-up within.

"Hurry up and get in," Twyla hisses at me.

I step into the room, feeling the rush of air behind me as she quickly closes the door and locks it shut behind me. My eyes travel across the room to where a set of wax candles and a tiny cauldron surrounded by glass bottles and vials are placed atop a dark blanket.

I turn and glance at Twyla over my shoulder, raising a single brow in question at the impressive setup. She shrugs nonchalantly, but I don't miss the slight twist in her mouth as she subdues a smile.

"I help Yvie with potions from time to time," she explains.

"From time to time," I repeat teasingly, a hint of sarcasm in my voice as I glance back at the items.

Twyla is close behind me as I study the layout of her room. I draw in a deep breath, exhaling it slowly through my nose as I bring my hands together.

"So, how do we start?" I ask, shifting my attention to her.

She moves around me and steps over the contents on the blanket and drops to her knees, reaching for the book hiding behind the hand-sized cauldron. I sit down opposite her and silently watch as she opens the book and flicks through the pages as she searches for the spell she's after. My fingers drum against the floor as I watch her, until I notice her eyes brighten and she straightens her posture, swivelling the book around for me to read the pages.

"Luhta'gwaedh nauta," I read out loud. "This is an oath spell, Twyla."

I glance at Twyla, giving her a dubious look while she scrunches up her nose at my expression.

"It's the only thing I could find that will allow you to communicate with others without something that belongs to them," she reasons.

"It will have to do for now. I just hope it does what we need it to," I reply.

I heave a sigh and meet her eye, nerves fluttering in my stomach. "What do I have to do?"

She swivels the book back around and she skims the page before she looks back at me.

"This spell requires a few drops of blood and a memory to work. It has to be your blood, your memory that tethers you to him for the spell to work," she explains, her expression serious.

"...alright," I say finally, processing her words.

Together we silently begin prepping the spell, adding each ingredient to the small cauldron and lighting a flat candle beneath to heat the substances. The acidic smell of powders sizzling wafts into the air as Twyla reads through the final instructions.

"This is the part where you add three drops of blood, as you focus on a particular memory. You'll need to say these words aloud as well," Twyla explains, handing me the book.

"If this works—" I start.

"—which it will," Twyla cuts in.

"Then how can we trust him? He works for Barilius, his hands are stained with just as much blood," I point out.

"Maybe, but information is still information. Lie or not, we can warn the others and make a plan," she reasons.

I peer at the book, heaving a sigh of acceptance as I unsheath Stormtip. In my mind, I pull up a memory of Lysan, doing my best to fight the anger burning in the base of my stomach as I think of all the wrong he's done, the monstrosity he'd allied himself with.

With the pointed edge, I prick the skin on my index finger, the tiny wound beading with my blood. I force out the three droplets required, listening as the crimson liquid sizzles against the powder as I read from the book.

"With this offering, I create a bond of mind and flesh. Luhta'gwaedh nauta orthanc mennai'metta," I speak clearly, repeating the text before me.

The contents in the cauldron flare, as do the flickering candles around us, but the effects only last a few seconds. A thick purple smoke wafts up from within the iron pot, the smell reminding me of something similar to burnt pine and mint. Without meaning to, I inhale the fumes, coughing and spluttering as the aroma burns the back of my throat.

Just as I'm about to ask Twyla what happens now, my eyes shut on their own and I feel a light tether tug at me, pulling my conscious thoughts away from the present, away from Twyla and the potion, and into a blanketed darkness.

When I come to, Twyla peers down at me with a concerned expression. Her dark eyes study me closely as I groan and I sit up, rubbing my temple.

"What happened? Did it work?" she asks, her tone insistent.

I search within myself, trying to recall the events, but come up blank. I feel no different other than a throbbing headache encircling my head. My neck aches as I crane my head back to face her and shake my head, defeated.

"Nothing happened. It just knocked me out," I answer.

"Dammit. I'm not sure what else we can try short of leaving the base and finding him," she replies, blowing out a frustrated breath.

"And even then we can't be sure he'd even tell the truth," I add.

"So, that's it then," Twyla breathes, slumping back.

Silence passes between us, our failure hanging heavily over our heads. Despite myself, I think back to the dream and wonder if I'd somehow made it up in my own mind, or projected my fears into some kind of a warning. But nothing tells me I'm wrong, somehow, for some unknown reason, he'd tried to contact me. I just had to figure out why.

"No," I say aloud, drawing Twyla's attention to me. "We'll try again tomorrow night."

My head continues to pound as I make my way back to my room, eager for a few hours of rest before I start the day. As I walk, I mentally go over the spell we'd used, trying to remember if I'd made any type of mistake for it to backfire the way it had. I'm so engrossed in my own thoughts that I walk straight into the person standing outside of my door. I stumble back several steps, blinking in surprise as I look up. My heart constricts as my uncle looks down at me with a resigned expression. I feel my throat tighten as we stand awkwardly outside of my door, shifting uncomfortably in the thick silence.

"Uncle, I don't really have time for this right now," I'm the first to speak, knowing why he's come to me so early in the day.

I step around him to reach my door, feeling him turn after me as I go.

"We need to talk, Nix. This can't go on forever," he reasons.

"No, it can't," I sigh, turning to give him a deadpan look. "But you can't force it, Uncle. I'm tired of being forced to bend to the will of others."

Uncle Erathon blinks, the hurt evident in his eyes, but I find myself free of guilt, too busy guarding the little of myself I feel I have left.

"I'm not trying to—" he starts.

I lift a hand to stop him, shaking my head as I close my eyes for a moment and take a deep breath. When I open my eyes, he is already studying me closely, his lips pressed into a thin line.

"Let me try to put things into perspective for you," I begin, my expression muted. "I can understand why you kept me in the dark about all of this, about what my parents helped build. I know that it was to protect me, but a lie is still a lie, Uncle." I speak, my voice calm yet firm. "But what I struggle to understand, what I grapple with the most, is how you took a part of me and hid it away from me. My abilities, where they came from. You took a vital part of me away, something that could have protected me, protected the others—" I falter, my voice growing thick with emotion.

I clench my fists, feeling them tremble with the anger running through me as I blink away the vicious tears that threaten to spill down my face. I release a shuddering breath and return my gaze to my uncle's. He remains frozen where he stands, unmoving. If it wasn't for the light flutter of his chest, I'd wonder if he was even breathing.

"These powers—*my* powers—could have changed the fate of so many, including mine," I say quietly, glancing down to study my hands.

"What I've done was unforgivable and I'm truly sorry. Can you at least let me try to make amends, Nix?" Uncle Erathon cuts in.

I shake my head, the curls bouncing as I lift my gaze back to his and he falters. "No, you don't get to decide how we do this. I love you, you're my uncle and the only family I've got, but my anger is too strong and your betrayal is too great."

The shuddering breath I release sounds more like a cry as I try to rein in the pain radiating in my chest and the colossal lump in my throat constricting my words. As I get a hold of myself, my uncle stands frozen to the spot, his parted lips unable to utter a syllable. Once I've regained my composure, I make sure to keep my voice level.

"There is a fight coming, and our focus needs to be on that. The others need us right now and Barilius must fall. That is as much as we can agree on right now, I'm sorry," I say.

I swerve to move around him, half-expecting him to put up one last attempt at fighting my decision, but he doesn't. Instead, he remains rooted to the spot as I glance back over my shoulder at him.

"I'm not ready for forgiveness," I say before I walk away.

'*It's retribution you seek,*' the little voice murmurs in my head.

I throw my weight around as I spar with the dummy standing before me. Beads of sweat slip down my temples and along my jaw as I thrust out my arm with another forceful punch.

My body aches with exhaustion, but I continue to push myself, running on anger and fumes whilst fighting through the storm brewing in my mind.

I think of what's to come, of the political dangers I've been drawn into. I think of how little I understand my abilities as a

Starweaver still, despite my training. I find myself afraid of what will be expected of me in the days to come. Wylan's proposal flits through my mind and for at least the hundredth time, I consider the offer, weighing up what it would mean, what responsibilities would befall me.

Then I think of him.

Lysan's face somehow weasels its way to the forefront of my mind. I think of his place at Barilius's side, of his role and the duty that comes with it. Then I consider the memory of him carrying me from the tower, to safety. To freedom.

I scowl and punch the dummy again, shaking my head as I fail to make sense of how the weapon that the king wields is the very same man that saved my life.

"You should maybe work on your form, it's a little sloppy," a female voice breaks through my jumbled thoughts.

I straighten, dropping my hands as I look around to find Farren watching me from the doorway, wearing a lopsided grin that quite suits her.

"I'm not great at my hand-to-hand," I explain. "I just needed to let off some steam."

"I can see that. You really let him have it," she answers with a knowing smirk.

"You're… Farren. I saw you at the meet," I point out, changing the subject. "I'm Nesryn."

I reach out my hand and wait as she crosses the space between us and takes my hand, shaking it once. She smiles, a glint in her eye.

"I know who you are," she answers.

I drop my arm back down as she takes a step back and folds her arms across her chest. "But then a lot of people know who *you* are, Nesryn Havenore. Word travels fast around here," she continues.

I shift on my feet, suddenly uncomfortable under her studying gaze. Perplexed, I tilt my head as her words sink in. "What do you mean by that?"

"As I'm sure you've been told, people who go into that palace scarcely ever come back out. And yet somehow, you and five others managed to free yourselves from that tyrant. That type of thing will catch people's interest," she explains, a flash of something in her hazel eyes that I'm not quick enough to read.

"People like you?"

The glint in her eyes fades, her smile slipping as if she's remembering something she'd rather not, and I find myself regretting the question.

"I have my own interests to contend with," she says before moving towards the door.

I watch her go, my brow knitting together in confusion when she pauses in the doorway and looks back at me over her shoulder. "But you have caught my attention."

Then she's gone and I'm alone once more.

My room is a welcome place when I finish throwing my weight around the training room. The exhaustion has fully crept up on me and it takes the very last dregs of my energy to run myself a hot bath and climb into my slim cot, praying no one disturbs me for a few hours. It doesn't matter that the quilt is scratching and the frame creaks with each movement as I shift into a more comfortable position. My heavy lids close almost as soon as my head hits the pillow, slipping into a welcome slumber.

I feel myself floating, a pull drawing me somewhere through the air and landing in a familiar, foreboding place. As I glance down at myself, I realise I'm wearing the black glittering gown from my final night in the palace. I blink, trying to clear my vision, but realise after several attempts that the world around me isn't completely in focus.

I look around and take in the high hedges and gloomy paths winding into the maze beyond, recognising it almost instantly despite the heaviness accumulating in my head. My skin prickles with a tingling sensation as I feel a presence behind me.

"What is this?" the voice asks, the sharpness somehow softened in this strange place.

I turn to see a familiar face several yards away, looking around as though seeing it all for the first time. A wave of strong emotions attempt to claw at me, and yet somehow I still feel calm, their strength not enough to penetrate the invisible walls around me. As I look at him, I try to take in the clearer features:

his dark hair which falls over his forehead, his tall frame, and the darkened leathers.

As if he's finally realised he's not alone, he stops, his attention falling on me. His seafoam eyes are clear and bright despite the rest of him being dreamlike and blurred. I note that they're rather striking as I stare back at him.

"Nesryn," his disbelieving voice is nothing more than a whisper.

"Didn't think you'd be seeing me again?" I ask, my voice sounding unfamiliar to my ears.

I draw out my hand from behind me, my attention shifting to my open palm as I bring to life miniature flares of light that float about my hand, moving in slow circles. Lysan stiffens on the spot and I feel his eyes move over me as I display my power.

"I knew what you were, from that moment," he says, voice soft. He speaks as though it's a moment that I would remember.

I curl my fingers into my palm, the gentle flecks of light shimmering into nothing. I take a step back, then another as I turn my attention to him.

"And what is that? What am I, Shadowcaster?" I ask before twirling around and striding into the dense maze before us, glancing over my shoulder with a secretive smile as I wait for him to follow.

"Wait!" I hear him call after me.

But I don't. My legs move faster, my feet picking up the pace until I'm flying through the maze, the wind in my hair. It's all a game, it's not real.

Nothing here is real.

I hear him as he calls after me, the ground vibrating beneath my bare feet and I sense him following me into the depths of rich hunter green and warm brown. Danger never feels far, and yet I feel light—lucid and dazed all at once. The sensation is intoxicating.

"Nesryn! Nesryn, where are we?" I hear him call through the swirling mist.

I finally stop when we reach a clearing in the maze, the hedges opening up to a rounded space filled with clusters of snowdrops. A stark contrast to the rich dark colours surrounding us. I spin around, my chest heaving as I try to catch my breath, waiting with anticipation for Lysan to appear.

When he does, his eyes find mine instantaneously. He breathes heavily through his nose as he steps into the clearing, the noise echoing softly through the air. I tilt my head as I study him, aware of the danger, yet unconcerned at the thought. I don't trust him. He helped massacre the girls I'd come to call friends. He stood idly by as they died, and yet something doesn't seem to add up. The memory of his arms around me sends a shiver running down my spine and momentarily scatters my thoughts. I contemplate this as I watch him, the edges of him still soft and fuzzy.

"What *is* this place? What are we doing here?" he tries again, but I've already dismissed his words. I feel my anger trying to make its way through the invisible wall around me, to no avail. I know who he is, I know what he's done. My thirst for revenge is still there within me somewhere, hidden away.

I step closer to where he stands, moving until we're practically touching, until I have to crane my head up to look at him. I watch the swirls of blue closely, trying to read them, to draw out their secrets. I feel his eyes move down, grazing my lips and I note how the colour darkens ever so slightly. I draw Stormtip, lifting the point to graze his chin. I feel his sharp intake of breath, his body involuntarily brushing against mine.

"You support the opposing side. You have supported your king's slaughter of those Chosen. I'm your enemy and you're a monster," I say, my voice quietly even.

"Your point, princess?" he asks, a dark smirk coating his lips despite the point of my blade cutting into his skin.

"Why save me?"

CHAPTER FORTYFOUR

"Why save me?"

Her question reverberates through me as we stand only millimetres apart, my smirk faltering.

With every breath she inhales, her chest brushes against me and I lose track of my thoughts. I keep my gaze fixed on her eyes, their colour bright and clear. Her face is so soft, her full lips parted in anticipation of my answer. An answer I can't seem to find. Nothing about this feels right, the hazed outline of our surroundings and rich colours like something out of a dreamscape. I feel as though my head is in the clearest water, able to see and hear within reason, yet I'm unable to come up for air, drunk on the lack of oxygen.

She grips her blade tighter and the sting sharpens but I'm unable to form the words.

Thoughts of Loísia threaten to break through but somehow don't, as though there is a wall between my lucid thoughts and this right here. I fight the effects of whatever this place is, mentally grasping at anything to stay grounded. I try to hold my usual mask in place, but I feel it slip. Her words hit me again.

'*What part do you play*?' A little voice in my head speaks up.

When I finally open my mouth to speak, I'm not expecting the words that come out. "You should be more worried about what is coming, princess. Those like you are in danger, there are much darker forces at play here."

Her eyes widen at my words, my ominous warning enough for her to pull back, and as she does, it's as though a band has snapped, yanking me back into serene darkness.

I launch into an upright position, suddenly awake.

My bedsheets are tangled around my legs, my hands gripping the edges of the slim cot as I slowly recall my surroundings. My heart thrums evenly in my chest, but it feels at odds with the strong pulse of magic running through me.

Blinking my eyes into focus, I realise I'm using my power, the shadows curling and coiling softly through the space around me like a darkened void. A single point under my chin stings and I brush my fingers underneath, pulling them away and noting the coating of blood across them.

'*Nesryn*,' I realise, recalling the dream.

"That was no regular dream…"

'*It was real*,' the voice in my head says.

"But how?" I consider, moving towards the window.

Leaning on the windowsill, I stare out at the view of the harbour, listening to the gulls caw above as I watch the water, reflecting the peach skies of dawn. I think of the strangeness of the dream, the way everything had felt real and yet also like a dream. The only thing that had seemed clear and *real*, was her.

"She must have found a way to communicate… which means she got my message," I realise, feeling a tinge of relief.

'*What spell could she have used*?' I wonder whether it had been the very same one I'd planned on using.

"But why seek me out? What has she got to gain?" I ask myself, as I think back over her words and the question that had me frozen.

"It doesn't matter for now," I dismiss my own questions, relief blooming in my stomach at the thought of being able to warn her of what was coming.

My relief is short-lived as I hear the marching of the soldiers outside and move back into the room, reaching for a shirt. Moving into the tiny cubby washroom, I splash my face with water and hold the edges of the basin as I stare at my reflection, the blood from the cut on my chin swirling around the bottom of the basin.

Keelhan would be moving them into Talló in the next few hours to make good on the king's orders, meaning I have very little time to try and get another message across before it's too late.

I consider trying to reason with him but I soon realise this will be a fruitless effort. Straightening, I pace back into my small room and arm myself before shrugging on my jacket and tying my boots, my mind racing with the plan now unfurling. There is work to be done, and I'm running out of time.

As I stand, I glance at the crumpled parchment on the desk, memorising each name before I make my way to the door, calling upon my shadows to shroud me from prying eyes.

"It's time to cause a little havoc," I murmur to myself, a small smile curling my lips.

STARWEAVER

NESRYN

CHAPTER FORTYFIVE

I feel on edge, my mind swimming with unwanted thoughts as I try to focus on the conversation going on around me. I try my best, but the events of last night have me all worked up and I'm unable to sit still, though no one else seems to notice. I woke with a start, my heart pummelling rapidly in my chest as though it may burst free at any given moment. Shock douses the anger in the pit of my stomach, my mouth dry as memories of my dream creep back into my mind.

The spell had worked and I needed to speak to Twyla.

I've never jumped out of bed so fast, rushing to throw my clothes on, eager to find her as soon as physically possible.

The plan doesn't last long at all.

Wylan finds me as I leave my room, still in an uneasy fit of panic from the dream. He finds me, carrying some freshly made rolls that waft towards me, causing my mouth to water. His smile falters as he sees my hurried state.

"Have I caught you at a bad time?"

I blink, swallowing the urgency humming through me and trying to relax my shoulders. "No, not at all," I lie.

"Are you sure? You seem like you're in a hurry," he replies, glancing briefly behind us.

"No, it can wait," I insist, swallowing my panic. I could hold it together, for now, then I'd find Twyla. "What can I help you with, Wylan?"

He spins on his feet, gesturing for me to follow him as he walks. I fall into step beside him.

"I know you haven't exactly agreed to the position yet, and we're still a way off from completing what I'm here to do, but

Row and a few others have set up a meeting. I think I'd benefit from having you in on it," he explains while passing me a roll.

"Of course, then lead the way," I say, earning a grateful grin.

I soon find my way back to the room where the last gathering had been held, only this time, there are only four other people waiting for us.

My uncle eyes me warily from across the small space as I enter, Wylan close behind me. There are bags beneath his dark eyes, and his dreads are stacked into a messy bun balancing on top of his head. I shift my attention away from his gaze, ignoring my twisting gut. My eyes travel across the room, acknowledging Rowena, Yvie and Jaeg, the latter lifts a hand in welcome before turning his focus back to the strange-looking metal contraption in his hand.

As I step inside, Wylan swallows his mouthful of bread and clears his throat. "Now that we're all here, shall we begin?"

I'm sitting towards the back of the room, the table now in even more disarray than when I'd arrived, piled high with parchment and maps. Rowena has decided to drag chairs in and even though it's a tight fit, I can't complain— I'm just glad to be sitting down after so long, standing in the same spot.

Hours pass by and I listen to them talk plans and tactics for so long, with so little to say myself, that I simply sit back and let my thoughts stray back to the dream.

'You should be more worried about what is coming, princess. Those like you are in danger, there are much darker forces at play here.'

"Those like me…" I trail off, fiddling with the corner of the closest unrolled parchment.

'But what could that mean?' I wonder glancing around the room at the others.

'A member of The Righteous Hand? A Starweaver? A survivor?'

The possibilities seem vast and I can't help but feel frustrated as I try to unravel Lysan's words, only to come up blank.

"—be prepared. This meet in Madmire is vital for our cause," Rowena's voice trickles through my thoughts.

My distracted brain dashes all thoughts of Lysan and the strange dreams as my attention snaps back to the meeting.

"I agree, it will give us an edge against the oncoming tides of change," my uncle chimes in.

"How is our meet to happen?" Wylan speaks up, his brow furrowed as he leans on the table, scrutinising the two leaders.

"Getting past the Aslitír will be the hardest part, though the way through the mountain pass isn't going to be a walk in the park," Yvie says, though her eyes are focused on the maps splayed out before her.

"The plan is that we leave for Mire Port as soon as possible. From there, we'll sail to Madmire and meet our correspondents at the fortress there.

I sit straighter in my chair, my eyes flitting from one person to the next, engrossed in the events unfolding around me.

"Are we sure that is still a good idea?" Wylan speaks up, his gaze shifting to me.

"Despite the slight setback of the Aslitír being sent our way, we can't say it was an unexpected factor. Madmire will offer us allies outside of these borders, allies we will need if war is to come," Rowena speaks.

"Which it *will*," my uncle cuts in.

"Have I missed something?" I speak up, suddenly finding five pairs of eyes trained on me.

"This is why I brought you along, Nesryn," Wylan starts, pausing to glance at Rowena. "A small group of us will be travelling to Madmire to meet with the seven nations. We want to build a treaty before we go head to head with Barilius."

"I gathered, but what does that have to do with me?" I ask, curiosity mingling with uncertainty.

"Consider it a practice run, should you accept my proposition," he answers.

My eyes widen and my stomach flips at the thought of being above ground once again. The tangle of emotion is momentarily washed away by the pride of being chosen for something so important.

"This is an incredibly dangerous mission, but it is crucial to our cause," Rowena warns me, her bright eyes alert as she holds my stare.

"Once there, if you can, I'll need you to relay some of your findings and experiences of your time in Barilius's palace,"

Wylan says, facing me with a sympathetic smile.

Unease coils in my stomach at the thought of relaying the horrors, of reliving those memories aloud for all to see me fall apart.

"Your powers must be kept under wraps though, we don't want to draw any attention to ourselves," Rowena adds.

I curl my fingers into fists in silent frustration. I understand why this would need to be said, but after finally being able to master my abilities, not using them seemed like an unnecessary waste.

"Your truth will help to open their eyes and back Wylan as the true heir of Akhozia," Yvie cuts in, her voice as gentle as the reassuring smile on her lips.

"If you can't handle it then—" Rowena starts.

I silence her with a dark glare before she can finish her sentence, my knuckles turning white against the table as I do my best to keep a firm grasp of my power.

"Who is going?"

"You, me, Row, Jaeg, Farren and maybe a few of her men," he answers.

I nod once, already set on a decision.

"If I'm going, Ria comes," I counter.

"No chance, we want to be small and unseen. We don't need any of the blood crown's men catching a scent of this. One liability is enough," Rowena argues, rising from her chair.

Everyone in the room goes quiet at her hostile words. I note the look my uncle sends her which she decidedly ignores. It only riles me further. I don't need anyone to fight my battles, especially if they involve a cocky bitch who needs to remember who she's dealing with.

Despite the urge to kick back my chair and launch myself at her, I lift my hand, fashioning a deadly glowing blade for all to see, my eyes sliding from it to Rowena as I glower at her.

"If you think I'm such a liability, why don't you come and test your theory? Come see how dangerous I really can be?" I suggest darkly.

I watch with concealed smugness how she moves to speak, fire burning in her eyes, but eventually thinks better of it, her mouth set in a thin line.

'I didn't think so,' I think to myself.

"You said it yourself, this will be a dangerous mission. And if we succeed, we then need to convince the seven nations that my word is true. Two voices speaking the same truth weighs more than one," I point out, closing my hand on the fabricated blade. "If my powers can't be used despite all my training, then fine," I start, turning to Wylan. "I may be well-versed in the sword, but I want someone watching my back while I watch yours."

"Spoken like a true Second," he observes.

Wylan's smile grows and pride swells in my chest. I watch as he slowly turns his attention back to Rowena. I follow suit, an expectant expression on my face as she looks at each of us, then sighs.

"Alright, fine. Prepare yourselves and get some rest. We leave tonight."

The air is sharper than expected as we traverse the road where the mountain meets land. Steephelm Rok looms over us even in the darkness, its solid shape is still visible under the dim light of the stars above. Despite the worry of Aslitír littering the streets of Tralló harbour, there had been none to trouble us as we were smuggled from the busy streets by a pair of allied merchants travelling the eastern road, to a small village north of Treberg.

Horses had been waiting for us when we'd reached the checkpoint, where the mountains met the river. Ria rides to my right on a chestnut mare, her bright eyes peering into the darkness as she grips the reins. I look past the blackened head of my own steed at the rest of the group. Rowena and Fareen lead, followed by Wylan and Jaeg, then Ria and myself, before ending the line with Farren's men: Elex and Theon.

The night is still full and heavy around us as we move in unison. There is no moon tonight, the dark landscape only illuminated by the twinkling stars. Clusters of trees break up the rocky landscape, the sounds of rushing water drowning out the little sound that we do make. I shift slightly in my saddle, my legs and back protesting as I readjust the leather bag strapped across my back and shoulders. For the third time tonight, I mentally kick myself for not speaking to Twyla before I left. In all the commotion of finding Ria and relaying the meeting to her,

I had forgotten about the dream and Lysan. Now, however, with nothing but the sound of hooves hitting the loose pebble road beneath us, it is all I can think of. I pick apart the encounter again, running through each moment, each distorted feeling and emotion that I had felt. His second warning, both ominous and clear in its intent to unnerve. When I finally come out of my train of thought, I'm feeling even more confused than before. I sense more than see Ria's concerned gaze on me, but I pretend not to notice, feeling strangely protective of this secret. No need to unsettle her with talk about dreaming of the enemy. Not when I feel unsettled enough on my own.

Up ahead there seems to be some quiet murmurs that I can barely make out. It's only when Wylan circles back that I realise those ahead are slowing down. He trots along my left side, the light of the stars reflecting in his eyes as he leans over.

"Nothing to worry about, we're just going to rest for a short while," he explains.

Relief floods my chest as I glance towards Ria to see that she's already overheard. Without another word, we follow Wylan and I mentally thank the goddess, my aching body grateful to be returning to solid ground.

The small campfire crackles, the orange and yellow flames flickering through the night, illuminating the faces around it. Conversation is scarce, with only Rowena and Farren discussing routes and making good time. I try my best to sit amongst them all, but I feel the fear blooming within me at the close proximity. Ria's silent, but not-so-subtle glances my way only speed up the unsettling fear growing within me, and before it becomes suffocating, I mumble an excuse and quickly get to my feet.

Moving with purpose, I return to the side of my mare, running my hand in a gentle stroke along her flank as I focus on a point and breathe slowly, feeling my heart slow with each intake. The sound of gravel underfoot snags my attention and I falter halfway through an intake, turning to find Wylan striding towards me.

"Ria told me I would find you over here," he says gently, handing me a pouch.

I take it and knock a mouthful back, expecting water. Instead, something stronger and spicier hits the back of my throat and I choke, holding the pouch away from me. Wylan laughs at me as my eyes water from the alcohol coating my tongue.

"What is that?" I croak to the future king.

"Something perhaps a bit too strong for the likes of you," he replies with another bark of laughter.

"Maybe for someone who thought she was drinking water," I grumble, swerving his hand as I take another swig, now welcoming the burn that hits the back of my throat before it warms in my stomach.

Despite myself, a wry grin finds its way onto my face as I pass it back to my amused companion. I watch, slightly impressed, as he brings it to his lips, a hiss escaping him after he swallows.

"Buckle for your thoughts?" he asks after a moment.

My smile falters and I find myself looking away from him, trying to quell the sudden bombardment of thoughts running around my head. I inhale deeply, letting out a long sigh before I return my gaze to him. He is curious yet patient.

"Sometimes the simplest things seem the hardest," I answer finally.

Wylan nods as if in understanding.

"Then just as you think you're getting the hang of it..." I trail off, unable to find the words.

"You're thrown off the deep end?" he suggests, tilting his head.

I nod once and silence envelopes us. I welcome it.

"If this is about my proposal... don't feel like you have to say yes. I will understand," he says softly.

I shake my head. "It's a huge responsibility, yes, but that isn't all. So much has happened and changed. I was this person I knew inside out, I knew her morals, goals, everything. Now I'm this new person, and everything around me has changed, including me."

I let out a shaky breath and glance back at him, searching his eyes.

"How do you deal with it? The pressure?" The question slips free.

"Just take it one day at a time I guess," he says with a shrug, offering me the pouch again.

"Is that all?" I reply dubiously, taking it and stealing another mouthful before passing it back.

He drops his head and smiles a secretive sort of smile before looking at me again. He searches my face thoughtfully as if deciding something.

"Remember you're not alone."

We're back on the road, now hours into our journey. I hear someone ahead say we're not too far from the checkpoint where the boat will meet us. I notice how the terrain shifts and changes as we move further into the mountains, the gravelled path becoming much less grassy around the edges. It begins to give way to the rockier terrain as we carefully make our way through the space between two of the Steephelm Rok peaks, alongside the roaring river as it continues to travel southwest. Its deadly current swirls viciously over the sharp rocks jutting out from the surface and we move in single file, guiding our steeds slowly through the treacherous path.

The hair on my neck stands on edge as we make it through onto the other side where the feeling intensifies. I feel my horse shift as though she can feel it too. Ahead, I hear shouts of surprise as disorder spreads throughout our group. I stand up in my saddle trying to get a good look at what's ahead, but there is too much going on to see properly.

"We're surrounded," one of Farren's men calls from behind us and I look back over my shoulder with widening eyes as I see what's there, swirling in the darkness.

Unease claws through my veins as I recognise the familiar sight of the inky shadows.

Our horses are spooked, whinnying and stamping their hooves. I try to find a way out of this but I come up blank. The river flows to our right; its deathly current is not worth the plunge. The harsh mountainous cliffs to our left are too perilous to risk. And the writhing shadows are creeping in behind us.

As the group splits apart, I'm given a perfect view of him and the fear is replaced immediately with burning anger and bitter distaste.

'*How the fuck did he find us?*' I dare to wonder, afraid I already know the answer.

There is nowhere for us to go but forwards, right into the hands of a somewhat smug-looking Shadowcaster.

CHAPTER FORTYSIX

Time isn't on my side. But in the last twenty-four hours, I'd managed enough of a delay to hinder my collection of the next Chosen. Aslitír now filled the streets while Keelhan had been sent away on a convenient tip-off at the market on the other side of the city. It would keep him busy for the rest of the day at least, as long as the rest of my plan went smoothly.

When I'd had a moment to myself, I'd tested the fragile connection between Nesryn and I, sensing more than feeling the thin spider silk string attaching us. I hadn't yet dreamt of her since our last meeting, but I found myself trying regardless, eager to elaborate on my warning. I had focused all my efforts into the line of communication between us, acutely aware that she may sense me probing the magic she'd clearly conjured. When I'd sensed that I'd broken through, I felt a brush of her presence on the other side: jasmine and something else I couldn't quite grasp. It wasn't what I had expected.

There had been nothing, nothing but a feeling of determination and the tiniest whisper of a name.

A place.

Madmire.

I'd processed this information with surprise and decided to formulate a plan.

Hours filter by, the day drawing into the evening by the time I begin to put my plan into action. In my mind, I go over every detail and analyse every possible outcome. I'm aware that what

I'm about to do is potentially reckless and dangerous, but it's not so different to most of my plans. Only that now there is no denying the king would have my head on a spike if he knew.

Loísia's voice filters through my mind, the soft voice sending a shiver along my spine as I remember who I'm doing this for, why I'm risking it all. A bitter laugh bubbles out of me, surprising me with the dark feeling that settles in my chest. I turn to see my reflection in the mirror in the washroom, seeing the determination lurking beneath the clouded green-blue. Stray dark hairs fall across my furrowed brow and my lips draw into a thin line, bracing myself for what's to come.

"The Choosing will end," I vow to myself, to Loísia.

I turn away, glancing toward my scabbard and sheathed sword, reaching for it before making my way out of the door, to the next stage of my plan.

The tavern is far less busy than I expected. Small groups of Aslitír cluster around tables with steins of frothed ale. The fireplace crackles with heat and the air smells warm, the scent of meaty stew wafting past my nose as I scour the tables for a particular face.

Initially, I'm surprised at how few there are here, wondering if any have decided to pay a visit to the local brothels. Then I realise that Keelhan probably ordered the men to continue patrolling the streets until dark, especially with the threat of the rebels growing stronger.

'And stronger still,' a little voice whispers in my head.

I feel the eyes of the men as I move through the room, my presence halting several conversations. I know how they think, all brave in their little packs and armed with their steel. They see themselves as the predators, watching me like the prey they believe me to be. They forget themselves. I am the wolf in sheep's clothing, the most dangerous thing in this room with a blow far more lethal than anything they could possibly attempt. The thought gives me a dark lick of satisfaction that settles in my chest.

I catch sight of a group of five men, sitting around two tables pushed together, their half-drunk drinks in their hands as they talk amongst themselves. Their conversation dies down as I make my way towards them, their gazes narrowing as I stop at the end of their tables.

"It's your lucky day, boys. You've got a new mission, so you'll all be joining me tonight," I say, my eyes flashing with dark excitement.

"The captain hasn't given us any new orders, Shadowcaster," says one of the men, Crell, before taking another large swig of his ale.

"Leave us be, you aren't welcome," another, Talix, dismisses me.

"Who said anything about the captain?" I respond, choosing to ignore the last soldier's comment.

They hesitate for only a moment before they each pick their drinks back up. Crell turns back to me with an unnecessarily loud sigh.

"Second or not, your orders aren't shit. We're not doing what you want, Shadowcaster, so forget it," he says, dismissing me as he turns his attention back to the others.

I swallow a growl. I refuse to let them see how their disrespect affects me.

"I don't really have time for your bullshit tonight, boys. But seeing as you aren't interested in orders from your king, I'll just have to find some who are," I say indifferently, my bored tone well-rehearsed.

I can tell by the way they shift in their seats that I have their attention.

"Order's from the king?" the Aslitír in the far corner speaks up, his tone unsure.

"There seems to be a matter that needs seeing to, a matter concerning some runaways from the rebel group. I've been told to gather some tag-alongs. So what do you say, boys?" I ask, arching my brow.

I watch as they glance between each other, sharing the same look. I know I've piqued their interest. A wry smile creeps across my mouth as I look at each of them before turning and making my way back outside.

"Good. We leave in five minutes," I call to them over my shoulder.

We arrive at nightfall, the wind catching between two peaks of the mountain. I ignore the protests and cursing from the Aslitír and scope out the area. Unsure as to why despite following the pull of our connection, I find myself having shadowfolded to the middle of nowhere.

I mentally try to place where we are on a map, taking in the rocky path, the towering mountains and the fast-paced river with its swirling current. The night sky is moonless, the grass and surrounding space illuminated only by the twinkling stars above. There is no one and nothing but the natural elements around, but something in my gut says that this is where we're meant to be.

"Where the fuck are we, Shadowcaster?" Crell spits, aiming the point of his blade at my throat.

I tut at him, lowering the point away from the exposed skin with a finger. "I wouldn't do that if I were you."

My eyes travel past him to where the mountains close towards each other, leaving only a narrow pass, and an idea sparks in my head. Meanwhile, the soldier glowers at me, his distrust visible even in the darkness.

"Don't suppose you boys are familiar with an ambush?" I ask dryly.

They share a look, their mouths twisting up into half-smiles that resemble sneers more than anything. I send each of them to a post, spread out in a semi-circle, to wait in silence.

Soon enough, beneath the sound of the raging river, I hear the sound of hooves. I inhale a breath and prepare myself for what is about to come, reminding myself again of the plan.

As they come closer, I step forwards and draw out my shadows, encircling us and the group heading toward us in a binding circle of writhing shadow. Their panic comes next as I hear the shouts of the rebels and the unease of the horses as they begin to break form. I smile at the unfurling chaos, settling in until they're close enough to see me standing here.

There are more of them than I anticipated but that doesn't matter. I see her and sudden relief floods me as I realise that my plan has worked.

Suddenly, the world unfolds into chaos as my men appear from the shadows with war cries leaving their lips, blades raised. I step forward and falter for a moment as some of the rebels jump from their horses, rushing towards the Aslitír with unyielding rage. The song of clashing steel fills the air as battle commences between the two sides, but my attention is still fixated on Nesryn who has melded into the crowd.

My feet begin to move on their own as I try to seek her out, blood pumping in my ears as the adrenaline burns in my veins. Suddenly, a blonde woman breaks from the cluster and comes rushing towards me, her face splattered with blood.

"Reverie?" I say, recognising the woman's face.

"I'll kill you! I'll kill you for what you've done!" she screams.

She throws a swing at me which I evade easily, but she carries on, unrelenting in her attack, swinging the sharpened blade this way and that. I block her with my shadows, letting them swallow each impact.

"Shadowcasting bastard! Murderer!" she screams at me, hot angry tears in her eyes.

A frustrated cry pours out of her as she keeps pushing, beads of sweat appearing on her temple as she tries to break through my barriers.

In the next move, I manipulate a shadow to wrap around the blade and snatch it away from her, throwing it several yards away.

"I'm not here to fight you," I say simply to her, my expression deadpan despite the turmoil rolling within.

"Coward!"

"Clearly I'm wasting my breath," I sigh.

Furious, she attempts to throw a punch at me but I shadowfold away from her, my attention focused on finding who I came for. The fighting is still in full swing as I search for Nesryn, though I notice two bodies crumpled on the floor. One I recognise immediately as one of the Aslitír, and I find myself feeling a little desperate as I run out of time.

I see a rush of movement and turn to see the fight moving across the grass, foe versus foe. Crell roars as he rushes towards a young blond man who I realise is unarmed. Then I see her, wrestling with another of my men, before jabbing a blade under his arm and kicking him roughly away with a fearsome look in her eye. Shrouded in shadow to avoid being picked out by another of the rebels, I move towards Nesryn, who notices her companion in need and rushes to aid the blond man. Even from here, I can see he's a good fighter, but he's no match for the soldier he's up against. Aslitír were made of stronger stuff and much darker morals. Especially Crell.

As my soldier moves to strike the final deathly blow, Nesryn reaches the wide-eyed man and a bright flash of golden light appears before disappearing altogether, Nesryn and the blond man with it, causing my vision to become momentarily impaired.

My sure steps falter in surprise as I realise she's lightjumped.

"Impossible," I breathe in disbelief.

I scan the area, searching frantically for her to reappear. I see three more of the men fall to the swords of the rebels, their bodies crumpling to the ground as I scour the darkened landscape.

There is a sudden burst of light out of the corner of my eye. I track it and quickly shadowfold towards her. She is tending to the blond man, wounded but alive when I grab her shoulder and drag her backwards. I hear his plea as he tries to reach out for her. She bucks beneath my grasp, struggling to free herself.

Before he can reach us, or she can free herself, I shadowfold us away from the onslaught unfolding, separating us from outside with an impenetrable wall of shadow. Once it's stable, I free her and she scrambles to her feet, trying to get as far away from me as she possibly can.

"You son of a bitch," she growls, the glint of her dagger catching my eye.

"Nice to see you too, princess," I reply, folding my arms across my chest.

I don't miss the darkening of her eyes as she sees this gesture for what it is.

"Free me!" she demands.

"Not until you've heard what I need to say," I reason.

She scowls, pacing back and forth like a caged wild animal before she suddenly launches herself at me. She throws kicks and punches my way, which at first, I deflect easily, then, out of nowhere she adds in random attacks with her magic.

'They're not random,' I decide. 'They're strategic.'

Deathly sharp blades of light come flying my way, too quick for me to deflect them all. I wince as some miss my evasion and slice through my skin, burning.

I retaliate by shoving her away from me with a wave of darkness, causing her to stumble back several steps. This only ignites her wrath further, her eyes illuminated with rage.

"There will be a second Choosing," I tell her.

She falters, her powers sputtering out as she frowns at me. "You're lying."

"Am I?" I tilt my head to the side, feeling the cuts across my skin ooze blood.

"Even if you are telling the truth, what in the name of Asteria would make me trust your word?"

I lean in close enough for me to notice how she holds her breath, how the golden flecks in her eyes shift with the light.

"Been having any strange dreams lately?"

Her lips part in surprise as I straighten, a knowing smirk pulling my lips upwards.

"You don't have to trust me, you only need to trust yourself," I say with a nonchalant shrug.

She doesn't speak and I dare to push my luck, leaning forward with a knowing smile on my face. "Consider this a little heads up."

I pull my shadows towards myself as I watch Nesryn's eyes widen. Then I shadowfold out of sight.

NESRYN

CHAPTER FORTYSEVEN

I stare at the spot where Lysan has just vanished in front of my eyes. Adrenaline courses through me, mixed with a tinge of nausea from using my power to move Wylan to safety. Sweat, grime and blood, not entirely my own, coat my skin, but I hardly notice as I stare into the now empty space where Lysan's tall frame was.

Far behind me, I hear the gurgled cry of the final Aslitír as Farren's blade brings him to his end.

I hear the others regrouping, as well as a barrage of cursing that I can only assume is coming from Rowena. I, however, can't move.

'There will be a second Choosing.'

My ears ring as I replay his words over and over in my head, my anger multiplying as a sick feeling expands within me. I panic at the thought of more girls unknowingly walking through those palace gates, suffering the same fate as us.

"Asteria above, what the fuck was that?" Ria cries as she storms towards me.

I slowly turn towards her, staring right through her.

"He was in your grasp and you let him get away!"

She launches herself at me, taking me down with a force that knocks the wind out of me as the back of my head collides with the hard floor, ricocheting from the force. The shock snaps me out of my daze and I try my best to fend her off as she throws wild punches and yells obscenities at me.

I feel my power bloom in me, growing with my frustration.

"Stop!" I order her, fending off the blows that she throws at me.

"You could have ended him! Why did you let him go?" she screams in blind anger.

"Ria, stop it!" I say more forcefully, trying to grab at her hands.

"It's his fault—she's gone—she's gone and it's all his fault," she continues, her voice breaking.

"Ria, *enough*!" I yell, my power expelling from me in one large burst.

The force throws her off me, landing her a few feet away as I scramble into a sitting position. She does the same and we stare at each other across the short distance. I take in her glossy eyes, her wetted cheeks and I feel a pang of guilt.

"I'm not the enemy here," I say, my voice shaky.

I feel someone come up beside me and I glance up to find a bloodied Wylan smiling down at me, though it doesn't reach his eyes. I gratefully take his hand and smile at him before turning back to Ria. I hate the way she's looking at me, I hate the hurt that she's feeling, but anger comes swifter than patience.

"You don't think I would have happily ended him if I'd had the chance?" I demand, my tone cold.

"I—"

"You think after *everything* he's done, everything that he's helped the king pull off, I wouldn't want to rip his throat out myself? Because if that's the case *clearly* you don't know me very fucking well," I shout.

She narrows her eyes, her lips parting as she moves to speak, but a voice from behind me cuts her off. I spin on my heels to find Rowena assessing me darkly, blood trickling down her cheek as she speaks.

"I don't know about anyone else, but I can't help but wonder how in the hell he knew where we'd be. And then *conveniently* I see you and that devil together right before the darkness sweeps in around you," she argues.

"You think *I* had something to do with this?" I reply incredulously.

"What happened back there was no random attack, girl, and you were in that thing long enough to share words," Rowena continues.

"*What*?" I demand.

"Nesryn, you were in there for a while. It's understandable why we'd be suspicious," Farren cuts in quietly, not meeting my eye.

"This is fucking unbelievable," I mutter, chuckling bitterly to myself.

"Nes, what happened in there?" Wylan steps in, his tone gentle.

"He blocked me in, taunted me. Naturally, I attacked him," I answer, giving Ria a pointed look that she turns away from.

"A likely story... if you're telling the truth," Rowena growls.

"I am," I snap back, giving her a warning glare as I flex my hand.

"Did he say anything to you?" Farren speaks up, her serious eyes trained on me.

I think back to his words, to the warning that he'd made enough times for me to notice, enough times to take seriously. The tension around me is thick enough to cut through and I quickly realise there isn't a single person I trust right now as I feel their eyes boring into me.

"He—he was trying to take me back with him. To the palace," I lie.

"What?" Ria is the first to speak.

"Clearly Barilius wants to finish what he started," I comment bitterly. "But I won't go back there, I won't."

Wylan places a hand on my shoulder. My skin begins to crawl beneath his touch but I resist the urge to pull away. He studies me for several moments before his features relax. "I believe you."

No one else speaks, but some of their hardened gazes soften.

"Alright, well now this is cleared up, let's get out of here. I don't want to be here if they come back," Wylan adds, heading towards the horses.

"Oh no, this isn't over," Rowena steps in, getting in my face.

I clench my fists and meet her glare with one of my own. "Yes, it is," I reply, ready to push past her.

"Wylan's right," Farren says stepping in. "Let's bury our dead and move on before any other unwanted visitors come snooping around," she continues.

"Our dead?" I hear Ria ask behind me.

"Elex," Farren answers quietly with a muted expression.

"Oh," is all I hear Ria reply.

The tension disappears for a moment as our eyes move to where the fallen man lies, Theon at his side, his head bowed low. Silence falls over us all as we slowly begin to part the crowd. Without a word, I move around Rowena and stride after Wylan towards the cluster of horses on the other side of the wide plain.

My anger takes over, but a cool sensation of surprise spreads through me as I think of my lie. Lysan's words haunt me as I follow Wylan, though my own falsehood is as confusing to me as him saving me. Behind me I hear rushed footsteps, followed by Ria calling my name. She catches up with me, stopping in front of me with teary eyes.

"Nes—I—I don't know what came over me. I just—"

"Insinuated I was working with the enemy," I cut her off with a cold, defensive tone.

Her face falls. "I'm sorry."

"Just—don't," I say, tiredness creeping into my voice.

This time she lets me go.

I feel the eyes of the others fall on me, looking away quickly when I dare to look back. A heaviness settles over me as I press my lips into a grim line. Thoughts of Lysan come back to me as I climb upon my mare, and I make a mental note to find Twyla as soon as we make it back. I relive the moment over and over, his voice repeating the same six words.

I wonder why I lied, and why it felt like I was protecting him.

CHAPTER FORTYEIGHT

As soon as I arrive, stumbling back into my small lodgings, hands grab me by the cuff of my leathers, forcing me back against the wall with a thud before I can react. The wind is knocked from me as I try to catch my bearings, my wounds screaming from another beating. I take in the assailant, recognising his bright blue eyes.

"Keelhan?" I croak.

"Are you out of your fucking mind?! Where the hell have you been?" he demands.

"If you'd be so kind as to let me go then maybe we could talk like civilised men," I reply.

Keelhan's answering growl says he doesn't plan on letting me go any time soon, so I'm surprised when the pressure finally eases at my throat. He steps back, pacing in front of me. He's pissed, the anger rolling off him in heated waves.

"I was on a mission," I explain, rubbing my throat.

"Bullshit!" he snaps, pointing a finger at me.

"Rebels were seen leaving the city. So I acted," I answer with a serious expression.

Keelhan stops pacing and faces me again. "And the men you took with you, *my* men?"

"Yes, well that *was* unfortunate. None of us could've predicted them overpowering us, but it happens," I answer, my tone grim.

"Yet you're still breathing," he comments, his gaze dark.

The captain's calm fury puts me on edge. I know I have to tread carefully, too deep into my plans to turn back now. In my head, Loísia's voice whispers words of encouragement, enough for me to put aside our rocky friendship and feed him the rest of what this plan demands of me.

"They tried taking me prisoner. I didn't take kindly to that, as you can imagine," I reply dryly.

"They tried to take you prisoner?" Keelhan scoffs in disbelief, his tone bitter.

I'm prepared for his scrutiny and from behind my back, I pull out a familiar circlet, only the clasp is damaged and the magical stones embedded into the silver are cracked, some smashed. I throw it toward him, watching as he catches it in the air and drops his gaze to the silver collar he turns in his hands.

He looks to me again, this time his anger shifts into solemn surprise. "How did they get this?"

"Hell if I know. I got out of there before they happened to throw any more of their tricks," I answer.

"And the king. He knows?" Keelhan asks quietly.

I shake my head. "Not yet, but I will be returning to the palace —"

"—Lysan you may like to hold onto your secrets, but Barilius won't take kindly to being kept in the dark about this. You know that," Keelhan cuts in.

"Don't try to lecture me, Keel," I say, moving past him and snatching the collar back. "I came back out of respect, don't make me regret my decision."

"What?" he replies, turning towards me, surprise registering on his face.

"Your men did their part and lost their lives in the process. You had a right to know before I went to report back to the king," I tell him earnestly as I pack my bag.

As I swing it over my back and turn to face the door, I notice Keelhan's speechless expression. He barely breathes as he stares at me, his blue eyes unmoving as if the words that had left my lips hadn't been anything he'd expected.

"Why?" he asks, cutting through the silence he'd created.

"Keel, you may be the captain, but you're also my friend. I hold enough respect for you and care for you enough to report back to you the loss of your men," I answer, peering at him.

Silence fills the room as I attach my scabbard to my belt, wincing as I accidentally reopen the wound on my hand.

"But you've never liked any of them," he speaks up again, his voice distant.

"I don't have to like them. But they were good soldiers and they followed orders well enough."

It's the first honest thing I've said yet. When he doesn't move to speak, I finish up what I'm doing and pull the strap of my bag further up my shoulder. I inhale and sigh as I rake a hand through my hair, looking around to see if anything has been left before my gaze settles on Keelhan.

"I'll be gone for a few days, but I'll return with news from the palace," I tell him.

I'm gone before he can even utter a word.

I make it to one of the portal bridges where I stumble out of the shadows, heaving gasping breaths as I fight to stay on my feet. Almost as soon as my feet touch the ground, I feel the sudden depletion of my power; I'd pushed my body into shadowfolding too far a distance to manage in one go. Nausea rises in a wave and exhaustion hits me but I fight the bile climbing my throat and steady myself. With a shaky breath, I pull my strap further up my shoulder and surge through the howling wind as icy blasts cut across my face. I always forgot how cool it was at these altitudes, out in the open.

My knees threaten to buckle, my body begging for rest and I find myself almost relenting to its pleas. Only the sharp thoughts of my plan coming to life keeps me going until I've reached the doors and made my way into the palace.

The halls are quiet after several days in Trulló, but I welcome the peace as it gives me a chance to clear my mind and to prepare for what is coming next. I waste no time, dropping my belongings in the hall outside my door before slowly making my way towards the steps to Barilius's private quarters.

When I reach the doors, I see Melek and two soldiers stationed outside. I straighten as they notice me, Melek's eyes widening slightly as he looks me up and down.

Melek looks at me, his expression solemn. "The king does not wish to be disturbed."

"He's going to want to hear what I've learnt, Melek. So step aside," I argue as I come closer, holding my ground.

"Goddess above, surely you would think to clean up before attempting to address the king!"

"I doubt he'll give a shit about the way I look, Melek. Now move," I demand.

When he doesn't move, I invade his personal space, towering over him. Despite the drain of my power, I summon the shadows to rest in my hands, twisting them around and over my fingertips.

"Step. Aside. Before I make you," I repeat.

I feel him hesitate for only a moment before he mumbles something under his breath and steps aside, waving a hand to the Aslitír behind him to open the doors for me.

"Don't say you weren't warned," he calls after me as I walk through.

I find Barilius in his private dining room, gorging himself on rich red wine and exquisite-looking food. The scent of it all wafts towards me, causing my stomach to clench with hunger. He ignores my presence for a few minutes as he shovels food into his mouth, washing it down with his goblet of wine. When his eyes finally flick to me standing in the open archway of black and gold marble, I can tell he's not happy with the intrusion. Unease erases the hunger in my stomach, temporarily.

"I didn't want to be disturbed, boy," he says after swallowing the wine and smacking his lips.

"I bring news that couldn't wait, Your Highness. Things that may delay your plans," I answer as I bow.

"Oh?"

"I intercepted a message between the rebel group. They had made plans to leave the Akhozian kingdom and were making their way to Mire Port," I explain.

"Mire Port?" His eyes flash with interest.

"Yes, my king. I took a handful of men and we intercepted them, but we lacked numbers and were unable to overpower them," I continue, bracing myself for his steely gaze.

"I see. Your usefulness is beginning to run dry with all these disappointments, boy," he says after a moment of thought.

"But you see, I know where they're going, and what they intend to do, Your Highness," I add quickly, hoping it will be enough to swerve his wrath.

"And what is that?" he bites.

"They have called a meet of the seven nations," I announce.

At this, Barilius's bored gaze sharpens and his amber eyes darken as he absorbs my words. I watch him silently, waiting for him to speak as he lowers his goblet from his lips.

"It seems I may have to put the preparations for The Choosing on hold for the time being," he murmurs as if to himself. "If they seek to try and take the crown from my head, then they've begun a war they won't soon forget," he vows, turning to me, his dark tone causing the skin to prickle down my spine.

CHAPTER FORTYNINE

The rest of our journey is made in tense silence. The whole group is on high alert, reacting to each snap of a twig beyond the line of trees, all the way to Mire Port.

From there, in the small, quiet little town, we meet the previously notified boatman who stores our horses and invites us onto his boat. If it wasn't for the many things plaguing my mind and the distrust I felt simmering around me, I'd feel elation and curiosity at finally seeing a fraction of the world past Akhozia's borders. Borders which had been illegal to cross for over a decade.

The boat is a humble thing, sturdy and silent as it crosses the water towards the small island across the bay. Some of the others rest, moving below deck to gather their strength for the upcoming meet. I know I should join Wylan and mentally prepare for the story that I must share with leaders of the continent, but I don't. I watch as, one by one, Rowena, Wylan, Ria climb down the narrow steps. I watch as the latter turns to meet my gaze, her eyes searching mine, silently imploring. A plea I ignore as I cling to my anger, a bitter sensation coiling within my stomach as I turn away from her. I walk over to the ledge, prop my arms up on it, and look out across the water. Mist floats across the surface below, twisting with the swirling current. Despite my best efforts, Lysan's words lodge themselves in my mind, replaying over and over.

"Goddess above…"

A sigh escapes me as I run a hand over my face and continue to stare out at the water as if the darkened depths hold all the answers that I need.

"If he's telling the truth then more innocents will die," I mutter to myself.

The weight of that thought sits heavily on my shoulders as I contemplate what to do with this knowledge, how to proceed should his words, in fact, be true. I want so badly to disregard him, to pin him as a liar and the deceitful bastard that I know him to be, and yet a small voice calls to listen.

For a long moment, I wish the past twelve hours hadn't occurred, that Wylan hadn't asked so much of me, that Lysan hadn't come to me, that I hadn't been dragged into all this madness.

'But you weren't dragged,' that same voice whispers in my head. *'You went willingly into the king's twisted games, didn't you?'*

I scowl, trying to ignore my own thoughts as I focus on the island growing ever closer through the mist. Through the rich blues and blacks of the night, I see a tower jutting out of a rock at the highest point of the island. Surrounded by trees and shrubbery illuminated only by the stars above, it looks like an impenetrable force, standing tall and solitary on its isle. As I glance up, I tilt my head, making out the parapet lining the top of the tower. A small smile pulls at my lips as I look at it. In the darkness, it looks like a crown atop the tower, the standing king of the hill.

We dock rather quickly and disembark with a renewed sense of urgency. Our boots hit the wooden planks, ricocheting through the quiet of the night, breaking the serenity. This time I only seem to sense Rowena's distrustful gaze as we follow the beaten path towards our destination: Madmire Fortress. I ignore the piercing stare, knowing it to be a battle for later. Right now, the pressing matter is before us and I feel my nerves begin to take precedence as I look up to the building looming above us. I falter for a moment, before feeling someone stop beside me. Wylan looks down at me with a reassuring grin that loosens the tightness in my chest slightly. My eyes drift past him and find Ria's nervous face peering at me, a tentative smile on her lips. My stomach squeezes as I look away, the sudden sensation of betrayal lingering over me.

When we reach the large gated doors to the fortress we stop, standing in a loose cluster with Rowena at the front of our group. I stand between Wylan and Farren, who watch the fortress ahead with steely expressions. From here, the place looks abandoned. Not a single light flickers from within the walls and we are met with complete and utter silence. That is until Rowena raps her fist against the door in four heavy blows. Suddenly, the torches on either side of the doors erupt to life, igniting a flickering light that cuts through the darkness. Slowly, one by one, the arched windows glow with light and warmth and the surprise in me fizzles as my attention returns to the doors ahead, the hinges groaning from the strain of opening. Curiosity gets the better of me and I peer ahead to find four guards stationed just past the entry point, two on either side of the open doors. In the centre of the archway is a man, but as Rowena steps forward to speak with him, she blocks my view of his face. When she finally steps away, a slim, tawny skinned man stands before us, his eyes travelling across our group as he addresses us.

"Welcome to you all, we have been anticipating your arrival," the deepness of his voice surprises me, given his small stature.

I feel Wylan shift beside me, his eyes peering down at me as I lift my gaze to his.

"Ready?"

"As I'll ever be."

The man, Mykal, is introduced to us as the Steward of Madmire Fortress, and soon leads us inside.

Our footsteps echo through the wide, empty corridors as he directs us to what he refers to as the Hall of Counsel. With each step bringing us closer, my nerves grow and I feel my heart begin to pick up the pace, despite my feeble fights to remain calm and collected. I'm completely taken aback when we're led into the Hall of Counsel, my breath catching as I take in the sheer size and height of the circular room. The ceiling is a beautiful mosaic of coloured stones depicting Askrhea; the lands of the seven nations we call home. As my eyes move south, I notice the tapestries next, spanning the entirety of the walls. Each tells a tale of our continent's history. Our triumphs, our failure, our wars and our eras of peace all hung on the walls around us.

As a reminder, or a warning.

A fire pit sits in the centre, warming the room, encircled by a curved table in the shape of a c. There is a narrow opening in the woodwork for one to reach the pit, and eight seats carefully tucked under the table on the outer edge. I notice on each section of the curved table, there is a symbol scorched into the surface, but I'm distracted by those already seated in their designated spots. I find myself calling upon my tutor sessions as I try to name each of the leaders before us.

The closest is a giant of a man with rich, thick red hair that flows over his shoulders. His lips are hidden by a thick moustache and his long beard is subdued by beads that hold it together in a roped length, ending in a tight twist. His eyes, in contrast, are deep and dark, a seriousness in them that makes you look twice. I glance at the chair, surprised it can even hold someone of his size.

'*Valdeamar, ruler of Elderwharf,*' I recognise him almost instantly.

My eyes move along the table to the man seated in the next chair. This man is vastly different to Valdeamar, with olive skin and narrow almond-shaped eyes that quietly survey the room. His pin-straight hair is a glossed black and pinned into a perfect bun atop his head, not a single hair astray. He is tall and slim, his clean shaved face all sharp angles and harsh features. His calculating eyes are the deepest onyx and they throw me for only a moment as they remind me of another and my gut twists.

'*Zander of Lúllah,*' I mentally note.

My attention strays from him, taking in the woman with ebony skin and rich chocolate curls bound tightly with glittering silver ribbons. Everything about her screams elegance, from the way she holds herself, to the shimmering furs she wears. Her eyes are a striking grey, almost as silver as the ribbons she wears, but deeper, and far more thoughtful than the two pairs of eyes I'd met before hers.

'*Queen Kyrith from Sómmyn.*' I recall her name from the texts I'd read of the northeast.

A voice draws my attention. The man talking is sitting in the Chair of Arburg's seat, meaning he can only be Kaius. But as I take him in, he reminds me so much of Uncle Erathon that I feel a jolt rush through me. He bears the same rich dark skin, the same wide eyes, only a few shades lighter than my uncle's. His full lips are wider, showing his teeth more, but his twisted dreadlocks are the same length as his, and worn in the same manner.

Quelling my shock, I tear my eyes away to peer at the man that Kaius is speaking with, recognising him as the ruler of Rhóglen in the southeast. He too is a large man with a stature that makes me think that he is a born warrior. His golden curls are bound in a half-up style, the top messily scraped back and coiled into a small bun, while the rest stretches down, brushing his broad shoulders. His tan skin is awash with silver scars across his hands that disappear beneath his navy tunic. I can't help but wonder what King Lowen had done to deserve them.

Finally, my eyes turn to meet a pair of icy blue ones. Ones that already seem to have found me. Shock pools in my stomach as I stare at the woman with clear porcelain skin and white-blonde hair. Her angular face is both sharp and soft, giving her quite striking features as we stare across the space at one another.

'*Polaris, Queen of the frosted north,*' I recall from my texts of the Hoaken ruler.

As if she hears my thoughts, the corners of her lips curl up in a knowing smile. I don't realise we're moving until Wylan seats himself in the seat of Akhozia and motions for me to stand by his side. I stop just behind the right of his chair, as the rest of the room settles into silence.

Mykal steps forwards once again, where the table breaks away. "I, Steward of Madmire, welcome you all, seven nations, to a place of peace and neutrality. From this moment on, let us speak openly and without remorse. With this, the meet of our seven nations will begin."

Discussions are well and truly underway by the time Wylan has called on me to recount the events from my time as a Chosen and I do my best to speak my truth, despite the bundled nerves tightening in my chest. I feel the leaders' eyes on me as I speak, recounting each unspeakable act, each gruelling trial, and finally each of the lives lost at his hand. As I do, I hear Ria speak up behind me, backing my claims with her own snippets of truth.

With each piece relayed, I see the eyes watching me darken and widen with shock.

When I finish, I feel my hands trembling and quickly hold them behind my back, my fingers squeezing my hands together tightly.

"And this is why we feel it is too dangerous to leave Barilius on the throne. He is too reckless... too desensitised," Wylan speaks, leaning against the table as he stands.

I look at him with newfound awe. The way he holds himself, the complete belief in this cause. He speaks like a true king.

'A king I would follow, a king I would proudly serve,' I realise.

"These claims are worrisome, and it has been too long since Barilius closed his borders to us," King Zander declares.

"But this is treason you speak of. How do you plan to overthrow him?" King Kaius leans in, scrutinising the young heir.

"With the blood that runs through my veins, but if that isn't enough then..." Wylan trails off, meeting each of the understanding gazes thrown his way across the curved table.

At this revelation, Rowena steps away from the rest of the group who stand idly against the far wall and stop on the other side of Wylan, glancing around the table before she speaks up.

"Wylan's last name is Ginemoux. Some of you will be familiar with that name," she speaks, giving the rulers time to absorb her words.

Confusion fills me as I take in their expressions as they look at Wylan in a seemingly new light. I look at him myself, unsure of what this means until Rowena speaks again.

"King Torren was a great leader and served the Akhozian kingdom well. No one knew what happened to him when Barilius took the crown all that time ago. He was presumed dead, and perhaps he was," she shrugs before she glances down at Wylan. "But he had a daughter, a daughter who birthed a son."

"Torren Ginemoux, Second of His Name, was my grandfather," Wylan declares.

"Claim to the throne or not, Barilius will not relinquish his crown without a fight. We're talking war here, boy," Valdeamar speaks up.

"I know. This is why we have called this meet. Why we seek your aid," he explains.

"The bloodshed must end," I add.

"With what? More bloodshed? It sounds to me that this is an internal affair. One that doesn't benefit the rest of us," Valdeamar counters.

"I think you'll change your mind when you hear what I have planned for Akhozia. Borders will be opened, new trading and shipping deals will bless these lands with prosperity and opportunity. All I ask is that if we seek your aid, you will grant us your support," Wylan speaks, his voice carrying across the large room.

"The boy seems set upon this path," Queen Kyrith says thoughtfully.

"He has the rightful claim to the throne, it seems. We are in a position to back his claims," Queen Polaris cuts in.

"This path may cause destruction of our nations, but change is coming, this I sense, is inevitable," King Lowen agrees, his wise words surprising.

Hope blooms in my chest as I listen to the kings and queens of Askrhea discuss the options before them. I look at Wylan with a hopeful smile, which he mirrors in his hazel eyes.

'This may actually work,' I think.

Mykal clears his throat, raising his hands just as the clock chimes thrice. I blink in surprise, not releasing how quickly the night had bled into a new day.

"There is much to consider, much left to discuss, but let us reconvene after food and rest. Many of you have travelled far to meet here tonight," he says, searching the faces of those around us. "I am aware these are pressing matters, but refreshing the mind will only help a swifter answer," he reasons, gaining the approval of several leaders.

All of a sudden, the room fills with the pungent smell of magic and people draw their weapons despite the pleas from Mykal reminding them that this is a place of peace. I reach for Stormtip all the same, unease washing over me. The pit in the centre of the table dims before flames roar high into the air, earning cries and shouts of surprise from the leaders around the table. The flames burn black and white, shaping into a figure with glowing silver eyes that pierce the room as it turns this way and that, the pit crackling and hissing with each movement of the figure.

Eventually, the creature of flame finally stops his gaze on Wylan, anger flickering in the flames.

A bitter, acidic smell fills the room as the apparition points a flickering finger at Wylan, who stands frozen on the spot.

"Little boy, you are a fool with your wishful thinking. You cannot play the game of kings, you cannot defeat me!" his voice roars.

A gasp escapes me as I immediately recognise the voice, fear spreading through me.

"Barilius? How!" Wylan answers, his voice even despite the slight tremble in his hands.

Barilius's flaming outline sneers at him before he turns around the room, as though he can't step foot outside of the burning pit.

"And all of you! You dare meet and conspire, I will see you all fall!" he yells, his fury projected across the room.

"What is this dark magic, Barilius?" King Kaius bellows, his brows knitted, and his sword raised.

"I hold power you couldn't even begin to imagine," he answers with a contemptuous smile.

"You dare to hurl threats in a sacred place of neutrality, you dare to taint these walls with your dark magic?" Queen Polaris spits in disgust.

"Neutrality?" Barilis's burning mouth repeats bitterly. "You plan and plot behind my back, like traitorous vermin!"

He twists back around and glares at Wylan with an accusing finger. "Mark my words, *boy*. You may have evaded me until now. But you have my attention, and you *will* meet my sword," he vows.

Before another word is uttered, the flames fly high, causing shouts of terror as people throw themselves backwards. Before I know what I'm doing, I've wrapped Wylan in my light and throw him backwards to safety. When I finally draw back the bubble, the wretched king is gone. Glancing up, I note how the black flames have scorched the mural on the ceiling above, watching as the lingering flames are sucked down with an overwhelming, deafening noise before disappearing into the fading glow of the ashes.

CHAPTER FIFTY

My mind runs a mile a minute as I walk the halls beside Keelhan. Neither of us speaks, our shoes clipping against the stone as we move in unison. I read the solemn expression on my friend's face as an invitation to keep my thoughts and taunts to myself today. For once, I listen to the signs. I'm in no mood for playful banter either.

He'd arrived that morning by horseback after a direct message of summons from the king. I'd bumped into him in the halls en route to answer the summons Barilius had sent to me through a most solemn Vilkha. Barilius had been unhinged since I'd shared the news of the meet in Madmire, his usual foul temper tripled. In all my years of servitude, I'd never seen him quite like this, and the visual unnerved me more than I care to admit. And with the dangerous game I'm playing, I'd be a fool to not feel slightly afraid. In the hours that followed, he'd sent me away, giving me plenty of time to hone my emotions and make my plan. I knew from the moment the information had passed my lips that there was no going back now, and from the way both Keelhan and I had been summoned, I'd been right.

As we make our way up the stairs into Barilius's quarters, I'm surprised to find newly appointed Aslitír lining the hallways, rather than the usual faces I see. Keelhan and I share a concerned glance as we continue on. Just before we reach the doors leading into a common room, we're stopped and led by two more new guards who lead us into the space and watch silently as we hover by the lounge chairs, glancing over at them as they take up posts on either side of the doorway.

"I wasn't aware you'd appointed new guards to the king," I comment, my eyes not leaving the two impassive faces standing across the room.

"Neither was I," Keelhan replies, his tone clipped.

I immediately notice the drawn expression tightening his face. He's usually good at keeping up appearances, almost politically so, but anyone who looks at him at this moment would be able to tell that he's pissed.

Minutes drag by and no one appears. Eventually, I start to notice Keelhan's thin stream of patience running dry, not that I blamed him. I fight the urge to pace the room or rain down my shadows upon the unsuspecting sentinel. As if just in time, Vilkha returns, his expression still drawn as he calls us and leads us back through the hall, turning instead towards the war room. Keelhan and I stop before the doors and glance at one another in silent understanding as the messenger turns back to us.

"Go careful, he's rather… animated today," Vilkha says, choosing his words carefully.

This only encourages another shared look before our attention falls back on the door. Behind it, we can hear the scuffing of boots and the rummaging of papers. I move first, reaching out my hands to push open the doors, and I walk into what can only be described as chaos.

Parchment maps and schematics lie scattered about the floor and across the strategy table. The room is dark, lit only by candlelight and the floating elvynlights dispersed about the room. At the far side of the room, a fire burns brightly in the fireplace, warming the room to almost uncomfortable temperatures. The air is stale and I wrinkle my nose at the scent of spilt red wine, following the smell to the knocked over, and smashed, glasses in the far corner of the room. Dust particles float through the air, visible in the blue hue of light, and I wonder how long he's been holed up in this room.

My wariness deepens when my attention finally shifts to the king. Barilius seems deranged the way he paces back and forth, randomly gathering scrolls that he quickly scours through and discards before reaching for another in an odd frenzy. As we both step into the room, I don't need to look at Keelhan to know his brow has creased in concern at the sight of his king. A king who has yet to acknowledge our presence in the room. We step further in, our feet brushing over discarded scrolls before Keelhan drops to his knee.

"My king, you sent for us," he says with a bowed head.

I glance toward him with a raised brow as he returns to his feet. He gives me a pointed look as though he expects me to do the same, but I only roll my eyes and turn instead to face Barilius. He waves his hand impatiently at us to join him at the table. He doesn't look up from his feverish scribbling.

"Is everything alright, Sire?" I ask tentatively when we reach the edge of the table.

"It has begun, there is no stopping it now," he says hurriedly.

My stomach drops. I feel Keelhan move closer to the table, leaning over to try and read the rushed writing. I only realise he's come up blank when he straightens, his lips set in a thin line.

"Those *halfwits* think they can make a fool of me. *Me*," he continues.

"What is this about, Your Highness?" I raise my voice.

Barilius stills, his gaze finally lifting to acknowledge us. For several moments his glowing amber eyes flicker between us with an unnervingly manic look in them. Beneath his unusually unkempt facial hair, his lips curl into a cruel smile as he stares through us, his mind whirring as he calculates. As quickly as he has slipped back into his own thoughts, he blinks and is suddenly back with us. His focus shifts to Keelhan who stiffens to attention beside me.

"Captain," Barilius addresses him.

"Yes, my king," he answers.

"Reach out to our allies, rally the men. I want every free Aslitír training as of today. I expect recruitment to double also," the king explains.

"Y-yes, my king. But what of my orders to deal with the rebels?" Keelhan asks, his shock evident.

"Didn't you hear me? Or do I need to assign a new captain?" he snipes back, eyes narrowed.

"No, Sire, of course not. Consider it done," Keelhan answers, standing to attention.

Barilius dismisses him with an impatient wave, turning his gaze to me as he pushes himself away from the strategy table and moves to where the roaring fire burns in the hearth. The door clicks shut behind Keelhan and I listen as his footsteps fade down the hall. All too suddenly, I watch Barilius's manic demeanour change into something calmer, something calculated and deadly.

"As for you my Shadowcaster, you are to continue gathering these whispers you seem to collect so well. Report back to me your findings regarding collecting the girls for the second Choosing," he says, his voice distant.

"Are we under attack?" I dare to ask.

Barilius hesitates for only a fraction of a second. "Your news of the meet proved to be true. And now that they have shown their hand, I will not show weakness. We must prepare for war."

"Is it wise for The Choosing to go ahead?" I press.

The king stiffens where he stands and I brace myself for the onslaught. But it doesn't come.

I watch closely as his grip on his fingers tighten at his back, and I swallow, suddenly feeling on edge.

"It is vital. The Choosing *must* happen, despite these new developments. I will *not* allow these traitors to dismantle that which I have created," he says through gritted teeth.

I inhale deeply as I absorb his words, feeling the bitter tang of failure as my mind races through my new orders, reconstructing my plan in my head.

"You may go," he says, cutting through the silence.

As I turn to leave, mind racing, the king stops me, turning to face me with glowering eyes.

"And Lysander, don't fail me."

I'm gently closing the doors behind me, noting how the sentinels have gone, most likely due to a shift change, when through the slit in the door I see Barilius turn and reach for a black candle. My heart races as he holds it out to the open flames, the black flame bursting from the wick.

My eyes widen as the air shifts with magic and I see Barilius's lips move. Quickly, I shroud myself in shadow, not keen on the thought of unwanted eyes, and turn my head so that my ear is to the door.

I strain my ear but I struggle to hear what he says beyond the scuffle of papers and the heavy echo of the king's clipped boots as he paces.

"The spell must be completed. I'm intrigued by this Starweaver you speak of," a voice says.

A female voice that I've never heard before.

"She was there with them. Her power nearly obliterated me! She owes me in blood," Barilius scowls.

"Patience, my dear king, with time you will have what you seek," the voice says.

The female's promise has my stomach clenching and my feet moving before I even know I've left the doors. I leave with more questions than answers and the chilling fear of impending war.

NESRYN

CHAPTER FIFTYONE

Chaos had ensued after the flames died down into the ashes. Security measures had seemingly doubled in the blink of an eye, with everyone on edge at the sudden appearance of Barilius and his threat that lingered in the air.

I remain close to Wylan, both of us still sprawled on the ground, ears ringing and power singing in my veins as I scan the room. My heart races, panic fights to be released, and my hands still tremble even as the shock of the last few moments passes.

"How in the name of the goddess did he discover us?" Kaius demands amongst the chaos.

"That whispering snake of his. The Shadowcaster," Rowena answers, gritting her teeth.

She flashes me a dark look that I ignore as I help Wylan to his feet. As we dust ourselves off, the leaders of the other six nations talk at each other, their voices loud and bombarding as they overlap. The sound fills the large room, their arguments and fears bouncing off the charred ceiling. Frustration fills me as I watch them silently, the dread accompanied by Barilius's threat of war, a heavy shadow hanging over us all.

"We need to stop this," Wylan murmurs, voicing my thoughts.

He turns to me, his hand gently reaching for mine. "Do you think you can get their attention?"

I smile, nodding once. It's easy enough to draw upon my power, sending it out in coiling tendrils, forcing the kings and queens to step apart as my light moves around them, illuminating the room. When their voices die down, and their attention shifts towards me, I pull in my light and force it to fade into glittering air. The silence that follows is thick and tense, but it only lasts a moment as Wylan steps forwards.

"Now is not the time for rash decisions. Now is the time for rest and deep consideration," he states, his voice clear as it penetrates the silence.

For a few moments, no one speaks, no one seems to breathe. I watch as they blink at his words, as though they haven't quite sunk in. Then, footsteps break the spell and Mykal steps forwards, straightening his tunic as he surveys the room.

"The boy is right, we will tackle this issue and make a final decision in the daybreak. I would normally suggest several days before reconvening, but these are worrisome times and this is a pressing matter. For now, there are enough rooms to hold you all for the night," he announces.

"But—" Valdeamar begins to protest.

"—We will all be safe here, we have the magical measures of security and we are safer as a united front than scattered," Mykal cuts in as he holds up his hand.

"He's right. Steward, please lead the way," Queen Kyrith sighs, presumably nodding towards her company, who collect themselves and join her.

With a single dip of his head, Mykal turns and leads us from the Hall of Counsel, directing each leader and their companions into quarters on each level, one by one they and their parties disappear behind the doors until it's only Wylan and the rest of our party left.

We're escorted into a cosy common room with doors leading off it, presumably into several bedrooms and washrooms. The fire at the other end of the room is lit and the space is warm despite the cool stone surrounding us. The room is furnished with rich leather-cushioned seats by the fireplace, while across the space six chairs are tucked beneath a large table, covered with an array of fruit, nuts, dried meats and pitchers of water and wine.

"I hope that it will be to your liking, my lord," Mykal says with a bow of his head.

"Yes, thank you. We're truly grateful for your hospitality," Wylan answers, with a wide smile for our host.

"Until tomorrow then," he says.

"Until then, Mykal," Rowena answers.

As the door clicks shut, the group visibly begins to relax. Rowena mumbles something about booze and bed before grabbing the pitcher of wine and disappearing behind one of the adjoining doors. Farren and Theon murmur their goodnights after having their fill from the table, shortly followed by Ria who hesitates at her door.

She glances back at me, but I turn away, moving towards the farthest bedroom, leaving her and Wylan watching after me.

Hours later, I find myself unable to sleep, so I leave the safety of my humble room and sit in the empty common room, settled beneath a throw, tossing stray peanuts into the twisting flames.

My whole body feels tense and on edge.

I'm so engrossed in my own head that I don't hear the click of the latch or the footsteps that follow. I start when Ria stands beside the cushioned seat, facing the fire, her eyes trained on me.

"Can't sleep? Nightmares?" she probes.

When I don't answer, she sighs and sits across from me, studying the side of my face as I toss another nut to the flames. I watch as it crackles and pops before the flames transform it to ash.

"You seem rather calm considering what the last twenty-four hours have thrown at us," she observes.

"Wylan thinks we should keep a level head until tomorrow's meeting," I answer.

Silence fills the room until Ria cuts into it with a heavy sigh. "Nes, I came to find you because of what happened. I don't want you to think I meant what I said out of pain and anger."

I send Ria a sharp look.

"I've been attacked, raped, almost killed, taken a blade to friends, watched them die as I stood and did *nothing*! But out of all of that, nothing cuts deeper than my truest friend labelling me a traitor!" I spit, my words taking me by surprise. "If you think that I don't feel pain, that I'm not angry... that fire doesn't boil my blood to dust as they speak politics around a table, well then you're sorely mistaken," I continue staring into the flames.

"I-I didn't know," she falters, the fight in her tone abandoning her.

"Yes, well, there's a lot you don't know," I cut back.

"I can't know, Nes. Not unless you let me in, unless you trust me," she tries to reason.

"I never thought to question the trust I had in you. You doubted me instead," I answer, a lump forming in my throat.

"I know and I've tried to tell you I'm sorry—"

"—After everything we've been through together, every suffering, you should *know* that I want to watch that man burn to ashes. My loyalties should *never* have come into question, no matter what you thought you saw in that plain," I argue, my hands curling into fists.

"I know, I just—" she tries to grapple with words, running a hand through her blonde tresses as she heaves a sigh, shoulders slumping. "I know."

Before I can utter another word, she gets up from her seat and turns away, heading back to her room. As she stops before her door, she turns her head over her shoulder.

"Know that I'm truly sorry. And I pray with time you'll see that, and learn to forgive my lapse in judgement."

Guilt tugs at me as I watch her slip back into her room, staring at the closed door for a long while before eventually returning my attention to the flames, a bitter taste in my mouth.

More time passes but I'm unable to leave my seat, still covered in a thick throw despite the heat emanating from the fire.

The day's events run over and over as I stare gormlessly past the flickering dance of the flames burning bright oranges and yellows, the wood cracking and splintering beneath its heated force.

Though it's my thoughts of Lysan which plague me the most.

I think back to his warning and then to Barilius's little show, wondering if the two were somehow connected. I wonder if Lysan's words and attempts to reach out had only been a diversion, to draw my attention away from what his master was planning, to distract me from the possibility of war.

'*Whose side are you on?*' I ask, the image of Lysan staring back at me in my mind's eye.

Exhaustion and frustration fill me. Lysan is playing a game, a game of wits that I find myself tired of playing.

I consider Wylan and his incredible ability to adapt to the politics and strategies around him. He made it look so easy, yet here I was struggling to decipher Lysan's goal in all of this.

Why had he saved me?

Why had he contacted me?

If his warnings proved to be the truth, why had he shared them?

And why with me of all people?

I didn't have any answers and too many questions plagued me. Curiosity and the need for answers fuel my growing frustrations. So much is happening and changing around me, I'm beginning to feel like I'm drowning in the complexities of it all. I'm sick of the questions swimming around my head, demanding answers. Questions that *he* could answer. And in that split second of realisation, clarity washes over me and I rush to my feet, suddenly eager to return to my room.

I know what I have to do.

CHAPTER FIFTYTWO

I keep my palm straight as I wrap the lengths of cloth around it, wrapping it tightly and neatly around my knuckles and my palm, before tying it off at my wrist and starting with the other side. Once I'm satisfied, I step towards the dummy, my eyes focused on my opponent.

It had been quite some time since I found myself seeking the release that training gifted me. At first, I had considered paying a visit to The Velvet Feather, then I thought better of it. Visiting Loísia's mound served no purpose either, and I was avoiding all thoughts of her, the self-loathing I felt for failing her driving me to steer clear for now.

I jab at the dummy, throwing curved punches and sharp uppercuts and drawing back lightning-fast. I focus on the connection, on each precise blow as I throw my body weight into it, keeping my balance on the balls of my feet. Sweat beads at my brow, rolling down along my temples as I push myself, forcing myself to focus on the distraction. I inhale deeply through my nose, blowing the air out of my mouth as I centre myself, ready for the next blow.

I know Keelhan expects me to meet him in a few hours, but until then, the training room is my haven. Night has crept in on me as I move onto another training exercise, sweat pouring off me as I push myself to my limits, eager to keep my mind away from The Choosing and lurking thoughts of Loísia. Elvynlight glows in the walls illuminating the darkening room, the blue skies shifting into rich navy tones and eventually into an inky black sky through the arched windows. I lose all sense of time as I train, glad to be busy with something physical. Glad to be finally alone even if only for a few hours.

Refocusing on my next target, I falter as I feel a brush of something against my subconscious. Hairs rise along my neck as I blink in surprise, the encounter is gone as quickly as it comes, but it disarms me almost immediately and I find my curiosity triggered. I drop the weights in my hands and straighten, my breaths becoming ragged as I heave them in and out, waiting, anticipating the sensation washing over me again. My eyes flicker across the room, searching for something, anything, to show itself to me. Shifting my stance, I wait, letting myself have a few long moments before I dismiss the feeling and continue on.

Then I feel it again.

The softest brush of something trying to reach me, only this time I can almost hear the whispered words beneath the new sensation. As I strain to hear, to understand it, the door on the other side of the room swings open and clatters loudly against the wall. My attention snaps towards the silhouette in the door, recognising his outline almost immediately.

"You're terrible at keeping time you know," Keelhan observes.

Scratching my head and feeling slightly sheepish, I turn back to him and shrug lazily, giving him a lopsided grin.

"I may have gotten a little carried away," I admit.

"I'll say. I told you to meet me hours ago, and spent most of them perusing the halls searching for you," he points out, stepping into the large space.

"I only meant to clear my mind before we spoke," I say, stalling as I rake a hand through my dripping hair, mentally searching for the sensation once more.

"You must have a lot on your mind for you to be training this heavily for this long," Keelhan observes.

"Takes a lot more to tackle a Shadowcaster of my strength," I wink.

This time when the sensation comes, I'm ready for it. I meet it with a brush of my own essence. As they connect, I feel the line between us spring to life and the scent, not of jasmine, this time, but of warm spice and the strong scent of nebiulas hits me. *Nesryn.*

Keelhan answers back, but I'm so wrapped up in this moment of pure sensory bliss, that I miss what I presume is a sarcastic retort.

'*But how*?' I dare to wonder.

"Come on, Lysan, are you even listening to a fucking word I'm saying or did you exert yourself just a little *too* much?" Keelhan grumbles.

"No. Yes, of course, I'm coming," I say, stumbling over my words.

She answers my response with another brush of her against this fragile line between us, the whispered words still just out of my reach.

"Well, come on then. And get yourself cleaned up, we have a lot we need to discuss," Keelhan gestures for me to join him.

I do as he asks, stifling the shudder that runs along my spine as I feel her again. Just as I fall into line beside Keelhan, I manage to absorb the words whispered along the connection.

"*Meet... equal grounds... tomorrow night.*"

CHAPTER FIFTYTHREE

Giddiness swarms me as I open my eyes and blink them back into focus.

"I wasn't even sure that would work," I admit, biting back a hysteric laugh born of pure disbelief.

I had only thought the spell would connect us through dream, but the spell Twyla had obtained must have been much stronger than either of us ever could have anticipated. My giddiness is quickly replaced with an uneasy feeling at this realisation, and suddenly I'm not sure it had been a good idea to cast this spell in the first place.

'*Progress is progress, even if it means you must delve into the mind of your enemy,*' I reason.

It hadn't been as difficult as I'd initially thought when I'd found myself hurrying back to my room with newfound determination. As soon as I'd really focused, sending my feelers out to follow the delicate silk thread to the other end, I'd come colliding with a powerful essence of smoke and midnight. It was musky and old, yet new.

His surprise ringing along the thread tying us together gave me the confirmation I needed. It had worked. I tried not to think about how this could potentially work both ways and instead focused on relaying the message. Just one simple sentence is all he would need, for now. I had focused on the words, replaying them over and over until I sensed he'd understood the message.

'We *meet on equal grounds tomorrow night, tell no one.*'

I wondered if he'd received the full message. I wondered long enough for dawn to finally break across the horizon. But I no longer felt tired, too wired to even attempt to rest my eyes. Unable to sleep, I take my energy back into the common room, pacing up and down whilst chewing on dried meat, as I consider what I'll say when I see him. If I can even manage to utter a word in the face of that bastard.

Muffled footsteps and the soft click of a door has me halting mid-step, eyes darting up from the ground and ahead to a weary-looking Wylan. His hair is more tousled than usual and there is a shadow beneath his eyes that hints at his night. When he finally notices I'm there, he sends me a tired smile before making his way towards me.

"You're up early," he observes, reaching past me for one of the thin slices of cheese.

"I couldn't sleep. It seems I wasn't the only one," I comment, looking him up and down.

I watch as he glances down at his dishevelled shirt before returning my gaze, his smirk brightening his face. "We live in unsettling times, I doubt this will be our last bout of sleeplessness."

"Are you ready for what the other nations may tell us?" I ask tentatively.

Wylan sighs and rakes a hand across his face, the slice of cheese forgotten in the other. His eyes lose their shine as his brows knit together in a deeply thoughtful expression. "I'm not sure what will come. Barilius has instilled fear with his little tactic last night. I can feel it."

"Fear hastens decisions, though we can't guarantee they will be choices which benefit our cause," Farren joins the conversation, emerging from her doorway.

I blink as my attention shifts to her, surprised that I hadn't heard her leave her room. Her eyes slide from Wylan to me, her wavy hair loose and swaying with each step. With her ears hidden, she looks more human than ever and the image throws me slightly as she stops between us, reaching forward and grabbing a handful of grapes. She pops a single grape into her mouth before moving toward the sofas.

"All we can do is hope for the best and prepare ourselves for the worst," I say, meeting Wylan's eye.

"So it would seem," he mutters in response, a shadow moving over his face.

"We will need time to decide, regardless of last night's theatrics. We can't promise you aid after a single day of deliberation," Queen Kyrith states.

"Our lands, while a part of Askrhea, do not touch the borders of which you fight. I'm sorry but I won't risk the lives of my people to settle your war. I can provide ordnance, but that is all the support I may give I'm afraid." King Lowen follows, his voice echoing through the room.

The Hall of Counsel had been full since daybreak, and although the leaders of the seven nations speak calmly across the table, there is a tension in everyone that could shatter into chaos at any moment. Fear pollutes the air, thick and potent after last night's surprise.

"We also cannot promise our support without deliberating with our council first. It is our law," Queen Polaris speaks, her voice now dominating the room.

"We are on the cusp of war, there is little time for such politics," Wylan argues.

Frustration radiates from him and I note the desperate pitch entering his tone as his eyes travel along the table. He is right, but although I agree with him, even I realise that this is not how things are done.

"You are young, boy, and eager to ascend the throne. Know that we don't do this to spite you or your cause," King Zander speaks up, his eyes tender and earnest.

"There are ways that these matters are handled. Traditions that span centuries, young heir. We only ask for your patience. You will have our answers soon enough," Valdeamar steps in, his voice booming yet calm.

"Wylan, we may not have a choice but to let them deliberate and hope we still have time," I murmur to him.

He meets my gaze, but they are missing their usual calm expression. I inhale a sharp breath as I note the anger and bitter disappointment there, hovering just beneath the surface.

"There is no time, why can't they see that? They would let us drown in the blood in our own people before—"

"—*Enough*, Wylan," Rowena cuts in.

Without thinking, I gently place a reassuring hand over his and watch his gaze flicker to the top of my hand, before resting on me. My lips set in a thin line, I nod once in reassurance and after a moment he returns the gesture.

Mykal steps into the centre of the room, holding his hands out. "If this is what has come to be agreed upon then I say the final decision is to be made on the seventh day. No earlier, no later."

"Let's just hope we're still standing by then," Rowena sighs quietly.

For once we're all in agreement.

The trip back across the water and through the mountain is thick with tense silence but otherwise uneventful. We keep to the shadows of the late afternoon sun blazing down into the horizon. No one speaks, the only sound to be heard aside from the elements is the clipping of the horses' hooves against the loose stone. Rowena leads us, while Farren and Theon take up the rear.

I find my thoughts drifting from the disappointing counsel to the secret meeting with Lysan and I try my best to ignore the nervous tension growing in my stomach. I try to focus only on what I plan to say and what information I intend to draw out of him. By the time we finally sneak back into Trilló, I feel prepared for anything he plans to throw at me. As we return to the underground base, hidden beneath a lighthouse, I excuse myself from the briefing with my uncle, giving Wylan an apologetic look. I feel Ria's eyes on me as I rush away, but I push that to one side. For now, I have a Shadowcaster to meet.

I head straight for Yvie's room, rapping my knuckles impatiently against the door. Silence ensues after the third round of knocking and I sigh in defeat, supposing that she's somewhere with Twyla. With nowhere left to go, I head back to my room to ready myself. I lock the door behind me and quickly change out of my clothes and into darker, thicker leathers. I grab several of the small bottles of enhancer potion Yvie had given me during one of our training sessions. If I'm to meet with a deadly, tricky Shadowcaster, I need an edge. I can't afford not to have one. Stormtip is already safely secured to my leg and I welcome the feel of it there, knowing that if I need it, it will be only inches from my fingertips.

Shoving the small bottles into my pocket, I take one last look around the room before I leave. I remember to inhale and exhale slowly as I focus on honing my abilities, feeling the spark of power igniting within me, the current running along my veins like static.

Then, in the next moment, just as my breath hitches, I'm no longer in my room. I'm not even in the base anymore.

I land in the small clearing, stumbling across the grassy floor before righting myself and taking in my surroundings. I allow myself a mental cheer for making the jump.

The sky is dark, only made darker by the trees' canopies arching high above my head, but I can still see through the gloom enough to know that for now, I'm alone. I attune myself to the sound of nature around me, feeling almost at one with my current surroundings. The glade I'd chosen is within a forest just past the borders of Trálló, close enough for me to lightjump, yet far enough away to avoid unwanted visitors. Having grown up here, I knew this place like the back of my hand and knew it would be the best place to hold the upper hand, Asteria above knows I need it.

As I wait, I feel a change in the air, sending a shiver rolling down my spine. In the next moment, it's gone and I stop reaching for my blade.

"You aren't going to try and kill me this time?" he purrs as he appears in the darkness.

He stops in the centre of the glade, a sliver of light bathing him, giving his features a sharper outline. His seafoam eyes pierce me even in the darkness and despite the dreamlike surreality I feel at seeing him here, I step out of the shadows, swallowing the anger that tries to break free.

"Now why would I do that when you need to be alive for that tongue to waggle," I answer dryly.

"You've been listening to my warnings, how… quaint," he replies. "Is that why I'm here?"

"I hope you aren't creating false leads for me, Shadowcaster. It will only speed up your death," I counter as we begin to slowly circle one another.

He barks a laugh which bounces off the trees. "Such bold words from such a naive little girl. There will be a second Choosing, mark my words. Six girls to replace the six lost," he states.

My burning anger turns to my veins to ice. I force myself to continue, never letting my eyes stray from him.

"War and another Choosing? My, my, your king will be busy," I drawl. "That isn't what he wants though, is it?" I press after a breath of silence. "It will only cause speculation. He's slipping."

When he doesn't answer, I keep talking. "All he wants is bloodshed while his people are rebelling. They dream of peace, of Barilius gone."

"Wanting, dreaming? Such notions are just a distraction. It's for the meek and weak-minded" he cuts, his eyes narrowing.

"You don't seriously believe that?" I argue incredulously. "If you do then you're as sick as he is."

"We are headed for war, Nesryn. Hoping and dreaming for the alternative is a fool's errand," he points out with a shrug.

"Just because a path seems bent towards destruction doesn't mean that is your destination," I growl, my temper getting the better of me. "What is he planning? Why a second Choosing? When?" I demand, my eyes piercing his.

"Hope and wish all you like, but I know Barilius, and war will come... whether you like it or not," he replies darkly, ignoring my questions, a grim smile touching his lips.

We continue to circle one another, silence filling the space as he evades my questions.

"What I want to know is what is his Second up to? What does he hope to achieve by slipping his king's secrets to those who seek to destroy him," I say, breaking the silence as I probe again. "You realise the king will kill you for fraternising with the enemies like this?" I point out, my disgust evident. "How can you even stand to serve him?"

"People can do worse things than kill you," he says, a sudden bitter edge to his voice. "But then I might say the same about the people you've entangled yourself with," he continues, recovering his dark, playful smirk quickly.

"What is that supposed to mean?" I demand.

I feel the air shift and stare at Lysan wide-eyed as I realise he's drawing in his shadows.

"I've enjoyed our little chat. It's been quite... insightful. Until next time, princess," he winks.

"No, wait!" I shout after him.

But with no power to stop him, I can only watch helplessly as he pulls away, drawing free from our decided neutral grounds. It takes everything in me not to scream out in frustration as I throw an untimely punch at the closest tree trunk. My simmering anger only worsens as I send out feelers along our connecting thread, only to feel him close off the connection.

I scowl and curse under my breath as I look to the sky, his answers bringing me no closer to understanding anything.

LYSAN

CHAPTER FIFTYFOUR

Satisfaction coats my lips as I slip back into my room, my mind whirring from my encounter with Nesryn.

She had changed, I could feel it. Her power, just simmering beneath the surface, is so much more collected than it was mere days ago. I had sensed how on edge she was, despite her attempts at a nonchalant appearance. But there was a question that lingered at the back of my mind, one that couldn't be answered by anyone I knew, not even her.

Because despite everything that has happened to her, she has remained a Starweaver. Something which should have changed. It hasn't and I find myself desperate to know why. What level of spell had been strong enough to not only bind her powers, but to maintain them through the traumas she had faced? Because the alternative was impossible to even consider.

I sigh and step further into my room, only to stiffen immediately after the first step. Alarm bells ring in my head as I glance warily around the room, my gaze stopping on the man sitting stiffly at my desk, his face hidden by the darkness.

But he forgot one thing. The darkness belongs to me.

"Inconspicuous reveals have never been your thing, Keelhan. But I'd like to know how you got in here," I say casually as I stride past him.

The chair creaks as Keelhan stands, his eyes dark and pensive as he follows after me. His shoulders are tense and his jaw clenches, the muscle twitching from his attempt at maintaining some sort of calm. Something he seems to be visibly failing at.

"Where were you?" he asks sharply.

"That is of no concern to you," I answer.

"*Where* have you been?" he asks again, his voice firm.

"Gathering whispers," I answer simply as I unbuckle my scabbard.

"Like *hell* you were," Keelhan growls, hovering over me in an attempt at intimidating me.

"The king requested that I follow the whispers and report back. If you don't like the way I do things, maybe you should take it up with him," I answer, my tone calm but my gaze sharp. "Because frankly, I don't give a fuck."

He scowls and curses under his breath at me, something that brings an amused smile to my lips. I place the scabbard and blade into the wardrobe.

"The king has many angles to play, it seems, I'm simply playing my part. I suggest you focus on yours," I warn him.

"But that isn't the only order he gave you, was it?" Keelhan argues.

I stiffen where I stand, my eyes travelling to meet his stony gaze. Even from here, I can see how the anger radiates off him in waves. I can't understand why he is so riled up over his own doubts and misconceptions, no matter how true some may be.

"Spit it out already, Keel," I sigh.

I push past him with my shoulder as I make my way over to my desk, and pick up the half-full bottle of wine I'd left there from the previous night. With little effort I pull the cork free with my teeth and spit it across the room, the cylinder bouncing across the rug before colliding with the far wall.

"When do you plan on collecting those girls, or are you too busy trying to avoid it at all costs? Don't think I haven't noticed how you've been acting around the notion of a second Choosing," he points out.

The mouthful of rich red wine turns to vinegar in my mouth as I swallow, my mood souring along with it as I turn back to Keelhan.

"I don't question the methods you use to do your job, I would suggest you do the with me, Captain," I warn him as I place the bottle back on the desk.

I watch as Keelhan's eyes narrow and he takes several steps towards me until he's right in my face, close enough for me to see the flecks of grey in his blue eyes. I stand my ground as the tension rises in the air around us.

"Whose side are you on, Lysander?" he asks, his breath lined with the stench of ale. "What are you fighting for?"

The question ricochets through me as I consider his loaded question and what it would mean for me to answer truthfully. Something I have no intention of doing, especially when my so-called friend is not only *not* in his right state of mind, but severely suspicious of my actions.

"The right one," I answer.

Keelhan blinks, as though he wasn't expecting a simple answer, or any answer at all.

He quickly recovers and takes a step back, surveying me from where he stands, his arms folded across his plated chest. I can sense that there is more he wants to say.

"What about you, Captain, who are you fighting for?" I ask the question calmly, but there is a steely note behind the question.

I watch as he manages to steer himself away from the anger I'd hoped he would unleash, eager to remind him of his place and knock him back down to it. I knew what I was doing, I knew it was a dangerous risk, but a vow was a vow and I intended on seeing this through until the end, irrespective of the events unfurling around us.

"My fight is for the king. I will defend the crown as I said in my oath," he replies, clenching his jaw.

"Then I suggest you stop trying to walk this path, because it will only lead to my wrath, Captain," I tell him, snatching the bottle once again. "You forget who outranks who here, and your constant questioning of my morals and loyalties are beginning to grate on me," I continue. "Something we both know Barilius will view as insolence, should I bring the matter to his attention."

"Lys—" Keelhan starts, his eyes glowing with rage.

"—So, how about you focus on your recruitment and training our new Aslitír. I will come and find you when it is time to collect The Chosen," I cut him off, walking over to the door.

He glares at me as I open the door for him and gesture with the bottle for him to leave. As I shut the door behind him, I swallow the bitter lump in my throat. Keelhan was coming dangerously close to the truth, a truth that would tear our currently unsteady friendship apart, and for now, I couldn't let that happen.

I was becoming too comfortable jumping between my morals and duties, and it was only bringing me more trouble. Sighing, I take another deep swig of the bottle and make the decision I'd been avoiding for too long. Keelhan was right, the king would only keep being distracted by his war efforts for so long before he demanded the six girls he'd ordered me to collect.

The Choosing could no longer be ignored, despite my will for it to simply disappear. It was time.

CHAPTER FIFTYFIVE

I'm full of angst as I tread the halls towards Wylan's room.

I've barely slept after my encounter with Lysan, which brought nothing but more questions and unease in his wake.

Unable to settle, I'd instead made my way to Twyla's room, finding her half-asleep, hair dishevelled and Yvie asleep in her bed. I'd chosen not to say anything about the latter and instead focused on telling her about Lysan. After which she'd quickly snapped out of her sleepy demeanour into something far more alert and sombre.

In little time, we'd come up with a plan on how to tell the others, and she left me to the rest, promising me that she'd be there when the time came. I could do little else but wait until the night slowly crept into dawn, my impatience and unsettled state doing nothing but adding more wear to the section of the floor I'd been pacing about in my room. Now I consider what I'm going to say to Wylan and how I'm going to say it. All I can think of is how unaware those six girls are, most likely excited and busily packing for what they believe will be the chance of a lifetime, something that will change their lives for the better.

Just like I had.

The realisation sends an ice-cold shiver running down my back at the memory of my own packing, my own excitement, and my mouth sours at my previous self and her eagerness to enter that blood house.

Pushing the thoughts to one side, I finally reach Wylan's door and knock twice before stepping back and waiting, tapping my foot impatiently against the ground. The door opens and my head snaps up to see Maz. He frowns when he sees me. I open my mouth to speak when he draws the door open further and steps out, wrapping me in his strong embrace. I stand awkwardly as he holds me, my face burning at the amount of skin he has on show and holding my breath as my skin begins to crawl.

I'm almost grateful to tears when he lets me go and steps back, my skin still prickling with disgust at being so physically close to him. I swallow the bile in my throat as I fight against where my mind wants to take me. Maz starts to speak but my head is underwater, fighting the memory of *him* and the smell of ale on his breath as I try to remember where I am, remember how far I've come since that bleak, twisted moment.

"—so grateful to you for bringing him back safely," Maz continues, his eyes shining with gratitude.

I blink as I tune into the conversation and draw in a breath, forcing a half-hearted smile. I shake my head gently as I meet his eyes.

"He would have done the same for me," I answer, my voice thicker than expected as I piece together what he said.

"I hope you agree to the position. You would be an incredible asset to him, and I know he'll be safe with you around, someone he can trust," he continues.

A knot forms in my stomach at this and I shift slightly on my feet, suddenly uncomfortable again. Sensing this, Maz stops, watching me for a moment before he steps to the side.

"Come on in, Wylan should be back any moment with tea," he explains.

I blink in surprise, curious as to why he would be up as early as me.

"Thanks," I say after a moment, stepping into the room.

Wylan returns with a tray of steaming tea, his eyes flicking across to me sitting on the sofa. He simply finishes up his conversation with Maz as he sets the tray down. I glance through the steam at Wylan, feeling unsettled again as I think of what I'm about to tell him.

"You're up early, Nes," he comments as he sits down, Maz joining him.

"I could say the same to you," I reply, a wry smile curling the edges of my lips.

"I certainly wasn't expecting a visit from you, either," he adds, reaching out with one of the steaming cups.

"Any news from the other nations?" I query, taking it from him and settling it into my lap.

"As eager as I am to hear news, I know that they won't have made a decision yet. What has you so impatient?" he asks with a chuckle.

I stare at the dark liquid within the cup in my lap.

"You're stalling," he observes.

I look up then, my expression serious enough for Wylan to lose his half-smile, his brow furrowing with concern.

"There's going to be a second Choosing."

Beside him, Maz chokes on his mouthful of tea. Wylan's expression darkens. I hold my breath as he digests my words, his hazel eyes pensive and his lips set in a thin line.

"Are you sure?" he asks finally, meeting my gaze.

I nod.

"I'll gather the others. If this is true, then this matter can't wait," he states, as he gets to his feet.

Before the hour is up, Wylan has us gathered in a larger room, his expression unchanged since I'd told him the news. In the room are Rowena, Uncle Erathon, Farren, me, Wylan, Maz, Jaeg, and upon my request, Twyla.

Before Rowena can ask for the third time why Wylan has gathered us all here, he clears his throat.

"I've gathered us here because it's come to my attention that the king plans a second Choosing," Wylan announces, his eyes flicking to where I stand.

The room goes eerily silent as they're hit with the bombshell news. For several long moments, no one utters a word and the tension in the room only grows with each second of silence that passes.

"Who told you this?" Uncle Erathon asks, his tone grave.

"I did," I say before Wylan has a chance.

All eyes fall on me, their penetrating gazes causing me discomfort. Surprise and wariness cloud most of their faces, only Twyla and Wylan are serious.

"Please, do tell how you've come about this information, when I've heard nothing of this until now," Rowena speaks up.

"We received word of another Choosing, several days gone," I start.

"And you didn't think to tell us then?" she cuts in.

"We wanted to confirm that this was in fact a real lead and not false, to steer our attention from Barilius's pledge of war," I answer, my tone clipped.

"Who is this *we*?" Uncle Erathon cuts in.

"Twyla and I," I answer, my gaze flitting to Twyla.

The attention of the others shifts to Twyla, but she holds her ground, her head held high even as Wylan glances between the two of us, as though trying to understand this new piece of information. A part of me regrets not warning him beforehand.

"Who gave you both this information?" Rowena speaks up, her voice even.

Twyla and I share a look of understanding before she turns to Rowena with a serious face.

"It's the same informant within the palace that I mentioned before, Row," she explains.

"And are you sure that—" Rowena begins, but she's quickly interrupted.

"—They can be trusted on this, there is no doubt," Twyla argues.

"And if we don't do anything, more innocent young women will die," I add, glancing around the room.

"That can't be allowed to happen," Wylan states, slamming a hand against the table between us.

"How can we stop this when we have no idea when it will take place?" Farren speaks up.

"We cut them off before they even arrive," I answer, the basic idea of a plan already forming in my mind.

"Go on," Farren waves at me, quietly impressed.

"If we know anything about The Choosing, we all know that there are only two paths they can take back to the kingdom," I explain as I reach for my power.

"The king will send his Second, Lysan, to escort the girls back to the palace. He is one of the few that he trusts…"

They lean forwards as I close my eyes and recall the long stretches of winding country roads, shaping them out before the group in brilliant glowing light. Once it's done, I point at the makeshift map I've created, floating just above the table.

"I suggest we prepare for both routes and jump them. They won't be expecting it," I reason.

"The Shadowcaster may prove to be an issue. I've heard of his abilities," Uncle Erathon speaks up.

A murmur of agreement ripples across the room and my nerves return.

"I doubt he'll expect what my brother and I have been working on. We've called them hand-cannons, and they pack a punch," Jaeg cuts in.

"Regardless of his abilities, we'll be catching him and his men off guard, plus with Jaeg's weapons and Nesryn with us, we'll hold equal, if not higher ground," Twyla says, scanning the faces in the room.

"This is all great, but we don't know when this will take place. We could be out there waiting for days," Rowena argues, gesturing to the map, which sways slightly with her violent gesture.

"That's where my informant comes in. We'll know when soon enough," Twyla cuts in, her tone reassuring before she glances across the table at me.

"We'll need to be ready, with two teams covering each route," I add.

"Getting two large groups out of the city may prove difficult," Wylan points out, my uncle nodding in agreement beside him.

"Can Yvie lightjump?" I ask Twyla, who nods.

"But she'd probably prefer to be at the base, you know, in case we needed any answers from her extensive library."

"I'll lead the other group," Farren says, standing proud.

I nod. "Then I'll move both groups past the city's borders. We can make the rest of the way on foot. It may take some time and drain my power, but if we're well-prepared, I can rest while we wait for them to reach the ambush point," I suggest.

"Yes... yes, that could work," my uncle agrees. "I'll put the teams together, starting with you two," he adds, glancing between me and Twyla, who nods with me.

"And Ria and the others, if they choose," I suggest, to which my uncle dips his head in agreement.

"Then we await the news from your informant, Twyla," Wylan speaks up, his attention moving from her as he turns to me. "Well done for bringing this to our attention, Nes."

With the meeting over, I find myself simultaneously full of nervous energy and heavy with exhaustion. I contemplate where I'm headed, but my thoughts distract me, leaving my feet to guide me along the corridor.

I hear a familiar pair of footsteps head towards me and I turn my head to find Wylan already watching me, contemplating something.

"Talk of the king's Shadowcaster has you on edge," he observes.

"It has everyone on edge," I counter.

"Yes, that is true," he smiles, his nose wrinkling as he nods. "But my guess is this runs deeper for you."

When I say nothing, he falls into step with me, glancing at me every once in a while, trying to read my expression.

"Is there history?" he probes.

I falter mid-step, turning to look at Wylan with an incredulous expression plastered across my face.

"Asteria above, *no!*" I answer.

He holds his hands up, fighting the grin that threatens to spread across his lips.

"I'm sorry if I misread the situation," he tells me, fighting a chuckle.

"He's an insufferable, cruel bastard, and the king's dog. Anything Barilius demands, he does without question," I answer, my mind travelling to my last encounter with Lysan. "The only history there is the suffering he's caused me and my friends by serving that tyrant."

"I see," he says quietly.

"He deserves what's coming to him," I say, as his words from last night resurface in my mind.

'People can do worse things than kill you.'

Hours later, I'm hard at work in the training ring, the space empty except for me. I focus on the dummy, letting all of my nervous energy out as I replay last night, and the earlier meeting as I hone my combat skills.

I'm only partly aware of Ria as she strides purposefully into the room. Anger flares in her eyes.

"It's Lysan, isn't it? Twyla's informant. It has to be… why else would he find us back there in the gorge? Who else would hold that type of information?" she demands, bursting into the room.

"How do you know about Twyla's informant?" I ask, dropping my fists.

"Words going around the base that the king is setting up a second Choosing," Ria ignores my question.

"He is," I confirm.

"Why would you lie about this?" she demands.

"I never lied about him being our informant," I reason, my tone warning.

"Oh, so he's *our* informant now, is he? What next? Our ally?" she scoffs as she paces.

"Don't insult me. He is sharing information, goddess knows why, but we need it. Don't you dare tell me we don't!" I snap.

She says nothing, her steps faltering as she stares wide-eyed at me.

"Before you start lecturing me, you know that I know better than anyone who he is and what he's done. But I also know for certain that his word can be shaped into a tool to take down the king. We take what information we need from him, make him think that we share the same goal," I tell her.

"Then what?" she spits.

I let out a shaky sigh, letting my own anger simmer down. "Then, when he's no longer of use, when he has no more information to give, he dies."

I look away, swallowing the disgust at my own words. In what way was I any better than him when I was throwing around threats like that?

"Alright… but Nesryn," Ria says, drawing me from my darkened train of thought.

"What?" I sigh, suddenly tired.

"No more secrets," she eyes me, offering me a tentative half-smile.

I shake my head. "There were never any. I've already requested you to be on one of the teams."

She blinks at this news as if surprised by my choice.

"Good," she nods decisively. "Because you never had a choice. I was coming anyway."

LYSAN

Chapter FiftySix

The war room is messier than before, something I never thought possible. There is a stronger scent of red wine and a staleness in the air that I can't quite put my finger on. Whatever the cause, it has gotten steadily worse since Barilius has begun to hole himself up in here, though it's a vast improvement from the tower high above the rest of the palace.

Crimson and black candles litter the space, balancing in groups upon the large table and dripping down onto rolls of spread out maps and parchment, scrawled with ink. Some glow with a normal golden flame, but a few scattered about the room burn black, and I can't help the sinister feeling that I get when I see those flames. I recall what I'd seen up in Barilius's tower and shudder.

'The blooded moon is coming into alignment. Be ready or be undone. The Black Orchid.'

The words on that note burn brightly in my memory and I find myself baffled at the idea of Barilius seeking aid in this way, and the name, The Black Orchid. It sounds too ominous to not be of some importance, plus it begs the question: who is this person hiding behind darkened candles and willing to help the king in his twisted escapades?

I stand side by side with Keelhan, just past the entryway. Neither of us have spoken to each other since our last disagreement and I find myself in no mood to continue the same narrative, so for once, I've decidedly kept my mouth shut, something that has earned me several harrowed looks from the captain.

Barilius has his back to us, muttering incoherent babble under his breath. His ponytail is loose and unkempt, strands clumps together, glossy from the greasiness. His clothes are crumpled and untucked, the edges of his tunic hanging free. His rich coloured, gold-buttoned suit jacket is slumped over the nearest chair beneath another stack of rolled-up parchment. When he turns to face us, I swallow my shock. His face is drawn, with heavy bags lining the underside of his eyes. The bright glowing amber of his eyes is muted to a dull brown shade, and his usually preened beard is loose and scraggly, with snakes of silver lining the dark tint. In fact, as I watch him pour over the maps, I notice how many strands of silver line his ponytail, how a handful of sunspots cover his hands, his skin fading into shadowed wrinkles. I turn to gauge Keelhan's reaction. The captain purses his lips as he watches the king, his eyes flickering wide for a split second before he catches himself and tries to smooth a calm, impassive expression back onto his face. In all the time that I've served him, in the decade that I've known him, Barilius has always looked the same, always the epitome of strict perfection, not a hair out of place. But now, it's as though the years have caught up with him and he's beginning to unravel.

I don't deny the wild look I see in his eyes, he looks desperate.

'*But why?*'

I open my mouth to speak, desperate to end the silence, but before I get the chance, the king finally looks up, his eyes flickering between us.

"The Choosing cannot wait any longer, you must collect The Chosen before the seventh day," he demands.

"I have already planned and secured our route through the forest path. I just need to speak with the captain as to how many men he can spare at this time, my king,"

I feel Keelhan stiffen in surprise at my side but his face remains impassive as we look at the king.

"And you, how goes the recruitment?" Barilius addresses Keelhan.

"Not as well as we'd hoped, Sire, most of the men within the age guidelines have already joined our numbers. The recruitment process is slow going," he explains.

"Forget the age gap, in fact, abolish it," Barilius says in rushed tones.

"My king—" Keelhan starts to protest.

"—We need the numbers! I want no fight from you on this, Captain, have you forgotten we are at war?" Barilius spits, his head snapping up from scouring the pages before him.

"Yes, my king. I will see to it that it is done," Keelhan answers after a split second.

"Go now, both of you. I have matters to attend to and old friends to speak with," the king waves us away, half-distracted.

Keelhan throws a concerned glance my way as we turn and leave, hearing the doors click shut behind us.

Without hesitation we continue on our way, leaving the king's quarters and heading out towards the courtyard, our steps clipping against the stone floor in unison.

"I received word from the king of Elderwharf this morning. They have offered their services and steel towards the war effort, providing their lands remain untouched by battle," Keelhan tells me solemnly as we walk.

"And you didn't mention this to the king?" I raise a brow, somewhat curious.

"The king doesn't seem himself," he answers.

"Keeping this news to yourself will only bring his temper down upon you," I warn him.

"I will inform him of the news once the girls have arrived safely," he answers pointedly, his eyes shifting to me.

My steps falter and I come to a stop, watching him with a furrowed brow. "You doubt my ability?"

"I'm right to have my doubts. You've hardly shown your utmost dedication since the last girls escaped," he stops, turning back to me.

"I'm growing very tired of your sudden suspicious mentality. You know I don't remember the last time we joked together?" I say plainly, tired of his mood towards me.

"I don't know what to tell you Lysan, you've brought it upon yourself," he answers.

"You know, we once shared the same opinions of the king's dealings," I point out.

He pauses, breathing a heavy sigh through his nose as he searches my face.

"That was before The Choosing went awry before you started fooling around like an incompetent child," he argues.

"Holding four years over me doesn't give you the right to insult me as though you have the moral high ground," I snipe, gritting my teeth. "If you keep this up, you'll quickly find yourself in hot water," I warn him.

"I'm not afraid of you, Lysan."

"You should be, you know what I'm capable of," I say coldly.

"I'm starting to," he murmurs, loud enough for me to hear.

I narrow my eyes. "How many men will you spare?"

"A dozen."

I grumble under my breath, knowing it isn't enough, but I can't be arsed to argue with him, my temper already fraying. I nod and start to walk away, already reaching along the mental thread to Nesryn when Keelhan stops me.

"There was a time I knew you as a brother, but now I don't know what exactly you've become, you've forgotten your place. This is your last warning. Pick a side, Lysan," he shows his blade, the metal glinting under the light. "Or I'll pick for you."

CHAPTER FIFTYSEVEN

I breathe heavily as I run through the base, towards Ria's room. My heart pounds heavily in my chest as I weave the halls, narrowly dodging people who shout after me as I rush past. Faces blur past as I go, my eagerness taking over as I skid to a stop outside Ria's door and begin banging on it, rattling the lock.

I hear shuffling on the other side before the lock clicks back and the door opens to a squinting Ria. Her hair is bedraggled and her clothes are no better as she blinks several times, before taking in me standing in her doorway.

"Nes? What—" she starts.

"—No time. There's been word from the other nations," I tell her breathlessly.

She rushes back into her room suddenly and I blink in surprise as I hear her scuffling and rummaging about behind the partly closed door before appearing again, this time dressed and far more awake.

"Well, what are we waiting for?" she demands.

We arrive at the gathering of people in the main food hall just in time to spot Wylan pacing back and forth, rubbing his jaw with his hand, whilst beside him, Rowena reads one of the letters in her hands.

Ria and I weave into the room, moving around the surprising number of people that have gathered in the time that it's taken for me to fetch Ria. We push through to the front, the nervous buzz in the air, thick and unavoidable. When we reach the front, Farren is there to greet us before turning her attention back to the front where my uncle joins Wylan and Rowena.

People mutter and murmur as I lean towards Farren, her eyes set ahead to where Rowena stands with the letter in hand.

"Have they announced anything yet?" I ask quietly.

"Not yet, but I don't think it's all good from the look of Row," she answers, tensely.

Just as the anticipation in the room thickens, Rowena walks to Wylan and says something that causes him to grimace. I can only watch on with jittering nerves for the outcome. After a moment of quiet chatter, they nod at one another and Rowena steps back while Wylan greets the crowd of people.

"As you all well know, some of us ventured past the borders of these lands to seek aid from our fellow nations," he begins. "Barilius's reign must end, and it will, but I cannot guarantee there won't be bloodshed," he goes on. "War is coming."

An eruption of chatter cuts into his speech and I feel the mixture of fear and eagerness swirling about the room. As the chatter builds and grows louder, Wylan holds up a hand in an attempt to subdue the spectators long enough to finish what he needs to say. When they don't, we watch as Rowena steps in, demanding to her followers that they listen.

"I know you all have your reservations and views on this, but Barilius has declared war, and we need to be ready," she holds the stares of the crowd, her authoritative stance unwavering. "Go on, Wylan."

"As I was saying, we sought aid from our fellow nations and we have received news that four of them will support us in our fight for the crown!" he pumps his fist into the air as an enormous cheer erupts through the room.

Farren, Ria and I stand amongst the chaos, but I keep my eyes trained on Wylan, noting the hollow expression in his eye despite the triumphant grin on his face.

'*What has him so worried?*' I wonder.

"That means another nation is refusing to help," Farren sighs.

"Or maybe they're simply refusing to help us," Ria adds pointedly, glancing sideways at us.

"*Barilius,*" I realise, my stomach coiling into a knot.

People are filtering out of the room when I sense it.

Like a tug on an invisible string, words filter into my mind and a sickening realisation with it. The connection between us was never severed.

I swallow the lump in my throat, worried about what he may have learned unwittingly through me when the words come through.

'... collection... tomorrow...'

As I process this, my eyes widen in understanding.

I turn to look at where Ria and Farren are standing with Yvie and Twyla, the latter noticing my expression and frowning in concern.

"What is it?" she asks, stepping towards me.

"We need to prepare the teams, we have a Choosing to stop," I tell her.

"You're sure?" she whispers before glancing back towards the others.

"It's happening tomorrow, we need to leave tonight," I assure her.

A determined look washes over her face and she spins on her heels.

"There's been a development," she announces, catching everyone's attention.

I join her side as Rowena, Wylan, and my uncle join us beside Farren and the others. They look to Twyla with anticipation as she surveys the group, her gaze resting on Rowena.

"My source tells me that the Shadowcaster will be collecting the girls tomorrow, we need to be ready," she tells them.

"That's so soon," Ria gasps.

"With the threat of war, we must have forced Barilius's hand," Wylan surmises.

"What are we waiting for then?" Farren asks, glancing around at each of our faces.

"Pay a visit to Jaeg before you go, he's finished his tweaks on those devices of his, something which may prove useful," my uncle speaks up.

"No one's seen the likes of these before. I call them hand-cannons," Jaeg explains to us in his workshop, showing off the metal contraption in his hands.

"The likes of you don't need 'em," he says, gesturing to Zariya and I. "It's for us simple kind who only have the strength of our hand in a fight."

I glance towards the girl beside me again, nerves fluttering in my chest. "Are you sure you don't want to sit this one out?"

She frowns. "Just because I'm blind, doesn't mean I'm incapable. Besides, my powers give me the ability to see, in a way. I've been training for months, Nesryn, this is my chance to show you all what I can do."

"Alright," I sigh, still uneasy with the idea.

"How do they work?" Ria asks the young man.

"Simple really, you load these in here," he explains, showing us how he places a handful of metal balls into the chamber. "...click it shut, aim, and then…"

He lifts the hand-cannon and aims it at the target across the room. With a single finger, he pulls the trigger and a blast erupts, causing everyone except Jaeg to jump back in surprise.

He turns to us, grinning, the mouth of the device smoking as he points at the target. We follow his finger to see the hole in the centre of the target.

"Impressive," Farren comments. "But I think I'll stick with what I'm familiar with."

She pats her twin blades and walks away as Ria, Theon and several others begin asking Jaeg a barrage of questions, all eager to try out the new weapon.

I follow after Farren with Zariya close behind, her shadows stretching out around her gently as she goes. The sight causes me to think of Lysan. Then the thought of what is about to happen causes a shiver to run down my spine.

"Are you ready?" Farren asks me with a doubtful look.

"I don't know," I admit, giving her a half-smile.

"Your bravery will shine true when the time comes, little warrior," she answers with a wink.

And with that she marches off, leaving me with her lingering words as I think of all we have to come, and the thought of war that hangs over us all.

I'm restless, we all are.

We had left as one group, splitting into two when the time came, still unsure as to which path Lysan would lead the party through. Farren's group head to the rockier path, while I lead mine into the forested path. One of us would send word to the other group when the time came.

There are seven of us: me, Twyla, Ria, Maz; as well as Trevil and Morey; two of Farren's men who'd volunteered. Farren's group is made up of Zariya, Ovie, Farren and the rest of her men. We hide out in our little makeshift camp, waiting impatiently. We're all on edge, and it's hard to ignore the restlessness rising within us as we wait for our scout, Maz, to come back with news.

I'm sharpening Stormtip when I hear rustling through the trees. Ria immediately douses the fire and we watch the trees, weapons at the ready when Maz comes flying through the trees, sweat slipping down his temple.

"They've taken this route. There's a dozen Aslitír, two carriages, and only one Shadowcaster amongst them," he explains through panted breaths.

"Lysan? The king's Second?" I ask.

He nods his confirmation and I get to my feet.

"Alright. Be at the ready, but wait for me to return," I order, waiting for them to agree before I disappear before their eyes.

I appear in Farren's camp at the sharp end of their blades and with the barrels of Jaeg's hand-cannons pointed at me. When they realise it's me, they lower their weapons. I give Farren a pointed look.

"They've taken the forest path," she says.

It's not a question, but I nod all the same, holding my arm out.

"Ready?" I ask.

Each of them grab a hold of me, determined expressions lining their faces. I take a deep breath and hone my power, drawing in its strength before we jump, arriving in a stumbling tangle, a stone's throw away from the others.

After dusting ourselves off, we follow Maz through the greenery, trying our best to maintain as much quiet as we can, stopping in sight of the road. We crouch down, waiting with bated breath as the sound of horses approaches. As the carriages come into sight, I stand still, watching. So many emotions fly through me all at once, but rage is the strongest as I think of what those girls within the carriages are being taken to, what fate awaits them if we fail today.

I refuse to let that happen.

I fall deathly still as our target moves closer and closer. My breaths come slow and steady until the target is right where I want them.

"Now!"

And just like that, as they follow my order into a surprise attack I join them as we descend into chaos and the clashing of steel.

LYSAN

CHAPTER FIFTYEIGHT

I don't know what I expected, but whatever it was, nothing compares to this. They come from both sides, erupting from the trees, war cries on their lips.

The Aslitír respond immediately to the threat as I jump down for the carriage and make my way quickly around to the side. As the door tries to open, I push it shut with a rough hand.

"Stay inside," I shout to them as a man runs at me.

I manage to hold him back, blocking his attacks with my shadows whilst trying to lead him away from the girls.

Nesryn has come armed and ready, she's outnumbered us and I fight the dark smile that threatens to appear on my lips. My opponent gets an opening and takes it while I'm distracted, thrusting his blade forwards. I move to dodge it but the edge of his blade catches me beneath my arm, slicing along my ribs. I hiss with pain, feeling blood ebb from the wound. I thrust out a hand, sending him sprawling with my shadows and flinging him backwards into a tree.

The cries of battle break the serenity, blood spattering the ground, as one by one, my men fall to the enemies' blades. I hear their gurgled cries as they fall whilst I run around the carriage, ready to fight back. A woman, however, stands in my way, her hazel eyes flash with bloodlust as she tilts her twin blades towards me. Blood stains her braided hair and drips from her chin as she sends me a dark smile, a loose wave slipping from behind her half-pointed ear.

"A mixed-blood wants to be a rebel. How refreshing," I comment, holding out my hands, slithering with shadows.

"Come quietly now, Shadowcaster, and I won't have to ruin that pretty face of yours," she answers, spinning her blades in her hands as she steps towards me.

"And ruin the fun?" I tease.

She scoffs only once, before her whole demeanour shifts and she launches herself at me, quick and lethal like a true warrior. But I'm ready for her, countering her moves with attacks of my own, weaving the shadows through her when she leaves an opening.

We're a blur as we fight. Her blades singing with each swing, my shadows striking and blocking in return. Just as I think I'm gaining the upper hand, an immense pain shoots through the back of my head.

"Congratulations, Shadowcaster, it seems you'll live to fight another day," the mixed-blood taunts me.

Disoriented, I lift my hand to my head, drawing it back to see blood as black spots crowd my vision. I half-turn, dropping to my knees as I look at the girl wielding shadows with eyes of black steel and lengths of dark hair. The noblewoman's gown is covered in muck and grime.

"Tula?" I manage, surprise tinging my tone.

Behind her lay the bodies of the Aslitír, massacred without hesitation. I had not expected such brutality from Nesryn and her band of rebels. An underestimation I won't soon make again.

As my vision worsens, she appears before me, leaning in to study my face, her own equally as filthy, blood smeared across her delicate features, highlighting her spring-green eyes.

"You're coming with us," she says softly, but I detect triumph in her voice.

They're the last words I hear before I collapse to the floor.

NESRYN

CHAPTER FIFTYNINE

I pace up and down the food hall, still bloodied and grimy from fighting.

The six girls we saved are in another room with Rowena and my uncle, understandably confused and wary. Although the original plan was to send them home, the dark-haired Shadowcaster, Tula, had refused, convincing us that the king would only send more of his men to collect them if they didn't show.

Tula led the frightened girls with Uncle Erathon and Rowena upon arrival, while I recounted what happened to a solemn Wylan. He'd listened attentively before getting to his feet and telling me that he'd be back to find me soon.

So I waited, letting the clock chime out, then again a while later, listening as time moved on around me while I sat and stewed in my own thoughts.

While I waited, I replayed every moment of the fight in my head, every slide of my sword, every twist of my dagger. In every one of the Aslitír I'd faced, I'd seen his face, smelt the stench of ale and I'd felt no fury or disgust like it. I stare down at my shaking hands, feeling queasy at how easily I tore those men apart, how I watched the light fade from their eyes as they'd fallen to the ground. I prayed that Asteria would forgive me when I ascended because, despite everything, I'm not sure I could ever truly forgive myself. Telling myself the bloodshed was necessary did nothing to help how I felt inside.

It's past six chimes when Wylan returns with Farren at his side. I stand immediately when they arrive, the food I'd been brought by Ovie forgotten.

"The Shadowcaster won't tell us anything. He demands to speak with you, Nesryn. *Only* you," Wylan explains, raking a hand through his hair.

I can sense he's irritated but Lysan's demand captures my attention, cool surprise washing over me.

"Me?" I repeat, dubious.

"He's holed up in one of the cells, refusing to cooperate with our questioning. He'll only speak to you," Farren explains.

I sigh. "Alright, I'll speak to him."

"Are you sure you want to do that? Remember you don't owe him shit," Wylan peers at me, reading my eyes.

"If it's the only way he'll cooperate, then I'll do it. I can handle myself, trust me," I reply, meeting his gaze.

"I don't know how I feel about giving him what he wants," he admits.

"We'll be right outside the door, Wylan, I've seen her out there. She can handle herself," Farren reassures Wylan, sending a wink my way. I smile gratefully at her.

Wylan hesitates for a few moments before eventually releasing a heavy sigh. "Alright, fine. You talk to him. Starweaver to Shadowcaster."

I'm led down into a lower section of the base, towards one of the few lit rooms. It's colder down here and I fight the urge to shiver as my skin prickles from the change in temperature.

"We'll be right outside," Farren reassures me as we arrive, Ria appearing beside her.

"Find out all you can," Wylan tells me, meeting my gaze with concern.

I nod once, enter the room, and pull it shut behind me with a soft click. The room is cold and dark, save for several lit torches embedded in the wall. Ahead, the room is separated by steel bars buried into the stone, both in the ceiling and floor, unyielding. He sits on the small wooden bench on the far side of the cell, beyond the bars. He looks like hell. His hands bound tightly with some sort of coil or rope. He looks like he's been beaten since I last laid eyes on him, with half his face bloodied and bruised. One eye is swollen shut, and his lips are split, equally as swollen.

There isn't a single part of him that isn't covered in blood or grime. I notice how the knock to his head has left quite the lump, his raven hair clumped together with dried blood. I'm also aware of the way his bound hands holds his ribs, blood seeping between his fingers.

"Lysan," I greet him.

"I see you've gotten quite cosy with the wannabe king," he taunts as I step closer.

"Wylan is a friend, and he'll be a far better leader than the bastard occupying the throne now," I spit back.

"Wylan?" he scoffs. "On a first name basis already? He sure does move quickly."

"You don't know anything about him," I answer coldly.

"I know what his angle is, what he hopes to achieve. Let me guess, he's asked you to join his cause?" he asks with a knowing smile.

When I don't answer, he lets out a bark of laughter.

"These seekers of the crown are all the same. We're just pawns, Nesryn, ready to use when and how our crown-wielders see fit. Nothing more," he chuckles bitterly, bringing on a bout of coughing that splatters blood across the stone floor.

"The others want to know what you're trying to achieve," I say, tactfully changing the subject. "So am I actually. You aren't being very clear about whose side you're really on."

"I'm on yours," he answers with a playful smirk that quickly turns into a painful grimace.

I scoff, shaking my head in disgust. "Whose side are you really on, Lysan?"

"You sound like someone else I know," he mutters, evidently bored of the question.

"Then tell me what you know. What your *master's* plans are," I order him, stepping forwards to grab the bars.

He tilts his head, his good eye studying me carefully. Silence ensues as we stay like this; him sitting, observing me; me standing against the bars, staring him down.

"I know that he still haunts you, doesn't he?" he says finally.

My hands drop from the bars and I take a step back. My heart begins to speed up in my chest as I stare at him warily.

"Olin. The one who—" he starts.

"—Shut. The. Fuck. Up," my words are sharp and cold as they leave my lips.

"I killed him, you know," he continues casually.

I freeze.

"What?" My eyes are as wide as saucers.

"I found him. I asked him what he did, and then reduced him to blood and dust," his seafoam eyes, swirling with danger, hold mine.

I stare at a spot on the wall as I try to process this information, swallowing the lump clogging my throat.

"*Ask him why,*" the little voice in my head urges me.

"You can do right here, choose the right side. There *is* good in you, Lysan," I say, choosing to ignore the little voice.

He flinches at my words, turning his face away from me, a shadow falling across his eyes. "No, there isn't. That died with her last breath. But I made a promise, one that I intend to see through."

His words catch my attention, but before I can ask him who he's speaking about, who he lost, he turns back to me, the shadow still there in his eyes.

"But there *is* a darkness in you," he says quietly.

"There is no darkness in me, Lysan, you only wish there was," I spit back.

"Like calls to like, we aren't so different you and I," he continues.

"You conniving bastard, I'm nothing like you," I yell.

My rage evaporates, the air going from my lungs as I blink in disbelief. Stepping forward, I take a closer look. The only things left are the empty bonds and the fading tendrils of dark smoke.

He's gone.

CHAPTER SIXTY

The exhaustion from shadowfolding back to the palace is so immense that I drop to my knees upon arrival, bringing up the contents of my stomach and blood, until there is nothing but bile and retching left.

I try to conjure a wisp of shadow only to stare shakily at my empty hand. I chuckle bitterly to myself. Without realising, I've managed to drain my power almost completely. I know it will be a while before it returns. All I can do is muster my strength and get to my feet, groaning with effort. I stagger through the empty halls, slipping and falling every few feet as my knees give out under me. Looking ahead with my good eye, I notice there is no one around to help, so I force myself back up, moving on with only grit and determination to keep me going. After what feels like an eternity, I stumble through the throne room doors, making it only a quarter of the way into the room before I collapse on my knees, breathing heavily. I look up to see Barilius standing at the base of the steps to his impressive throne.

Keelhan stands beside him with a group of Aslitír all looking down at me with cruel sneers and visible disgust—even their captain looks at me in disappointment, wrinkling his nose. But it's what is standing beside the king, leering behind him that catches my attention as my next inhale catches just at the sight of it.

Whatever it is, it's not human. Though its shape is vaguely human, it's made of shadow and twisting darkness, not dissimilar to my shadows. Where the thing should have eyes, there are only two large holes. It looks like some sort of unearthly golem fashioned from dark magic. It taints the room and my skin crawls at the mere sight of it.

I look to the king, noting how the silver in his hair is gone, the brightness has returned to his amber eyes with a vengeance, and he looks as I'd always known him. A shiver runs down my spine.

"You dare show up empty-handed?" he roars across the room.

"I-I'm sorry, my king, we were ambushed," I begin.

"I have heard this excuse. It won't work a second time, boy," Barilius's voice booms across the hall.

"I only did what you asked of me," I rasp.

"You have failed me! And now I hear how you have fallen into close encounters with them, the enemy!" he roars, his fury palpable.

"Bhok, show him how I deal with failures," he orders the creature in a clipped voice.

Despite its size, the creature moves quickly, striding towards me. Within moments it's upon me, and there is nowhere for me to go. Its huge arms beat down on me, raining punches before rolling me over as it kicks me across the room into the far wall. The air rushes from my lungs and my head slams against the hard surface, causing black spots to dance at the edges of my vision and sending me into a dizzying state.

As I manage to right myself on all fours, I retch, blood dripping from my lips. The creature is upon me again before I can even glance up from the floor. It grabs me by the scruff and hurls me across the room. I slam against the hard, cold floor, as another of my bones snap and a scream tries to erupt from my lips, only to surface as a gurgled gasp.

"Wait!" I shout, sounding more like a groan as I hold up my hand.

The creature relents, stepping back as Barilius commands it to stop with a simple hand gesture.

I sway on all fours as I gather my scrambled thoughts, fighting to remain conscious despite the golem's beatings.

"I didn't bring you *nothing*," I spit a mouthful of blood.

"My patience is growing thin boy and I don't deal well with traitors," he cuts back.

"I haven't betrayed you, my king," I plead.

This captures his attention and I hear his footsteps as he stops before me. I force myself to my knees, leaning back as I sway, the room spinning as I try to focus on the glowing amber eyes glaring down at me.

"Speak now, or die!" he yells after another second passes.

I manage a sickly smile, feeling blood spill over my chin as I give him my most triumphant look despite the beating I've endured.

"I know where they are. The Chosen, the Starweaver, the rebels, all of them," I tell him, watching as his eyes fill with greed and vengeance. "And I can lead you straight to them."

CHAPTER SIXTYONE

I glare at the bonds, now lying empty on the small bench within the cell. Lysan's swollen, bloodied face stares back at me tauntingly in my mind from where he had been sitting only mere moments ago, and before I know what's happening, frustration fills my every bone and quickly evolves into anger.

A roar of fury erupts from me as I stare at the now empty cell, my power exploding from me, drowning every inch of the room in bright, burning white light. My power streams from me, coming in wave after wave of dazzling light until I have no more to release, slumping to the floor, and panting on all fours.

As I catch my breath, the door behind me bursts open and Ria, Wylan and Farren rush into the room.

"What happened? Where is he?" Ria demands, peering past the metal bars.

"The bastard slipped out under my nose," I growl, my voice thick with anger.

Wylan and Farren stare at me in disbelief as Ria walks back over to me and helps me to my feet. She searches my face, but I scowl at the empty bonds. I thought he'd been too beaten, too weak to shadowfold, but I'd been wrong.

"Did you get anything useful out of him at least?" Ria asks, turning toward me.

With my lips set in a thin line, I shake my head, angry at myself.

"Damn it," I snap, kicking the bars.

"It's ok, Nes, this isn't your fault. We know how slippery he can be," Wylan sighs, turning his attention back to the empty cell.

"He's had us running in circles," Farren adds, shaking her head.

"We have no idea where he's gone," I point out, folding my arms over my chest.

"More than likely he's gone crawling back to Barilius," Ria spits.

"Wouldn't put it past him, he *is* the king's lapdog," Farren agrees with a shrug.

"Well, wherever he's disappeared to, we know that he can't be trusted," Wylan adds.

For the first time in a while, I falter, thinking of what he'd shared with me and finding myself slightly unconvinced.

'But he is up to something,' a little voice whispers in my head.

"I guess I'd better go and tell the others," Wylan sighs.

He strolls back towards the door, stopping beside me and putting a hand on my shoulder, looking at me earnestly.

"Get some rest, Nes. You're going to need it."

My room feels claustrophobic when I step through the door. I look around the space, from my single cot to the humble desk and chair, to the door leading into the darkened washroom. It all looks the same, yet feels different. Somehow everything has changed over the last several days and it seems like there is a dark cloud that hangs over me and my thoughts.

I trudge over to my desk and drag the chair out, the legs grinding against the hard floor before I sit down, staring at the door, deep in thought.

"I know that he still haunts you, doesn't he?"

"Olin. The one who—"

"—Shut. The. Fuck. Up."

"I killed him, you know."

"What?"

"I found him. I asked him what he did, and then reduced him to blood and dust."

I dare to reach down the thread connecting us, only to come up empty, a deathly silence that I'm not prepared for.

Unable to sit here any longer, I kick back my chair and leave the room, ignoring the order to remain within these four walls. I march down the halls, climbing the stairs until I reach the two doors, one leading outside, the other up into the lighthouse.

Choosing the latter, I make my way up the winding steps all the way to the top. Skirting around the enormous light at the centre of the circular room, I make my way towards the small lookout, welcoming the sharp winds that whip across my face as I stare out at the vast seas before me.

I can feel my power simmering beneath the surface of my skin, waiting patiently to be released. I pull away from the ledge and glance down at my clenched fist, my brows knitting together as I heave a sigh and raise my gaze back to the horizon.

Thinking of everything I have been through, everything that I've dealt with, everything that will undoubtedly try to tear me apart with the threat of war hanging over us like an ominous promise. Determination fills me as I take a deep breath. Let Barilius bring war, let him try to rain down hell upon us. He can try.

Because, as I remind myself of the strength I've discovered within me, I realise something.

I wasn't brought into this world to be silent and gentle. I had been made to make the world tremble and quake at my fingertips, and in time, Barilius and his men would come to know this.

When the time comes, I'll be ready.

COMING SOON!

A *Sea* OF *Black & Gold*

ELORA BURRELL
eloraburrell.com

BLOTTED
QUILL
PUBLISHING

A Sea of Black & Gold

COMING SOON

NESRYN IS AN OUTCAST

After recently discovering her extraordinary power she never knew existed. Once a Chosen, now a Starweaver and valued member of the Righteous Hand, she finds herself an outlaw with a price on her head after fleeing the palace. But she is a survivor and will stop at nothing to remove the crown from Barilius's treacherous head.

LYSAN IS A TRAITOR

No longer the second to the King, the disgraced Shadowcaster has a hard truth to face. He is her enemy, but with his doubts growing about the King and his methods, Lysan must decide what side of the fight he wants to be on.

WAR IS ON THE HORIZON

With the Righteous Hand's plans coming into play, both Nesryn and Lysan will be drawn into the depths of war. Blood will be spilt and lives will be lost as enemies' swords clash. But will they raise their swords together or let their differences tear them apart?

ACKNOWLEDGEMENTS

Wow, A Spell of Dust and Smoke is finally finished and here I am looking back at the past year and what I've accomplished. Though of course, I certainly couldn't have done it alone!

Reflecting on the journey this book has led me on, it has been one hell of a rollercoaster and to finally be at the finish line is a satisfaction I just can't put into words. I can't deny that writing this book has been one of the most challenging tasks I've put myself through.

This book is raw, emotional and full of matters close to my heart.

Introducing you to this whole new set of characters, and to a world far beyond anything I've ever imagined before, has been a terrifying thing to do. But as a storyteller, it is my duty to share it with you, my readers.

There are six people in particular I would like to thank, starting with my fabulous and ever-dedicated editor, Britt from Folio Freelance. As always you are an incredible person to work with! You are so patient and encouraging and without your diligent work, this book would only be half the book I would want it to be!

Secondly, I'd like to thank my fellow authors, Des and Rae, for their constant encouragement and for pushing me to keep going when all I wanted to do was give up. Thank you for the long chats and always being so eager and willing to read the numerous snippets I sent your way! (Especially with the time difference!)

Thirdly thank you to Amy; my bestie, confidant, and the best proofreader a writer could ask for! Thank you so much for sitting up all hours reading through the many drafts of

ASODAS, for putting up with reading it on a screen rather than your preferred printed version, though you WILL be getting a copy, I promise!

Thank you to my dear friend, Rachel (who some may know as Enchantedwoodbooks on Bookstagram) for agreeing to be a Beta reader. Thank you for all your praise and support, I'm honoured that you were willing to read it so early on in its drafted, messy state!

I can't forget to thank Art By K Huggs. Thank you my lovely, talented friend for your incredible contribution to this book. All of the beautiful and stunning artwork and illustrations that make this book as eye-catching as it is, is all thanks to you. As always, you have created a showstopper of a book cover and I cannot wait to share what is inside, waiting to be discovered, with my readers.

Thank you to my family for their support and my two boys, Mason and Phylo, who though are still young, are able to still somehow cheer me one. I love you both.

Last of all, I'd like to thank you, my wonderful readers.

Thank you for your patience and your eagerness for this book. I appreciate every message and every comment on my ASODAS posts. Without you all, I would not be here, living my dream and sharing these stories with you.

I appreciate every single bit of support you give me, whether that be keeping up to date with my socials, buying copies of my books, or leaving reviews. I am truly grateful for it all.

So, thank you for taking these characters into your hearts, and for cherishing them as much as I do. It means the world to me.

ABOUT THE AUTHOR

Elora Burrell is an emerging author of speculative fiction. She has worked a variety of jobs and is now the co-founder of a growing publishing business. She has a Master's Degree in Creative Writing from Teeside University, as well as a Bachelors in English Literature & Creative Writing from the University of Chester. When not reading or writing, she enjoys gaming, dog walks, a long list of television series', and spending time with her family.

She lives in Wiltshire, with woodlands and Salisbury Plains on her back doorstep.